Hateship,

Friendship,

Courtship,

Loveship,

Marriage

ALSO BY ALICE MUNRO

Hateship,
Friendship,
Courtship,
Loveship,
Marriage

Stories by

ALICE MUNRO

⟦A DOUGLAS GIBSON BOOK⟧

M&S

NATIONAL LIBRARY OF CANADA CATALOGUING IN PUBLICATION DATA

Munro, Alice, 1931–
Hateship, friendship, courtship, loveship, marriage

"A Douglas Gibson book"
ISBN 0-7710-6525-6

I. Title.

PS8576.U57H38 2001   C813'.54   C2001-901826-6
PR9199.3.M8H38 2001a

We acknowledge the financial support of the Government of Canada through the Book
Publishing Industry Development Program for our publishing activities. We further
acknowledge the support of the Canadian Council for the Arts and the Ontario Arts
Council for our publishing program.

Some of the stories in this collection were originally published as follows:
"Floating Bridge," "Family Furnishings," "Nettles," "Post and Beam," and "The Bear
Came Over the Mountain" in *The New Yorker*; "Queenie" in the *London Review of Books*
and subsequently in book form by Profile Books Ltd., London.

Typeset in Fournier
Printed and bound in Canada
This book is printed on acid-free paper that is
100% ancient forest friendly (100% post-consumer recycled)

A Douglas Gibson Book

McClelland & Stewart Ltd.
The Canadian Publishers
481 University Avenue
Toronto, Ontario
M5G 2E9
www. mcclelland.com

1 2 3 4 5 6   06 05 04 03 02 01

With gratitude
to
Sarah Skinner

Contents

Hateship,

Friendship,

Courtship,

Loveship,

Marriage

Hateship, Friendship, Courtship, Loveship, Marriage

Years ago, before the trains stopped running on so many of the branch lines, a woman with a high, freckled forehead and a frizz of reddish hair came into the railway station and inquired about shipping furniture.

The station agent often tried a little teasing with women, especially the plain ones who seemed to appreciate it.

"Furniture?" he said, as if nobody had ever had such an idea before. "Well. Now. What kind of furniture are we talking about?"

A dining-room table and six chairs. A full bedroom suite, a sofa, a coffee table, end tables, a floor lamp. Also a china cabinet and a buffet.

"Whoa there. You mean a houseful."

"It shouldn't count as that much," she said. "There's no kitchen things and only enough for one bedroom."

Her teeth were crowded to the front of her mouth as if they were ready for an argument.

"You'll be needing the truck," he said.

"No. I want to send it on the train. It's going out west, to Saskatchewan."

She spoke to him in a loud voice as if he was deaf or stupid, and there was something wrong with the way she pronounced her words. An accent. He thought of Dutch—the Dutch were moving in around here—but she didn't have the heft of the Dutch women or the nice pink skin or the fair hair. She might have been under forty, but what did it matter? No beauty queen, ever.

He turned all business.

"First you'll need the truck to get it to here from wherever you got it. And we better see if it's a place in Saskatchewan where the train goes through. Otherways you'd have to arrange to get it picked up, say, in Regina."

"It's Gdynia," she said. "The train goes through."

He took down a greasy-covered directory that was hanging from a nail and asked how she would spell that. She helped herself to the pencil that was also on a string and wrote on a piece of paper from her purse: *G D Y N I A.*

"What kind of nationality would that be?"

She said she didn't know.

He took back the pencil to follow from line to line.

"A lot of places out there it's all Czechs or Hungarians or Ukrainians," he said. It came to him as he said this that she might be one of those. But so what, he was only stating a fact.

"Here it is, all right, it's on the line."

"Yes," she said. "I want to ship it Friday—can you do that?"

"We can ship it, but I can't promise what day it'll get there," he said. "It all depends on the priorities. Somebody going to be on the lookout for it when it comes in?"

"Yes."

"It's a mixed train Friday, two-eighteen p.m. Truck picks it up Friday morning. You live here in town?"

She nodded, writing down the address. 106 Exhibition Road.

It was only recently that the houses in town had been numbered, and he couldn't picture the place, though he knew where

Exhibition Road was. If she'd said the name McCauley at that time he might have taken more of an interest, and things might have turned out differently. There were new houses out there, built since the war, though they were called "wartime houses." He supposed it must be one of those.

"Pay when you ship," he told her.

"Also, I want a ticket for myself on the same train. Friday afternoon."

"Going same place?"

"Yes."

"You can travel on the same train to Toronto, but then you have to wait for the Transcontinental, goes out ten-thirty at night. You want sleeper or coach? Sleeper you get a berth, coach you sit up in the day car."

She said she would sit up.

"Wait in Sudbury for the Montreal train, but you won't get off there, they'll just shunt you around and hitch on the Montreal cars. Then on to Port Arthur and then to Kenora. You don't get off till Regina, and there you have to get off and catch the branch-line train."

She nodded as if he should just get on and give her the ticket.

Slowing down, he said, "But I won't promise your furniture'll arrive when you do, I wouldn't think it would get in till a day or two after. It's all the priorities. Somebody coming to meet you?"

"Yes."

"Good. Because it won't likely be much of a station. Towns out there, they're not like here. They're mostly pretty rudimentary affairs."

She paid for the passenger ticket now, from a roll of bills in a cloth bag in her purse. Like an old lady. She counted her change, too. But not the way an old lady would count it—she held it in her hand and flicked her eyes over it, but you could tell she didn't miss a penny. Then she turned away rudely, without a good-bye.

"See you Friday," he called out.

She wore a long, drab coat on this warm September day, also a pair of clunky laced-up shoes, and ankle socks.

He was getting a coffee out of his thermos when she came back and rapped on the wicket.

"The furniture I'm sending," she said. "It's all good furniture, it's like new. I wouldn't want it to get scratched or banged up or in any way damaged. I don't want it to smell like livestock, either."

"Oh, well," he said. "The railway's pretty used to shipping things. And they don't use the same cars for shipping furniture they use for shipping pigs."

"I'm concerned that it gets there in just as good a shape as it leaves here."

"Well, you know, when you buy your furniture, it's in the store, right? But did you ever think how it got there? It wasn't made in the store, was it? No. It was made in some factory someplace, and it got shipped to the store, and that was done quite possibly by train. So that being the case, doesn't it stand to reason the railway knows how to look after it?"

She continued to look at him without a smile or any admission of her female foolishness.

"I hope so," she said. "I hope they do."

The station agent would have said, without thinking about it, that he knew everybody in town. Which meant that he knew about half of them. And most of those he knew were the core people, the ones who really were "in town" in the sense that they had not arrived yesterday and had no plans to move on. He did not know the woman who was going to Saskatchewan because she did not go to his church or teach his children in school or work in any store or restaurant or office that he went into. Nor was she married to any of the men he knew in the Elks or the Oddfellows or the Lions

Club or the Legion. A look at her left hand while she was getting the money out had told him—and he was not surprised—that she was not married to anybody. With those shoes, and ankle socks instead of stockings, and no hat or gloves in the afternoon, she might have been a farm woman. But she didn't have the hesitation they generally had, the embarrassment. She didn't have country manners—in fact, she had no manners at all. She had treated him as if he was an information machine. Besides, she had written a town address—Exhibition Road. The person she really reminded him of was a plainclothes nun he had seen on television, talking about the missionary work she did somewhere in the jungle—probably they had got out of their nuns' clothes there because it made it easier for them to clamber around. This nun had smiled once in a while to show that her religion was supposed to make people happy, but most of the time she looked out at her audience as if she believed that other people were mainly in the world for her to boss around.

One more thing Johanna meant to do she had been putting off doing. She had to go into the dress shop called Milady's and buy herself an outfit. She had never been inside that shop—when she had to buy anything, like socks, she went to Callaghans Mens Ladies and Childrens Wear. She had lots of clothes inherited from Mrs. Willets, things like this coat that would never wear out. And Sabitha—the girl she looked after, in Mr. McCauley's house—was showered with costly hand-me-downs from her cousins.

In Milady's window there were two mannequins wearing suits with quite short skirts and boxy jackets. One suit was a rusty-gold color and the other a soft deep green. Big gaudy paper maple leaves were scattered round the mannequins' feet and pasted here and there on the window. At the time of year when most people's concern was to rake up leaves and burn them, here they were the chosen thing. A sign written in flowing black script was stuck diagonally across the glass. It said: *Simple Elegance, the Mode for Fall*.

She opened the door and went inside.

Right ahead of her, a full-length mirror showed her in Mrs. Willets's high-quality but shapeless long coat, with a few inches of lumpy bare legs above the ankle socks.

They did that on purpose, of course. They set the mirror there so you could get a proper notion of your deficiencies, right away, and then—they hoped—you would jump to the conclusion that you had to buy something to alter the picture. Such a transparent trick that it would have made her walk out, if she had not come in determined, knowing what she had to get.

Along one wall was a rack of evening dresses, all fit for belles of the ball with their net and taffeta, their dreamy colors. And beyond them, in a glass case so no profane fingers could get at them, half a dozen wedding gowns, pure white froth or vanilla satin or ivory lace, embroidered in silver beads or seed pearls. Tiny bodices, scalloped necklines, lavish skirts. Even when she was younger she could never have contemplated such extravagance, not just in the matter of money but in expectations, in the preposterous hope of transformation, and bliss.

It was two or three minutes before anybody came. Maybe they had a peephole and were eyeing her, thinking she wasn't their kind of customer and hoping she would go away.

She would not. She moved beyond the mirror's reflection—stepping from the linoleum by the door to a plushy rug—and at long last the curtain at the back of the store opened and out stepped Milady herself, dressed in a black suit with glittery buttons. High heels, thin ankles, girdle so tight her nylons rasped, gold hair skinned back from her made-up face.

"I thought I could try on the suit in the window," Johanna said in a rehearsed voice. "The green one."

"Oh, that's a lovely suit," the woman said. "The one in the window happens to be a size ten. Now you look to be—maybe a fourteen?"

She rasped ahead of Johanna back to the part of the store where the ordinary clothes, the suits and daytime dresses, were hung.

"You're in luck. Fourteen coming up."

The first thing Johanna did was look at the price tag. Easily twice what she'd expected, and she was not going to pretend otherwise.

"It's expensive enough."

"It's very fine wool." The woman monkeyed around till she found the label, then read off a description of the material that Johanna wasn't really listening to because she had caught at the hem to examine the workmanship.

"It feels as light as silk, but it wears like iron. You can see it's lined throughout, lovely silk-and-rayon lining. You won't find it bagging in the seat and going out of shape the way the cheap suits do. Look at the velvet cuffs and collar and the little velvet buttons on the sleeve."

"I see them."

"That's the kind of detail you pay for, you just do not get it otherwise. I love the velvet touch. It's only on the green one, you know—the apricot one doesn't have it, even though they're exactly the same price."

Indeed it was the velvet collar and cuffs that gave the suit, in Johanna's eyes, its subtle look of luxury and made her long to buy it. But she was not going to say so.

"I might as well go ahead and try it on."

This was what she'd come prepared for, after all. Clean underwear and fresh talcum powder under her arms.

The woman had enough sense to leave her alone in the bright cubicle. Johanna avoided the glass like poison till she'd got the skirt straight and the jacket done up.

At first she just looked at the suit. It was all right. The fit was all right—the skirt shorter than what she was used to, but then what she was used to was not the style. There was no problem with the suit. The problem was with what stuck out of it. Her neck and her face and her hair and her big hands and thick legs.

"How are you getting on? Mind if I take a peek?"

Peek all you want to, Johanna thought, it's a case of a sow's ear, as you'll soon see.

The woman tried looking from one side, then the other.

"Of course, you'll need your nylons on and your heels. How does it feel? Comfortable?"

"The suit feels fine," Johanna said. "There's nothing the matter with the suit."

The woman's face changed in the mirror. She stopped smiling. She looked disappointed and tired, but kinder.

"Sometimes that's just the way it is. You never really know until you try something on. The thing is," she said, with a new, more moderate conviction growing in her voice, "the thing is you have a fine figure, but it's a strong figure. You have large bones and what's the matter with that? Dinky little velvet-covered buttons are not for you. Don't bother with it anymore. Just take it off."

Then when Johanna had got down to her underwear there was a tap and a hand through the curtain.

"Just slip this on, for the heck of it."

A brown wool dress, lined, with a full skirt gracefully gathered, three-quarter sleeves and a plain round neckline. About as plain as you could get, except for a narrow gold belt. Not as expensive as the suit, but still the price seemed like a lot, when you considered all there was to it.

At least the skirt was a more decent length and the fabric made a noble swirl around her legs. She steeled herself and looked in the glass.

This time she didn't look as if she'd been stuck into the garment for a joke.

The woman came and stood beside her, and laughed, but with relief.

"It's the color of your eyes. You don't need to wear velvet. You've got velvet eyes."

That was the kind of soft-soaping Johanna would have felt bound to scoff at, except that at the moment it seemed to be true. Her eyes were not large, and if asked to describe their color she would have said, "I guess they're a kind of a brown." But now they looked to be a really deep brown, soft and shining.

It wasn't that she had suddenly started thinking she was pretty or anything. Just that her eyes were a nice color, if they had been a piece of cloth.

"Now, I bet you don't wear dress shoes very often," the woman said. "But if you had nylons on and just a minimum kind of pump— And I bet you don't wear jewelry, and you're quite right, you don't need to, with that belt."

To cut off the sales spiel Johanna said, "Well, I better take it off so you can wrap it up." She was sorry to lose the soft weight of the skirt and the discreet ribbon of gold around her waist. She had never in her life had this silly feeling of being enhanced by what she had put on herself.

"I just hope it's for a special occasion," the woman called out as Johanna was hastening into her now dingy-looking regular clothes.

"It'll likely be what I get married in," said Johanna.

She was surprised at that coming out of her mouth. It wasn't a major error—the woman didn't know who she was and would probably not be talking to anybody who did know. Still, she had meant to keep absolutely quiet. She must have felt she owed this person something—that they'd been through the disaster of the green suit and the discovery of the brown dress together and that was a bond. Which was nonsense. The woman was in the business of selling clothes, and she'd just succeeded in doing that.

"Oh!" the woman cried out. "Oh, that's wonderful."

Well, it might be, Johanna thought, and then again it might not. She might be marrying anybody. Some miserable farmer who wanted a workhorse around the place, or some wheezy old half-cripple looking for a nurse. This woman had no idea what kind of man she had lined up, and it wasn't any of her business anyway.

"I can tell it's a love match," the woman said, just as if she had read these disgruntled thoughts. "That's why your eyes were shining in the mirror. I've wrapped it all in tissue paper, all you have to do is take it out and hang it up and the material will fall out beautifully. Just give it a light press if you want, but you probably won't even need to do that."

Then there was the business of handing over the money. They both pretended not to look, but both did.

"It's worth it," the woman said. "You only get married the once. Well, that's not always strictly true—"

"In my case it'll be true," Johanna said. Her face was hotly flushed because marriage had not, in fact, been mentioned. Not even in the last letter. She had revealed to this woman what she was counting on, and that had perhaps been an unlucky thing to do.

"Where did you meet him?" said the woman, still in that tone of wistful gaiety. "What was your first date?"

"Through family," Johanna said truthfully. She wasn't meaning to say any more but heard herself go on. "The Western Fair. In London."

"The Western Fair," the woman said. "In London." She could have been saying "the Castle Ball."

"We had his daughter and her friend with us," said Johanna, thinking that in a way it would have been more accurate to say that he and Sabitha and Edith had her, Johanna, with them.

"Well, I can say my day has not been wasted. I've provided the dress for somebody to be a happy bride in. That's enough to justify my existence." The woman tied a narrow pink ribbon around the dress box, making a big, unnecessary bow, then gave it a wicked snip with the scissors.

"I'm here all day," she said. "And sometimes I just wonder what I think I'm doing. I ask myself, What do you think you're doing here? I put up a new display in the window and I do this and that to entice the people in, but there are days—there are *days*—when I do not see one soul come in that door. I know—people think these clothes are too expensive—but they're *good*. They're good clothes. If you want the quality you have to pay the price."

"They must come in when they want something like those," said Johanna, looking towards the evening dresses. "Where else could they go?"

"That's just it. They don't. They go to the city—that's where they go. They'll drive fifty miles, a hundred miles, never mind the gas, and tell themselves that way they get something better than I've got here. And they haven't. Not better quality, not better selection. Nothing. Just that they'd be ashamed to say they bought their wedding outfits in town. Or they'll come in and try something on and say they have to think about it. I'll be back, they say. And I think, Oh, yes, I know what that means. It means they'll try to find the same thing cheaper in London or Kitchener, and even if it isn't cheaper, they'll buy it there once they've driven all that way and got sick of looking."

"I don't know," she said. "Maybe if I was a local person it would make a difference. It's very clique-y here, I find. You're not local, are you?"

Johanna said, "No."

"Don't you find it clique-y?"

Cleeky.

"Hard for an outsider to break in, is what I mean."

"I'm used to being on my own," Johanna said.

"But you found somebody. You won't be on your own anymore and isn't that lovely? Some days I think how grand it would be, to be married and stay at home. Of course, I used to be married, and I worked anyway. Ah, well. Maybe the man in the moon will walk in here and fall in love with me and then I'll be all set!"

Johanna had to hurry—that woman's need for conversation had delayed her. She was hurrying to be back at the house, her purchase stowed away, before Sabitha got home from school.

Then she remembered that Sabitha wasn't there, having been carried off on the weekend by her mother's cousin, her Aunt Roxanne, to live like a proper rich girl in Toronto and go to a rich girl's school. But she continued to walk fast—so fast some smart aleck holding up the wall of the drugstore called out to her, "Where's the fire?" and she slowed down a bit, not to attract attention.

The dress box was awkward—how could she have known the store would have its own pink cardboard boxes, with *Milady's* written across them in purple handwriting? A dead giveaway.

She felt a fool for mentioning a wedding, when he hadn't mentioned it and she ought to remember that. So much else had been said—or written—such fondness and yearning expressed, that the actual marrying seemed just to have been overlooked. The way you might speak about getting up in the morning and not about having breakfast, though you certainly intended to have it.

Nevertheless she should have kept her mouth shut.

She saw Mr. McCauley walking in the opposite direction up the other side of the street. That was all right—even if he had met her head-on he would never have noticed the box she carried. He would have raised a finger to his hat and passed her by, presumably noticing that she was his housekeeper but possibly not. He had

other things on his mind, and for all anybody knew might be looking at some town other than the one they saw. Every working
day—and sometimes, forgetfully, on holidays or Sundays—he got
dressed in one of his three-piece suits and his light overcoat or his
heavy overcoat, and his gray fedora and his well-polished shoes,
and walked from Exhibition Road uptown to the office he still
maintained over what had been the harness and luggage store. It
was spoken of as an Insurance Office, though it was quite a long
time since he had actively sold insurance. Sometimes people
climbed the stairs to see him, maybe to ask some question about
their policies or more likely about lot boundaries, the history of
some piece of real estate in town or farm out in the country. His
office was full of maps old and new, and he liked nothing better
than to lay them out and get into a discussion that expanded far
beyond the question asked. Three or four times a day he emerged
and walked the street, as now. During the war he had put the
McLaughlin-Buick up on blocks in the barn, and walked everywhere to set an example. He still seemed to be setting an example,
fifteen years later. Hands clasped behind his back, he was like a
kind landlord inspecting his property or a preacher happy to
observe his flock. Of course, half the people that he met had no
idea who he was.

The town had changed, even in the time Johanna had been here.
Trade was moving out to the highway, where there was a new discount store and a Canadian Tire and a motel with a lounge and
topless dancers. Some downtown shops had tried to spruce themselves up with pink or mauve or olive paint, but already that paint
was curling on the old brick and some of the interiors were empty.
Milady's was almost certain to follow suit.

If Johanna was the woman in there, what would she have done?
She'd never have gotten in so many elaborate evening dresses, for
a start. What instead? If you made the switch to cheaper clothes
you'd only be putting yourself in competition with Callaghans and

the discount place, and there probably wasn't trade enough to go around. So what about going into fancy baby clothes, children's clothes, trying to pull in the grandmothers and aunts who had the money and would spend it for that kind of thing? Forget about the mothers, who would go to Callaghans, having less money and more sense.

But if it was her in charge—Johanna—she would never be able to pull in anybody. She could see what needed to be done, and how, and she could round up and supervise people to do it, but she could never charm or entice. Take it or leave it, would be her attitude. No doubt they would leave it.

It was the rare person who took to her, and she'd been aware of that for a long time. Sabitha certainly hadn't shed any tears when she said good-bye—though you could say Johanna was the nearest thing Sabitha had to a mother, since her own mother had died. Mr. McCauley would be upset when she left because she'd given good service and it would be hard to replace her, but that would be all he thought about. Both he and his granddaughter were spoiled and self-centered. As for the neighbors, they would no doubt rejoice. Johanna had had problems on both sides of the property. On one side it was the neighbors' dog digging in her garden, burying and retrieving his supply of bones, which he could better have done at home. And on the other it was the black cherry tree, which was on the McCauleys' property but bore most of its cherries on the branches hanging over into the next yard. In both cases she had raised a fuss, and won. The dog was tied up and the other neighbors left the cherries alone. If she got up on the stepladder she could reach well over into their yard, but they no longer chased the birds out of the branches and it made a difference to the crop.

Mr. McCauley would have let them pick. He would have let the dog dig. He would let himself be taken advantage of. Part of the reason was that these were new people and lived in new houses and so he preferred not to pay attention to them. At one time there had been just three or four large houses on Exhibition Road. Across from them were the fairgrounds, where the fall fair was held (officially called the Agricultural Exhibition, hence the name), and in between were orchard trees, small meadows. A dozen years ago or so that land had been sold off in regular lot sizes and houses had been put up—small houses in alternating styles, one kind with an upstairs and the other kind without. Some were already getting to look pretty shabby.

There were only a couple of houses whose occupants Mr. McCauley knew and was friendly with—the schoolteacher, Miss Hood, and her mother, and the Shultzes, who ran the Shoe Repair shop. The Shultzes' daughter, Edith, was or had been Sabitha's great friend. It was natural, with their being in the same grade at school—at least last year, once Sabitha had been held back—and living near each other. Mr. McCauley hadn't minded—maybe he had some idea that Sabitha would be removed before long to live a different sort of life in Toronto. Johanna would not have chosen Edith, though the girl was never rude, never troublesome when she came to the house. And she was not stupid. That might have been the problem—she was smart and Sabitha was not so smart. She had made Sabitha sly.

That was all over now. Now that the cousin, Roxanne—Mrs. Huber—had shown up, the Schultz girl was all part of Sabitha's childish past.

I am going to arrange to get all your furniture out to you on the train as soon as they can take it and prepaid as soon as they tell me what it will cost. I have been thinking you will need it now. I guess it will not be that much of a surprise that I thought you would not mind it if I went along to be of help to you as I hope I can be.

This was the letter she had taken to the Post Office, before she went to make arrangements at the railway station. It was the first letter she had ever sent to him directly. The others had been slipped in with the letters she made Sabitha write. And his to her had come in the same way, tidily folded and with her name, Johanna, typed on the back of the page so there would be no mistaking. That kept the people in the Post Office from catching on, and it never hurt to save a stamp. Of course, Sabitha could have reported to her grandfather, or even read what was written to Johanna, but Sabitha was no more interested in communicating with the old man than she was in letters—the writing or the receiving of them.

The furniture was stored back in the barn, which was just a town barn, not a real barn with animals and a granary. When Johanna got her first look at everything a year or so ago, she found it grimy with dust and splattered with pigeon droppings. The pieces had been piled in carelessly without anything to cover them. She had hauled what she could carry out into the yard, leaving space in the barn to get at the big pieces she couldn't carry—the sofa and buffet and china cabinet and dining table. The bedstead she could take apart. She went at the wood with soft dustrags, then lemon oil, and when she was finished it shone like candy. Maple candy—it was bird's-eye maple wood. It looked glamorous to her, like satin bedspreads and blond hair. Glamorous and modern, a total contrast to all the dark wood and irksome carving of the furniture she cared for in the house. She thought of it as *his* furniture then, and still did when she got it out this Wednesday. She had put old quilts over the bottom layer to protect everything there from what was piled on top, and sheets over what was on top to protect that from the birds, and as a result there was only a light dust. But she wiped everything and lemon-oiled it before she put it back, protected in the same way, to wait for the truck on Friday.

Dear Mr. McCauley,
I am leaving on the train this afternoon (Friday). I realize this is without giving my notice to you, but I will wave my last pay, which would be three weeks owing this coming Monday. There

is a beef stew on the stove in the double boiler that just needs warming up. Enough there for three meals or maybe could be stretched to a fourth. As soon as it is hot and you have got all you want, put the lid on and put it away in the fridge. Remember, put the lid on at once not to take chances with it getting spoiled. Regards to you and to Sabitha and will probably be in touch when I am settled. Johanna Parry.

P.S. I have shipped his furniture to Mr. Boudreau as he may need it. Remember to make sure when you reheat there is enough water in bottom part of the double boiler.

Mr. McCauley had no trouble finding out that the ticket Johanna had bought was to Gdynia, Saskatchewan. He phoned the station agent and asked. He could not think how to describe Johanna— was she old or young-looking, thin or moderately heavy, what was the color of her coat?—but that was not necessary when he mentioned the furniture.

When this call came through there were a couple of people in the station waiting for the evening train. The agent tried to keep his voice down at first, but he became excited when he heard about the stolen furniture (what Mr. McCauley actually said was "and I believe she took some furniture with her"). He swore that if he had known who she was and what she was up to he would never have let her set foot on the train. This assertion was heard and repeated and believed, nobody asking how he could have stopped a grown woman who had paid for her ticket, unless he had some proof right away that she was a thief. Most people who repeated his words believed that he could and would have stopped her— they believed in the authority of station agents and of upright-walking fine old men in three-piece suits like Mr. McCauley.

The beef stew was excellent, as Johanna's cooking always was, but Mr. McCauley found he could not swallow it. He disregarded the instruction about the lid and left the pot sitting open on the stove and did not even turn off the burner until the water in the bottom pot boiled away and he was alerted by a smell of smoking metal.

This was the smell of treachery.

He told himself to be thankful at least that Sabitha was taken care of and he did not have that to worry about. His cousin—his wife's cousin, actually, Roxanne—had written to tell him that from what she had seen of Sabitha on her summer visit to Lake Simcoe the girl was going to take some handling.

"Frankly I don't think you and that woman you've hired are going to be up to it when the boys come swarming around."

She did not go so far as to ask him whether he wanted another Marcelle on his hands, but that was what she meant. She said she would get Sabitha into a good school where she could be taught manners at least.

He turned on the television for a distraction, but it was no use.

It was the furniture that galled him. It was Ken Boudreau.

The fact was that three days before—on the very day that Johanna had bought her ticket, as the station agent had now told him—Mr. McCauley had received a letter from Ken Boudreau asking him to (a) advance some money against the furniture belonging to him (Ken Boudreau) and his dead wife, Marcelle, which was stored in Mr. McCauley's barn, or (b) if he could not see his way to doing that, to sell the furniture for as much as he could get and send the money as quickly as he could to Saskatchewan. There was no mention of the loans that had already been made by father-in-law to son-in-law, all against the value of this furniture and amounting to more than it could ever be sold for. Could Ken Boudreau have forgotten all about that? Or did he simply hope—and this was more probable—that his father-in-law would have forgotten?

He was now, it seemed, the owner of a hotel. But his letter was full of diatribes against the fellow who had formerly owned it and who had misled him as to various particulars.

"If I can just get over this hurdle," he said, "then I am convinced I can still make a go of it." But what was the hurdle? A need for immediate money, but he did not say whether it was owing to the former owner, or to the bank, or to a private mortgage holder, or what. It was the same old story—a desperate, wheedling tone mixed in with some arrogance, some sense of its being what was owed him, because of the wounds inflicted on him, the shame suffered, on account of Marcelle.

With many misgivings but remembering that Ken Boudreau was after all his son-in-law and had fought in the war and been through God-knows-what trouble in his marriage, Mr. McCauley had sat down and written a letter saying that he did not have any idea how to go about getting the best price for the furniture and it would be very difficult for him to find out and that he was enclosing a check, which he would count as an outright personal loan. He wished his son-in-law to acknowledge it as such and to remember the number of similar loans made in the past—already, he believed, exceeding any value of the furniture. He was enclosing a list of dates and amounts. Apart from fifty dollars paid nearly two years ago (with a promise of regular payments to follow), he had received nothing. His son-in-law must surely understand that as a result of these unpaid and interest-free loans Mr. McCauley's income had declined, since he would otherwise have invested the money.

He had thought of adding, "I am not such a fool as you seem to think," but decided not to, since that would reveal his irritation and perhaps his weakness.

And now look. The man had jumped the gun and enlisted Johanna in his scheme—he would always be able to get around women—and got hold of the furniture as well as the check. She had paid for the shipping herself, the station agent had said. The flashy-looking modern maple stuff had been overvalued in the deals already made and they would not get much for it, especially when you counted what the railway had charged. If they had been cleverer they would simply have taken something from the house, one of the old cabinets or parlor settees too uncomfortable to sit on, made and bought in the last century. That, of course, would have been plain stealing. But what they had done was not far off.

He went to bed with his mind made up to prosecute.

He woke in the house alone, with no smell of coffee or breakfast coming from the kitchen—instead, there was a whiff of the burned pot still in the air. An autumn chill had settled in all the high-ceilinged, forlorn rooms. It had been warm last evening and on preceding evenings—the furnace had not been turned on yet, and when Mr. McCauley did turn it on the warm air was accompanied by a blast of cellar damp, of mold and earth and decay. He washed and dressed slowly, with forgetful pauses, and spread some peanut butter on a piece of bread for his breakfast. He belonged to a generation in which there were men who were said not to be able even to boil water, and he was one of them. He looked out the front windows and saw the trees on the other side of the racetrack swallowed up in the morning fog, which seemed to be advancing, not retreating as it should at this hour, across the track itself. He seemed to see in the fog the looming buildings of the old Exhibition Grounds—homely, spacious buildings, like enormous barns. They had stood for years and years unused—all through the war—and he forgot what happened to them in the end. Were they torn down, or did they fall down? He abhorred the races that took place now, the crowds and the loudspeaker and the illegal drinking and the ruinous uproar of the summer Sundays. When he thought of that he thought of his poor girl Marcelle, sitting on the verandah steps and calling out to grown schoolmates who had got out of their parked cars and were hurrying to see the races. The fuss she made, the joy she expressed at being back in town, the hugging and holding people up, talking a mile a minute, rattling on about childhood days and how she'd missed everybody. She had

said that the only thing not perfect about life was missing her husband, Ken, left out west because of his work.

She went out there in her silk pajamas, with straggly, un-
combed, dyed-blond hair. Her arms and legs were thin, but her
face was somewhat bloated, and what she claimed was her tan
seemed a sickly brown color not from the sun. Maybe jaundice.

The child had stayed inside and watched television—Sunday
cartoons that she was surely too old for.

He couldn't tell what was wrong, or be sure that anything was.
Marcelle went away to London to have some female thing done
and died in the hospital. When he phoned her husband to tell him,
Ken Boudreau said, "What did she take?"

If Marcelle's mother had been alive still, would things have
been any different? The fact was that her mother, when she was
alive, had been as bewildered as he was. She had sat in the kitchen
crying while their teenage daughter, locked into her room, had
climbed out the window and slid down the verandah roof to be
welcomed by carloads of boys.

The house was full of a feeling of callous desertion, of deceit.
He and his wife had surely been kind parents, driven to the wall by
Marcelle. When she had eloped with an airman, they had hoped
that she would be all right, at last. They had been generous to the
two of them as to the most proper young couple. But it all fell
apart. To Johanna Parry he had likewise been generous, and look
how she too had gone against him.

He walked to town and went into the hotel for his breakfast.
The waitress said, "You're bright and early this morning."

And while she was still pouring out his coffee he began to tell
her about how his housekeeper had walked out on him without any
warning or provocation, not only left her job with no notice but
taken a load of furniture that had belonged to his daughter, that
now was supposed to belong to his son-in-law but didn't really,
having been bought with his daughter's wedding money. He told

her how his daughter had married an airman, a good-looking, plausible fellow who wasn't to be trusted around the corner.

"Excuse me," the waitress said. "I'd love to chat, but I got people waiting on their breakfast. Excuse me——"

He climbed the stairs to his office, and there, spread out on his desk, were the old maps he had been studying yesterday in an effort to locate exactly the very first burying ground in the county (abandoned, he believed, in 1839). He turned on the light and sat down, but he found he could not concentrate. After the waitress's reproof—or what he took for a reproof—he hadn't been able to eat his breakfast or enjoy his coffee. He decided to go out for a walk to calm himself down.

But instead of walking along in his usual way, greeting people and passing a few words with them, he found himself bursting into speech. The minute anybody asked him how he was this morning he began in a most uncharacteristic, even shameful way to blurt out his woes, and like the waitress, these people had business to attend to and they nodded and shuffled and made excuses to get away. The morning didn't seem to be warming up in the way foggy fall mornings usually did; his jacket wasn't warm enough, so he sought the comfort of the shops.

People who had known him the longest were the most dismayed. He had never been anything but reticent—the well-mannered gentleman, his mind on other times, his courtesy a deft apology for privilege (which was a bit of a joke, because the privilege was mostly in his recollections and not apparent to others). He should have been the last person to air wrongs or ask for sympathy—he hadn't when his wife died, or even when his daughter died—yet here he was, pulling out some letter, asking if it wasn't a shame the way this fellow had taken him for money over and over again, and even now when he'd taken pity on him once more the fellow had connived with his housekeeper to steal the furniture. Some thought it was his own furniture he was talking about—they believed the old man had been left without a bed or a chair in his house. They advised him to go to the police.

"That's no good, that's no good," he said. "How can you get blood from a stone?"

He went into the Shoe Repair shop and greeted Herman Shultz.

"Do you remember those boots you resoled for me, the ones I got in England? You resoled them four or five years ago."

The shop was like a cave, with shaded bulbs hanging down over various workplaces. It was abominably ventilated, but its manly smells—of glue and leather and shoe-blacking and fresh-cut felt soles and rotted old ones—were comfortable to Mr. McCauley. Here his neighbor Herman Shultz, a sallow, expert, spectacled workman, bent-shouldered, was occupied in all seasons—driving in iron nails and clinch nails and, with a wicked hooked knife, cutting the desired shapes out of leather. The felt was cut by something like a miniature circular saw. The buffers made a scuffing noise and the sandpaper wheel made a rasp and the emery stone on a tool's edge sang high like a mechanical insect and the sewing machine punched the leather in an earnest industrial rhythm. All the sounds and smells and precise activities of the place had been familiar to Mr. McCauley for years but never identified or reflected upon before. Now Herman, in his blackened leather apron with a boot on one hand, straightened up, smiled, nodded, and Mr. McCauley saw the man's whole life in this cave. He wished to express sympathy or admiration or something more that he didn't understand.

"Yes, I do," Herman said. "They were nice boots."

"Fine boots. You know I got them on my wedding trip. I got them in England. I can't remember now where, but it wasn't in London."

"I remember you telling me."

"You did a fine job on them. They're still doing well. Fine job, Herman. You do a good job here. You do honest work."

"That's good." Herman took a quick look at the boot on his hand. Mr. McCauley knew that the man wanted to get back to his work, but he couldn't let him.

"I've just had an eye-opener. A shock."

"Have you?"

The old man pulled out the letter and began to read bits of it aloud, with interjections of dismal laughter.

"Bronchitis. He says he's sick with bronchitis. He doesn't know where to turn. *I don't know who to turn to.* Well he always knows who to turn to. When he's run through everything else, turn to me. *A few hundred just till I get on my feet.* Begging and pleading with me and all the time he's conniving with my housekeeper. Did you know that? She stole a load of furniture and went off out west with it. They were hand in glove. This is a man I've saved the skin of, time and time again. And never a penny back. No, no, I have to be honest and say fifty dollars. Fifty out of hundreds and hundreds. Thousands. He was in the Air Force in the war, you know. Those shortish fellows, they were often in the Air Force. Strutting around thinking they were war heroes. Well, I guess I shouldn't say that, but I think the war spoiled some of those fellows, they never could adjust to life afterwards. But that's not enough of an excuse. Is it? I can't excuse him forever because of the war."

"No you can't."

"I knew he wasn't to be trusted the first time I met him. That's the extraordinary thing. I knew it and I let him rook me all the same. There are people like that. You take pity on them just for being the crooks they are. I got him his insurance job out there, I had some connections. Of course he mucked it up. A bad egg. Some just are."

"You're right about that."

Mrs. Shultz was not in the store that day. Usually she was the one at the counter, taking in the shoes and showing them to her husband and reporting back what he said, making out the slips, and taking the payment when the restored shoes were handed back.

Mr. McCauley remembered that she had had some kind of operation during the summer.

"Your wife isn't in today? Is she well?"

"She thought she'd better take it easy today. I've got my
girl in."

Herman Shultz nodded towards the shelves to the right of
the counter, where the finished shoes were displayed. Mr.
McCauley turned his head and saw Edith, the daughter, whom he
hadn't noticed when he came in. A childishly thin girl with straight
black hair, who kept her back to him, rearranging the shoes. That
was just the way she had seemed to slide in and out of sight when
she came to his house as Sabitha's friend. You never got a good
look at her face.

"You're going to help your father out now?" Mr. McCauley
said. "You're through with school?"

"It's Saturday," said Edith, half turning, faintly smiling.

"So it is. Well, it's a good thing to help your father, anyway. You
must take care of your parents. They've worked hard and they're
good people." With a slight air of apology, as if he knew he was
being sententious, Mr. McCauley said, "Honor thy father and thy
mother, that thy days may be long in the—"

Edith said something not for him to hear. She said, "Shoe
Repair shop."

"I'm taking up your time, I'm imposing on you," said Mr.
McCauley sadly. "You have work to do."

"There's no need for you to be sarcastic," said Edith's father
when the old man had gone.

He told Edith's mother all about Mr. McCauley at supper.

"He's not himself," he said. "Something's come over him."

"Maybe a little stroke," she said. Since her own operation—for
gallstones—she spoke knowledgeably and with a placid satisfaction about the afflictions of other people.

Now that Sabitha had gone, vanished into another sort of life that had, it seemed, always been waiting for her, Edith had reverted to being the person she had been before Sabitha came here. "Old for her age," diligent, critical. After three weeks at high school she knew that she was going to be very good at all the new subjects—Latin, Algebra, English Literature. She believed that her cleverness was going to be recognized and acclaimed and an important future would open out for her. The past year's silliness with Sabitha was slipping out of sight.

Yet when she thought about Johanna's going off out west she felt a chill from her past, an invasive alarm. She tried to bang a lid down on that, but it wouldn't stay.

As soon as she had finished washing the dishes she went off to her room with the book they had been assigned for literature class. *David Copperfield.*

She was a child who had never received more than tepid reproofs from her parents—old parents to have a child of her age, which was said to account for her being the way she was—but she felt in perfect accord with David in his unhappy situation. She felt that she was one like him, one who might as well have been an orphan, because she would probably have to run away, go into hiding, fend for herself, when the truth became known and her past shut off her future.

It had all begun with Sabitha saying, on the way to school, "We have to go by the Post Office. I have to send a letter to my dad."

They walked to and from school together every day. Sometimes they walked with their eyes closed, or backwards. Sometimes when they met people they gabbled away softly in a nonsense language, to cause confusion. Most of their good ideas were Edith's. The only idea Sabitha introduced was the writing down of a boy's name and your own, and the stroking out of all letters that were duplicated and the counting of the remainder. Then you ticked off the counted number on your fingers, saying, *Hateship, friendship, courtship, loveship, marriage,* till you got the verdict on what could happen between you and that boy.

"That's a fat letter," said Edith. She noticed everything, and she remembered everything, quickly memorizing whole pages of the textbooks in a way the other children found sinister. "Did you have a lot of things to write to your dad?" she said, surprised, because she could not credit this—or at least could not credit that Sabitha would get them on paper.

"I only wrote on one page," Sabitha said, feeling the letter.

"A-ha," said Edith. "Ah. Ha."

"Aha what?"

"I bet she put something else in. Johanna did."

The upshot of this was that they did not take the letter directly to the Post Office, but saved it and steamed it open at Edith's house after school. They could do such things at Edith's house because her mother worked all day at the Shoe Repair shop.

Dear Mr. Ken Boudreau,

I just thought I would write and send my thanks to you for the nice things you said about me in your letter to your daughter. You do not need to worry about me leaving. You say that I am a person you can trust. That is the meaning I take and as far as I know it is true. I am grateful to you for saying that, since some people feel that a person like me that they do not know the background of is Beyond the Pale. So I thought I would tell you something about myself. I was born in Glasgow, but my mother had to give me up when she got married. I was taken to the Home at the age of five. I looked for her to come back, but she didn't and I got used to it there and they weren't Bad. At the age of eleven I was brought to Canada on a Plan and lived with the Dixons, working on their Market Gardens. School was in the Plan, but I didn't see much of it. In winter I worked in the house for the Mrs. but circumstances made me think of leaving, and being big and strong for my age got taken on at a Nursing Home looking after the old people. I did not mind the work, but for better money went and worked in a Broom Factory. Mr. Willets that owned it had an old mother that came in to see how things were going, and she and I took to each other some way. The atmosphere was giving me breathing troubles so she said I should come and work for her and I did. I lived with her 12 yrs. on a lake called Mourning Dove Lake up north. There was only the two of us, but I could take care of everything outside and in, even running the motorboat and driving the car. I learned to read properly because her eyes were going bad and she liked me to read to her. She died at the age of 96. You might say what a life for a young person, but I was happy. We ate together every meal and I slept in her room the last year and a half. But after she died the family gave me one wk. to pack up. She had left me some money and I guess they did not like that. She wanted me to use it for Education but I would have to go in with kids. So when I saw the ad Mr. McCauley put in the Globe and Mail I came to see about it. I needed work to get over missing Mrs. Willets. So I guess I have bored you long enough with my History and you'll be relieved I have got up to the Present. Thank you for your good opinion and for taking me along to the Fair. I am not one for the rides or for eating the stuff but it was still certainly a pleasure to be included.

Your friend, Johanna Parry.

Edith read Johanna's words aloud, in an imploring voice and with a woebegone expression.

"I was born in Glasgow, but my mother had to give me up when she took one look at me—"

"Stop," said Sabitha. "I'm laughing so hard I'll be sick."

"How did she get her letter in with yours without you knowing?"

"She just takes it from me and puts it in an envelope and writes on the outside because she doesn't think my writing is good enough."

Edith had to put Scotch tape on the flap of the envelope to make it stick, since there wasn't enough sticky stuff left. "She's in love with him," she said.

"Oh, puke-puke," said Sabitha, holding her stomach. "She can't be. Old Johanna."

"What did he say about her, anyway?"

"Just about how I was supposed to respect her and it would be too bad if she left because we were lucky to have her and he didn't have a home for me and Grandpa couldn't raise a girl by himself and blah-blah. He said she was a lady. He said he could tell."

"So then she falls in lo-ove."

The letter remained with Edith overnight, lest Johanna discover that it hadn't been posted and was sealed with Scotch tape. They took it to the Post Office the next morning.

"Now we'll see what he writes back. Watch out," said Edith.

No letter came for a long time. And when it did, it was a disappointment. They steamed it open at Edith's house, but found nothing inside for Johanna.

Dear Sabitha,

Christmas finds me a bit short this year, sorry I don't have more than a two-dollar bill to send you. But I hope you are in good health and have a Merry Christmas and keep up your school-work. I have not been feeling so well myself, having got Bronchitis, which I seem to do every winter, but this is the first time it landed me in bed before Christmas. As you see by the address I am in a new place. The apartment was in a very noisy location and too many people dropping in hoping for a party.

This is a boardinghouse, which suits me fine as I was never good at the shopping and the cooking.

Merry Christmas and love, Dad.

"Poor Johanna," said Edith. "Her heart will be bwoken."
Sabitha said, "Who cares?"
"Unless we do it," Edith said.
"What?"
"*Answer* her."

They would have to type their letter, because Johanna would notice that it was not in Sabitha's father's handwriting. But the typing was not difficult. There was a typewriter in Edith's house, on a card table in the front room. Her mother had worked in an office before she was married and she sometimes earned a little money still by writing the sort of letters that people wanted to look official. She had taught Edith the basics of typing, in the hope that Edith too might get an office job someday.

"Dear Johanna," said Sabitha, "I am sorry I cannot be in love with you because you have got those ugly spots all over your face."

"I'm going to be serious," said Edith. "So shut up."

She typed, "I was so glad to get the letter—" speaking the words of her composition aloud, pausing while she thought up more, her voice becoming increasingly solemn and tender. Sabitha sprawled on the couch, giggling. At one point she turned on the television, but Edith said, "Pul-eeze. How can I concentrate on my e-motions with all that shit going on?"

Edith and Sabitha used the words "shit" and "bitch" and "Jesus Christ" when they were alone together.

Dear Johanna,
I was so glad to get the letter you put in with Sabitha's and to find out about your life. It must often have been a sad and lonely one

though Mrs. Willets sounds like a lucky person for you to find. You have remained industrious and uncomplaining and I must say that I admire you very much. My own life has been a checkered one and I have never exactly settled down. I do not know why I have this inner restlessness and loneliness, it just seems to be my fate. I am always meeting people and talking to people but sometimes I ask myself, Who is my friend? Then comes your letter and you write at the end of it, Your friend. So I think, Does she really mean that? And what a very nice Christmas present it would be for me if Johanna would tell me that she is my friend. Maybe you just thought it was a nice way to end a letter and you don't really know me well enough. Merry Christmas anyway.

Your friend, Ken Boudreau.

The letter went home to Johanna. The one to Sabitha had ended up being typed as well because why would one be typed and not the other? They had been sparing with the steam this time and opened the envelope very carefully so there would be no telltale Scotch tape.

"Why couldn't we type a new envelope? Wouldn't he do that if he typed the letter?" said Sabitha, thinking she was being clever.

"Because a new *envelope* wouldn't have a *postmark* on it. Dumb-dumb."

"What if she answers it?"

"We'll read it."

"Yah, what if she answers it and sends it direct to *him*?"

Edith didn't like to show she had not thought of that.

"She won't. She's sly. Anyway, you write him back right away to give her the idea she can slip it in with yours."

"I hate writing stupid letters."

"Go on. It won't kill you. Don't you want to see what she says?"

Dear Friend,

You ask me do I know you well enough to be your friend and my answer is that I think I do. I have only had one Friend in my life, Mrs. Willets who I loved and she was so good to me but she is dead. She was a lot older than me and the trouble with Older Friends is they die and leave you. She was so old she would call me sometimes by another person's name. I did not mind it though.

I will tell you a strange thing. That picture that you got the photographer at the Fair to take, of you and Sabitha and her friend Edith and me, I had it enlarged and framed and set in the living room. It is not a very good picture and he certainly charged you enough for what it is, but it is better than nothing. So the day before yesterday I was dusting around it and I imagined I could hear you say Hello to me. Hello, you said, and I looked at your face as well as you can see it in the picture and I thought, Well, I must be losing my mind. Or else it is a sign of a letter coming. I am just fooling, I don't really believe in anything like that. But yesterday there was a letter. So you see it is not asking too much of me to be your friend. I can always find a way to keep busy but a true Friend is something else again.

Your Friend, Johanna Parry.

Of course, that could not be replaced in the envelope. Sabitha's father would spot something fishy in the references to a letter he had never written. Johanna's words had to be torn into tiny pieces and flushed down the toilet at Edith's house.

When the letter came telling about the hotel it was months and months later. It was summer. And it was just by luck that Sabitha had picked that letter up, since she had been away for three weeks, staying at the cottage on Lake Simcoe that belonged to her Aunt Roxanne and her Uncle Clark.

Almost the first thing Sabitha said, coming into Edith's house, was, "Ugga-ugga. This place stinks."

"Ugga-ugga" was an expression she had picked up from her cousins.

Edith sniffed the air. "I don't smell anything."

"It's like your dad's shop, only not so bad. They must bring it home on their clothes and stuff."

Edith attended to the steaming and opening. On her way from the Post Office, Sabitha had bought two chocolate eclairs at the bakeshop. She was lying on the couch eating hers.

"Just one letter. For you," said Edith. "Pore old Johanna. Of course he never actually *got* hers."

"Read it to me," said Sabitha resignedly. "I've got sticky guck all over my hands."

Edith read it with businesslike speed, hardly pausing for the periods.

Well, Sabitha, my fortunes have taken a different turn, as you can see I am not in Brandon anymore but in a place called Gdynia. And not in the employ of my former bosses. I have had an exceptionally hard winter with my chest troubles and they, that is my bosses, thought I should be out on the road even if I was in danger of developing pneumonia so this developed into quite an argument so we all decided to say farewell. But luck is a strange thing and just about that time I came into possession of a Hotel. It is too complicated to explain the ins and outs but if your grandfather wants to know about it just tell him a man who owed me money which he could not pay let me have this hotel instead. So here I am moved from one room in a boardinghouse to a twelve-bedroom building and from not even owning the bed I slept in to owning several. It's a wonderful thing to wake up in the morning and know you are your own boss. I have some fixing up to do, actually plenty, and will get to it as soon as the weather warms up. I will need to hire somebody to help and later on I will hire a good cook to have a restaurant as well as the beverage room. That ought to go like hotcakes as there is none in this town. Hope you are well and doing your schoolwork and developing good habits.

Love, Your Dad.

Sabitha said, "Have you got some coffee?"

"Instant," said Edith. "Why?"

Sabitha said that iced coffee was what everybody had been drinking at the cottage and they were all crazy about it. She was crazy about it too. She got up and messed around in the kitchen, boiling the water and stirring up the coffee with milk and ice cubes. "What we really ought to have is vanilla ice cream," she said. "Oh, my Gad, is it ever wonderful. Don't you want your eclair?"

Oh, my Gad.

"Yes. All of it," said Edith meanly.

All these changes in Sabitha in just three weeks—during the time Edith had been working in the shop and her mother recovering at home from her operation. Sabitha's skin was an appetizing golden-brown color, and her hair was cut shorter and fluffed out around her face. Her cousins had cut it and given her a permanent. She wore a sort of playsuit, with shorts cut like a skirt and buttons down the front and frills over the shoulders in a becoming blue color. She had got plumper, and when she leaned over to pick up her glass of iced coffee, which was on the floor, she displayed a smooth, glowing cleavage.

Breasts. They must have started growing before she went away, but Edith had not noticed. Maybe they were just something you woke up with one morning. Or did not.

However they came, they seemed to indicate a completely unearned and unfair advantage.

Sabitha was full of talk about her cousins and life at the cottage. She would say, "Listen, I've got to tell you about this, it's a scream—" and then ramble on about what Aunt Roxanne said to Uncle Clark when they had the fight, how Mary Jo drove with the top down and without a license in Stan's car (who was Stan?) and took them all to a drive-in—and what was the scream or the point of the story somehow never became clear.

But after a while other things did. The real adventures of the summer. The older girls—that included Sabitha—slept in the upstairs of the boathouse. Sometimes they had tickling fights— they would all gang up on someone and tickle her till she shrieked for mercy and agreed to pull her pajama pants down to show if she had hair. They told stories about girls at boarding school who did things with hairbrush handles, toothbrush handles. *Ugga-ugga.* Once a couple of cousins put on a show—one girl got on top of the other and pretended to be the boy and they wound their legs around each other and groaned and panted and carried on.

Uncle Clark's sister and her husband came to visit on their honeymoon, and he was seen to put his hand inside her swimsuit.

"They really loved each other, they were at it day and night," said Sabitha. She hugged a cushion to her chest. "People can't help it when they're in love like that."

One of the cousins had already done it with a boy. He was one of the summer help in the gardens of the resort down the road. He took her out in a boat and threatened to push her out until she agreed to let him do it. So it wasn't her fault.

"Couldn't she swim?" said Edith.

Sabitha pushed the cushion between her legs. "Oooh," she said. "Feels so nice."

Edith knew all about the pleasurable agonies Sabitha was feeling, but she was appalled that anybody would make them public. She herself was frightened of them. Years ago, before she knew what she was doing, she had gone to sleep with the blanket between her legs and her mother had discovered her and told her about a girl she had known who did things like that all the time and had eventually been operated on for the problem.

"They used to throw cold water on her, but it didn't cure her," her mother had said. "So she had to be cut."

Otherwise her organs would get congested and she might die.

"Stop," she said to Sabitha, but Sabitha moaned defiantly and said, "It's nothing. We all did it like this. Haven't you got a cushion?"

Edith got up and went to the kitchen and filled her empty iced-coffee glass with cold water. When she got back Sabitha was lying limp on the couch, laughing, the cushion flung on the floor.

"What did you think I was doing?" she said. "Didn't you know I was kidding?"

"I was thirsty," Edith said.

"You just drank a whole glass of iced coffee."

"I was thirsty for water."

"Can't have any fun with you." Sabitha sat up. "If you're so thirsty why don't you drink it?"

They sat in a moody silence until Sabitha said, in a conciliatory but disappointed tone, "Aren't we going to write Johanna another letter? Let's write her a lovey-dovey letter."

Edith had lost a good deal of her interest in the letters, but she was gratified to see that Sabitha had not. Some sense of having power over Sabitha returned, in spite of Lake Simcoe and the breasts. Sighing, as if reluctantly, she got up and took the cover off the typewriter.

"My darlingest Johanna—" said Sabitha.

"No. That's too sickening."

"She won't think so."

"She will so," said Edith.

She wondered whether she should tell Sabitha about the danger

of congested organs. She decided not to. For one thing, that information fell into a category of warnings she had received from her
mother and never known whether to wholly trust or distrust. It
had not fallen as low, in credibility, as the belief that wearing foot-
rubbers in the house would ruin your eyesight, but there was no
telling—someday it might.

And for another thing—Sabitha would just laugh. She laughed
at warnings—she would laugh even if you told her that chocolate
eclairs would make her fat.

"Your last letter made me so happy—"

"Your last letter filled me with rap-ture—" said Sabitha.

"—made me so happy to think I did have a true friend in the
world, which is you—"

"I could not sleep all night because I was longing to crush you
in my arms—" Sabitha wrapped her arms around herself and
rocked back and forth.

"*No.* Often I have felt so lonely in spite of a gregarious life and
not known where to turn—"

"What does that mean—'gregarious'? She won't know what it
means."

"*She* will."

That shut Sabitha up and perhaps hurt her feelings. So at the
end Edith read out, "I must say good-bye and the only way I can
do it is to imagine you reading this and blushing—" "Is that more
what you want?"

"Reading it in bed with your nightgown on," said Sabitha,
always quickly restored, "and thinking how I would crush you in
my arms and I would suck your titties—"

My Dear Johanna,
Your last letter made me so happy to think I have a true friend in
the world, which is you. Often I have felt so lonely in spite of a
gregarious life and not known where to turn.

Well, I have told Sabitha in my letter about my good fortune and how I am going into the hotel business. I did not tell her actually how sick I was last winter because I did not want to worry her. I do not want to worry you, either, dear Johanna, only to tell you that I thought of you so often and longed to see your dear sweet face. When I was feverish I thought that I really did see it bending over me and I heard your voice telling me I would soon be better and I felt the ministrations of your kind hands. I was in the boardinghouse and when I came to out of my fever there was a lot of teasing going on as to, who is this Johanna? But I was sad as could be to wake and find you were not there. I really wondered if you could have flown through the air and been with me, even though I knew that could not have happened. Believe me, believe me, the most beautiful movie star could not have been as welcome to me as you. I don't know if I should tell you the other things you were saying to me because they were very sweet and intimate but they might embarrass you. I hate to end this letter because it feels now as if I have my arms around you and I am talking to you quietly in the dark privacy of our room, but I must say good-bye and the only way I can do it is to imagine you reading this and blushing. It would be wonderful if you were reading it in bed with your nightgown on and thinking how I would like to crush you in my arms.

L-v-, Ken Boudreau.

Somewhat surprisingly, there was no reply to this letter. When Sabitha had written her half-page, Johanna put it in the envelope and addressed it and that was that.

When Johanna got off the train there was nobody to meet her. She did not let herself worry about that—she had been thinking that her letter might not, after all, have got here before she did. (In fact it had, and was lying in the Post Office, uncollected, because Ken Boudreau, who had not been seriously sick last winter, really did have bronchitis now and for several days had not come in for his mail. On this day it had been joined by another envelope, containing the check from Mr. McCauley. But payment on that had already been stopped.)

What was of more concern to her was that there did not appear to be a town. The station was an enclosed shelter with benches along the walls and a wooden shutter pulled down over the window of the ticket office. There was also a freight shed—she supposed it was a freight shed—but the sliding door to it would not budge. She peered through a crack between the planks until her eyes got used to the dark in there, and she saw that it was empty, with a dirt floor. No crates of furniture there. She called out, "Anybody here? Anybody here?" several times, but she did not expect a reply.

She stood on the platform and tried to get her bearings.

About half a mile away there was a slight hill, noticeable at once because it had a crown of trees. And the sandy-looking track that she had taken, when she saw it from the train, for a back lane into a farmer's field—that must be the road. Now she saw the low shapes of buildings here and there in the trees—and a water tower, which looked from this distance like a toy, a tin soldier on long legs.

She picked up her suitcase—this would not be too difficult; she had carried it, after all, from Exhibition Road to the other railway station—and set out.

There was a wind blowing, but this was a hot day—hotter than the weather she had left in Ontario—and the wind seemed hot as well. Over her new dress she was wearing her same old coat, which would have taken up too much room in the suitcase. She looked with longing to the shade of the town ahead, but when she got there she found that the trees were either spruce, which were too tight and narrow to give much shade, or raggedy thin-leaved cottonwoods, which blew about and let the sun through anyway.

There was a discouraging lack of formality, or any sort of organization, to this place. No sidewalks, or paved streets, no imposing buildings except a big church like a brick barn. A painting over its door, showing the Holy Family with clay-colored faces and staring blue eyes. It was named for an unheard-of saint—Saint Voytech.

The houses did not show much forethought in their situation or planning. They were set at different angles to the road, or street, and most of them had mean-looking little windows stuck here and there, with snow porches like boxes round the doors. Nobody was out in the yards, and why should they be? There was nothing to tend, only clumps of brown grass and once a big burst of rhubarb, gone to seed.

The main street, if that's what it was, had a raised wooden walk on one side only, and some unconsolidated buildings, of which a grocery store (containing the Post Office) and a garage seemed to be the only ones functioning. There was one two-story building that she thought might be the hotel, but it was a bank and it was closed.

The first human being she saw—though two dogs had barked at her—was a man in front of the garage, busy loading chains into the back of his truck.

"Hotel?" he said. "You come too far."

He told her that it was down by the station, on the other side of the tracks and along a bit, it was painted blue and you couldn't miss it.

She set the suitcase down, not from discouragement but because she had to have a moment's rest.

He said he would ride her down there if she wanted to wait a minute. And though it was a new kind of thing for her to accept such an offer, she soon found herself riding in the hot, greasy cab of his truck, rocking down the dirt road that she had just walked up, with the chains making a desperate racket in the back.

"So—where'd you bring this heat wave from?" he said.

She said Ontario, in a tone that promised nothing further.

"Ontario," he said regretfully. "Well. There 'tis. Your hotel." He took one hand off the wheel. The truck gave an accompanying lurch as he waved to a two-story flat-roofed building that she hadn't missed but had seen from the train, as they came in. She had taken it then for a large and fairly derelict, perhaps abandoned, family home. Now that she had seen the houses in town, she knew that she should not have dismissed it so readily. It was covered with sheets of tin stamped to look like bricks and painted a light blue. There was the one word HOTEL, in neon tubing, no longer lit, over the doorway.

"I am a dunce," she said, and offered the man a dollar for the ride.

He laughed. "Hang on to your money. You never know when you'll need it."

Quite a decent-looking car, a Plymouth, was parked outside this hotel. It was very dirty, but how could you help that, with these roads?

There were signs on the door advertising a brand of cigarettes, and of beer. She waited till the truck had turned before she knocked—knocked because it didn't look as if the place could in any way be open for business. Then she tried the door to see if it was open, and walked into a little dusty room with a staircase, and then into a large dark room in which there was a billiard table and a bad smell of beer and an unswept floor. Off in a side room she could see the glimmer of a mirror, empty shelves, a counter. These rooms had the blinds pulled tightly down. The only light she saw was coming through two small round windows, which turned out to be set in double swinging doors. She went on through these into a kitchen. It was lighter, because of a row of high—and dirty— windows, uncovered, in the opposite wall. And here were the first signs of life—somebody had been eating at the table and had left a plate smeared with dried ketchup and a cup half full of cold black coffee.

One of the doors off the kitchen led outside—this one was locked—and one to a pantry in which there were several cans of food, one to a broom closet, and one to an enclosed stairway. She climbed the steps, bumping her suitcase along in front of her because the space was narrow. Straight ahead of her on the second floor she saw a toilet with the seat up.

The door of the bedroom at the end of the hall was open, and in there she found Ken Boudreau.

She saw his clothes before she saw him. His jacket hanging up on a corner of the door and his trousers on the doorknob, so that they trailed on the floor. She thought at once that this was no way to treat good clothes, so she went boldly into the room—leaving her suitcase in the hall—with the idea of hanging them up properly.

He was in bed, with only a sheet over him. The blanket and his shirt were lying on the floor. He was breathing restlessly as if about to wake up, so she said, "Good morning. Afternoon."

The bright sunlight was coming in the window, hitting him almost in the face. The window was closed and the air horribly stale—smelling, for one thing, of the full ashtray on the chair he used as a bed table.

He had bad habits—he smoked in bed.

He did not wake up at her voice—or he woke only part way. He began to cough.

She recognized this as a serious cough, a sick man's cough. He struggled to lift himself up, still with his eyes closed, and she went over to the bed and hoisted him. She looked for a handkerchief or a box of tissues, but she saw nothing so she reached for his shirt on the floor, which she could wash later. She wanted to get a good look at what he spat up.

When he had hacked up enough, he muttered and sank down into the bed, gasping, the charming cocky-looking face she remembered crumpled up in disgust. She knew from the feel of him that he had a fever.

The stuff that he had coughed out was greenish-yellow—no rusty streaks. She carried the shirt to the toilet sink, where rather to her surprise she found a bar of soap, and washed it out and hung it on the door hook, then thoroughly washed her hands. She had to dry them on the skirt of her new brown dress. She had put that on in another little toilet—the *Ladies* on the train—not more than a couple of hours ago. She had been wondering then if she should have got some makeup.

In a hall closet she found a roll of toilet paper and took it into his room for the next time he had to cough. She picked up the blanket and covered him well, pulled the blind down to the sill and raised the stiff window an inch or two, propping it open with the ashtray she had emptied. Then she changed, out in the hall, from the brown dress into old clothes from her suitcase. A lot of use a nice dress or any makeup in the world would be now, in these surroundings.

She was not sure how sick he was, but she had nursed Mrs. Willets—also a heavy smoker—through several bouts of bronchitis, and she thought she could manage for a while without having to think about getting a doctor. In the same hall closet was a pile of clean, though worn and faded, towels, and she wet one of these and wiped his arms and legs, to try to get his fever down. He came half awake at this and began to cough again. She held him up and made him spit into the toilet paper, examined it once more and threw it down the toilet and washed her hands. She had a towel now to dry them on. She went downstairs and found a glass in the kitchen, also an empty, large ginger-ale bottle, which she filled with water. This she attempted to make him drink. He took a little, protested, and she let him lie down. In five minutes or so she tried again. She kept doing this until she believed he had swallowed as much as he could hold without throwing up.

Time and again he coughed and she lifted him up, held him with one arm while the other hand pounded on his back to help loosen the load in his chest. He opened his eyes several times and seemed to take in her presence without alarm or surprise—or gratitude, for that matter. She sponged him once more, being careful to cover immediately with the blanket the part that had just been cooled.

She noticed that it had begun to get dark, and she went down into the kitchen, found the light switch. The lights and the old electric stove were working. She opened and heated a can of chicken-with-rice soup, carried it upstairs and roused him. He swallowed a little from the spoon. She took advantage of his momentary wakefulness to ask if he had a bottle of aspirin. He nodded yes, then became very confused when trying to tell her where. "In the wastebasket," he said.

"No, no," she said. "You don't mean wastebasket."

"In the— in the—"

He tried to shape something with his hands. Tears came into his eyes.

"Never mind," Johanna said. "Never mind."

His fever went down anyway. He slept for an hour or more without coughing. Then he grew hot again. By that time she had found the aspirin—they were in a kitchen drawer with such things as a screwdriver and some lightbulbs and a ball of twine—and she got a couple into him. Soon he had a violent coughing fit, but she didn't think he threw them up. When he lay down she put her ear to his chest and listened to the wheezing. She had already looked for mustard to make a plaster with, but apparently there wasn't any. She went downstairs again and heated some water and brought it in a basin. She tried to make him lean over it, tenting him with towels, so that he could breathe the steam. He would cooperate only for a moment or so, but perhaps it helped—he hacked up quantities of phlegm.

His fever went down again and he slept more calmly. She dragged in an armchair she had found in one of the other rooms and she slept too, in snatches, waking and wondering where she was, then remembering and getting up and touching him—his fever seemed to be staying down—and tucking in the blanket. For her own cover she used the everlasting old tweed coat that she had Mrs. Willets to thank for.

He woke. It was full morning. "What are you doing here?" he said, in a hoarse, weak voice.

"I came yesterday," she said. "I brought your furniture. It isn't here yet, but it's on its way. You were sick when I got here and you were sick most of the night. How do you feel now?"

He said, "Better," and began to cough. She didn't have to lift him, he sat up on his own, but she went to the bed and pounded his back. When he finished, he said, "Thank you."

His skin now felt as cool as her own. And smooth—no rough moles, no fat on him. She could feel his ribs. He was like a delicate, stricken boy. He smelled like corn.

"You swallowed the phlegm," she said. "Don't do that, it's not good for you. Here's the toilet paper, you have to spit it out. You could get trouble with your kidneys, swallowing it."

"I never knew that," he said. "Could you find the coffee?"

The percolator was black on the inside. She washed it as well as she could and put the coffee on. Then she washed and tidied herself, wondering what kind of food she should give him. In the pantry there was a box of biscuit mix. At first she thought she would have to mix it with water, but she found a can of milk powder as well. When the coffee was ready she had a pan of biscuits in the oven.

As soon as he heard her busy in the kitchen, he got up to go to the toilet. He was weaker than he'd thought—he had to lean over and put one hand on the tank. Then he found some underwear on the floor of the hall closet where he kept clean clothes. He had figured out by now who this woman was and recalled her writing him some kind of friendly letter he couldn't take the time to answer. She had said she came to bring him his furniture, though he hadn't asked her or anybody to do that—hadn't asked for the furniture at all, just the money. He should know her name, but he couldn't remember it. That was why he opened her purse, which was on the floor of the hall beside her suitcase. There was a name tag sewn to the lining.

Johanna Parry, and the address of his father-in-law, on Exhibition Road.

Some other things. A cloth bag with a few bills in it. Twenty-seven dollars. Another bag with change, which he didn't bother to count. A bright blue bankbook. He opened it up automatically, without expectations of anything unusual.

A couple of weeks ago Johanna had been able to transfer the whole of her inheritance from Mrs. Willets into her bank account, adding it to the amount of money she had saved. She had explained to the bank manager that she did not know when she might need it.

The sum was not dazzling, but it was impressive. It gave her substance. In Ken Boudreau's mind, it added a sleek upholstery to the name Johanna Parry.

"Were you wearing a brown dress?" he said, when she came up with the coffee.

"Yes, I was. When I first got here."

"I thought it was a dream. It was you."

"Like in your other dream," Johanna said, her speckled forehead turning fiery. He didn't know what that was all about and hadn't the energy to inquire. Possibly a dream he'd wakened from when she was here in the night—one he couldn't now remember. He coughed again in a more reasonable way, with her handing him some toilet paper.

"Now," she said, "where are you going to set your coffee?" She pushed up the wooden chair that she had moved to get at him more easily. "There," she said. She lifted him under the arms and wedged the pillow in behind him. A dirty pillow, without a case, but she had covered it last night with a towel.

"Could you see if there's any cigarettes downstairs?"

She shook her head, but said, "I'll look. I've got biscuits in the oven."

Ken Boudreau was in the habit of lending money, as well as borrowing it. Much of the trouble that had come upon him—or that he had got into, to put it another way—had to do with not being able to say no to a friend. Loyalty. He had not been drummed out of the peacetime Air Force, but had resigned out of loyalty to the friend who had been hauled up for offering insults to the C.O. at a mess party. At a mess party, where everything was supposed to be a joke and no offense taken—it was not fair. And he had lost the job with the fertilizer company because he took a company truck across the American border without permission, on a Sunday, to pick up a buddy who had got into a fight and was afraid of being caught and charged.

Part and parcel of the loyalty to friends was the difficulty with bosses. He would confess that he found it hard to knuckle under. "Yes, sir," and "no, sir" were not ready words in his vocabulary. He had not been fired from the insurance company, but he had been passed over so many times that it seemed they were daring him to quit, and eventually he did.

Drink had played a part, you had to admit that. And the idea that life should be a more heroic enterprise than it ever seemed to be nowadays.

He liked to tell people he'd won the hotel in a poker game. He was not really much of a gambler, but women liked the sound of that. He didn't want to admit that he'd taken it sight unseen in payment of a debt. And even after he saw it, he told himself it could be salvaged. The idea of being his own boss did appeal to him. He did not see it as a place where people would stay—except perhaps hunters, in the fall. He saw it as a drinking establishment and a restaurant. If he could get a good cook. But before anything much could happen money would have to be spent. Work had to be done—more than he could possibly do himself though he was not unhandy. If he could live through the winter doing what he could by himself, proving his good intentions, he thought maybe he could get a loan from the bank. But he needed a smaller loan just to get through the winter, and that was where his father-in-law came into the picture. He would rather have tried somebody else, but nobody else could so easily spare it.

He had thought it a good idea to put the request in the form of a proposal to sell the furniture, which he knew the old man would never bestir himself enough to do. He was aware, not very specifically, of loans still outstanding from the past—but he was able to think of those as sums he'd been entitled to, for supporting Marcelle during a period of bad behavior (hers, at a time when his own hadn't started) and for accepting Sabitha as his child when he had his doubts. Also, the McCauleys were the only people he knew who had money that nobody now alive had earned.

I brought your furniture.

He was unable to figure out what that could mean for him, at present. He was too tired. He wanted to sleep more than he wanted to eat when she came with the biscuits (and no cigarettes). To satisfy her he ate half of one. Then he fell dead asleep. He came only half awake when she rolled him on one side, then the other, getting the dirty sheet out from under him, then spreading the clean one and rolling him onto that, all without making him get out of bed or really wake up.

"I found a clean sheet, but it's thin as a rag," she said. "It didn't smell too good, so I hung it on the line awhile."

Later he realized that a sound he'd been hearing for a long time in a dream was really the sound of the washing machine. He wondered how that could be—the hot-water tank was defunct. She must have heated tubs of water on the stove. Later still, he heard the unmistakable sound of his own car starting up and driving away. She would have got the keys from his pants pocket.

She might be driving away in his only worthwhile possession, deserting him, and he could not even phone the police to nab her. The phone was cut off, even if he'd been able to get to it.

That was always a possibility—theft and desertion—yet he turned over on the fresh sheet, which smelled of prairie wind and grass, and went back to sleep, knowing for certain that she had only gone to buy milk and eggs and butter and bread and other supplies—even cigarettes—that were necessary for a decent life, and that she would come back and be busy downstairs and that the sound of her activity would be like a net beneath him, heaven-sent, a bounty not to be questioned.

There was a woman problem in his life right now. Two women, actually, a young one and an older one (that is, one of about his own age) who knew about each other and were ready to tear each other's hair out. All he had got from them recently was howling and complaining, punctuated with their angry assertions that they loved him.

Perhaps a solution had arrived for that, as well.

When she was buying groceries in the store, Johanna heard a train, and driving back to the hotel, she saw a car parked at the railway station. Before she had even stopped Ken Boudreau's car she saw the furniture crates piled up on the platform. She talked to the agent—it was his car there—and he was very surprised and irritated by the arrival of all these big crates. When she had got out of him the name of a man with a truck—a clean truck, she insisted—who lived twenty miles away and sometimes did hauling, she used the station phone to call the man and half bribed, half ordered him to come right away. Then she impressed upon the agent that he must stay with the crates till the truck arrived. By suppertime the truck had come, and the man and his son had unloaded all the furniture and carried it into the main room of the hotel.

The next day she took a good look around. She was making up her mind.

The day after that she judged Ken Boudreau to be able to sit up and listen to her, and she said, "This place is a sinkhole for money. The town is on its last legs. What should be done is to take out everything that can bring in any cash and sell it. I don't mean the furniture that was shipped in, I mean things like the pool table and the kitchen range. Then we ought to sell the building to somebody who'll strip the tin off it for junk. There's always a bit to be made off stuff you'd never think had any value. Then— What was it you had in mind to do before you got hold of the hotel?"

He said that he had had some idea of going to British Columbia, to Salmon Arm, where he had a friend who had told him one time he could have a job managing orchards. But he couldn't go because the car needed new tires and work done on it before he could undertake a long trip, and he was spending all he had just to live. Then the hotel had fallen into his lap.

"Like a ton of bricks," she said. "Tires and fixing the car would be a better investment than sinking anything into this place. It would be a good idea to get out there before the snow comes. And ship the furniture by rail again, to make use of it when we get there. We have got all we need to furnish a home."

"It's maybe not all that firm of an offer."

She said, "I know. But it'll be all right."

He understood that she did know, and that it was, it would be, all right. You could say that a case like his was right up her alley.

Not that he wouldn't be grateful. He'd got to a point where gratitude wasn't a burden, where it was natural—especially when it wasn't demanded.

Thoughts of regeneration were starting. *This is the change I need*. He had said that before, but surely there was one time when it would be true. The mild winters, the smell of the evergreen forests and the ripe apples. *All we need to make a home.*

He has his pride, she thought. That would have to be taken account of. It might be better never to mention the letters in which he had laid himself open to her. Before she came away, she had destroyed them. In fact she had destroyed each one as soon as she'd read it over well enough to know it by heart, and that didn't take long. One thing she surely didn't want was for them ever to fall into the hands of young Sabitha and her shifty friend. Especially the part in the last letter, about her nightgown, and being in bed. It wasn't that such things wouldn't go on, but it might be thought vulgar or sappy or asking for ridicule, to put them on paper.

She doubted they'd see much of Sabitha. But she would never thwart him, if that was what he wanted.

This wasn't really a new experience, this brisk sense of expansion and responsibility. She'd felt something the same for Mrs. Willets—another fine-looking, flighty person in need of care and management. Ken Boudreau had turned out to be a bit more that way than she was prepared for, and there were the differences you had to expect with a man, but surely there was nothing in him that she couldn't handle.

After Mrs. Willets her heart had been dry, and she had considered it might always be so. And now such a warm commotion, such busy love.

Mr. McCauley died about two years after Johanna's departure. His funeral was the last one held in the Anglican church. There was a good turnout for it. Sabitha—who came with her mother's cousin, the Toronto woman—was now self-contained and pretty and remarkably, unexpectedly slim. She wore a sophisticated black hat and did not speak to anybody unless they spoke to her first. Even then, she did not seem to remember them.

The death notice in the paper said that Mr. McCauley was survived by his granddaughter Sabitha Boudreau and his son-in-law Ken Boudreau, and Mr. Boudreau's wife Johanna, and their infant son Omar, of Salmon Arm, B.C.

Edith's mother read this out—Edith herself never looked at the local paper. Of course, the marriage was not news to either of them—or to Edith's father, who was around the corner in the front room, watching television. Word had got back. The only news was Omar.

"Her with a *baby,*" Edith's mother said.

Edith was doing her Latin translation at the kitchen table. *Tu ne quaesieris, scire nefas, quem mihi, quem tibi—*

In the church she had taken the precaution of not speaking to Sabitha first, before Sabitha could not speak to her.

She was not really afraid, anymore, of being found out—though she still could not understand why they hadn't been. And in a way, it seemed only proper that the antics of her former self should not be connected with her present self—let alone with the real self that she expected would take over once she got out of this town and away from all the people who thought they knew her. It was the whole twist of consequence that dismayed her—it seemed fantastical, but dull. Also insulting, like some sort of joke or inept warning, trying to get its hooks into her. For where, on the list of things she planned to achieve in her life, was there any mention of her being responsible for the existence on earth of a person named Omar?

Ignoring her mother, she wrote, "You must not ask, it is forbidden for us to know—"

She paused, chewing her pencil, then finished off with a chill of satisfaction, "—what fate has in store for me, or for you—"

Floating Bridge

One time she had left him. The immediate reason was fairly trivial. He had joined a couple of the Young Offenders (Yo-yos was what he called them) in gobbling up a gingerbread cake she had just made and intended to serve after a meeting that evening. Unobserved—at least by Neal and the Yo-yos—she had left the house and gone to sit in a three-sided shelter on the main street, where the city bus stopped twice a day. She had never been in there before, and she had a couple of hours to wait. She sat and read everything that had been written on or cut into those wooden walls. Various initials loved each other 4 ever. Laurie G. sucked cock. Dunk Cultis was a fag. So was Mr. Garner (Math).

Eat Shit H.W. Gange rules. Skate or Die. God hates filth. Kevin S. is Dead Meat. Amanda W. is beautiful and sweet and I wish they did not put her in jail because I miss her with all my heart. I want to fuck V.P. Ladies have to sit here and read this disgusting dirty things what you write.

Looking at this barrage of human messages—and puzzling in particular over the heartfelt, very neatly written sentence concerning Amanda W., Jinny wondered if people were alone when they wrote such things. And she went on to imagine herself sitting here or in some similar place, waiting for a bus, alone, as she would surely be if she went ahead with the plan she was set on now. Would she be compelled to make statements on public walls?

She felt herself connected at present with the way people felt when they had to write certain things down—she was connected by her feelings of anger, of petty outrage (perhaps it was petty?), and her excitement at what she was doing to Neal, to pay him back. But the life she was carrying herself into might not give her anybody to be angry at, or anybody who owed her anything, anybody who could possibly be rewarded or punished or truly affected by what she might do. Her feelings might become of no importance to anybody but herself, and yet they would be bulging up inside her, squeezing her heart and breath.

She was not, after all, somebody people flocked to in the world. And yet she was choosy, in her own way.

The bus was still not in sight when she got up and walked home.

Neal was not there. He was returning the boys to the school, and by the time he got back somebody had already arrived, early for the meeting. She told him what she'd done when she was well over it and it could be turned into a joke. In fact, it became a joke she told in company—leaving out or just describing in a general way the things she'd read on the walls—many times.

"Would you ever have thought to come after me?" she said to Neal.

"Of course. Given time."

The oncologist had a priestly demeanor and in fact wore a black turtle-necked shirt under a white smock—an outfit that suggested he had just come from some ceremonial mixing and dosing. His skin was young and smooth—it looked like butterscotch. On the dome of his head there was just a faint black growth of hair, a delicate sprouting, very like the fuzz Jinny was sporting herself. Though hers was brownish-gray, like mouse fur. At first Jinny had wondered if he could possibly be a patient as well as a doctor.

Then, whether he had adopted this style to make the patients more comfortable. More likely it was a transplant. Or just the way he liked to wear his hair.

You couldn't ask him. He came from Syria or Jordan or some place where doctors kept their dignity. His courtesies were frigid.

"Now," he said. "I do not wish to give a wrong impression."

She went out of the air-conditioned building into the stunning glare of a late afternoon in August in Ontario. Sometimes the sun burned through, sometimes it stayed behind thin clouds—it was just as hot either way. The parked cars, the pavement, the bricks of the other buildings, seemed positively to bombard her, as if they were all separate facts thrown up in ridiculous sequence. She did not take changes of scene very well these days, she wanted everything familiar and stable. It was the same with changes of information.

She saw the van detach itself from its place at the curb and make its way down the street to pick her up. It was a light-blue, shimmery, sickening color. Lighter blue where the rust spots had been painted over. Its stickers said I KNOW I DRIVE A WRECK, BUT YOU SHOULD SEE MY HOUSE, and HONOUR THY MOTHER—EARTH, and (this was more recent) USE PESTICIDE, KILL WEEDS, PROMOTE CANCER.

Neal came around to help her.

"She's in the van," he said. There was an eager note in his voice that registered vaguely as a warning or a plea. A buzz around him, a tension, that told Jinny it wasn't time to give him her news, if news was what you'd call it. When Neal was around other people, even one person other than Jinny, his behavior changed, becoming more animated, enthusiastic, ingratiating. Jinny was not bothered by that anymore—they had been together for twenty-one years. And she herself changed—as a reaction, she used to think— becoming more reserved and slightly ironic. Some masquerades were necessary, or just too habitual to be dropped. Like Neal's antique appearance—the bandanna headband, the rough gray ponytail, the little gold earring that caught the light like the gold rims 'round his teeth, and his shaggy outlaw clothes.

While she had been seeing the doctor, he had been picking up the girl who was going to help them with their life now. He knew her from the Correctional Institute for Young Offenders, where he was a teacher and she had worked in the kitchen. The Correctional Institute was just outside the town where they lived, about twenty miles away from here. The girl had quit her kitchen job a few months ago and taken a job looking after a farm household where the mother was sick. Somewhere not far from this larger town. Luckily she was now free.

"What happened to the woman?" Jinny had said. "Did she die?"

Neal said, "She went into the hospital."

"Same deal."

They had had to make a lot of practical arrangements in a fairly short time. Clear the front room of their house of all the files, the newspapers and magazines containing relevant articles that had not yet been put on disk—these had filled the shelves lining the room up to the ceiling. The two computers as well, the old type-writers, the printer. All this had to find a place—temporarily, though nobody said so—in somebody else's house. The front room would become the sickroom.

Jinny had said to Neal that he could keep one computer, at least, in the bedroom. But he had refused. He did not say, but she under-stood, that he believed there would not be time for it.

Neal had spent nearly all his spare time, in the years she had been with him, organizing and carrying out campaigns. Not just political campaigns (those too) but efforts to preserve historic buildings and bridges and cemeteries, to keep trees from being cut down both along the town streets and in isolated patches of old forest, to save rivers from poisonous runoff and choice land from developers and the local population from casinos. Letters and petitions were always being written, government departments lobbied, posters distributed, protests organized. The front room was the scene of rages of indignation (which gave people a lot of satisfaction, Jinny thought) and confused propositions and arguments, and Neal's nervy buoyancy. And now that it was suddenly emptied, it made her think of when she first walked into the house, straight from her parents' split-level with the swag curtains, and thought of all those shelves filled with books, wooden shutters on the windows, and those beautiful Middle Eastern rugs she always forgot the name of, on the varnished floor. The Canaletto print she had bought for her room at college on the one bare wall. *Lord Mayor's Day on the Thames.* She had actually put that up, though she never noticed it anymore.

They rented a hospital bed—they didn't really need it yet, but it was better to get one while you could because they were often in short supply. Neal thought of everything. He hung up some heavy curtains that were discards from a friend's family room. They had a pattern of tankards and horse brasses and Jinny thought them very ugly. But she knew now that there comes a time when ugly and beautiful serve pretty much the same purpose, when anything you look at is just a peg to hang the unruly sensations of your body on, and the bits and pieces of your mind.

She was forty-two, and until recently she had looked younger than her age. Neal was sixteen years older than she was. So she had thought that in the natural course of things she would be in the position he was in now, and she had sometimes worried about how she would manage it. Once when she was holding his hand in bed before they went to sleep, his warm and present hand, she had thought that she would hold, or touch this hand, at least once, when he was dead. And she would not be able to believe in that fact. The fact of his being dead and powerless. No matter how long this state had been foreseen, she would not be able to credit it. She would not be able to believe that, deep down, he had not some knowledge of this moment. Of her. To think of him not having that brought on a kind of emotional vertigo, the sense of a horrid drop.

And yet—an excitement. The unspeakable excitement you feel when a galloping disaster promises to release you from all responsibility for your own life. Then for shame you must compose yourself and stay very quiet.

"Where are you going?" he had said, when she withdrew her hand.

"No place. Just turning over."

She didn't know if Neal had any such feeling, now that it had happened to be her. She had asked him if he had got used to the idea yet. He shook his head.

She said, "Me neither."

Then she said, "Just don't let the Grief Counselors in. They could be hanging around already. Wanting to make a preemptive strike."

"Don't harrow me," he said, in a voice of rare anger.

"Sorry."

"You don't always have to take the lighter view."

"I know," she said. But the fact was that with so much going on and present events grabbing so much of her attention, she found it hard to take any view at all.

"This is Helen," Neal said. "This is who is going to look after us from now on. She won't stand for any nonsense, either."

"Good for her," said Jinny. She put out her hand, once she was sitting down. But the girl might not have seen it, low down between the two front seats.

Or she might not have known what to do. Neal had said that she came from an unbelievable situation, an absolutely barbaric family. Things had gone on that you could not imagine going on in this day and age. An isolated farm, a dead mother and a mentally deficient daughter and a tyrannical, deranged incestuous old father, and the two girl children. Helen the older one, who had run away at the age of fourteen after beating up on the old man. She had been sheltered by a neighbor who phoned the police, and the police had come and got the younger sister and made both children wards of the Children's Aid. The old man and his daughter—that is, their mother and their father—were both placed in a Psychiatric Hospital. Foster parents took Helen and her sister, who were mentally and physically normal. They were sent to school and had a miserable time there, having to be put into the first grade. But they both learned enough to be employable.

When Neal had started the van up the girl decided to speak.

"You picked a hot enough day to be out in," she said. It was the sort of thing she might have heard people say to start a conversation. She spoke in a hard, flat tone of antagonism and distrust, but even that, Jinny knew by now, should not be taken personally. It was just the way some people sounded—particularly country people—in this part of the world.

"If you're hot you can turn the air-conditioner on," Neal said. "We've got the old-fashioned kind—just roll down all the windows."

The turn they made at the next corner was one Jinny had not expected.

"We have to go to the hospital," Neal said. "Don't panic. Helen's sister works there and she's got something Helen wants to pick up. Isn't that right, Helen?"

Helen said, "Yeah. My good shoes."

"Helen's good shoes." Neal looked up at the mirror. "Miss Helen Rosie's good shoes."

"My name's not Helen Rosie," said Helen. It seemed as if she was saying this not for the first time.

"I just call you that because you have such a rosy face," Neal said.

"I have not."

"You do. Doesn't she, Jinny? Jinny agrees with me, you've got a rosy face. Miss Helen Rosie-face."

The girl did have a tender pink skin. Jinny had noticed as well her nearly white lashes and eyebrows, her blond baby-wool hair, and her mouth, which had an oddly naked look, not just the normal look of a mouth without lipstick. A fresh-out-of-the-egg look was what she had, as if there was one layer of skin still missing, and one final growth of coarser grown-up hair. She must be susceptible to rashes and infections, quick to show scrapes and bruises, to get sores around the mouth and sties between her white lashes. Yet she didn't look frail. Her shoulders were broad, she was lean but large-framed. She didn't look stupid, either, though she had a head-on expression like a calf's or a deer's. Everything must be right at the surface with her, her attention and the whole of her personality coming straight at you, with an innocent and—to Jinny—a disagreeable power.

They were going up the long hill to the hospital—the same place where Jinny had had her operation and undergone the first bout of chemotherapy. Across the road from the hospital buildings there was a cemetery. This was a main road and whenever they used to pass this way—in the old days when they came to this town just for shopping or the rare diversion of a movie—Jinny would say something like "What a discouraging view" or "This is carrying convenience too far."

Now she kept quiet. The cemetery didn't bother her. She realized it didn't matter.

Neal must realize that too. He said into the mirror, "How many dead people do you think there are in that cemetery?"

Helen didn't say anything for a moment. Then—rather sullenly—"I don't know."

"They're *all* dead in there."

"He got me on that too," said Jinny. "That's a Grade Four–level joke."

Helen didn't answer. She might never have made it to Grade Four.

They drove up to the main doors of the hospital, then on Helen's directions swung around to the back. People in hospital dressing gowns, some trailing their IV's, had come outside to smoke.

"You see that bench," said Jinny. "Oh, never mind, we're past it now. It has a sign—THANK YOU FOR NOT SMOKING. But it's out there for people to sit down on when they wander out of the hospital. And why do they come out? To smoke. Then are they not supposed to sit down? I don't understand it."

"Helen's sister works in the laundry," Neal said. "What's her name, Helen? What's your sister's name?"

"Lois," said Helen. "Stop here. Okay. Here."

They were in a parking lot at the back of a wing of the hospital. There were no doors on the ground floor except a loading door, shut tight. On the other three floors there were doors opening onto a fire escape.

Helen was getting out.

"You know how to find your way in?" Neal said.

"Easy."

The fire escape stopped four or five feet above the ground but she was able to grab hold of the railing and swing herself up, maybe wedging a foot against a loose brick, in a matter of seconds. Jinny could not tell how she did it. Neal was laughing.

"Go get 'em, girl," he said.

"Isn't there any other way?" said Jinny.

Helen had run up to the third floor and disappeared.

"If there is she ain't a-gonna use it," Neal said.

"Full of gumption," said Jinny with an effort.

"Otherwise she'd never have broken out," he said. "She needed all the gumption she could get."

Jinny was wearing a wide-brimmed straw hat. She took it off and began to fan herself.

Neal said, "Sorry. There doesn't seem to be any shade to park in. She'll be out of there fast."

"Do I look too startling?" Jinny said. He was used to her asking that.

"You're fine. There's nobody around here anyway."

"The man I saw today wasn't the same one I'd seen before. I think this one was more important. The funny thing was he had a scalp that looked about like mine. Maybe he does it to put the patients at ease."

She meant to go on and tell him what the doctor had said, but he said, "That sister of hers isn't as bright as she is. Helen sort of looks after her and bosses her around. This business with the shoes—that's typical. Isn't she capable of buying her own shoes? She hasn't even got her own place—she still lives with the people who fostered them, out in the country somewhere."

Jinny did not continue. The fanning took up most of her energy. He watched the building.

"I hope to Christ they didn't haul her up for getting in the wrong way," he said. "Breaking the rules. She is just not a gal for whom the rules was made."

After several minutes he let out a whistle.

"Here she comes now. Here-she-comes. Headin' down the homestretch. Will-she-will-she-will-she have enough sense to stop before she jumps? Look before she leaps? Will-she-will-she—nope. Nope. Unh-*unh*."

Helen had no shoes in her hands. She jumped into the van and banged the door shut and said, "Stupid idiots. First I get up there and this asshole gets in my way. Where's your tag? You gotta have a tag. You can't come in here without a tag. I seen you come in off the fire escape, you can't do that. Okay, okay, I gotta see my sister. You can't see her now she's not on her break. I know that, that's why I come in off the fire escape I just need to pick something up. I don't want to talk to her I'm not goin' to take up her time I just gotta pick something up. Well you can't. Well I can. Well you can't. And then I start to holler *Lois. Lois.* All their machines goin' it's two hundred degrees in there sweat runnin' all down their faces stuff goin' by and *Lois, Lois.* I don't know where she is can she hear me or not. But she comes tearing out and as soon as she sees me—Oh, shit. Oh shit, she says, I went and forgot. *She forgot to bring my shoes.* I phoned her up last night and reminded her but there she is, oh, shit, she *forgot.* I could've beat her up. Now you get out, he says. Go downstairs and out. Not by the fire escape because it's illegal. Piss on him."

Neal was laughing and laughing and shaking his head.

"So that's what she did? Left your shoes behind?"

"Out at June's and Matt's."

"What a tragedy."

Jinny said, "Could we just start driving now and get some air? I don't think fanning is doing a lot of good."

"Fine," said Neal. He backed and turned around, and once more they were passing the familiar front of the hospital, with the same or different smokers parading by in their dreary hospital clothes with their IV's. "Helen will just have to tell us where to go."

He called into the back seat, "Helen?"

"What?"

"Which way do we turn now to get to those people's place?"

"What people's?"

"Where your sister lives. Where your shoes are. Tell us how to get to their place."

"We're not goin' to their place so I'm not telling you."

Neal turned back the way they had come.

"I'm just driving this way till you can get your directions straight. Would it work better if I went out to the highway? Or in to the middle of town? Where should I start from?"

"Not starting anywhere. Not going."

"It's not so far, is it? Why aren't we going?"

"You done me one favor and that's enough." Helen sat as far forward as she could, pushing her head between Neal's seat and Jinny's. "You took me to the hospital and isn't that enough? You don't need to be driving all over doing me favors."

They slowed down, turned into a side street.

"That's silly," Neal said. "You're going twenty miles away and you might not get back here for a while. You might need those shoes."

No answer. He tried again.

"Or don't you know the way? Don't you know the way from here?"

"I know it, but I'm not telling."

"So we're just going to have to drive around. Drive around and around till you get ready to tell us."

"Well I'm not goin' to get ready. So I'm not."

"We could go back and see your sister. I bet she'd tell us. Must be about quitting time for her now, we could drive her home."

"She's on the late shift, so haw haw."

They were driving through a part of this town that Jinny had not seen before. They drove very slowly and made frequent turns, so that hardly any breeze went through the car. A boarded-up factory, discount stores, pawnshops. CASH, CASH, CASH, said a flashing sign above barred windows. But there were houses, disreputable-looking old duplexes, and the sort of single wooden houses that were put up quickly during the Second World War. One tiny yard was full of things for sale—clothes pegged to a line, tables stacked with dishes and household goods. A dog was nosing around under a table and could have knocked it over, but the woman who sat on the step, smoking and surveying the lack of customers, did not seem to care.

In front of a corner store some children were sucking on Popsicles. A boy who was on the edge of the group—he was probably no more than four or five years old—threw his Popsicle at the van. A surprisingly strong throw. It hit Jinny's door just below her arm and she gave a light scream.

Helen thrust her head out the back window.

"You want your arm in a sling?"

The child began to howl. He hadn't bargained on Helen, and he might not have bargained on the Popsicle's being gone for good.

Back in the van, Helen spoke to Neal.

"You're just wasting your gas."

"North of town?" Neal said. "South of town? North south east west, Helen tell us which is best."

"I already told you. You done all for me you are goin' to do today."

"And I told you. We're going to get those shoes for you before we head home."

No matter how strictly he spoke, Neal was smiling. On his face there was an expression of conscious, but helpless, silliness. Signs of an invasion of bliss. Neal's whole being was invaded, he was brimming with silly bliss.

"You're just stubborn," Helen said.

"You'll see how stubborn."

"I am too. I'm just as stubborn as what you are."

It seemed to Jinny that she could feel the blaze of Helen's cheek, which was so close to hers. And she could certainly hear the girl's breathing, hoarse and thick with excitement and showing some trace of asthma. Helen's presence was like that of a domestic cat that should never be brought along in any vehicle, being too high-strung to have sense, too apt to spring between the seats.

The sun had burned through the clouds again. It was still high and brassy in the sky.

Neal swung the car onto a street lined with heavy old trees, and somewhat more respectable houses.

"Better here?" he said to Jinny. "More shade for you?" He spoke in a lowered, confidential tone, as if what was going on with the girl could be set aside for a moment, it was all nonsense.

"Taking the scenic route," he said, pitching his voice again towards the back seat. "Taking the scenic route today, courtesy of Miss Helen Rosie-face."

"Maybe we ought to just go on," Jinny said. "Maybe we ought to just go on home."

Helen broke in, almost shouting. "I don't want to stop nobody from getting home."

"Then you can just give me some directions," Neal said. He was trying hard to get his voice under control, to get some ordinary sobriety into it. And to banish the smile, which kept slipping back in place no matter how often he swallowed it. "Just let's go to the place and do our errand and head home."

Half a slow block more, and Helen groaned.

"If I got to I guess I got to," she said.

It was not very far that they had to go. They passed a subdivision, and Neal, speaking again to Jinny, said, "No creek that I can see. No estates, either."

Jinny said, "What?"

"*Silver Creek Estates.* On the sign."

He must have read a sign that she had not seen.

"Turn," said Helen.

"Left or right?"

"At the wrecker's."

They went past a wrecking yard, with the car bodies only partly hidden by a sagging tin fence. Then up a hill and past the gates to a gravel pit that was a great cavity in the center of the hill.

"That's them. That's their mailbox up ahead," Helen called out with some importance, and when they got close enough she read out the name.

"Matt and June Bergson. That's them."

A couple of dogs came barking down the short drive. One was

large and black and one small and tan-colored, puppylike. They bumbled around at the wheels and Neal sounded the horn. Then another dog—this one more sly and purposeful, with a slick coat and bluish spots—slid out of the long grass.

Helen called to them to shut up, to lay down, to piss off.

"You don't need to bother about any of them but Pinto," she said. "Them other two just cowards."

They stopped in a wide, ill-defined space where some gravel had been laid down. On one side was a barn or implement shed, tin-covered, and over to one side of it, on the edge of a cornfield, an abandoned farmhouse from which most of the bricks had been removed, showing dark wooden walls. The house inhabited nowadays was a trailer, nicely fixed up with a deck and an awning, and a flower garden behind what looked like a toy fence. The trailer and its garden looked proper and tidy, while the rest of the property was littered with things that might have a purpose or might just be left around to rust or rot.

Helen had jumped out and was cuffing the dogs. But they kept on running past her, and jumping and barking at the car, until a man came out of the shed and called to them. The threats and names he called were not intelligible to Jinny, but the dogs quieted down.

Jinny put on her hat. All this time she had been holding it in her hand.

"They just got to show off," said Helen.

Neal had got out too and was negotiating with the dogs in a resolute way. The man from the shed came towards them. He wore a purple T-shirt that was wet with sweat, clinging to his chest and stomach. He was fat enough to have breasts and you could see his navel pushing out like a pregnant woman's. It rode on his belly like a giant pincushion.

Neal went to meet him with his hand out. The man slapped his own hand on his work pants, laughed and shook Neal's. Jinny could not hear what they said. A woman came out of the trailer and opened the toy gate and latched it behind her.

"Lois went and forgot she was supposed to bring my shoes," Helen called to her. "I phoned her up and everything, but she went and forgot anyway, so Mr. Lockyer brought me out to get them."

The woman was fat too, though not as fat as her husband. She wore a pink muumuu with Aztec suns on it and her hair was streaked with gold. She moved across the gravel with a composed and hospitable air. Neal turned and introduced himself, then brought her to the van and introduced Jinny.

"Glad to meet you," the woman said. "You're the lady that isn't very well?"

"I'm okay," said Jinny.

"Well, now you're here you better come inside. Come in out of this heat."

"Oh, we just dropped by," said Neal.

The man had come closer. "We got the air-conditioning in there," he said. He was inspecting the van and his expression was genial but disparaging.

"We just came to pick up the shoes," Jinny said.

"You got to do more than that now you're here," said the woman—June—laughing as if the idea of their not coming in was a scandalous joke. "You come in and rest yourself."

"We wouldn't like to disturb your supper," Neal said.

"We had it already," said Matt. "We eat early."

"But all kinds of chili left," said June. "You have to come in and help clean up that chili."

Jinny said, "Oh, thank you. But I don't think I could eat anything. I don't feel like eating anything when it's this hot."

"Then you better drink something instead," June said. "We got ginger ale, Coke. We got peach schnapps."

"Beer," Matt said to Neal. "You like a Blue?"

Jinny waved Neal to come close to her window.

"I can't do it," she said. "Just tell them I can't."

"You know you'll hurt their feelings," he whispered. "They're trying to be nice."

"But I can't. Maybe you could go."

He bent closer. "You know what it looks like if you don't. It looks like you think you're too good for them."

"You go."

"You'd be okay once you got inside. The air-conditioning really would do you good."

Jinny shook her head.

Neal straightened up.

"Jinny thinks she better just stay and rest here where it's in the shade."

June said, "But she's welcome to rest in the house—"

"I wouldn't mind a Blue, actually," Neal said. He turned back to Jinny with a hard smile. He seemed to her desolate and angry. "You sure you'll be okay?" he said for them to hear. "Sure? You don't mind if I go in for a little while?"

"I'll be fine," said Jinny.

He put one hand on Helen's shoulder and one on June's shoulder, walking them companionably towards the trailer. Matt smiled at Jinny curiously, and followed.

This time when he called the dogs to come after him Jinny could make out their names.

Goober. Sally. Pinto.

The van was parked under a row of willow trees. These trees were big and old, but their leaves were thin and gave a wavering shade. But to be alone was a great relief.

Earlier today, driving along the highway from the town where they lived, they had stopped at a roadside stand and bought some early apples. Jinny got one out of the bag at her feet and took a small bite—more or less to see if she could taste and swallow and hold it in her stomach. She needed something to counteract the thought of chili, and Matt's prodigious navel.

It was all right. The apple was firm and tart, but not too tart, and if she took small bites and chewed seriously she could manage it.

She'd seen Neal like this—or something like this—a few times before. It would be over some boy at the school. A mention of the name in an offhand, even belittling way. A mushy look, an apologetic yet somehow defiant bit of giggling.

But that was never anybody she had to have around the house, and it could never come to anything. The boy's time would be up, he'd go away.

So would this time be up. It shouldn't matter.

She had to wonder if it would have mattered less yesterday than it did today.

She got out of the van, leaving the door open so that she could hang on to the inside handle. Anything on the outside was too hot to hang on to for any length of time. She had to see if she was steady. Then she walked a little in the shade. Some of the willow leaves were already going yellow. Some were lying on the ground. She looked out from the shade at all the things there were around the yard.

A dented delivery truck with both headlights gone and the name on the side painted out. A baby's stroller that the dogs had chewed the seat out of, a load of firewood dumped but not stacked, a pile of huge tires, a great number of plastic jugs and some oil cans and pieces of old lumber and a couple of orange plastic tarpaulins crumpled up by the wall of the shed. In the shed itself there was a heavy GM truck and a small beat-up Mazda truck and a garden tractor, as well as implements whole or broken and loose wheels, handles, rods that would be useful or not useful depending on the uses you could imagine. What a lot of things people could find themselves in charge of. As she had been in charge of all those photographs, official letters, minutes of meetings, newspaper clippings, a thousand categories that she had devised and was putting on disk when she had to go into chemo and everything got taken away. It might end up being thrown out. As all this might, if Matt died.

The cornfield was the place she wanted to get to. The corn was higher than her head now, maybe higher than Neal's head—she wanted to get into the shade of it. She made her way across the yard with this one thought in mind. The dogs thank God must have been taken inside.

There was no fence. The cornfield just petered out into the yard. She walked straight ahead into it, onto the narrow path between two rows. The leaves flapped into her face and against her arms like streamers of oilcloth. She had to remove her hat so they would not knock it off. Each stalk had its cob, like a baby in a shroud. There was a strong, almost sickening smell of vegetable growth, of green starch and hot sap.

What she'd thought she'd do, once she got in here, was lie down. Lie down in the shade of these large coarse leaves and not come out till she heard Neal calling her. Perhaps not even then. But the rows were too close together to permit that, and she was too busy thinking about something to take the trouble. She was too angry.

It was not about anything that had happened recently. She was remembering how a group of people had been sitting around one evening on the floor of her living room—or meeting room—playing one of those serious psychological games. One of those games that were supposed to make a person more honest and resilient. You had to say just what came into your mind as you looked at each of the others. And a white-haired woman named Addie Norton, a friend of Neal's, had said, "I hate to tell you this, Jinny, but whenever I look at you all I can think of is—*Nice Nellie.*"

Jinny didn't remember making any response at the time. Maybe you weren't supposed to. What she said, now, in her head, was "Why do you say you hate to say that? Haven't you noticed that whenever people say they hate to say something, they actually love to say it? Don't you think since we're being so honest we could at least start with that?"

It was not the first time she had made this mental reply. And mentally pointed out to Neal what a farce that game was. For when it came Addie's turn, did anyone dare say anything unpleasant to her? Oh, no. "Feisty," they said or "Honest as a dash of cold water." They were scared of her, that was all.

She said, "Dash of cold water," out loud, now, in a stinging voice.

Other people had said kinder things to her. "Flower child" or "Madonna of the springs." She happened to know that whoever said that meant "Manon of the Springs," but she offered no correction. She was outraged at having to sit there and listen to people's opinions of her. Everyone was wrong. She was not timid or acquiescent or natural or pure.

When you died, of course, these wrong opinions were all there was left.

While this was going through her mind she had done the easiest thing you could do in a cornfield—got lost. She had stepped over one row and then another and probably got turned around. She tried going back the way she had come, but it obviously wasn't the right way. There were clouds over the sun again so she couldn't tell where west was. And she had not known which direction she was going when she entered the field, so that would not have helped anyway. She stood still and heard nothing but the corn whispering away, and some distant traffic.

Her heart was pounding just like any heart that had years and years of life ahead of it.

Then a door opened, she heard the dogs barking and Matt yelling and the door slammed shut. She pushed her way through stalks and leaves in the direction of that noise.

And it turned out that she had not gone far at all. She had been stumbling around in one small corner of the field all the time.

Matt waved at her and warned off the dogs.

"Don't be scairt of them, don't be scairt," he called. He was going towards the car just as she was, though from another direction. As they got closer to each other he spoke in a lower, perhaps more intimate voice.

"You shoulda come and knocked on the door."

He thought that she had gone into the corn to have a pee.

"I just told your husband I'd come out and make sure you're okay."

Jinny said, "I'm fine. Thank you." She got into the van but left the door open. He might be insulted if she closed it. Also, she felt too weak.

"He was sure hungry for that chili."

Who was he talking about?

Neal.

She was trembling and sweating and there was a hum in her head, as on a wire strung between her ears.

"I could bring you some out if you'd like it."

She shook her head, smiling. He lifted up the bottle of beer in his hand—he seemed to be saluting her.

"Drink?"

She shook her head again, still smiling.

"Not even drink of water? We got good water here."

"No thanks."

If she turned her head and looked at his purple navel, she would gag.

"You know, there was this fellow," he said, in a changed voice. A leisurely, chuckling voice. "There was a fellow going out the door and he's got a jar of horseradish in one hand. So his dad says to him, Where you goin' with that horseradish?

"Well I'm goin' to get a horse, he says.

"You're not goin' to catch a horse with no horseradish.

"Comes back next morning, nicest horse you ever want to see. Lookit my horse here. Puts it in the barn."

I do not wish to give the wrong impression. We must not get carried away with optimism. But it looks as if we have some unexpected results here.

"Next day the dad sees him goin' out again. Roll of duct tape under his arm. Where you goin' now?

"Well I heard my mom say she'd like a nice duck for dinner.

"You damn fool, you didn't think you're goin' to catch a duck with duct tape?

"Wait and see.

"Comes back next morning, nice fat duck under his arm."

It looks as if there has been a very significant shrinkage. What we hoped for of course but frankly we did not expect it. And I do not mean that the battle is over, just that this is a favorable sign.

"Dad don't know what to say. Just don't know what to say about it.

"Next night, very next night, sees his son goin' out the door with big bunch of branches in his hand."

Quite a favorable sign. We do not know that there may not be more trouble in the future but we can say we are cautiously optimistic.

"What's them branches you got in your hand?

"Them's pussy willows.

"Okay, Dad says. You just hang on a minute.

"You just hang on a minute, I'm gettin' my hat. I'm gettin' my hat and I'm comin' with you!"

"It's too much," Jinny said out loud.

Talking in her head to the doctor.

"What?" said Matt. An aggrieved and babyish look had come over his face while he was still chuckling. "What's the matter now?"

Jinny was shaking her head, squeezing her hand over her mouth.

"It was just a joke," he said. "I never meant to offend you."

Jinny said, "No, no. I— No."

"Never mind, I'm goin' in. I'm not goin' to take up no more of your time." And he turned his back on her, not even bothering to call to the dogs.

She had not said anything like that to the doctor. Why should she? Nothing was his fault. But it was true. It was too much. What he had said made everything harder. It made her have to go back and start this year all over again. It removed a certain low-grade freedom. A dull, protecting membrane that she had not even known was there had been pulled away and left her raw.

Matt's thinking she had gone into the cornfield to pee had made her realize that she actually wanted to. She got out of the van, stood cautiously, and spread her legs and lifted her wide cotton skirt. She had taken to wearing big skirts and no panties this summer because her bladder was no longer under perfect control.

A dark stream trickled away from her through the gravel. The sun was down now, evening was coming on. A clear sky overhead, the clouds had vanished.

One of the dogs barked halfheartedly, to say that somebody was coming, but it was somebody they knew. They had not come over to bother her when she got out—they were used to her now. They went running out to meet whoever it was without any alarm or excitement.

It was a boy, or young man, riding a bicycle. He swerved towards the van and Jinny went round to meet him, a hand on the cooled-down but still-warm metal to support herself. When he spoke to her she did not want it to be across her puddle. And maybe to distract him from even looking on the ground for such a thing, she spoke first.

She said, "Hello—are you delivering something?"

He laughed, springing off the bike and dropping it to the ground, all in one motion.

"I live here," he said. "I'm just getting home from work."

She thought that she should explain who she was, tell him how she came to be here and for how long. But all this was too difficult. Hanging on to the van like this, she must look like somebody who had just come out of a wreck.

"Yeah, I live here," he said. "But I work in a restaurant in town. I work at Sammy's."

A waiter. The bright white shirt and black pants were waiter's clothes. And he had a waiter's air of patience and alertness.

"I'm Jinny Lockyer," she said. "Helen. Helen is—"

"Okay, I know," he said. "You're who Helen's going to work for. Where's Helen?"

"In the house."

"Didn't nobody ask you in, then?"

He was about Helen's age, she thought. Seventeen or eighteen. Slim and graceful and cocky, with an ingenuous enthusiasm that would probably not get him as far as he hoped. She had seen a few like that who ended up as Young Offenders.

He seemed to understand things, though. He seemed to understand that she was exhausted and in some kind of muddle.

"June in there too?" he said. "June's my mom."

His hair was colored like June's, gold streaks over dark. He wore it rather long, and parted in the middle, flopping off to either side.

"Matt too?" he said.

"And my husband. Yes."

"That's a shame."

"Oh, no," she said. "They asked me. I said I'd rather wait out here."

Neal used sometimes to bring home a couple of his Yo-yos, to be supervised doing lawn work or painting or basic carpentry. He thought it was good for them, to be accepted into somebody's home. Jinny had flirted with them occasionally, in a way that she could never be blamed for. Just a gentle tone, a way of making them aware of her soft skirts and her scent of apple soap. That wasn't why Neal had stopped bringing them. He had been told it was out of order.

"So how long have you been waiting?"

"I don't know," Jinny said. "I don't wear a watch."

"Is that right?" he said. "I don't either. I don't hardly ever meet another person that doesn't wear a watch. Did you never wear one?"

She said, "No. Never."

"Me neither. Never ever. I just never wanted to. I don't know why. Never ever wanted to. Like, I always just seemed to know what time it was anyway. Within a couple minutes. Five minutes the most. And I know where all the clocks are, too. I'm riding in to work, and I think I'll check, you know, just be sure what time it is really. And I know the first place I can see the courthouse clock in between the buildings. Always not more than three/four minutes out. Sometimes one of the diners asks me, do you know the time, and I just tell them. They don't even notice I'm not wearing a watch. I go and check as soon as I can, clock in the kitchen. But I never once had to go in there and tell them any different."

"I've been able to do that too, once in a while," Jinny said. "I guess you do develop a sense, if you never wear a watch."

"Yeah, you really do."

"So what time do you think it is now?"

He laughed. He looked at the sky.

"Getting close to eight. Six/seven minutes to eight? I got an advantage, though. I know when I got off of work and then I went to get some cigarettes at the 7-Eleven and then I talked to some

guys a couple of minutes and then I biked home. You don't live in
town, do you?"

Jinny said no.

"So where do you live?"

She told him.

"You getting tired? You want to go home? You want me to go in
and tell your husband you want to go home?"

"No. Don't do that," she said.

"Okay. Okay. I won't. June's probably telling their fortunes in
there anyway. She can read hands."

"Can she?"

"Sure. She goes in the restaurant a couple of times a week. Tea
too. Tea leaves."

He picked up his bike and wheeled it out of the way of the van.
Then he looked in through the driver's window.

"Left the keys in," he said. "So—you want me to drive you
home or what? I can put my bike in the back. Your husband can get
Matt to drive him and Helen when they get ready. Or if it don't
look like Matt can, June can. June's my mom but Matt's not my
dad. You don't drive, do you?"

"No," said Jinny. She had not driven for months.

"No. I didn't think so. Okay then? You want me to? Okay?"

"This is just a road I know. It'll get you there as soon as the highway."

They had not driven past the subdivision. In fact they had
headed the other way, taking a road that seemed to circle the gravel
pit. At least they were going west now, towards the brightest part
of the sky. Ricky—that was what he'd told her his name was—
had not yet turned the car lights on.

"No danger meeting anybody," he said. "I don't think I ever
met a single car on this road, ever. See—not so many people even
know this road is here."

"And if I was to turn the lights on," he said, "then the sky would go dark and everything would go dark and you wouldn't be able to see where you were. We just give it a little while more, then when it gets we can see the stars, that's when we turn the lights on."

The sky was like very faintly colored red or yellow or green or blue glass, depending on which part of it you looked at.

"That okay with you?"

"Yes," said Jinny.

The bushes and trees would turn black, once the lights were on. There would just be black clumps along the road and the black mass of trees crowding in behind them, instead of, as now, the individual still identifiable spruce and cedar and feathery tamarack and the jewelweed with its flowers like winking bits of fire. It seemed close enough to touch, and they were going slowly. She put her hand out.

Not quite. But close. The road seemed hardly wider than the car.

She thought she saw the gleam of a full ditch ahead.

"Is there water down there?" she said.

"Down there?" said Ricky. "Down there and everywhere. There's water to both sides of us and lots of places water underneath us. Want to see?"

He slowed the van. He stopped. "Look down your side," he said. "Open the door and look down."

When she did that she saw that they were on a bridge. A little bridge no more than ten feet long, of crossway-laid planks. No railings. And motionless water underneath it.

"Bridges all along here," he said. "And where it's not bridges it's culverts. 'Cause it's always flowing back and forth under the road. Or just laying there and not flowing anyplace."

"How deep?" she said.

"Not deep. Not this time of year. Not till we get to the big pond—it's deeper. And then in spring it's all over the road, you can't drive here, it's deep then. This road goes flat for miles and miles, and it goes straight from one end to the other. There isn't even any roads that cuts across it. This is the only road I know of through the Borneo Swamp."

"Borneo Swamp?" Jinny repeated.

"That's what it's supposed to be called."

"There is an island called Borneo," she said. "It's halfway round the world."

"I don't know about that. All I ever heard of was just the Borneo Swamp."

There was a strip of dark grass now, growing down the middle of the road.

"Time for the lights," he said. He switched them on and they were in a tunnel in the sudden night.

"Once I did that," he said. "I turned the lights on like that and there was this porcupine. It was just sitting there in the middle of the road. It was sitting straight up kind of on its hind legs and looking right at me. Like some little old man. It was scared to death and it couldn't move. I could see its little old teeth chattering."

She thought, This is where he brings his girls.

"So what do I do? I tried beeping the horn and it still didn't do nothing. I didn't feel like getting out and chasing it. He was scared, but he still was a porcupine and he could let fly. So I just parked there. I had time. When I turned the lights on again he was gone."

Now the branches really did reach close and brush against the door, but if there were flowers she could not see them.

"I am going to show you something," he said. "I'm going to show you something like I bet you never seen before."

If this was happening back in her old, normal life, it was possible that she might now begin to be frightened. If she was back in her old, normal life she would not be here at all.

"You're going to show me a porcupine," she said.

"Nope. Not that. Something there's not even as many of as there is porcupines. Least as far as I know there's not."

Maybe half a mile farther on he turned off the lights.

"See the stars?" he said. "I told you. Stars."

He stopped the van. Everywhere there was at first a deep silence. Then this silence was filled in, at the edges, by some kind of humming that could have been faraway traffic, and little noises that passed before you properly heard them, that could have been made by night-feeding animals or birds or bats.

"Come in here in the springtime," he said, "you wouldn't hear nothing but the frogs. You'd think you were going deaf with the frogs."

He opened the door on his side.

"Now. Get out and walk a ways with me."

She did as she was told. She walked in one of the wheel tracks, he in the other. The sky seemed to be lighter ahead and there was a different sound—something like mild and rhythmical conversation.

The road turned to wood and the trees on either side were gone.

"Walk out on it," he said. "Go on."

He came close and touched her waist as if he was guiding her. Then he took his hand away, left her to walk on these planks which were like the deck of a boat. Like the deck of a boat they rose and fell. But it wasn't a movement of waves, it was their footsteps, his and hers, that caused this very slight rising and falling of the boards beneath them.

"Now do you know where you are?" he said.

"On a dock?" she said.

"On a bridge. This is a floating bridge."

Now she could make it out—the plank roadway just a few inches above the still water. He drew her over to the side and they looked down. There were stars riding on the water.

"The water's very dark," she said. "I mean—it's dark not just because it's night?"

"It's dark all the time," he said proudly. "That's because it's a swamp. It's got the same stuff in it tea has got and it looks like black tea."

She could see the shoreline, and the reed beds. Water in the reeds, lapping water, was what was making that sound.

"Tannin," he said, sounding the word proudly as if he'd hauled it up out of the dark.

The slight movement of the bridge made her imagine that all the trees and the reed beds were set on saucers of earth and the road was a floating ribbon of earth and underneath it all was water. And the water seemed so still, but it could not really be still because if you tried to keep your eye on one reflected star, you saw how it winked and changed shape and slid from sight. Then it was back again—but maybe not the same one.

It was not until this moment that she realized she didn't have her hat. She not only didn't have it on, she hadn't had it with her in the car. She had not been wearing it when she got out of the car to pee and when she began to talk to Ricky. She had not been wearing it when she sat in the car with her head back against the seat and her eyes closed, when Matt was telling his joke. She must have dropped it in the cornfield, and in her panic left it there.

When she had been scared of seeing the mound of Matt's navel with the purple shirt plastered over it, he had not minded looking at her bleak knob.

"It's too bad the moon isn't up yet," Ricky said. "It's really nice here when the moon is up."

"It's nice now, too."

He slipped his arms around her as if there was no question at all about what he was doing and he could take all the time he wanted to do it. He kissed her mouth. It seemed to her that this was the first time ever that she had participated in a kiss that was an event in itself. The whole story, all by itself. A tender prologue, an efficient pressure, a wholehearted probing and receiving, a lingering thanks, and a drawing away satisfied.

"Oh," he said. "Oh."

He turned her around, and they walked back the way they had come.

———

"So was that the first you ever been on a floating bridge?"

She said yes it was.

"And now that's what you're going to get to drive over."

He took her hand and swung it as if he would like to toss it.

"And that's the first time ever I kissed a married woman."

"You'll probably kiss a lot more of them," she said. "Before you're done."

He sighed. "Yeah," he said. Amazed and sobered by the thought of what lay ahead of him. "Yeah, I probably will."

Jinny had a sudden thought of Neal, back on dry land. Neal giddy and doubtful, opening his hand to the gaze of the woman with the bright-streaked hair, the fortune teller. Rocking on the edge of his future.

No matter.

What she felt was a lighthearted sort of compassion, almost like laughter. A swish of tender hilarity, getting the better of all her sores and hollows, for the time given.

Family Furnishings

Alfrida. My father called her Freddie. The two of them were first cousins and lived for a while on adjoining farms. One day they were out in the fields of stubble playing with my father's dog, whose name was Mack. That day the sun shone, but did not melt the ice in the furrows. They stomped on the ice and enjoyed its crackle underfoot.

How could she remember a thing like that? my father said. She made it up, he said.

"I did not," she said.

"You did so."

"I did not."

All of a sudden they heard bells pealing, whistles blowing. The town bell and the church bells were ringing. The factory whistles were blowing in the town three miles away. The world had burst its seams for joy, and Mack tore out to the road, because he was sure a parade was coming. It was the end of the First World War.

Three times a week, we could read Alfrida's name in the paper. Just her first name—Alfrida. It was printed as if written by hand, a flowing, fountain-pen signature. Round and About the Town, with

Alfrida. The town mentioned was not the one close by, but the city to the south, where Alfrida lived, and which my family visited perhaps once every two or three years.

Now is the time for all you future June brides to start registering your preferences at the China Cabinet, and I must tell you that if I were a bride-to-be—which alas I am not—I might resist all the patterned dinner sets, exquisite as they are, and go for the pearly-white, the ultra-modern Rosenthal . . .

Beauty treatments may come and beauty treatments may go, but the masques they slather on you at Fantine's Salon are guaranteed— speaking of brides—to make your skin bloom like orange blossoms. And to make the bride's mom—and the bride's aunts and for all I know her grandmom—feel as if they'd just taken a dip in the Fountain of Youth . . .

You would never expect Alfrida to write in this style, from the way she talked.

She was also one of the people who wrote under the name of Flora Simpson, on the Flora Simpson Housewives' Page. Women from all over the countryside believed that they were writing their letters to the plump woman with the crimped gray hair and the forgiving smile who was pictured at the top of the page. But the truth—which I was not to tell—was that the notes that appeared at the bottom of each of their letters were produced by Alfrida and a man she called Horse Henry, who otherwise did the obituaries. The women gave themselves such names as Morning Star and Lily-of-the-Valley and Green Thumb and Little Annie Rooney and Dishmop Queen. Some names were so popular that numbers had to be assigned to them—Goldilocks 1, Goldilocks 2, Goldilocks 3.

Dear Morning Star, Alfrida or Horse Henry would write,

Eczema is a dreadful pest, especially in this hot weather we're having, and I hope the baking soda does some good. Home treatments certainly ought to be respected, but it never hurts to seek out your doctor's advice. It's splendid news to hear your hubby is up and about again. It can't have been any fun with both of you under the weather . . .

In all the small towns of that part of Ontario, housewives who belonged to the Flora Simpson Club would hold an annual summer picnic. Flora Simpson always sent her special greetings but explained that there were just too many events for her to show up at all of them and she did not like to make distinctions. Alfrida said that there had been talk of sending Horse Henry done up in a wig and pillow bosoms, or perhaps herself leering like the Witch of Babylon (not even she, at my parents' table, could quote the Bible accurately and say "Whore") with a ciggie-boo stuck to her lipstick. But, oh, she said, the paper would kill us. And anyway, it would be too mean.

She always called her cigarettes ciggie-boos. When I was fifteen or sixteen she leaned across the table and asked me, "How would you like a ciggie-boo, too?" The meal was finished, and my younger brother and sister had left the table. My father was shaking his head. He had started to roll his own.

I said thank you and let Alfrida light it and smoked for the first time in front of my parents.

They pretended that it was a great joke.

"Ah, will you look at your daughter?" said my mother to my father. She rolled her eyes and clapped her hands to her chest and spoke in an artificial, languishing voice. "I'm like to faint."

"Have to get the horsewhip out," my father said, half rising in his chair.

This moment was amazing, as if Alfrida had transformed us into new people. Ordinarily, my mother would say that she did not like to see a woman smoke. She did not say that it was indecent, or unladylike—just that she did not like it. And when she said in a certain tone that she did not like something it seemed that she was not making a confession of irrationality but drawing on a private source of wisdom, which was unassailable and almost sacred. It was when she reached for this tone, with its accompanying expression of listening to inner voices, that I particularly hated her.

As for my father, he had beaten me, in this very room, not with a horsewhip but his belt, for running afoul of my mother's rules and wounding my mother's feelings, and for answering back. Now it seemed that such beatings could occur only in another universe.

My parents had been put in a corner by Alfrida—and also by me—but they had responded so gamely and gracefully that it was really as if all three of us—my mother and my father and myself—had been lifted to a new level of ease and aplomb. In that instant I could see them—particularly my mother—as being capable of a kind of lightheartedness that was scarcely ever on view.

All due to Alfrida.

Alfrida was always referred to as a career girl. This made her seem to be younger than my parents, though she was known to be about the same age. It was also said that she was a city person. And the city, when it was spoken of in this way, meant the one she lived and worked in. But it meant something else as well—not just a distinct configuration of buildings and sidewalks and streetcar lines or even a crowding together of individual people. It meant something more abstract that could be repeated over and over, something like a hive of bees, stormy but organized, not useless or deluded exactly, but disturbing and sometimes dangerous. People went into such a place when they had to and were glad when they got out. Some, however, were attracted to it—as Alfrida must have been, long ago, and as I was now, puffing on my cigarette and trying to hold it in a nonchalant way, though it seemed to have grown to the size of a baseball bat between my fingers.

My family did not have a regular social life—people did not come to the house for dinner, let alone to parties. It was a matter of class, maybe. The parents of the boy I married, about five years after this scene at the dinner table, invited people who were not related to them to dinner, and they went to afternoon parties that they spoke of, unselfconsciously, as cocktail parties. It was a life such as I had read of in magazine stories, and it seemed to me to place my in-laws in a world of storybook privilege.

What our family did was put boards in the dining-room table two or three times a year to entertain my grandmother and my aunts—my father's older sisters—and their husbands. We did this at Christmas or Thanksgiving, when it was our turn, and perhaps also when a relative from another part of the province showed up on a visit. This visitor would always be a person rather like the aunts and their husbands and never the least bit like Alfrida.

My mother and I would start preparing for such dinners a couple of days ahead. We ironed the good tablecloth, which was as heavy as a bed quilt, and washed the good dishes, which had been sitting in the china cabinet collecting dust, and wiped the legs of the dining-room chairs, as well as making the jellied salads, the pies and cakes, that had to accompany the central roast turkey or baked ham and bowls of vegetables. There had to be far too much to eat, and most of the conversation at the table had to do with the food, with the company saying how good it was and being urged to have more, and saying that they couldn't, they were stuffed, and then the aunts' husbands relenting, taking more, and the aunts taking just a little more and saying that they shouldn't, they were ready to bust.

And dessert still to come.

There was hardly any idea of a general conversation, and in fact there was a feeling that conversation that passed beyond certain understood limits might be a disruption, a showing-off. My mother's understanding of the limits was not reliable, and she sometimes could not wait out the pauses or honor the aversion to follow-up. So when somebody said, "Seen Harley upstreet yesterday," she was liable to say, perhaps, "Do you think a man like Harley is a confirmed bachelor? Or he just hasn't met the right person?"

As if, when you mentioned seeing a person you were bound to have something further to say, something *interesting*.

Then there might be a silence, not because the people at the table meant to be rude but because they were flummoxed. Till my father would say with embarrassment, and oblique reproach, "He seems to get on all right by hisself."

If his relatives had not been present, he would more likely have said "himself."

And everybody went on cutting, spooning, swallowing, in the glare of the fresh tablecloth, with the bright light pouring in through the newly washed windows. These dinners were always in the middle of the day.

The people at that table were quite capable of talk. Washing and drying the dishes, in the kitchen, the aunts would talk about who had a tumor, a septic throat, a bad mess of boils. They would tell about how their own digestions, kidneys, nerves were functioning. Mention of intimate bodily matters seemed never to be so out of place, or suspect, as the mention of something read in a magazine, or an item in the news—it was improper somehow to pay attention to anything that was not close at hand. Meanwhile, resting on the porch, or during a brief walk out to look at the crops, the aunts' husbands might pass on the information that somebody was in a tight spot with the bank, or still owed money on an expensive piece of machinery, or had invested in a bull that was a disappointment on the job.

It could have been that they felt clamped down by the formality of the dining room, the presence of bread-and-butter plates and dessert spoons, when it was the custom, at other times, to put a piece of pie right onto a dinner plate that had been cleaned up with bread. (It would have been an offense, however, not to set things out in this proper way. In their own houses, on like occasions, they would put their guests through the same paces.) It may have been just that eating was one thing, and talking was something else.

When Alfrida came it was altogether another story. The good cloth would be spread and the good dishes would be out. My mother would have gone to a lot of trouble with the food and she would be nervous about the results—probably she would have abandoned the usual turkey-and-stuffing-and-mashed-potatoes menu and made something like chicken salad surrounded by mounds of molded rice with cut-up pimientos, and this would be followed by a dessert involving gelatin and egg white and whipped cream, taking a long, nerve-racking time to set because we had no refrigerator and it had to be chilled on the cellar floor. But the constraint, the pall over the table, was quite absent. Alfrida not only accepted second helpings, she asked for them. And she did this almost absentmindedly, and tossed off her compliments in the same way, as if the food, the eating of the food, was a secondary though agreeable thing, and she was really there to talk, and make other people talk, and anything you wanted to talk about—almost anything—would be fine.

She always visited in summer, and usually she wore some sort of striped, silky sundress, with a halter top that left her back bare. Her back was not pretty, being sprinkled with little dark moles, and her shoulders were bony and her chest nearly flat. My father would always remark on how much she could eat and remain thin. Or he turned truth on its head by noting that her appetite was as picky as ever, but she still hadn't been prevented from larding on the fat. (It was not considered out of place in our family to comment about fatness or skinniness or pallor or ruddiness or baldness.)

Her dark hair was done up in rolls above her face and at the sides, in the style of the time. Her skin was brownish-looking, netted with fine wrinkles, and her mouth wide, the lower lip rather thick, almost drooping, painted with a hearty lipstick that left a smear on the teacup and water tumbler. When her mouth was opened wide—as it nearly always was, talking or laughing—you could see that some of her teeth had been pulled at the back. Nobody could say that she was good-looking—any woman over twenty-five seemed to me to have pretty well passed beyond the possibility of being good-looking, anyway, to have lost the right to be so, and perhaps even the desire—but she was fervent and dashing. My father said thoughtfully that she had zing.

Alfrida talked to my father about things that were happening in the world, about politics. My father read the paper, he listened to the radio, he had opinions about these things but rarely got a chance to talk about them. The aunts' husbands had opinions too, but theirs were brief and unvaried and expressed an everlasting distrust of all public figures and particularly all foreigners, so that most of the time all that could be gotten out of them were grunts of dismissal. My grandmother was deaf—nobody could tell how much she knew or what she thought about anything, and the aunts themselves seemed fairly proud of how much they didn't know or didn't have to pay attention to. My mother had been a school-teacher, and she could readily have pointed out all the countries of Europe on the map, but she saw everything through a personal haze, with the British Empire and the royal family looming large and everything else diminished, thrown into a jumble-heap that was easy for her to disregard.

Alfrida's views were not really so far away from those of the uncles. Or so it appeared. But instead of grunting and letting the subject go, she gave her hooting laugh, and told stories about prime ministers and the American president and John L. Lewis and the mayor of Montreal—stories in which they all came out badly. She told stories about the royal family too, but there she made a distinction between the good ones like the king and queen and the beautiful Duchess of Kent and the dreadful ones like the Windsors and old King Eddy, who—she said—had a certain disease and had marked his wife's neck by trying to strangle her, which was why she always had to wear her pearls. This distinction coincided pretty well with one my mother made but seldom spoke about, so she did not object—though the reference to syphilis made her wince.

I smiled at it, knowingly, with a foolhardy composure.

Alfrida called the Russians funny names. Mikoyan-sky. Uncle Joe-sky. She believed that they were pulling the wool over everybody's eyes, and that the United Nations was a farce that would never work and that Japan would rise again and should have been finished off when there was the chance. She didn't trust Quebec either. Or the pope. There was a problem for her with Senator McCarthy—she would have liked to be on his side, but his being a Catholic was a stumbling block. She called the pope the poop. She relished the thought of all the crooks and scoundrels to be found in the world.

Sometimes it seemed as if she was putting on a show—a display, maybe to tease my father. To rile him up, as he himself would have said, to get his goat. But not because she disliked him or even wanted to make him uncomfortable. Quite the opposite. She might have been tormenting him as young girls torment boys at school, when arguments are a peculiar delight to both sides and insults are taken as flattery. My father argued with her, always in a mild steady voice, and yet it was clear that he had the intention of goading her on. Sometimes he would do a turnaround, and say that maybe she was right—that with her work on the newspaper, she must have sources of information that he couldn't have. You've put me straight, he would say, if I had any sense I'd be obliged to you. And she would say, Don't give me that load of baloney.

"You two," said my mother, in mock despair and perhaps in real exhaustion, and Alfrida told her to go and have a lie-down, she deserved it after this splendiferous dinner, she and I would manage the dishes. My mother was subject to a tremor in her right arm, a stiffness in her fingers, that she believed came when she got overtired.

While we worked in the kitchen Alfrida talked to me about celebrities—actors, even minor movie stars, who had made stage appearances in the city where she lived. In a lowered voice still broken by wildly disrespectful laughter she told me stories of their bad behavior, the rumors of private scandals that had never made it into the magazines. She mentioned queers, man-made bosoms, household triangles—all things that I had found hints of in my reading but felt giddy to hear about, even at third or fourth hand, in real life.

Alfrida's teeth always got my attention, so that even in these confidential recitals I sometimes lost track of what was being said. Those teeth that were left, across the front, were each of a slightly different color, no two alike. Some with a fairly strong enamel tended towards shades of dark ivory, others were opalescent, shadowed with lilac, and giving out fish-flashes of silver rims, occasionally a gleam of gold. People's teeth in those days seldom made such a solid, handsome show as they do now, unless they were false. But these teeth of Alfrida's were unusual in their individuality, clear separation, and large size. When Alfrida let out some jibe that was especially, knowingly outrageous, they seemed to leap to the fore like a palace guard, like jolly spear-fighters.

"She always did have trouble with her teeth," the aunts said. "She had that abscess, remember, the poison went all through her system."

How like them, I thought, to toss aside Alfrida's wit and style and turn her teeth into a sorry problem.

"Why doesn't she just have them all out and be done with it?" they said.

"Likely she couldn't afford it," said my grandmother, surprising everybody as she sometimes did, by showing that she had been keeping up with the conversation all along.

And surprising me with the new, everyday sort of light this shed on Alfrida's life. I had believed that Alfrida was rich—rich at least in comparison with the rest of the family. She lived in an apartment—I had never seen it, but to me that fact conveyed at least the idea of a very civilized life—and she wore clothes that were not

homemade, and her shoes were not Oxfords like the shoes of practically all the other grown-up women I knew—they were sandals
made of bright strips of the new plastic. It was hard to know
whether my grandmother was simply living in the past, when getting your false teeth was the solemn, crowning expense of a lifetime, or whether she really knew things about Alfrida's life that I
never would have guessed.

The rest of the family was never present when Alfrida had dinner at our house. She did go to see my grandmother, who was her
aunt, her mother's sister. My grandmother no longer lived at her
own house but lived alternately with one or the other of the aunts,
and Alfrida went to whichever house she was living in at the time,
but not to the other house, to see the other aunt who was as much
her cousin as my father was. And the meal she took was never with
any of them. Usually she came to our house first and visited
awhile, and then gathered herself up, as if reluctantly, to make the
other visit. When she came back later and we sat down to eat,
nothing derogatory was said outright against the aunts and their
husbands, and certainly nothing disrespectful about my grandmother. In fact, it was the way that my grandmother would be spoken of by Alfrida—a sudden sobriety and concern in her voice,
even a touch of fear (what about her blood pressure, had she been
to the doctor lately, what did he have to say?)—that made me
aware of the difference, the coolness or possibly unfriendly
restraint, with which she asked after the others. Then there would
be a similar restraint in my mother's reply, and an extra gravity in
my father's—a caricature of gravity, you might say—that showed
how they all agreed about something they could not say.

On the day when I smoked the cigarette Alfrida decided to take
this a bit further, and she said solemnly, "How about Asa, then? Is
he still as much of a conversation grabber as ever?"

My father shook his head sadly, as if the thought of this uncle's
garrulousness must weigh us all down.

"Indeed," he said. "He is indeed."

Then I took my chance.

"Looks like the roundworms have got into the hogs," I said.
"Yup."

Except for the "yup," this was just what my uncle had said, and
he had said it at this very table, being overcome by an uncharacteristic need to break the silence or to pass on something important
that had just come to mind. And I said it with just his stately
grunts, his innocent solemnity.

Alfrida gave a great, approving laugh, showing her festive
teeth. "That's it, she's got him to a *T*."

My father bent over his plate, as if to hide how he was laughing
too, but of course not really hiding it, and my mother shook her
head, biting her lips, smiling. I felt a keen triumph. Nothing was
said to put me in my place, no reproof for what was sometimes
called my sarcasm, my being smart. The word "smart" when it was
used about me, in the family, might mean intelligent, and then it
was used rather grudgingly—"oh, she's smart enough some
ways"—or it might be used to mean pushy, attention-seeking,
obnoxious. *Don't be so smart.*

Sometimes my mother said sadly, "You have a cruel tongue."

Sometimes—and this was a great deal worse—my father was
disgusted with me.

"What makes you think you have the right to run down decent
people?"

This day nothing like that happened—I seemed to be as free as
a visitor at the table, almost as free as Alfrida, and flourishing
under the banner of my own personality.

But there was a gap about to open, and perhaps that was the last
time, the very last time, that Alfrida sat at our table. Christmas
cards continued to be exchanged, possibly even letters—as long as

my mother could manage a pen—and we still read Alfrida's name in the paper, but I cannot recall any visits during the last couple of years I lived at home.

It may have been that Alfrida asked if she could bring her friend and had been told that she could not. If she was already living with him, that would have been one reason, and if he was the same man she had later, the fact that he was married would have been another. My parents would have been united in this. My mother had a horror of irregular sex or flaunted sex—of any sex, you might say, for the proper married kind was not acknowledged at all—and my father too judged these matters strictly at that time in his life. He might have had a special objection, also, to a man who could get a hold over Alfrida.

She would have made herself cheap in their eyes. I can imagine either one of them saying it. *She didn't need to go and make herself cheap.*

But she may not have asked at all, she may have known enough not to. During the time of those earlier, lively visits there may have been no man in her life, and then when there was one, her attention may have shifted entirely. She may have become a different person then, as she certainly was later on.

Or she may have been wary of the special atmosphere of a household where there is a sick person who will go on getting sicker and never get better. Which was the case with my mother, whose symptoms joined together, and turned a corner, and instead of a worry and an inconvenience became her whole destiny.

"The poor thing," the aunts said.

And as my mother was changed from a mother into a stricken presence around the house, these other, formerly so restricted females in the family seemed to gain some little liveliness and increased competence in the world. My grandmother got herself a hearing aid—something nobody would have suggested to her. One of the aunts' husbands—not Asa, but the one called Irvine—

died, and the aunt who had been married to him learned to drive the car and got a job doing alterations in a clothing store and no longer wore a hairnet.

They called to see my mother, and saw always the same thing— that the one who had been better-looking, who had never quite let them forget she was a schoolteacher, was growing month by month more slow and stiff in the movements of her limbs and more thick and importunate in her speech, and that nothing was going to help her.

They told me to take good care of her.

"She's your mother," they reminded me.

"The poor thing."

Alfrida would not have been able to say those things, and she might not have been able to find anything to say in their place.

Her not coming to see us was all right with me. I didn't want people coming. I had no time for them, I had became a furious housekeeper—waxing the floors and ironing even the dish towels, and this was all done to keep some sort of disgrace (my mother's deterioration seemed to be a unique disgrace that infected us all) at bay. It was done to make it seem as if I lived with my parents and my brother and my sister in a normal family in an ordinary house, but the moment somebody stepped in our door and saw my mother they saw that this was not so and they pitied us. A thing I could not stand.

I won a scholarship. I didn't stay home to take care of my mother or of anything else. I went off to college. The college was in the city where Alfrida lived. After a few months she asked me to come for supper, but I could not go, because I worked every evening of the week except on Sundays. I worked in the city library, down-town, and in the college library, both of which stayed open until nine o'clock. Some time later, during the winter, Alfrida asked me again, and this time the invitation was for a Sunday. I told her that I could not come because I was going to a concert.

"Oh—a date?" she said, and I said yes, but at the time it was not true. I would go to the free Sunday concerts in the college auditorium with another girl, or two or three other girls, for something to do and in the faint hope of meeting some boys there.

"Well you'll have to bring him around sometime," Alfrida said. "I'm dying to meet him."

Towards the end of the year I did have someone to bring, and I had actually met him at a concert. At least, he had seen me at a concert and had phoned me up and asked me to go out with him. But I would never have brought him to meet Alfrida. I would never have brought any of my new friends to meet her. My new friends were people who said, "Have you read *Look Homeward Angel*? Oh, you have to read that. Have you read *Buddenbrooks*?" They were people with whom I went to see *Forbidden Games* and *Les Enfants du Paradis* when the Film Society brought them in. The boy I went out with, and later became engaged to, had taken me to the Music Building, where you could listen to records at lunch hour. He introduced me to Gounod and because of Gounod I loved opera, and because of opera I loved Mozart.

When Alfrida left a message at my rooming house, asking me to call back, I never did. After that she didn't call again.

She still wrote for the paper—occasionally I glanced at one of her rhapsodies about Royal Doulton figurines or imported ginger biscuits or honeymoon negligees. Very likely she was still answering the letters from the Flora Simpson housewives, and still laughing at them. Now that I was living in that city I seldom looked at the paper that had once seemed to me the center of city life—and even, in a way, the center of our life at home, sixty miles away. The jokes, the compulsive insincerity, of people like Alfrida and Horse Henry now struck me as tawdry and boring.

I did not worry about running into her, even in this city that was not, after all, so very large. I never went into the shops that she mentioned in her column. I had no reason ever to walk past the newspaper building, and she lived far away from my rooming house, somewhere on the south side of town.

Nor did I think that Alfrida was the kind of person to show up at the library. The very word, "library," would probably make her turn down her big mouth in a parody of consternation, as she used to do at the books in the bookcase in our house—those books not bought in my time, some of them won as school prizes by my teenaged parents (there was my mother's maiden name, in her beautiful lost handwriting), books that seemed to me not like things bought in a store at all, but like presences in the house just as the trees outside the window were not plants but presences rooted in the ground. *The Mill on the Floss, The Call of the Wild, The Heart of Midlothian.* "Lot of hotshot reading in there," Alfrida had said. "Bet you don't crack those very often." And my father had said no, he didn't, falling in with her comradely tone of dismissal or even contempt and to some extent telling a lie, because he did look into them, once in a long while, when he had the time.

That was the kind of lie that I hoped never to have to tell again, the contempt I hoped never to have to show, about the things that really mattered to me. And in order not to have to do that, I would pretty well have to stay clear of the people I used to know.

At the end of my second year I was leaving college—my scholarship had covered only two years there. It didn't matter—I was planning to be a writer anyway. And I was getting married.

Alfrida had heard about this, and she got in touch with me again.

"I guess you must've been too busy to call me, or maybe nobody ever gave you my messages," she said.

I said that maybe I had been, or maybe they hadn't.

This time I agreed to visit. A visit would not commit me to anything, since I was not going to be living in this city in the future. I picked a Sunday, just after my final exams were over, when my fiancé was going to be in Ottawa for a job interview. The day was bright and sunny—it was around the beginning of May. I decided to walk. I had hardly ever been south of Dundas Street or east of Adelaide, so there were parts of the city that were entirely strange to me. The shade trees along the northern streets had just come out in leaf, and the lilacs, the ornamental crab apple trees, the beds of tulips were all in flower, the lawns like fresh carpets. But after a while I found myself walking along streets where there were no shade trees, streets where the houses were hardly an arm's reach from the sidewalk, and where such lilacs as there were—lilacs will grow anywhere—were pale, as if sun-bleached, and their fragrance did not carry. On these streets, as well as houses there were narrow apartment buildings, only two or three stories high—some with the utilitarian decoration of a rim of bricks around their doors, and some with raised windows and limp curtains falling out over their sills.

Alfrida lived in a house, not in an apartment building. She had the whole upstairs of a house. The downstairs, at least the front part of the downstairs, had been turned into a shop, which was closed, because of Sunday. It was a secondhand shop—I could see through the dirty front windows a lot of nondescript furniture with stacks of old dishes and utensils set everywhere. The only thing that caught my eye was a honey pail, exactly like the honey pail with a blue sky and a golden beehive in which I had carried my lunch to school when I was six or seven years old. I could remember reading over and over the words on its side.

All pure honey will granulate.

I had no idea then what "granulate" meant, but I liked the sound of it. It seemed ornate and delicious.

I had taken longer to get there than I had expected and I was very hot. I had not thought that Alfrida, inviting me to lunch, would present me with a meal like the Sunday dinners at home, but it was cooked meat and vegetables I smelled as I climbed the outdoor stairway.

"I thought you'd got lost," Alfrida called out above me. "I was about to get up a rescue party."

Instead of a sundress she was wearing a pink blouse with a floppy bow at the neck, tucked into a pleated brown skirt. Her hair was no longer done up in smooth rolls but cut short and frizzed around her face, its dark brown color now harshly touched with red. And her face, which I remembered as lean and summer-tanned, had got fuller and somewhat pouchy. Her makeup stood out on her skin like orange-pink paint in the noon light.

But the biggest difference was that she had gotten false teeth, of a uniform color, slightly overfilling her mouth and giving an anxious edge to her old expression of slapdash eagerness.

"Well—haven't you plumped out," she said. "You used to be so skinny."

This was true, but I did not like to hear it. Along with all the girls at the rooming house, I ate cheap food—copious meals of Kraft dinners and packages of jam-filled cookies. My fiancé, so sturdily and possessively in favor of everything about me, said that he liked full-bodied women and that I reminded him of Jane Russell. I did not mind his saying that, but usually I was affronted when people had anything to say about my appearance. Particularly when it was somebody like Alfrida—somebody who had lost all importance in my life. I believed that such people had no right to be looking at me, or forming any opinions about me, let alone stating them.

This house was narrow across the front, but long from front to back. There was a living room whose ceiling sloped at the sides and whose windows overlooked the street, a hall-like dining room with no windows at all because side bedrooms with dormers opened off it, a kitchen, a bathroom also without windows that got its daylight through a pebbled-glass pane in its door, and across the back of the house a glassed-in sunporch.

The sloping ceilings made the rooms look makeshift, as if they were only pretending to be anything but bedrooms. But they were crowded with serious furniture—dining-room table and chairs, kitchen table and chairs, living-room sofa and recliner—all meant for larger, proper rooms. Doilies on the tables, squares of embroidered white cloth protecting the backs and arms of sofa and chairs, sheer curtains across the windows and heavy flowered drapes at the sides—it was all more like the aunts' houses than I would have thought possible. And on the dining-room wall—not in the bathroom or bedroom but in the dining room—there hung a picture that was the silhouette of a girl in a hoopskirt, all constructed of pink satin ribbon.

A strip of tough linoleum was laid down on the dining-room floor, on the path from the kitchen to the living room.

Alfrida seemed to guess something of what I was thinking.

"I know I've got far too much stuff in here," she said. "But it's my parents' stuff. It's family furnishings, and I couldn't let them go."

I had never thought of her as having parents. Her mother had died long ago, and she had been brought up by my grandmother, who was her aunt.

"My dad and mother's," Alfrida said. "When Dad went off, your grandma kept it because she said it ought to be mine when I grew up, and so here it is. I couldn't turn it down, when she went to that trouble."

Now it came back to me—the part of Alfrida's life that I had forgotten about. Her father had married again. He had left the farm and got a job working for the railway. He had some other children, the family moved from one town to another, and sometimes Alfrida used to mention them, in a joking way that had something to do with how many children there had been and how close they came together and how much the family had to move around.

"Come and meet Bill," Alfrida said.

Bill was out on the sunporch. He sat, as if waiting to be summoned, on a low couch or daybed that was covered with a brown plaid blanket. The blanket was rumpled—he must have been lying on it recently—and the blinds on the windows were all pulled down to their sills. The light in the room—the hot sunlight coming through the rain-marked yellow blinds—and the rumpled rough blanket and faded, dented cushion, even the smell of the blanket, and of the masculine slippers, old scuffed slippers that had lost their shape and pattern, reminded me—just as much as the doilies and the heavy polished furniture in the inner rooms had done, and the ribbon-girl on the wall—of my aunts' houses. There, too, you could come upon a shabby male hideaway with its furtive yet insistent odors, its shamefaced but stubborn look of contradicting the female domain.

Bill stood up and shook my hand, however, as the uncles would never have done with a strange girl. Or with any girl. No specific rudeness would have held them back, just a dread of appearing ceremonious.

He was a tall man with wavy, glistening gray hair and a smooth but not young-looking face. A handsome man, with the force of his good looks somehow drained away—by indifferent health, or some bad luck, or lack of gumption. But he had still a worn courtesy, a way of bending towards a woman, that suggested the meeting would be a pleasure, for her and for himself.

Alfrida directed us into the windowless dining room where the lights were on in the middle of this bright day. I got the impression that the meal had been ready some time ago, and that my late arrival had delayed their usual schedule. Bill served the roast chicken and dressing, Alfrida the vegetables. Alfrida said to Bill, "Honey, what do you think that is beside your plate?" and then he remembered to pick up his napkin.

He had not much to say. He offered the gravy, he inquired as to whether I wanted mustard relish or salt and pepper, he followed the conversation by turning his head towards Alfrida or towards me. Every so often he made a little whistling sound between his teeth, a shivery sound that seemed meant to be genial and appreciative and that I thought at first might be a prelude to some remark. But it never was, and Alfrida never paused for it. I have since seen reformed drinkers who behaved somewhat as he did— chiming in agreeably but unable to carry things beyond that, helplessly preoccupied. I never knew whether that was true of Bill, but he did seem to carry around a history of defeat, of troubles borne and lessons learned. He had an air too of gallant accommodation towards whatever choices had gone wrong or chances hadn't panned out.

These were frozen peas and carrots, Alfrida said. Frozen vegetables were fairly new at the time.

"They beat the canned," she said. "They're practically as good as fresh."

Then Bill made a whole statement. He said they were better than fresh. The color, the flavor, everything was better than fresh. He said it was remarkable what they could do now and what would be done by way of freezing things in the future.

Alfrida leaned forward, smiling. She seemed almost to hold her breath, as if he was her child taking unsupported steps, or a first lone wobble on a bicycle.

There was a way they could inject something into a chicken, he told us, there was a new process that would have every chicken coming out the same, plump and tasty. No such thing as taking a risk on getting an inferior chicken anymore.

"Bill's field is chemistry," Alfrida said.

When I had nothing to say to this she added, "He worked for Gooderhams."

Still nothing.

"The distillers," she said. "Gooderhams Whisky."

The reason that I had nothing to say was not that I was rude or bored (or any more rude than I was naturally at that time, or more bored than I had expected to be) but that I did not understand that I should ask questions—almost any questions at all, to draw a shy male into conversation, to shake him out of his abstraction and set him up as a man of a certain authority, therefore the man of the house. I did not understand why Alfrida looked at him with such a fiercely encouraging smile. All of my experience of a woman with men, of a woman listening to her man, hoping and hoping that he will establish himself as somebody she can reasonably be proud of, was in the future. The only observation I had made of couples was of my aunts and uncles and of my mother and father, and those husbands and wives seemed to have remote and formalized connections and no obvious dependence on each other.

Bill continued eating as if he had not heard this mention of his profession and his employer, and Alfrida began to question me about my courses. She was still smiling, but her smile had changed. There was a little twitch of impatience and unpleasantness in it, as if she was just waiting for me to get to the end of my explanations so that she could say—as she did say—"You couldn't get me to read that stuff for a million dollars."

"Life's too short," she said. "You know, down at the paper we sometimes get somebody that's been through all that. Honors English. Honors Philosophy. You don't know what to do with them. They can't write worth a nickel. I've told you that, haven't I?" she said to Bill, and Bill looked up and gave her his dutiful smile.

She let this settle.

"So what do you do for fun?" she said.

A Streetcar Named Desire was being done in a theater in Toronto at that time, and I told her that I had gone down on the train with a couple of friends to see it.

Alfrida let the knife and fork clatter onto her plate.

"That filth," she cried. Her face leapt out at me, carved with disgust. Then she spoke more calmly but still with a virulent displeasure.

"You went *all the way to Toronto* to see that filth."

We had finished the dessert, and Bill picked that moment to ask if he might be excused. He asked Alfrida, then with the slightest bow he asked me. He went back to the sunporch and in a little while we could smell his pipe. Alfrida, watching him go, seemed to forget about me and the play. There was a look of such stricken tenderness on her face that when she stood up I thought she was going to follow him. But she was only going to get her cigarettes.

She held them out to me, and when I took one she said, with a deliberate effort at jollity, "I see you kept up the bad habit I got you started on." She might have remembered that I was not a child anymore and I did not have to be in her house and that there was no point in making an enemy of me. And I wasn't going to argue—I did not care what Alfrida thought about Tennessee Williams. Or what she thought about anything else.

"I guess it's your own business," Alfrida said. "You can go where you want to go." And she added, "After all—you'll pretty soon be a married woman."

By her tone, this could mean either "I have to allow that you're grown up now" or "Pretty soon you'll have to toe the line."

We got up and started to collect the dishes. Working close to each other in the small space between the kitchen table and counter and the refrigerator, we soon developed without speaking about it a certain order and harmony of scraping and stacking and putting the leftover food into smaller containers for storage and filling the sink with hot, soapy water and pouncing on any piece of cutlery that hadn't been touched and slipping it into the baize-lined drawer in the dining-room buffet. We brought the ashtray out to the kitchen and stopped every now and then to take a restorative, businesslike drag on our cigarettes. There are things women agree on or don't agree on when they work together in this way— whether it is all right to smoke, for instance, or preferable not to smoke because some migratory ash might find its way onto a clean dish, or whether every single thing that has been on the table has to be washed even if it has not been used—and it turned out that

Alfrida and I agreed. Also, the thought that I could get away, once the dishes were done, made me feel more relaxed and generous. I had already said that I had to meet a friend that afternoon.

"These are pretty dishes," I said. They were creamy-colored, slightly yellowish, with a rim of blue flowers.

"Well—they were my mother's wedding dishes," Alfrida said. "That was one other good thing your grandma did for me. She packed up all my mother's dishes and put them away until the time came when I could use them. Jeanie never knew they existed. They wouldn't have lasted long, with that bunch."

Jeanie. That bunch. Her stepmother and the half brothers and sisters.

"You know about that, don't you?" Alfrida said. "You know what happened to my mother?"

Of course I knew. Alfrida's mother had died when a lamp exploded in her hands—that is, she died of burns she got when a lamp exploded in her hands—and my aunts and my mother had spoken of this regularly. Nothing could be said about Alfrida's mother or about Alfrida's father, and very little about Alfrida herself—without that death being dragged in and tacked onto it. It was the reason that Alfrida's father left the farm (always somewhat of a downward step morally if not financially). It was a reason to be desperately careful with coal oil, and a reason to be grateful for electricity, whatever the cost. And it was a dreadful thing for a child of Alfrida's age, whatever. (That is—whatever she had done with herself since.)

If it hadn't've been for the thunderstorm she wouldn't ever have been lighting a lamp in the middle of the afternoon.

She lived all that night and the next day and the next night and it would have been the best thing in the world for her if she hadn't've.

And just the year after that the Hydro came down their road, and they didn't have need of the lamps anymore.

The aunts and my mother seldom felt the same way about anything, but they shared a feeling about this story. The feeling was in their voices whenever they said Alfrida's mother's name. The story seemed to be a horrible treasure to them, something our family could claim that nobody else could, a distinction that would never be let go. To listen to them had always made me feel as if there was some obscene connivance going on, a fond fingering of whatever was grisly or disastrous. Their voices were like worms slithering around in my insides.

Men were not like this, in my experience. Men looked away from frightful happenings as soon as they could and behaved as if there was no use, once things were over with, in mentioning them or thinking about them ever again. They didn't want to stir themselves up, or stir other people up.

So if Alfrida was going to talk about it, I thought, it was a good thing that my fiancé had not come. A good thing that he didn't have to hear about Alfrida's mother, on top of finding out about my mother and my family's relative or maybe considerable poverty. He admired opera and Laurence Olivier's *Hamlet*, but he had no time for tragedy—for the squalor of tragedy—in ordinary life. His parents were healthy and good-looking and prosperous (though he said of course that they were dull), and it seemed he had not had to know anybody who did not live in fairly sunny circumstances. Failures in life—failures of luck, of health, of finances—all struck him as lapses, and his resolute approval of me did not extend to my ramshackle background.

"They wouldn't let me in to see her, at the hospital," Alfrida said, and at least she was saying this in her normal voice, not preparing the way with any special piety, or greasy excitement. "Well, I probably wouldn't have let me in either, if I'd been in their shoes. I've no idea what she looked like. Probably all bound up like a mummy. Or if she wasn't she should have been. I wasn't there when it happened, I was at school. It got very dark and the teacher turned the lights on—we had the lights, at school—and we all had to stay till the thunderstorm was over. Then my aunt Lily—well, your grandmother—she came to meet me and took me to her place. And I never got to see my mother again."

I thought that was all she was going to say but in a moment she continued, in a voice that had actually brightened up a bit, as if she was preparing for a laugh.

"I yelled and yelled my fool head off that I wanted to see her. I carried on and carried on, and finally when they couldn't shut me up your grandmother said to me, 'You're just better off not to see her. You would not want to see her, if you knew what she looks like now. You wouldn't want to remember her this way.'

"But you know what I said? I remember saying it. I said, But she would want to see me. *She would want to see me.*"

Then she really did laugh, or make a snorting sound that was evasive and scornful.

"I must've thought I was a pretty big cheese, mustn't I? *She would want to see me.*"

This was a part of the story I had never heard.

And the minute that I heard it, something happened. It was as if a trap had snapped shut, to hold these words in my head. I did not exactly understand what use I would have for them. I only knew how they jolted me and released me, right away, to breathe a different kind of air, available only to myself,

She would want to see me.

The story I wrote, with this in it, would not be written till years later, not until it had become quite unimportant to think about who had put the idea into my head in the first place.

I thanked Alfrida and said that I had to go. Alfrida went to call Bill to say good-bye to me, but came back to report that he had fallen asleep.

"He'll be kicking himself when he wakes up," she said. "He enjoyed meeting you."

She took off her apron and accompanied me all the way down the outside steps. At the bottom of the steps was a gravel path leading around to the sidewalk. The gravel crunched under our feet and she stumbled in her thin-soled house shoes.

She said, "Ouch! Goldarn it," and caught hold of my shoulder.

"How's your dad?" she said.

"He's all right."

"He works too hard."

I said, "He has to."

"Oh, I know. And how's your mother?"

"She's about the same."

She turned aside towards the shop window.

"Who do they think is ever going to buy this junk? Look at that honey pail. Your dad and I used to take our lunch to school in pails just like that."

"So did I," I said.

"Did you?" She squeezed me. "You tell your folks I'm thinking about them, will you do that?"

Alfrida did not come to my father's funeral. I wondered if that was because she did not want to meet me. As far as I knew she had never made public what she held against me; nobody else would know about it. But my father had known. When I was home visiting him and learned that Alfrida was living not far away—in my grandmother's house, in fact, which she had finally inherited—I had suggested that we go to see her. This was in the flurry between my two marriages, when I was in an expansive mood, newly released and able to make contact with anyone I chose.

My father said, "Well, you know, Alfrida was a bit upset."

He was calling her Alfrida now. When had that started?

I could not even think, at first, what Alfrida might be upset about. My father had to remind me of the story, published several years ago, and I was surprised, even impatient and a little angry, to think of Alfrida's objecting to something that seemed now to have so little to do with her.

"It wasn't Alfrida at all," I said to my father. "I changed it, I wasn't even thinking about her. It was a character. Anybody could see that."

But as a matter of fact there was still the exploding lamp, the mother in her charnel wrappings, the staunch, bereft child.

"Well," my father said. He was in general quite pleased that I had become a writer, but there were reservations he had about what might be called my character. About the fact that I had ended my marriage for personal—that is, wanton—reasons, and the way I went around justifying myself—or perhaps, as he would have said, weaseling out of things. He would not say so—it was not his business anymore.

I asked him how he knew that Alfrida felt this way.

He said, "A letter."

A letter, though they lived not far apart. I did feel sorry to think that he had had to bear the brunt of what could be taken as my thoughtlessness, or even my wrongdoing. Also that he and Alfrida seemed now to be on such formal terms. I wondered what he was leaving out. Had he felt compelled to defend me to Alfrida, as he had to defend my writing to other people? He would do that now, though it was never easy for him. In his uneasy defense he might have said something harsh.

Through me, peculiar difficulties had developed for him.

There was a danger whenever I was on home ground. It was the danger of seeing my life through other eyes than my own. Seeing it as an ever-increasing roll of words like barbed wire, intricate, bewildering, uncomforting—set against the rich productions, the food, flowers, and knitted garments, of other women's domesticity. It became harder to say that it was worth the trouble.

Worth my trouble, maybe, but what about anyone else's?

My father had said that Alfrida was living alone now. I asked him what had become of Bill. He said that all of that was outside of his jurisdiction. But he believed there had been a bit of a rescue operation.

"Of Bill? How come? Who by?"

"Well, I believe there was a wife."

"I met him at Alfrida's once. I liked him."

"People did. Women."

I had to consider that the rupture might have had nothing to do with me. My stepmother had urged my father into a new sort of life. They went bowling and curling and regularly joined other couples for coffee and doughnuts at Tim Horton's. She had been a widow for a long time before she married him, and she had many friends from those days who became new friends for him. What had happened with him and Alfrida might have been simply one of the changes, the wearing-out of old attachments, that I understood so well in my own life but did not expect to happen in the lives of older people—particularly, as I would have said, in the lives of people at home.

My stepmother died just a little while before my father. After their short, happy marriage they were sent to separate cemeteries to lie beside their first, more troublesome, partners. Before either of those deaths Alfrida had moved back to the city. She didn't sell the house, she just went away and left it. My father wrote to me, "That's a pretty funny way of doing things."

There were a lot of people at my father's funeral, a lot of people I didn't know. A woman came across the grass in the cemetery to speak to me—I thought at first she must be a friend of my stepmother's. Then I saw that the woman was only a few years past my own age. The stocky figure and crown of gray-blond curls and floral-patterned jacket made her look older.

"I recognized you by your picture," she said. "Alfrida used to always be bragging about you."

I said, "Alfrida's not dead?"

"Oh, no," the woman said, and went on to tell me that Alfrida was in a nursing home in a town just north of Toronto.

"I moved her down there so's I could keep an eye on her."

Now it was easy to tell—even by her voice—that she was somebody of my own generation, and it came to me that she must be one of the other family, a half sister of Alfrida's, born when Alfrida was almost grown up.

She told me her name, and it was of course not the same as Alfrida's—she must have married. And I couldn't recall Alfrida's ever mentioning any of her half family by their first names.

I asked how Alfrida was, and the woman said her own eyesight was so bad that she was legally blind. And she had a serious kidney problem, which meant that she had to be on dialysis twice a week.

"Other than that—?" she said, and laughed. I thought, yes, a sister, because I could hear something of Alfrida in that reckless, tossed laugh.

"So she doesn't travel too good," she said. "Or else I would've brought her. She still gets the paper from here and I read it to her sometimes. That's where I saw about your dad."

I wondered out loud, impulsively, if I should go to visit, at the nursing home. The emotions of the funeral—all the warm and relieved and reconciled feelings opened up in me by the death of my father at a reasonable age—prompted this suggestion. It would have been hard to carry out. My husband—my second husband—and I had only two days here before we were flying to Europe on an already delayed holiday.

"I don't know if you'd get so much out of it," the woman said. "She has her good days. Then she has her bad days. You never know. Sometimes I think she's putting it on. Like, she'll sit there all day and whatever anybody says to her, she'll just say the same thing. *Fit as a fiddle and ready for love.* That's what she'll say all day long. *Fit-as-a-fiddle-and-ready-for-love.* She'll drive you crazy. Then other days she can answer all right."

Again, her voice and laugh—this time half submerged—reminded me of Alfrida, and I said, "You know I must have met you, I remember once when Alfrida's stepmother and her father dropped in, or maybe it was only her father and some of the children—"

"Oh, that's not who I am," the woman said. "You thought I was Alfrida's sister? Glory. I must be looking my age."

I started to say that I could not see her very well, and it was true. In October the afternoon sun was low, and it was coming straight into my eyes. The woman was standing against the light, so that it was hard to make out her features or her expression.

She twitched her shoulders nervously and importantly. She said, "Alfrida was my birth mom."

Mawm. Mother.

Then she told me, at not too great length, the story that she must have told often, because it was about an emphatic event in her life and an adventure she had embarked on alone. She had been adopted by a family in eastern Ontario; they were the only family she had ever known ("and I love them dearly"), and she had married and had her children, who were grown up before she got the urge to find out who her own mother was. It wasn't too easy, because of the way records used to be kept, and the secrecy ("It was kept one hundred percent secret that she had me"), but a few years ago she had tracked down Alfrida.

"Just in time too," she said. "I mean, it was time somebody came along to look after her. As much as I can."

I said, "I never knew."

"No. Those days, I don't suppose too many did. They warn you, when you start out to do this, it could be a shock when you show up. Older people, it's still heavy-duty. However. I don't think she minded. Earlier on, maybe she would have."

There was some sense of triumph about her, which wasn't hard to understand. If you have something to tell that will stagger someone, and you've told it, and it has done so, there has to be a balmy moment of power. In this case it was so complete that she felt a need to apologize.

"Excuse me talking all about myself and not saying how sorry I am about your dad."

I thanked her.

"You know Alfrida told me that your dad and her were walking home from school one day, this was in high school. They couldn't walk all the way together because, you know, in those days, a boy and a girl, they would just get teased something terrible. So if he got out first he'd wait just where their road went off the main road, outside of town, and if she got out first she would do the same, wait for him. And one day they were walking together and they heard all the bells starting to ring and you know what that was? It was the end of the First World War."

I said that I had heard that story too.

"Only I thought they were just children."

"Then how could they be coming home from high school, if they were just children?"

I said that I had thought they were out playing in the fields. "They had my father's dog with them. He was called Mack."

"Maybe they had the dog all right. Maybe he came to meet them. I wouldn't think she'd get mixed up on what she was telling me. She was pretty good on remembering anything involved your dad."

Now I was aware of two things. First, that my father was born in 1902, and that Alfrida was close to the same age. So it was much more likely that they were walking home from high school than that they were playing in the fields, and it was odd that I had never thought of that before. Maybe they had said they were in the fields, that is, walking home across the fields. Maybe they had never said "playing."

Also, that the feeling of apology or friendliness, the harmlessness that I had felt in this woman a little while before, was not there now.

I said, "Things get changed around."

"That's right," the woman said. "People change things around. You want to know what Alfrida said about you?"

Now. I knew it was coming now.

"What?"

"She said you were smart, but you weren't ever quite as smart as you thought you were."

I made myself keep looking into the dark face against the light.

Smart, too smart, not smart enough.

I said, "Is that all?"

"She said you were kind of a cold fish. That's her talking, not me. I haven't got anything against you."

That Sunday, after the noon dinner at Alfrida's, I set out to walk all the way back to my rooming house. If I walked both ways, I reckoned that I would have covered about ten miles, which ought to offset the effects of the meal I had eaten. I felt overfull, not just of food but of everything that I had seen and sensed in the apartment. The crowded, old-fashioned furnishings. Bill's silences. Alfrida's love, stubborn as sludge, and inappropriate, and hopeless—as far as I could see—on the grounds of age alone.

After I had walked for a while, my stomach did not feel so heavy. I made a vow not to eat anything for the next twenty-four hours. I walked north and west, north and west, on the streets of the tidily rectangular small city. On a Sunday afternoon there was hardly any traffic, except on the main thoroughfares. Sometimes my route coincided with a bus route for a few blocks. A bus might go by with only two or three people in it. People I did not know and who did not know me. What a blessing.

I had lied, I was not meeting any friends. My friends had mostly all gone home to wherever they lived. My fiancé would be away until the next day—he was visiting his parents, in Cobourg, on the way home from Ottawa. There would be nobody in the rooming house when I got there—nobody I had to bother talking to or listening to. I had nothing to do.

When I had walked for over an hour, I saw a drugstore that was open. I went in and had a cup of coffee. The coffee was reheated, black and bitter—its taste was medicinal, exactly what I needed. I was already feeling relieved, and now I began to feel happy. Such happiness, to be alone. To see the hot late-afternoon light on the sidewalk outside, the branches of a tree just out in leaf, throwing their skimpy shadows. To hear from the back of the shop the sounds of the ball game that the man who had served me was listening to on the radio. I did not think of the story I would make about Alfrida—not of that in particular—but of the work I wanted to do, which seemed more like grabbing something out of the air than constructing stories. The cries of the crowd came to me like big heartbeats, full of sorrows. Lovely formal-sounding waves, with their distant, almost inhuman assent and lamentation.

This was what I wanted, this was what I thought I had to pay attention to, this was how I wanted my life to be.

Comfort

Nina had been playing tennis in the late afternoon, on the high-school courts. After Lewis had left his job at the school she had boycotted the courts for a while, but that was nearly a year ago, and her friend Margaret—another retired teacher, whose departure had been routine and ceremonious, unlike Lewis's—had talked her into playing there again.

"Better get out a bit while you still can."

Margaret had already been gone when Lewis's trouble occurred. She had written a letter from Scotland in support of him. But she was a person of such wide sympathies, such open understanding and far-reaching friendships, that the letter perhaps did not carry much weight. More of Margaret's good-heartedness.

"How is Lewis?" she said, when Nina drove her home that afternoon.

Nina said, "Coasting."

The sun had already dropped nearly to the rim of the lake. Some trees that still held their leaves were flares of gold, but the summer warmth of the afternoon had been snatched away. The shrubs in front of Margaret's house were all bundled up in sacking like mummies.

This moment of the day made Nina think of the walks she and

Lewis used to take after school and before supper. Short walks, of necessity as the days got dark, along out-of-town lanes and old railway embankments. But crowded with all that specific observation, spoken or not spoken, that she had learned or absorbed from Lewis. Bugs, grubs, snails, mosses, reeds in the ditch and shaggy-manes in the grass, animal tracks, nannyberries, cranberries—a deep mix stirred up a little differently every day. And every day a new step towards winter, an increased frugality, a withering.

The house Nina and Lewis lived in had been built in the 1840s, close up to the sidewalk in the style of that time. If you were in the living room or dining room you could hear not only footsteps but conversations outside. Nina expected that Lewis would have heard the car door close.

She entered whistling, as well as she could. *See the conquering hero comes.*

"I won. I won. Hello?"

But while she was out, Lewis had been dying. In fact, he had been killing himself. On the bedside table lay four little plastic packets, backed with foil. Each had contained two potent painkillers. Two extra packets lay beside these, inviolate, the white capsules still plumping up the plastic cover. When Nina picked these up, later, she would see that one of them had a mark on the foil, as if he had started to dig in, with a fingernail, then had given up as if he'd decided he had already had enough, or had at that moment been drawn into unconsciousness.

His drinking glass was nearly empty. No water spilled.

This was a thing they had talked about. The plan had been agreed to, but always as a thing that could happen—would happen—in the future. Nina had assumed that she would be present and that there would be some ceremonial recognition. Music. The pillows arranged and a chair drawn up so that she could hold his hand. Two things she had not thought of—his extreme dislike of ceremony of any sort, and the burden such participation would put on her. The questions asked, the opinions passed, her jeopardy as a party to the act.

In doing it this way he had given her as little as possible that was worth covering up.

She looked for a note. What did she think it would say? She didn't need instructions. She certainly did not need an explanation, let alone an apology. There was nothing a note could tell her that she didn't know already. Even the question, Why so soon? was one she could figure out the answer for by herself. They had talked—or he had—about the threshold of intolerable helplessness or pain or self-disgust, and how it was important to recognize that threshold, not slide over it. Sooner, rather than later.

Just the same, it seemed impossible that he would not still have something to say to her. She looked first on the floor, thinking that he might have swiped the paper off the bedside table with his pajama sleeve when he set the water glass down for the last time. Or he could have taken special care not to do that—she looked under the base of the lamp. Then in the drawer of the table. Then under, and in, his slippers. She picked up and shook loose the pages of the book he had lately been reading, a paleontology book about what she believed was called the Cambrian explosion of multi-celled life-forms.

Nothing there.

She began rifling through the bedclothes. She stripped off the duvet, then the top sheet. There he lay, in the dark-blue silk pajamas which she had bought for him a couple of weeks ago. He had complained of feeling cold—he who had never been cold in bed before—so she went out and bought the most expensive pajamas in the store. She bought them because silk was both light and warm, and because all the other pajamas she saw—with their stripes, and their whimsical or naughty messages—made her think of old men, or comic-strip husbands, defeated shufflers. These were almost the same color as the sheets, so that little of him was revealed to her. Feet, ankles, shins. Hands, wrists, neck, head. He lay on his side, facing away from her. Still intent on the note, she moved the pillow, dragged it roughly away from under his head.

No. No.

Shifted from pillow to mattress, the head made a certain sound, a sound that was heavier than she would have expected. And it was that, as much as the blank expanse of the sheet, that seemed to be saying to her that the search was futile.

The pills would have put him to sleep, taken all his workings by stealth, so that there was no dead stare, no contortion. His mouth was slightly open, but dry. The last couple of months had altered him a great deal—it was really only now that she saw how much. When his eyes had been open, or even when he had been sleeping, some effort of his had kept up the illusion that the damage was temporary—that the face of a vigorous, always potentially aggressive sixty-two-year-old man was still there, under the folds of bluish skin, the stony vigilance of illness. It had never been bone structure that gave his face its fierce and lively character—it was all in the deep-set bright eyes and the twitchy mouth and the facility of expression, the fast-changing display of creases that effected his repertoire of mockery, disbelief, ironic patience, suffering disgust. A classroom repertoire—and not always confined there.

No more. No more. Now within a couple of hours of death (for he must have got down to business as soon as she had left, not wanting to risk the job's not being finished when she returned), now it was plain that the wasting and crumbling had won out and his face was deeply shrunken. It was sealed, remote, aged and infantile—perhaps like the face of a baby born dead.

The disease had three styles of onset. One involved the hands and arms. The fingers grew numb and stupid, their clasp awkward and then impossible. Or it could be the legs that weakened first, and the feet that started stumbling, soon refusing to lift themselves up steps or even over carpet edges. The third and probably the worst sort of attack was made on the throat and tongue. Swallowing became unreliable, fearful, a choking drama, and speech turned into a clotted flow of importunate syllables. It was the voluntary muscles that were affected, always, and at first that did indeed sound like a lesser evil. No misfirings in the heart or brain, no signals gone awry, no malicious rearrangements of the personality. Sight and hearing and taste and touch, and best of all intelligence, lively and strong as ever. The brain kept busy monitoring all the outlying shutdown, toting up the defaults and depletions. Wasn't that to be preferred?

Of course, Lewis had said. But only because of the chance it gives you, to take action.

His own problems had started with the muscles of his legs. He had enrolled in a Seniors Fitness class (though he hated the idea) to see if strength could be bullied back into them. He thought it was working, for a week or two. But then came the lead feet, the shuffling and tripping, and before long, the diagnosis. As soon as they knew that much, they had talked about what would be done when the time came. Early in the summer, he was walking with two canes. By the end of summer he was not walking at all. But his hands could still turn the pages of a book and manage, with difficulty, a fork or spoon or pen. His speech seemed to Nina almost unaffected, though visitors had trouble with it. He had decided anyway that visitors should be banned. His diet had been changed, to make swallowing easier, and sometimes days passed without any difficulty of that kind.

Nina had made inquiries about a wheelchair. He had not opposed this. They no longer talked about what they called the Big Shutdown. She had even wondered if they—or he—might be entering a phase she had read about, a change that came on people sometimes in the middle of a fatal illness. A measure of optimism struggling to the fore, not because it was warranted, but because the whole experience had become a reality and not an abstraction, the ways of coping had become permanent, not a nuisance.

The end is not yet. Live for the present. Seize the day.

That kind of development seemed out of character for Lewis. Nina would not have thought him capable of even the most useful self-deception. But she could never have imagined him overtaken by physical collapse, either. And now that one unlikely thing had happened, couldn't others? Was it not possible that the changes that happened with other people might occur with him too? The secret hopes, the turning aside, the sly bargains?

No.

She picked up the bedside phone book and looked for "Undertakers," which was a word that of course did not occur. "Funeral Directors." The exasperation she felt at that was of the sort she usually shared with him. Undertakers, for God's sake, what's wrong with undertakers? She turned to him and saw how she had left him, helplessly uncovered. Before she rang the number she got the sheet and the duvet back on.

A young man's voice asked her if the doctor was there, had the doctor been yet?

"He didn't need a doctor. When I came in I found him dead."

"When was that, then?"

"I don't know—twenty minutes ago."

"You found him passed away? So—who is your doctor? I'll phone and send him over."

In their matter-of-fact discussions of suicide, Nina and Lewis had never, as she remembered, talked about whether the fact was to be kept secret or made known. In one way, she was sure, Lewis would have wanted the facts known. He would have wanted to make it known that this was his idea of an honorable and sensible way to deal with the situation he had found himself in. But there was another way in which he might have preferred no such revelation. He would not want anybody to think that this resulted from the loss of his job, his failed struggle at the school. To have them think he had caved in like this on account of his defeat there—that would have set him raging.

She scooped the packets off the bedside table, the full ones as well as the empties, and flushed them down the toilet.

The undertaker's men were big local lads, former students, a bit more flustered than they wanted to show. The doctor was young, too, and a stranger—Lewis's regular doctor was on holiday, in Greece.

"A blessing, then," the doctor said when he had been filled in on the facts. She was a bit surprised to hear him so openly admit that, and thought that Lewis, if he could have heard, might have caught an unwelcome whiff of religion. What the doctor said next was less surprising.

"Would you like to talk to anybody? We have people now who can, just, you know, help you sort out your feelings."

"No. No. Thank you, I'm all right."

"You've lived here a long time? You have friends you can call on?"

"Oh, yes. Yes."

"Are you going to call somebody now?"

"Yes," said Nina. She was lying. As soon as the doctor, and the young bearers, and Lewis, had left the house—Lewis borne like a piece of furniture wrapped to protect it from knocks—she had to resume her search. It seemed now that she had been a fool to restrict it to the vicinity of the bed. She found herself going through the pockets of her dressing gown, which hung on the back of the bedroom door. An excellent place, since this was a garment she put on every morning before scurrying to make coffee, and she was always exploring its pockets to find a Kleenex, a lipstick. Except that he would have had to rise from his bed and cross the room—he who had not been able to take a step without her help for some weeks.

But why would the note have had to be composed and put in place yesterday? Would it not have made sense to write and hide it weeks ago, especially since he didn't know the rate at which his writing would deteriorate? And if that was the case it could be any-where. In the drawers of her desk—where she was rummaging now. Or under the bottle of champagne, which she had bought to drink on his birthday and set on the dresser, to remind him of that date two weeks hence—or between the pages of any of the books she opened these days. He had in fact asked her, not long ago, "What are you reading on your own now?" He meant, apart from the book she was reading to him—*Frederick the Great* by Nancy Mitford. She chose to read him entertaining history—he wouldn't put up with fiction—and left the science books for him to manage himself. She had told him, "Just some Japanese stories," and held up the book. Now she threw books aside to locate that one, to hold it upside down and shake the pages out. Every book she had pushed away then got the same treatment. Cushions on the chair where she habitually sat were thrown to the floor, to see what was behind them. Eventually all the cushions on the sofa were dispersed in the same way. The coffee beans shaken out of their tin, in case he had (whimsically?) concealed a farewell in there.

She had wanted no one with her, no one to observe this search—which she had been conducting, however, with all the lights on and the curtains open. No one to remind her that she had to get hold of herself. It had been dark for some time and she real-ized that she ought to have something to eat. She might phone Margaret. But she did nothing. She got up to close the curtains but instead turned out the lights.

Nina was slightly over six feet tall. Even when she was in her teens, gym teachers, guidance counselors, concerned friends of her mother's had been urging her to get rid of her stoop. She did her best, but even now, when she looked at photographs of herself, she was dismayed to see how pliant she had made herself—shoulders drawn together, head tilted to the side, her whole attitude that of a smiling attendant. When she was young she had got used to meetings being arranged, friends bringing her together with tall men. It seemed that nothing else much mattered about the man—if he was well over six feet tall, he must be paired off with Nina. Quite often he would be sulky about this situation—a tall man, after all, could pick and choose—and Nina, still stooping and smiling, would be swamped with embarrassment.

Her parents, at least, behaved as if her life was her own business. They were both doctors, living in a small city in Michigan. Nina lived with them after she had finished college. She taught Latin at the local high school. On her vacations she went off to Europe with those college friends who had not yet been skimmed off to marry and remarry, and probably wouldn't be. Hiking in the Cairngorms, she and her party fell in with a pack of Australians and New Zealanders, temporary hippies whose leader appeared to be Lewis. He was a few years older than the rest, less a hippie than a seasoned wanderer, and definitely the one to be called on when disputes and difficulties arose. He was not particularly tall—three or four inches shorter than Nina. Nevertheless, he attached himself to her, persuaded her to change her itinerary and go off with him—he himself cheerfully leaving his pack to their own devices.

It turned out that he was fed up with wandering, and also that he had a perfectly good Biology degree and a teaching certificate from New Zealand. Nina told him about the town on the east shore of Lake Huron, in Canada, where she had visited relatives when she was a child. She described the tall trees along the streets, the plain old houses, the sunsets over the lake—an excellent place for their life together, and a place where, because of Commonwealth connections, Lewis might find it easier to get a job. They did get jobs, both of them, at the high school—though Nina gave up teaching a few years later, when Latin was phased out. She could have taken upgrading courses, preparing herself to teach something else, but she was just as glad, secretly, to no longer be working in the same place, and at the same sort of job, as Lewis. The force of his personality, the unsettling style of his teaching, made enemies as well as friends, and it was a rest, for her, not to be in the thick of it.

They had left it rather late to have a child. And she suspected that they were both a little too vain—they didn't like the thought of wrapping themselves up in the slightly comic and diminished identities of Mom and Dad. Both of them—but particularly Lewis—were admired by the students for being unlike the adults around home. More energetic mentally and physically, more complex and vivid and capable of getting some good out of life.

She joined a choral society. Many of its recitals were given in churches, and it was then that she learned what a deep dislike Lewis had of these places. She argued that there often wasn't any other suitable space available and it didn't mean that the music was religious (though it was a bit hard to argue this when the music was the *Messiah*). She said that he was being old-fashioned and that there was little harm any religion could do nowadays. This started a great row. They had to rush around slamming down the windows, so that their roused voices might not be heard out on the sidewalk in the warm summer evening.

A fight like this was stunning, revealing not just how much he was on the lookout for enemies, but how she too was unable to abandon argument which escalated into rage. Neither of them would back off, they held bitterly to principles.

Can't you tolerate people being different, why is this so important?

If this isn't important, nothing is.

The air seemed to grow thick with loathing. All over a matter that could never be resolved. They went to bed speechless, parted speechless the next morning, and during the day were overtaken by fear—hers that he would never come home, his that when he did she would not be there. Their luck held, however. They came together in the late afternoon pale with contrition, shaking with love, like people who had narrowly escaped an earthquake and had been walking around in naked desolation.

That was not the last time. Nina, brought up to be so peaceable, wondered if this was normal life. She couldn't discuss it with him— their reunions were too grateful, too sweet and silly. He called her Sweet Nina-Hyena and she called him Merry Weather Lewis.

A few years ago, a new sort of sign started appearing on the road-side. For a long time there had been signs urging conversion, and those with large pink hearts and the flattening line of beats, meant to discourage abortion. What was showing up now were texts from Genesis.

> *In the beginning God created Heaven and Earth.*
> *God said, Let there be Light, and there was Light.*
> *God created Man in his own image. Male and Female created*
>   *he them.*

Usually there was a rainbow or a rose or some symbol of Edenic loveliness painted alongside the words.

"What is the meaning of all this?" said Nina. "It's a change anyway. From 'God so loved the world.'"

"It's creationism," said Lewis.

"I could figure that. I mean, why is it up on signs all over the place?"

Lewis said there was a definite movement now to reinforce belief in the literal Bible story.

"Adam and Eve. The same old rubbish."

He seemed not greatly disturbed about this—or any more affronted than he might be by the crèche that was put up every Christmas not in front of a church but on the lawn of the Town Hall. On church property was one thing, he said, town property another. Nina's Quaker teaching had not put much emphasis on Adam and Eve, so when she got home she took out the King James

Bible and read the story all the way through. She was delighted by the majestic progress of those first six days—the dividing of the waters and the installation of the sun and moon and the appearance of the things that creep upon the earth and the fowls of the air, and so on.

"This is beautiful," she said. "It's great poetry. People should read it."

He said that it was no better and no worse than any of the whole parcel of creation myths that had sprung up in all corners of the earth and that he was sick and tired of hearing about how beautiful it was, and the poetry.

"That's a smoke screen," he said. "They don't give a piss in a pot about the poetry."

Nina laughed. "Corners of the earth," she said. "What kind of talk is that for a scientist? I bet it's out of the Bible."

She would take a chance, once in a while, to tease him on this subject. But she had to be careful not to go too far. She had to watch out for the point at which he might sense the deadly threat, the dishonoring insult.

Now and then she found a pamphlet in the mail. She didn't read them through, and for a while she thought that everybody must be getting this sort of thing, along with the junk mail offering tropical holidays and other gaudy windfalls. Then she found out that Lewis was getting the same material at school—"creationist propaganda" as he called it—left on his desk or stuffed into his pigeonhole in the office.

"The kids have access to my desk, but who the hell is stuffing my mailbox in here?" he had said to the Principal.

The Principal had said that he couldn't figure it out, he was getting it too. Lewis mentioned the name of a couple of teachers on the staff, a couple of crypto-Christians as he called them, and the

Principal said it wasn't worth getting your shirt in a knot about, you could always throw the stuff away.

There were questions in class. Of course, there always had been. You could count on it, Lewis said. Some little sickly saint of a girl or a smart-arse of either sex trying to throw a monkey wrench into evolution. Lewis had his tried-and-true ways of dealing with this. He told the disrupters that if they wanted the religious interpretation of the world's history there was the Christian Separate School in the next town, which they were welcome to attend. Questions becoming more frequent, he added that there were buses to take them there, and they could collect their books and depart this day and hour if they had a mind to.

"And a fair wind to your—" he said. Later there was controversy—about whether he actually said the word "arse" or let it hang unspoken in the air. But even if he had not actually said it he had surely given offense, because everybody knew how the phrase could be completed.

The students were taking a new tack these days.

"It's not that we necessarily want the religious view, sir. It's just that we wonder why you don't give it equal time."

Lewis let himself be drawn into argument.

"It's because I am here to teach you science, not religion."

That was what he said he had said. There were those who reported him as saying, "Because I am not here to teach you crap." And indeed, indeed, said Lewis, after the fourth or fifth interruption, the posing of the question in whatever slightly different way ("Do you think it hurts us to hear the other side of the story? If we get taught atheism, isn't that sort of like teaching us some kind of religion?"), the word might have escaped his lips, and under such provocation he did not apologize for it.

"I happen to be the boss in this classroom and I decide what will be taught."

"I thought God was the boss, sir."

There were expulsions from the room. Parents arrived to speak to the Principal. Or they may have intended to speak to Lewis, but the Principal made sure that did not happen. Lewis heard about these interviews only later, from remarks passed, more or less jokingly, in the staff room.

"You don't need to get worried about it," said the Principal—his name was Paul Gibbings, and he was a few years younger than Lewis. "They just need to feel they're being listened to. Need a bit of jollying along."

"I'd have jollied them," Lewis said.

"Yeah. That's not quite the jollying I had in mind."

"There should be a sign. No dogs or parents on the premises."

"Something to that," said Paul Gibbings, sighing amiably. "But I suppose they've got their rights."

Letters started to appear in the local paper. One every couple of weeks, signed "Concerned Parent" or "Christian Taxpayer" or "Where Do We Go From Here?" They were well written, neatly paragraphed, competently argued, as if they might all have come from one delegated hand. They made the point that not all parents could afford the fees for the private Christian school, and yet all parents paid taxes. Therefore they deserved to have their children educated in the public schools in a way that was not offensive to, or deliberately destructive of, their faith. In scientific language, some explained how the record had been misunderstood and how discoveries that seemed to support evolution actually confirmed the Biblical account. Then came citing of Bible texts that predicted this present-day false teaching and its leading the way to the abandonment of all decent rules of life.

In time the tone changed; it grew wrathful. Agents of the Antichrist in charge of the government and the classroom. The claws of Satan stretched out towards the souls of children, who were actually forced to reiterate, on their examinations, the doctrines of damnation.

"What is the difference between Satan and the Antichrist, or is there one?" said Nina. "The Quakers were very remiss about all that."

Lewis said that he could do without her treating all this as a joke.

"Sorry," she said soberly. "Who do you think is really writing them? Some minister?"

He said no, it would be better organized than that. A masterminded campaign, some central office, supplying letters to be sent from local addresses. He doubted if any of it had started here, in his classroom. It was all planned, schools were targeted, probably in areas where there was some good hope of public sympathy.

"So? It's not personal?"

"That's not a consolation."

"Isn't it? I'd think it would be."

Someone wrote "Hellfire" on Lewis's car. It wasn't done with spray paint—just a finger-tracing in the dust.

His senior class began to be boycotted by a minority of students, who sat on the floor outside, armed with notes from their parents. When Lewis began to teach, they began to sing.

> *All things bright and beautiful*
> *All creatures great and small*
> *All things wise and wonderful*
> *The Lord God made them all—*

The principal invoked a rule about not sitting on the hall floor, but he did not order them back into the classroom. They had to go to a storage room off the gym, where they continued their singing—they had other hymns ready as well. Their voices mingled disconcertingly with the hoarse instructions of the gym teacher and the thump of feet on the gym floor.

On a Monday morning a petition appeared on the Principal's desk and at the same time a copy of it was delivered to the town newspaper office. Signatures had been collected not just from the

parents of the children involved but from various church con-
gregations around the town. Most were from fundamentalist
churches, but there were some from the United and Anglican and
Presbyterian churches as well.

There was no mention of hellfire in the petition. None whatever
of Satan or the Antichrist. All that was requested was to have the
Biblical version of creation given equal time, considered respect-
fully as an option.

"We the undersigned believe that God has been left out of the
picture too long."

"That's nonsense," Lewis said. "They don't believe in equal
time—they don't believe in options. Absolutists is what they are.
Fascists."

Paul Gibbings had come round to Lewis and Nina's house. He
didn't want to discuss the matter where spies might be listening.
(One of the secretaries was a member of the Bible Chapel.) He
hadn't much expectation of getting around Lewis, but he had to
give it a try.

"They've got me over the bloody barrel," he said.

"Fire me," said Lewis. "Hire some stupid bugger of a creationist."

The son of a bitch is enjoying this, Paul thought. But he controlled himself. What he seemed mostly to do these days was control himself.

"I didn't come over here to talk about that. I mean a lot of
people will think this bunch is just being reasonable. Including
people on the Board."

"Make them happy. Fire me. March in Adam and Eve."

Nina brought them coffee. Paul thanked her and tried to catch
her eye, to see where she stood on this. No go.

"Yeah sure," he said. "I couldn't do that if I wanted to. And I
don't want to. The Union would be after my ass. We'd have it all

over the province, could even be a strike issue, we have to think of the kids."

You'd think that might get to Lewis—thinking of the kids. But he was off on his own trip as usual.

"March in Adam and Eve. With or without the fig leaves."

"All I want to ask is a little speech indicating that this is a different interpretation and some people believe one thing and some people believe the other. Get the Genesis story down to fifteen or twenty minutes. Read it out loud. Only do it with respect. You know what it's all about, don't you? People feeling disregarded. People just don't like to feel they're being disregarded."

Lewis sat silent long enough to create a hope—in Paul, and maybe in Nina, who could tell?—but it turned out that this long pause was just a device to let the perceived iniquity of the suggestion sink in.

"What about it?" Paul said cautiously.

"I will read the whole book of Genesis aloud if you like, and then I will announce that it is a hodgepodge of tribal self-aggrandizement and theological notions mainly borrowed from other, better cultures—"

"Myths," said Nina. "A myth after all is not an untruth, it is just—"

Paul didn't see much point in paying attention to her. Lewis wasn't.

Lewis wrote a letter to the paper. The first part of it was temperate and scholarly, describing the shift of continents and the opening and closing of seas, and the inauspicious beginnings of life. Ancient microbes, oceans without fish and skies without birds. Flourishing and destruction, the reign of the amphibians, reptiles, dinosaurs; the shifting of climates, the first grubby little mammals. Trial and error, primates late and unpromising on the scene, the humanoids getting up on their hind legs and figuring out fire, sharpening stones, marking their territory, and finally, in a recent rush, building boats and pyramids and bombs, creating languages and gods and sacrificing and murdering each other. Fighting over whether their God was named Jehovah or Krishna (here the language was heating up) or whether it was okay to eat pork, getting down on their knees and howling out their prayers to some Old Codger in the sky who took a big interest in who won wars and football games. Finally, amazingly, working a few things out and getting a start on knowing about themselves and the universe they found themselves in, then deciding they'd be better off throwing all that hard-won knowledge out, bring back the Old Codger and force everybody down on their knees again, to be taught and believe the old twaddle, why not bring back the Flat Earth while they were at it?

Yours truly, Lewis Spiers.

The editor of the paper was an out-of-towner and a recent graduate of a School of Journalism. He was happy with the uproar and continued to print the responses ("God Is Not Mocked," over the signatures of every member of the Bible Chapel congregation, "Writer Cheapens Argument," from the tolerant but saddened United Church minister who was offended by *twaddle*, and the Old Codger) until the publisher of the newspaper chain let it be known that this kind of ruckus was old-fashioned and out of place and discouraged advertisers. Put a lid on it, he said.

Lewis wrote another letter, this one of resignation. It was accepted with regret, Paul Gibbings stated—this too in the paper— the reason being ill health.

That was true, though it was not a reason Lewis himself would have preferred to make public. For several weeks he had felt a weakness in his legs. At the very time when it was important for him to stand up before his class, and march back and forth in front of it, he had felt himself trembling, longing to sit down. He never gave in, but sometimes he had to catch hold of the back of his chair, as if for emphasis. And now and then he realized that he could not tell where his feet were. If there had been carpet, he might have tripped over the least wrinkle, and even in the classroom, where there was no carpet, a piece of fallen chalk, a pencil, would have meant disaster.

He was furious about this ailment, thinking it psychosomatic. He had never suffered from nerves in front of a class, or in front of any group. When he was given the true diagnosis, in the neurologist's office, what he felt first—so he told Nina—was a ridiculous relief.

"I was afraid I was neurotic," he said, and they both began to laugh.

"I was afraid I was neurotic, but I only have amyotrophic lateral sclerosis." They laughed, stumbling along the silent plush-floored corridor, and got into the elevator where they were stared at with astonishment—laughter being most uncommon in this place.

The LakeShore Funeral Home was an extensive new building of golden brick—so new that the field around it had not yet been transformed into lawns and shrubbery. Except for the sign, you might have thought it a medical clinic, or government office building. The name LakeShore did not mean that it overlooked the lake but was instead a sly incorporation of the family name of the undertaker—Bruce Shore. Some people thought this tasteless. When the business had been conducted in one of the large Victorian houses in town and had belonged to Bruce's father, it had been simply the Shore Funeral Home. And it had in fact been a home, with plenty of room for Ed and Kitty Shore and their five children on the second and third floors.

Nobody lived in this new establishment, but there was a bedroom with kitchen facilities, and a shower. This was in case Bruce Shore found it more convenient to stay overnight instead of driving fifteen miles to the country place where he and his wife raised horses.

Last night had been one of those nights because of the accident north of town. A car full of teenagers had crashed into a bridge abutment. This sort of thing—a newly licensed driver or one not licensed at all, everybody wildly drunk—usually happened in the spring around graduation time, or in the excitement of the first couple of weeks at school in September. Now was the time when you looked more for the fatalities of newcomers—nurses fresh from the Philippines last year—caught in the first altogether unfamiliar snow.

Nevertheless, on a perfectly fine night and dry road, it had been two seventeen-year-olds, both from town. And just before that, in came Lewis Spiers. Bruce had his hands full—the work he had to do on the kids, to make them presentable, took him far into the night. He had called up his father. Ed and Kitty, who still spent the summers in the house in town, had not yet left for Florida, and Ed had come in to tend to Lewis.

Bruce had gone for a run, to refresh himself. He hadn't even had breakfast and was still in his jogging outfit when he saw Mrs. Spiers pull up in her old Honda Accord. He hurried to the waiting room to get the door open for her.

She was a tall, skinny woman, gray-haired but youthfully speedy in her movements. She didn't appear too cut up this morning, though he noticed she hadn't bothered with a coat.

"Sorry. Sorry," he said. "I just got back from a little exercise. Shirley's not in yet, I'm afraid. We sure feel bad about your loss."

"Yes," she said.

"Mr. Spiers taught me Grade Eleven and Twelve Science, and he was one teacher I'll never forget. Would you like to sit down? I know you must have been prepared in a way, but it's still an experience you're never prepared for when it happens. Would you like me to go through the paperwork with you now or would you like to see your husband?"

She said, "All we wanted was a cremation."

He nodded. "Yes. Cremation to follow."

"No. He was supposed to be cremated immediately. That's what he wanted. I thought I could pick up his ashes."

"Well, we didn't have any instructions that way," said Bruce firmly. "We prepared the body for viewing. He looks very good, actually. I think you'll be pleased."

She stood and stared at him.

"Don't you want to sit down?" he said. "You did plan on having some sort of visitation, didn't you? Some sort of service? There's going to be an awful lot of people want to pay their respects to Mr. Spiers. You know, we have conducted other services here where there wasn't any religious persuasion. Just somebody to give a eulogy, instead of a preacher. Or if you don't even want it that formal, you can just have people getting up and voicing their thoughts. It's up to you whether you want the casket open or closed. But around here people usually seem to like to have it open. When you're going for cremation you don't have the same range of caskets, of course. We have caskets that look very nice, but they are only a fraction of the cost."

Stood and stared.

The fact was that the work had been done and there had been no instructions that the work was not to be done. Work like any other work that should be paid for. Not to mention materials.

"I am just talking about what I think you'll want, when you've had time to sit down and consider it. We are here to follow your wishes—"

Maybe saying that was going too far.

"But we went ahead this way because there were no instructions to the contrary."

A car stopped outside, a car door closed, and Ed Shore came into the waiting room. Bruce felt an enormous relief. There was still a lot he had to learn in this business. The dealing-with-the-survivor end of it.

Ed said, "Hello, Nina. I saw your car. I thought I'd just come in and say I'm sorry."

Nina had spent the night in the living room. She supposed she had slept, but her sleep was so shallow that she had been aware all the time of where she was—on the living-room sofa—and where Lewis was—in the funeral home.

When she tried to speak now, her teeth were chattering. This was a complete surprise to her.

"I wanted to have him cremated immediately," was what she was trying to say, and what she started to say, thinking that she was speaking normally. Then she heard, or felt, her own gasps and uncontrollable stuttering.

"I want—I want—he wanted—"

Ed Shore held her forearm and put his other arm around her shoulders. Bruce had lifted his arms but didn't touch her.

"I should've got her sitting down," he said plaintively.

"That's all right," Ed said. "You feel like walking out to my car, Nina? We'll get you a bit of fresh air."

Ed drove with the windows down, up into the old part of town and onto a dead-end street which had a turnaround overlooking the lake. During the day people drove here to look at the view— sometimes while eating their takeout lunches—but at night it was a place for lovers. The thought of this might have dawned on Ed, as it did on her, when he parked the car.

"That enough fresh air?" he said. "You don't want to catch cold, out without a coat on."

She said carefully, "It's getting warm. Like yesterday."

They had never sat together in a parked car either after dark or in the daylight; never sought out such a place to be alone together.

That seemed a tawdry reflection to be having now.

"I'm sorry," said Nina. "I lost control. I only meant to say that Lewis—that we—that he—"

And it began to happen again. All over again the chattering of her teeth, the shaking, the words splitting apart. The horrid piteousness of it. It was not even an expression of what she was really feeling. What she felt before was anger and frustration, from talking to—or listening to—Bruce. This time she felt—she had thought she felt—quite calm and reasonable.

And this time, because they were alone together, he didn't touch her. He simply began to talk. Don't worry about all that. I'll take care of it. Right away. I'll see that it goes all right. I understand. Cremation.

"Breathe," he said. "Breathe in. Now hold it. Now out."

"I'm all right."

"Sure you are."

"I don't know what's the matter."

"The shock," he said matter-of-factly.

"I'm not like this."

"Look at the horizon. That helps too."

He was taking something out of his pocket. A handkerchief? But she didn't need a handkerchief. She had no tears. All she had was the shakes.

It was a tightly folded piece of paper.

"I put this away for you," he said. "It was in his pajama pocket."

She put the paper in her purse, carefully and without excitement, as if it was a prescription. Then she realized all of what he was telling her.

"You were there when he was brought in."

"I looked after him. Bruce called me up. There was the car accident and he had a bit more than he could handle."

She didn't even say, What accident? She didn't care. All she wanted now was to be alone to read her message.

The pajama pocket. The only place she hadn't looked. She hadn't touched his body.

She drove her own car home, after Ed had returned her to it. As soon as he had waved her out of sight she pulled over to the curb.

One hand had been working the paper out of her purse even while she drove. She read what was written on it, with the engine running, then proceeded.

On the sidewalk in front of her house there was another message. *The Will of God.*

Hasty, spidery writing, in chalk. It would be easy to wipe off.

What Lewis had written and left for her to find was a poem. Several verses of scathing doggerel. It had a title—"The Battle of the Genesisites and the Sons of Darwin for the Soul of the Flabby Generation."

There was a Temple of Learning sat
Right on Lake Huron shore
Where many a dull-eyed Dunce did come
To listen to many a Bore.

And the King of the Bores was a Right Fine Chap
Did Grin from Ear to Ear
A Jerk with One Big Thought in his Head—
Tell 'em All What They'd Like to Hear!

One winter Margaret had got the idea of organizing a series of evenings at which people would talk—at not too great length—on whatever subject they knew and cared most about. She thought of it being for teachers ("Teachers are always the ones standing up blabbing away at a captive audience," she said. "They need to sit down and listen to somebody else telling *them* something, for a change"), but then it was decided that it would be more interesting if nonteachers were invited as well. There would be a potluck dinner and wine, first, at Margaret's house.

That was how, on a clear cold night, Nina found herself standing outside Margaret's kitchen door in the dark entryway packed with the coats and schoolbags and hockey sticks of Margaret's sons—it was back when they were all still at home. In the living room—from which no sound could reach Nina anymore—Kitty Shore was going on about her chosen subject, which was saints. Kitty and Ed Shore were among the "real people" invited into the group—they were also Margaret's neighbors. Ed had spoken on another night, about mountain climbing. He had done some himself, in the Rockies, but mostly he talked of the perilous and tragic expeditions he liked to read about. (Margaret had said to Nina, when they were getting the coffee that night, "I was a little worried he might talk about embalming," and Nina had giggled and said, "But that's not his favorite thing. It's not an *amateur* thing. I don't suppose you get too many amateur embalmers.")

Ed and Kitty were a good-looking couple. Margaret and Nina had agreed, confidentially, that Ed would have been a notable turn-on if it weren't for his profession. The scrubbed pallor of his long, capable hands was extraordinary and made you think, Where have those hands been? Curvy Kitty was often referred to as a dar-ling—she was a short, busty, warm-eyed brunette with a voice full of breathy enthusiasm. Enthusiasm about her marriage, her children, the seasons, the town, and especially about her religion. In the Anglican church, which she belonged to, enthusiasts like her were uncommon, and there were reports that she was a trial, with her strictness and fanciness and penchant for arcane ceremonies such as the Churching of Women. Nina and Margaret, also, found her hard to take, and Lewis thought she was poison. But most people were smitten.

This evening she wore a dark-red wool dress and the earrings that one of her children had made for her for Christmas. She sat in a corner of the sofa with her legs tucked under her. As long as she stuck to the historical and geographical incidence of saints it was all right—that is, all right for Nina, who was hoping that Lewis might not find it necessary to go on the attack.

Kitty said that she was compelled to leave out all the saints of Eastern Europe and concentrate mostly on the saints of the British Isles, particularly those of Cornwall and Wales and Ireland, the Celtic saints with the wonderful names, who were her favorites. When she got into the cures, the miracles, and especially as her voice became more joyous and confiding and her earrings tinkled, Nina grew apprehensive. She knew that people might think her frivolous, Kitty said, to talk to some saint when she had a cooking disaster, but that was what she really believed the saints were there for. They were not too high and mighty to take an interest in all those trials and tribulations, the details of our lives that we would feel shy about bothering the God of the Universe with. With the help of the saints, you could stay partly inside a child's world, with a child's hope of help and consolation. *Ye must become as little children.* And it was the small miracles— surely it was the small miracles that helped prepare us for the great ones?

Now. Were there any questions?

Somebody asked about the status of saints in an Anglican church. In a Protestant church.

"Well, strictly speaking I don't think the Anglican is a Protestant church," said Kitty. "But I don't want to get into that. When we say in the creed, 'I believe in the Holy Catholic Church,' I just take it to mean the whole big universal Christian church. And then we say, 'I believe in the Communion of Saints.' Of course we don't have statues in the church, though personally I think it would be lovely if we did."

Margaret said, "Coffee?" and it was understood that the formal part of the evening was over. But Lewis shifted his chair closer to Kitty and said almost genially, "So? Are we to understand that you believe in these miracles?"

Kitty laughed. "Absolutely. I couldn't exist if I didn't believe in miracles."

Then Nina knew what had to follow. Lewis moving in quietly and relentlessly, Kitty countering with merry conviction and what she might think of as charming and feminine inconsistencies. Her faith was in that, surely—in her own charm. But Lewis would not be charmed. He would want to know, What form do these saints take at the present moment? In Heaven, do they occupy the same territory as the merely dead, the virtuous ancestors? And how are they chosen? Isn't it by the attested miracles, the proven miracles? And how are you going to prove the miracles of someone who lived fifteen centuries ago? How prove miracles, anyway? In the case of the loaves and fishes, counting. But is that real counting, or is it perception? Faith? Ah, yes. So it all comes down to faith. In daily matters, in her whole life, Kitty lives by faith?

She does.

She doesn't rely on science in any way? Surely not. When her children are sick she doesn't give them medicine. She doesn't bother about gas in her car, she has faith—

A dozen conversations have sprung up around them and yet, because of its intensity and its danger—Kitty's voice now hopping about like a bird on a wire, saying don't be silly, and do you think I'm an absolute nutcase? and Lewis's teasing growing ever more contemptuous, more deadly—this conversation will be heard through the others, at all times, everywhere in the room.

Nina has a bitter taste in her mouth. She goes out to the kitchen to help Margaret. They pass each other, Margaret carrying in the coffee. Nina goes straight on through the kitchen and out into the passage. Through the little pane in the back door she peers at the moonless night, the snowbanks along the street, the stars. She lays her hot cheek against the glass.

She straightens up at once when the door from the kitchen opens, she turns and smiles and is about to say, "I just came out to check on the weather." But when she sees Ed Shore's face against the light, in the minute before he closes the door, she thinks that she doesn't have to say that. They greet each other with an abbreviated, sociable, slightly apologetic and disclaiming laugh, by which it seems many things are conveyed and understood.

They are deserting Kitty and Lewis. Just for a little while— Kitty and Lewis won't notice. Lewis won't run out of steam and Kitty will find some way—being sorry for Lewis could be one— out of the dilemma of being devoured. Kitty and Lewis won't get sick of themselves.

Is that how Ed and Nina feel? Sick of those others, or at least sick of argument and conviction. Tired of the never-letting-up of those striving personalities.

They wouldn't quite say so. They would only say they're tired.

Ed Shore puts an arm around Nina. He kisses her—not on the mouth, not on her face, but on her throat. The place where an agitated pulse might be beating, in her throat.

He is a man who has to bend to do that. With a lot of men, it might be the natural place to kiss Nina, when she's standing up. But he is tall enough to bend and so deliberately kiss her in that exposed and tender place.

"You'll get cold out here," he said.

"I know. I'm going in."

Nina has never to this day had sex with any man but Lewis. Never come near it.

Had sex. Have sex with. For a long time she could not say that. She said make love. Lewis did not say anything. He was an athletic and inventive partner and in a physical sense, not unaware of her. Not inconsiderate. But he was on guard against anything that verged on sentimentality, and from his point of view, much did. She came to be very sensitive to this distaste, almost to share it.

Her memory of Ed Shore's kiss outside the kitchen door did, however, become a treasure. When Ed sang the tenor solos in the Choral Society's performance of the *Messiah* every Christmas, that moment would return to her. "Comfort Ye My People" pierced her throat with starry needles. As if everything about her was recognized then, and honored and set alight.

Paul Gibbings had not expected trouble from Nina. He had always thought that she was a warm person, in her reserved way. Not caustic like Lewis. But smart.

"No," she said. "He wouldn't have wanted it."

"Nina. Teaching was his life. He gave a lot. There are so many people, I don't know if you understand how many people, who remember just sitting spellbound in his classroom. They probably don't remember another thing about high school like they remember Lewis. He had a presence, Nina. You either have it or you don't. Lewis had it in spades."

"I'm not arguing that."

"So you've got all these people wanting somehow to say good-bye. We all need to say good-bye. Also to honor him. You know what I'm saying? After all this stuff. Closure."

"Yes. I hear. *Closure.*"

A nasty tone there, he thought. But he ignored it. "There doesn't need to be a hint of religiosity about it. No prayers. No mention. I know as well as you do how he would hate that."

"He would."

"I know. I can sort of master-of-ceremony the whole thing, if that doesn't seem like the wrong word. I have a pretty good idea of the right sort of people to ask just to do a little appreciation. Maybe half a dozen, ending up with a bit by me. 'Eulogies,' I think that's the word, but I prefer 'appreciation'—"

"Lewis would prefer nothing."

"And we can have your participation at whatever level you would choose—"

"Paul. Listen. Listen to me now."

"Of course. I'm listening."

"If you go ahead with this I will participate."

"Well. Good."

"When Lewis died he left a—he left a poem, actually. If you go ahead with this I will read it."

"Yes?"

"I mean I'll read it there, out loud. I'll read a bit of it to you now."

"Right. Go ahead."

> *"There was a Temple of Learning sat*
> *Right on Lake Huron shore*
> *Where many a dull-eyed Dunce did come*
> *To listen to many a Bore."*

"Sounds like Lewis all right."

> *"And the King of the Bores was a Right Fine Chap*
> *Did Grin from Ear to Ear—"*

"Nina. Okay. Okay. I got you. So this is what you want, is it? Harper Valley P.T.A.?"

"There's more."

"I'm sure there is. I think you're very upset, Nina. I don't think you'd act this way if you weren't very upset. And when you're feeling better you're going to regret it."

"No."

"I think you're going to regret it. I'm going to hang up now. I'm going to have to say good-bye."

"Wow," said Margaret. "How did he take that?"

"He said he was going to have to say good-bye."

"Do you want me to come over? I could just be company."

"No. Thanks."

"You don't want company?"

"I guess not. Not right now."

"You're sure? You're okay?"

"I'm okay."

She was really not so pleased with herself, about that performance on the phone. Lewis had said to her, "Be sure you scotch it if they want to bugger around with any memorial stuff. That candy-ass is capable of it." So it had been necessary to stop Paul somehow, but the way she had done it seemed crudely theatrical. Outrage was what had been left up to Lewis, retaliation his specialty—all she had managed to do was quote him.

It was beyond her to think how she could live, with only her old pacific habits. Cold and muted, stripped of him.

Some time after dark Ed Shore knocked on her back door. He held a box of ashes and a bouquet of white roses.

He gave her the ashes first.

"Oh," she said. "It's done."

She felt a warmth through the heavy cardboard. It came not immediately but gradually, like the blood's warmth through the skin.

Where was she to set this down? Not on the kitchen table, beside her late, hardly touched supper. Scrambled eggs and salsa, a combination that she'd always looked forward to on nights when Lewis was kept late for some reason and was eating with the other teachers at Tim Horton's or the pub. Tonight it had proved a bad choice.

Not on the counter either. It would look like a bulky grocery item. And not on the floor, where it could more easily be disregarded but would seem to be relegated to a lowly position—as if it held something like kitty litter or garden fertilizer, something that should not come too close to dishes and food.

She wanted, really, to take it into another room, to set it down somewhere in the unlighted front rooms of the house. Better still, in a shelf in a closet. But it was somehow too soon for that banishment. Also, considering that Ed Shore was watching her, it might look like a brisk and brutal clearing of the decks, a vulgar invitation.

She finally set the box down on the low phone table.

"I didn't mean to keep you standing," she said. "Sit down. Please do."

"I've interrupted your meal."

"I didn't feel like finishing it."

He was still holding the flowers. She said, "Those are for me?" The image of him with the bouquet, the image of him with the box of ashes and the bouquet, when she opened the door—that seemed grotesque, now that she thought of it, and horribly funny. It was the sort of thing she could get hysterical about, telling somebody. Telling Margaret. She hoped she never would.

Those are for me?

They could as easily be for the dead. Flowers for the house of the dead. She started to look for a vase, then filled the kettle, saying, "I was just going to make some tea," went back to hunting for the vase and found it, filled it with water, found the scissors she needed to clip the stems, and finally relieved him of the flowers. Then she noticed that she hadn't turned on the burner under the kettle. She was barely in control. She felt as if she could easily throw the roses on the floor, smash the vase, squash the congealed mess in her supper plate between her fingers. But why? She wasn't angry. It was just such a crazy effort, to keep doing one thing after another. Now she would have to warm the pot, she would have to measure the tea.

She said, "Did you read what you took out of Lewis's pocket?"

He shook his head, not looking at her. She knew he was lying. He was lying, he was shaken, how far into her life did he mean to go? What if she broke down and told him about the astonishment she had felt—why not say it, the chill around her heart—when she saw what Lewis had written? When she saw that that was all that he had written.

"Never mind," she said. "It was just some verses."

They were a pair of people with no middle ground, nothing between polite formalities and an engulfing intimacy. What had been between them, all these years, had been kept in balance because of their two marriages. Their marriages were the real content of their lives—her marriage to Lewis, the sometimes harsh and bewildering, indispensable content of her life. This other thing depended on those marriages, for its sweetness, its consoling promise. It was not likely to be something that could hold up on its own, even if they were both free. Yet it was not nothing. The danger was in trying it, and seeing it fall apart and then thinking that it had been nothing.

She had the burner on, she had the teapot ready to warm. She said, "You've been very kind and I haven't even thanked you. You must have some tea."

"That would be nice," he said.

And when they were settled at the table, the cups filled, milk and sugar offered—at the moment when there could have been panic—she had a very odd inspiration.

She said, "What is it really that you do?"

"That I do?"

"I mean—what did you do to him, last night? Or don't you usually get asked that?"

"Not in so many words."

"Do you mind? Don't answer me if you mind."

"I'm just surprised. I don't mind."

"I'm surprised I asked."

"Well, okay," he said, replacing his cup in its saucer. "Basically what you have to do is drain the blood vessels and the body cavity, and there you can run into problems depending on clots and so on, so you do what you should to get around that. In most cases you can use the jugular vein, but sometimes you have to do a heart tap. And you drain out the body cavity with a thing called a trocar, it's more or less a long thin needle on a flexible tube. But of course it's different if there's been an autopsy and the organs taken out. You have to get some padding in, to restore the natural outline. . . ."

He kept an eye on her all the time he was telling her this, and proceeded cautiously. It was all right—what she felt awaken in herself was just a cool and spacious curiosity.

"Is this what you meant you wanted to know?"

"Yes," she said steadily.

He saw that it was all right. He was relieved. Relieved and perhaps grateful. He must be used to people shying away completely from what he did, or else making jokes about it.

"And then you inject the fluid, which is a solution of formaldehyde and phenol and alcohol, and often some dye added to it for the hands and the face. Everybody thinks of the face being important and there's a lot to be done there with the eye caps and wiring the gums. As well as massage and fussing with the eyelashes and special makeup. But people are just as apt to care about the hands and to want them soft and natural and not wrinkled at the fingertips. . . ."

"You did all that work."

"That's all right. It wasn't what you wanted. It's just cosmetic things we do, mostly. That's what we're concerned with today more than any long-term preservation. Even old Lenin, you know, they had to keep going in and re-injecting him so he wouldn't dessicate or discolor—I don't know if they do anymore."

Some expansion, or ease, combined with the seriousness in his voice, made her think of Lewis. She was reminded of Lewis the night before last, speaking to her weakly but with satisfaction about the single-celled creatures—no nucleus, no paired chromosomes, no what else?—that had been the only form of life on earth for nearly two-thirds of life-on-earth's history.

"Now with the ancient Egyptians," Ed said, "they had the idea that your soul went on a journey, and it took three thousand years to complete, and then it came back to your body and your body ought to be in reasonably good shape. So the main concern they had was preservation, which we have not got today to anything like the same extent."

No chloroplasts and no—mitochondria.

"Three thousand years," she said. "Then it comes back."

"Well, according to them," he said. He put down his empty cup and remarked that he had better be getting home.

"Thank you," said Nina. Then, hurriedly, "Do you believe in such a thing as souls?"

He stood with his hands pressed down on her kitchen table. He sighed and shook his head and said, "Yes."

Soon after he had gone she took the ashes out and set them on the passenger seat of the car. Then she went back into the house to get her keys and a coat. She drove about a mile out of town, to a crossroads, parked and got out and walked up a side road, carrying the box. The night was quite cold and still, the moon already high in the sky.

This road at first ran through boggy ground in which cattails grew—they were now dried out, tall and wintry-looking. There were also milkweeds, with their pods empty, shining like shells. Everything was distinct under the moon. She could smell horses. Yes—there were two of them close by, solid black shapes beyond the cattails and the farmer's fence. They stood brushing their big bodies against each other, watching her.

She got the box open and put her hand into the cooling ashes and tossed or dropped them—with other tiny recalcitrant bits of the body—among those roadside plants. Doing this was like wading and then throwing yourself into the lake for the first icy swim, in June. A sickening shock at first, then amazement that you were still moving, lifted up on a stream of steely devotion—calm above the surface of your life, surviving, though the pain of the cold continued to wash into your body.

Nettles

In the summer of 1979, I walked into the kitchen of my friend Sunny's house near Uxbridge, Ontario, and saw a man standing at the counter, making himself a ketchup sandwich.

I have driven around in the hills northeast of Toronto, with my husband—my second husband, not the one I had left behind that summer—and I have looked for the house, in an idly persistent way, I have tried to locate the road it was on, but I have never succeeded. It has probably been torn down. Sunny and her husband sold it a few years after I visited them. It was too far from Ottawa, where they lived, to serve as a convenient summer place. Their children, as they became teenagers, balked at going there. And there was too much upkeep work for Johnston—Sunny's husband—who liked to spend his weekends golfing.

I have found the golf course—I think it the right one, though the ragged verges have been cleaned up and there is a fancier clubhouse.

In the countryside where I lived as a child, wells would go dry in the summer. This happened once in about every five or six years, when there was not enough rain. These wells were holes dug in the ground. Our well was a deeper hole than most, but we needed a good supply of water for our penned animals—my father raised silver foxes and mink—so one day the well driller arrived with impressive equipment, and the hole was extended down, down, deep into the earth until it found the water in the rock. From that time on we could pump out pure, cold water no matter what the time of year and no matter how dry the weather. That was something to be proud of. There was a tin mug hanging on the pump, and when I drank from it on a burning day, I thought of black rocks where the water ran sparkling like diamonds.

The well driller—he was sometimes called the well digger, as if nobody could be bothered to be precise about what he did and the older description was the more comfortable—was a man named Mike McCallum. He lived in the town close by our farm but he did not have a house there. He lived in the Clark Hotel—he had come there in the spring, and he would stay until he finished up whatever work he found to do in this part of the country. Then he would move on.

Mike McCallum was a younger man than my father, but he had a son who was a year and two months older than I was. This boy lived with his father in hotel rooms or boardinghouses, wherever his father was working, and he went to whatever school was at hand. His name was Mike McCallum too.

I know exactly how old he was because that is something children establish immediately, it is one of the essential matters on which they negotiate whether to be friends or not. He was nine and I was eight. His birthday was in April, mine in June. The summer holidays were well under way when he arrived at our house with his father.

His father drove a dark-red truck that was always muddy or dusty. Mike and I climbed into the cab when it rained. I don't remember whether his father went into our kitchen then, for a smoke and a cup of tea, or stood under a tree, or went right on working. Rain washed down the windows of the cab and made a racket like stones on the roof. The smell was of men—their work clothes and tools and tobacco and mucky boots and sour-cheese socks. Also of damp long-haired dog, because we had taken Ranger in with us. I took Ranger for granted, I was used to having him follow me around and sometimes for no good reason I would order him to stay home, go off to the barn, leave me alone. But Mike was fond of him and always addressed him kindly and by name, telling him our plans and waiting for him when he took off on one of his dog-projects, chasing a groundhog or a rabbit. Living as he did with his father, Mike could never have a dog of his own.

One day when Ranger was with us he chased a skunk, and the skunk turned and sprayed him. Mike and I were held to be some-what to blame. My mother had to stop whatever she was doing and drive into town and get several large tins of tomato juice. Mike persuaded Ranger to get into a tub and we poured the tomato juice over him and brushed it into his hair. It looked as if we were wash-ing him in blood. How many people would it take to supply that much blood? we wondered. How many horses? Elephants?

I had more acquaintance with blood and animal-killing than Mike did. I took him to see the spot in the corner of the pasture near the barnyard gate where my father shot and butchered the horses that were fed to the foxes and mink. The ground was trod-den bare and appeared to have a deep blood-stain, an iron-red cast to it. Then I took him to the meat-house in the barnyard where the horse carcasses were hung before being ground up for feed. The meat-house was just a shed with wire walls and the walls were black with flies, drunk on the smell of carrion. We got shingles and smashed them dead.

Our farm was small—nine acres. It was small enough for me to have explored every part of it, and every part had a particular look and character, which I could not have put into words. It is easy to see what would be special about the wire shed with the long, pale horse carcasses hung from brutal hooks, or about the trodden blood-soaked ground where they had changed from live horses into those supplies of meat. But there were other things, such as the stones on either side of the barn gangway, that had just as much to say to me, though nothing memorable had ever occurred there. On one side there was a big smooth whitish stone that bulged out and dominated all the others, and so that side had to me an expansive and public air, and I would always choose to climb that way rather than on the other side, where the stones were darker and clung together in a more mean-spirited way. Each of the trees on the place had likewise an attitude and a presence—the elm looked serene and the oak threatening, the maples friendly and workaday, the hawthorn old and crabby. Even the pits on the river flats—where my father had sold off gravel years ago—had their distinct character, perhaps easiest to spot if you saw them full of water at the receding of the spring floods. There was the one that was small and round and deep and perfect; the one that was spread out like a tail; and the one that was wide and irresolute in shape and always with a chop on it because the water was so shallow.

Mike saw all these things from a different angle. And so did I, now that I was with him. I saw them his way and mine, and my way was by its very nature incommunicable, so that it had to stay secret. His had to do with immediate advantage. The large pale stone in the gangway was for jumping off, taking a short hard run and then launching yourself out into the air, to clear the smaller stones in the slope beneath and land on the packed earth by the stable door. All the trees were for climbing, but particularly the maple next to the house, with the branch that you could crawl out on, so as to drop yourself onto the verandah roof. And the gravel pits were simply for leaping into, with the shouts of animals leaping on their prey, after a furious run through the long grass. If it had been earlier in the year, Mike said, when these held more water, we could have built a raft.

That project was considered, with regard to the river. But the river in August was almost as much a stony road as it was a watercourse, and instead of trying to float down it or swim in it we took off our shoes and waded—jumping from one bare bone-white rock to another and slipping on the scummy rocks below the surface, plowing through mats of flat-leafed water lilies and other water plants whose names I can't recall or never knew (wild parsnip, water hemlock?). These grew so thick they looked as if they must be rooted on islands, on dry land, but they were actually growing out of river muck, and trapped our legs in their snaky roots.

This river was the same one that ran publicly through the town, and walking upstream, we came in sight of the double-span highway bridge. When I was by myself or just with Ranger I had never gone as far as the bridge, because there were usually town people there. They came to fish over the side, and when the water was high enough boys jumped from the railing. They wouldn't be doing that now, but it was more than likely some of them would be splashing around down below—loudmouthed and hostile as town children always were.

Tramps were another possibility. But I said nothing of this to Mike, who went ahead of me as if the bridge was an ordinary destination and there was nothing unpleasant or forbidden about it. Voices reached us, and as I expected they were the voices of boys yelling—you would think the bridge belonged to them. Ranger had followed us this far, unenthusiastically, but now he veered off towards the bank. He was an old dog by this time, and he had never been indiscriminately fond of children.

There was a man fishing, not off the bridge but from the bank, and he swore at the commotion Ranger made getting out of the water. He asked us whether we couldn't keep our arse of a dog at home. Mike went straight on as if this man had only whistled at us, and then we passed into the shadow of the bridge itself, where I had never been in my life.

The floor of the bridge was our roof, with streaks of sunlight showing between the planks. And now a car passed over, with a sound of thunder and a blotting out of the light. We stood still for this event, looking up. Under-the-bridge was a place on its own, not just a short stretch of the river. When the car had passed and the sun shone through the cracks again, its reflection on the water cast waves of light, queer bubbles of light, high on the cement pilings. Mike yelled to test the echo, and I did the same, but faintly, because the boys on the shore, the strangers, on the other side of the bridge scared me more than tramps would have done.

I went to the country school beyond our farm. Enrollment there had dwindled to the point where I was the only child in my class. But Mike had been going to the town school since spring and these boys were not strangers to him. He would probably have been playing with them, and not with me, if his father had not had the idea of taking him along on his jobs, so that he could—now and then—keep an eye on him.

There must have been some words of greeting passed, between these town boys and Mike.

Hey. What do you think you're doing here?

Nothing. What do you think you're doing?

Nothing. Who's that you got with you?

Nobody. Just her.

Nnya-nnya. Just her.

There was in fact a game going on, which was taking up everybody's attention. And everybody included girls—there were girls farther up on the bank, intent on their own business—though we were all past the age at which groups of boys and girls played together as a customary thing. They might have followed the boys out from town—pretending not to follow—or the boys might have come along after them, intending some harassment, but somehow when they all got together this game had taken shape and had needed everybody in it, so the usual restrictions had broken down. And the more people who were in it, the better the game was, so it was easy for Mike to become involved, and bring me in after him.

It was a game of war. The boys had divided themselves into two armies who fought each other from behind barricades roughly made of tree branches, and also from the shelter of the coarse, sharp grass, and of the bulrushes and water weeds that were higher than our heads. The chief weapons were balls of clay, mud balls, about the size of baseballs. There happened to be a special source of clay, a gray pit hollowed out, half hidden by weeds, partway up the bank (discovery of this might have been what suggested the game), and it was there that the girls were working, preparing the ammunition. You squeezed and patted the sticky clay into as hard a ball as you could make—there could be some gravel in it and binding material of grass, leaves, bits of twigs gathered at the spot, but no stones added on purpose—and there had to be a great many of these balls, because they were good for only one throw. There was no possibility of picking up the balls that had missed and packing them together and throwing them over again.

The rules of the war were simple. If you were hit by a ball—the official name for them was cannonballs—in the face, head, or body, you had to fall down dead. If you were hit in the arms or legs you had to fall down, but you were only wounded. Then another thing that girls had to do was crawl out and drag the wounded soldiers back to a trampled place that was the hospital. Leaves were plastered on their wounds and they were supposed to lie still till they counted to one hundred. When they'd done that they could get up and fight again. The dead soldiers were not supposed to get up until the war was over, and the war was not over till everybody on one side was dead.

The girls as well as the boys were divided into two sides, but since there were not nearly as many girls as boys we could not serve as munitions makers and nurses for just one soldier. There were alliances, just the same. Each girl had her own pile of balls and was working for particular soldiers, and when a soldier fell wounded he would call out a girl's name, so that she could drag him away and dress his wounds as soon as possible. I made weapons for Mike and mine was the name Mike called. There was so much noise going on—constant cries of "You're dead," either triumphant or outraged (outraged because of course people who were supposed to be dead were always trying to sneak back into the fighting) and the barking of a dog, not Ranger, who had somehow got mixed up in the battle—so much noise that you had to be always alert for the boy's voice that called your own name. There was a keen alarm when the cry came, a wire zinging through your whole body, a fanatic feeling of devotion. (At least it was so for me who, unlike the other girls, owed my services to only one warrior.)

I don't suppose, either, that I had ever played in a group, like this, before. It was such a joy to be part of a large and desperate enterprise, and to be singled out, within it, to be essentially pledged to the service of a fighter. When Mike was wounded he never opened his eyes, he lay limp and still while I pressed the slimy large leaves to his forehead and throat and—pulling out his shirt—to his pale, tender stomach, with its sweet and vulnerable belly button.

Nobody won. The game disintegrated, after a long while, in arguments and mass resurrections. We tried to get some of the clay off us, on the way home, by lying down flat in the river water. Our shorts and shirts were filthy and dripping.

It was late in the afternoon. Mike's father was getting ready to leave.

"For Christ's sake," he said.

We had a part-time hired man who came to help my father when there was a butchering or some extra job to be done. He had an elderly, boyish look and a wheezing asthmatic way of breathing. He liked to grab me and tickle me until I thought I would suffocate.

Nobody interfered with this. My mother didn't like it, but my father told her it was only a joke.

He was there in the yard, helping Mike's father.

"You two been rolling in the mud," he said. "First thing you know you gonna have to get married."

From behind the screen door my mother heard that. (If the men had known she was there, neither one of them would have spoken as he had.) She came out and said something to the hired man, in a low, reproving voice, before she said anything about the way we looked.

I heard part of what she said.

Like brother and sister.

The hired man looked at his boots, grinning helplessly.

She was wrong. The hired man was closer to the truth than she was. We were not like brother and sister, or not like any brother and sister I had ever seen. My one brother was hardly more than a baby, so I had no experience of that on my own. And we were not like the wives and husbands I knew, who were old, for one thing, and who lived in such separate worlds that they seemed barely to recognize one another. We were like sturdy and accustomed sweethearts, whose bond needs not much outward expression. And for me at least that was solemn and thrilling.

I knew that the hired man was talking about sex, though I don't think I knew the word "sex." And I hated him for that even more than I usually hated him. Specifically, he was wrong. We did not go in for any showings and rubbings and guilty intimacies—there was none of that bothered search for hiding places, none of the twiddling pleasure and frustration and immediate, raw shame. Such scenes had taken place for me with a boy cousin and with a couple of slightly older girls, sisters, who went to my school. I disliked these partners before and after the event and would angrily deny, even in my own mind, that any of these things had happened. Such escapades could never have been considered, with anybody for whom I felt any fondness or respect—only with people who disgusted me, as those randy abhorrent itches disgusted me with myself.

In my feelings for Mike the localized demon was transformed into a diffuse excitement and tenderness spread everywhere under the skin, a pleasure of the eyes and ears and a tingling contentment, in the presence of the other person. I woke up every morning hungry for the sight of him, for the sound of the well driller's truck as it came bumping and rattling down the lane. I worshipped, without any show of it, the back of his neck and the shape of his head, the frown of his eyebrows, his long, bare toes and his dirty elbows, his loud and confident voice, his smell. I accepted readily, even devoutly, the roles that did not have to be explained or worked out between us—that I would aid and admire him, he would direct and stand ready to protect me.

And one morning the truck did not come. One morning, of course, the job was all finished, the well capped, the pump reinstated, the fresh water marvelled at. There were two chairs fewer at the table for the noon meal. Both the older and the younger Mike had always eaten that meal with us. The younger Mike and I never talked and barely looked at each other. He liked to put ketchup on his bread. His father talked to my father, and the talk was mostly about wells, accidents, water tables. A serious man. All work, my father said. Yet he—Mike's father—ended nearly every speech with a laugh. The laugh had a lonely boom in it, as if he was still down the well.

They did not come. The work was finished, there was no reason for them ever to come again. And it turned out that this job was the last one that the well driller had to do in our part of the country. He had other jobs lined up elsewhere, and he wanted to get to them as soon as he could, while the good weather lasted. Living as he did, in the hotel, he could just pack up and be gone. And that was what he had done.

Why did I not understand what was happening? Was there no good-bye, no awareness that when Mike climbed into the truck on that last afternoon, he was going for good? No wave, no head turned towards me—or not turned towards me—when the truck, heavy now with all the equipment, lurched down our lane for the last time? When the water gushed out—I remember it gushing out, and everybody gathering round to have a drink—why did I not understand how much had come to an end, for me? I wonder now if there was a deliberate plan not to make too much of the occasion, to eliminate farewells, so that I—or we—should not become too unhappy and troublesome.

It doesn't seem likely that such account would be taken of children's feelings, in those days. They were our business, to suffer or suppress.

I did not become troublesome. After the first shock I did not let anybody see a thing. The hired man teased me whenever he caught sight of me ("Did your boyfriend run away on you?"), but I never looked his way.

I must have known that Mike would be leaving. Just as I knew that Ranger was old and that he would soon die. Future absence I accepted—it was just that I had no idea, till Mike disappeared, of what absence could be like. How all my own territory would be altered, as if a landslide had gone through it and skimmed off all meaning except loss of Mike. I could never again look at the white stone in the gangway without thinking of him, and so I got a feeling of aversion towards it. I had that feeling also about the limb of the maple tree, and when my father cut it off because it was too near the house, I had it about the scar that was left.

One day weeks afterwards, when I was wearing my fall coat, I was standing by the door of the shoe store while my mother tried on shoes, and I heard a woman call, "Mike." She ran past the store, calling, "Mike." I was suddenly convinced that this woman whom

I did not know must be Mike's mother—I knew, though not from him, that she was separated from his father, not dead—and that they had come back to town for some reason. I did not consider whether this return might be temporary or permanent, only—I was now running out of the store—that in another minute I would see Mike.

The woman had caught up with a boy about five years old, who had just helped himself to an apple out of a bushel of apples that was standing on the sidewalk in front of the grocery shop next door.

I stopped and stared at this child in disbelief, as if an outrageous, an unfair enchantment had taken place before my eyes.

A common name. A stupid flat-faced child with dirty blond hair.

My heart was beating in big thumps, like howls happening in my chest.

Sunny met my bus in Uxbridge. She was a large-boned, bright-faced woman, with silvery-brown, curly hair caught back by unmatched combs on either side of her face. Even when she put on weight—which she had done—she did not look matronly, but majestically girlish.

She swept me into her life as she had always done, telling me that she had thought she was going to be late because Claire had got a bug in her ear that morning and had to be taken to the hospital to have it flushed out, then the dog threw up on the kitchen step, probably because it hated the trip and the house and the country, and when she—Sunny—had left to get me Johnston was making the boys clean it up because they had wanted a dog, and Claire was complaining that she could still hear something going *bzz-bzz* in her ear.

"So suppose we go someplace nice and quiet and get drunk and never go back there?" she said. "We have to, though. Johnston invited a friend whose wife and kids are away in Ireland, and they want to go and play golf."

Sunny and I had been friends in Vancouver. Our pregnancies had dovetailed nicely, so that we could manage with one set of maternity clothes. In my kitchen or in hers, once a week or so, distracted by our children and sometimes reeling for lack of sleep, we stoked ourselves up on strong coffee and cigarettes and launched out on a rampage of talk—about our marriages, our fights, our personal deficiencies, our interesting and discreditable motives, our foregone ambitions. We read Jung at the same time and tried to keep track of our dreams. During that time of life that is supposed to be a reproductive daze, with the woman's mind all swamped by maternal juices, we were still compelled to discuss Simone de Beauvoir and Arthur Koestler and *The Cocktail Party*.

Our husbands were not in this frame of mind at all. When we tried to talk about such things with them they would say, "Oh, that's just literature" or "You sound like Philosophy 101."

Now we had both moved away from Vancouver. But Sunny had moved with her husband and her children and her furniture, in the normal way and for the usual reason—her husband had got another job. And I had moved for the newfangled reason that was approved of mightily but fleetingly and only in some special circles—leaving husband and house and all the things acquired during the marriage (except of course the children, who were to be parcelled about) in the hope of making a life that could be lived without hypocrisy or deprivation or shame.

I lived now on the second floor of a house in Toronto. The people downstairs—the people who owned the house—had come from Trinidad a dozen years before. All up and down the street, the old brick houses with their verandahs and high, narrow windows, the former homes of Methodists and Presbyterians who had names like Henderson and Grisham and McAllister, were full up with olive- or brownish-skinned people who spoke English in a way unfamiliar to me if they spoke it at all, and who filled the air at all hours with the smell of their spicy-sweet cooking. I was happy with all this—it made me feel as if I had made a true change, a long necessary voyage from the house of marriage. But it was too much to expect of my daughters, who were ten and twelve years old, that they should feel the same way. I had left Vancouver in the spring and they had come to me at the beginning of the summer holidays, supposedly to stay for the whole two months. They found the smells of the street sickening and the noise frightening. It was hot, and they could not sleep even with the fan I bought. We had to keep the windows open, and the backyard parties lasted sometimes till four o'clock.

Expeditions to the Science Centre and the C.N. Tower, to the Museum and the Zoo, treats in the cooled restaurants of department stores, a boat trip to Toronto Island, could not make up to them the absence of their friends or reconcile them to the travesty of a home that I provided. They missed their cats. They wanted their own rooms, the freedom of the neighborhood, the dawdling stay-at-home days.

For a while they did not complain. I heard the older one say to the younger one. "Let Mom think we're happy. Or she'll feel bad."

At last a blowup. Accusations, confessions of misery (even exaggerations of misery, as I thought, developed for my benefit). The younger wailing, "Why can't you just live at home?" and the older telling her bitterly, "Because she hates Dad."

I phoned my husband—who asked me nearly the same question and provided, on his own, nearly the same answer. I changed the tickets and helped my children pack and took them to the airport. All the way we played a silly game introduced by the older girl. You had to pick a number—27, 42—and then look out of the window and count the men you saw, and the 27th or 42nd man, or whatever, would be the one you had to marry. When I came back, alone, I gathered up all reminders of them—a cartoon the younger one had drawn, a *Glamour* magazine that the older one had bought, various bits of jewelry and clothing they could wear in Toronto but not at home—and stuffed them into a garbage bag. And I did more or less the same thing every time I thought of them—I snapped my mind shut. There were miseries that I could bear—those connected with men. And other miseries—those connected with children—that I could not.

I went back to living as I had lived before they came. I stopped cooking breakfast and went out every morning to get coffee and fresh rolls at the Italian deli. The idea of being so far freed from domesticity enchanted me. But I noticed now, as I hadn't done before, the look on some of the faces of the people who sat every morning on the stools behind the window or at the sidewalk tables—people for whom this was in no way a fine and amazing thing to be doing but the stale habit of a lonely life.

Back home, then, I would sit and write for hours at a wooden table under the windows of a former sunporch now become a makeshift kitchen. I was hoping to make my living as a writer. The sun soon heated up the little room, and the backs of my legs—I would be wearing shorts—stuck to the chair. I could smell the peculiar sweetish chemical odor of my plastic sandals absorbing the sweat of my feet. I liked that—it was the smell of my industry, and, I hoped, of my accomplishment. What I wrote wasn't any better than what I'd managed to write back in the old life while the potatoes cooked or the laundry thumped around in its automatic cycle. There was just more of it, and it wasn't any worse—that was all.

Later in the day I would have a bath and probably go to meet one or another of my women friends. We drank wine at the sidewalk tables in front of little restaurants on Queen Street or Baldwin Street or Brunswick Street and talked about our lives—chiefly about our lovers, but we felt queasy saying "lover," so we called them "the men we were involved with." And sometimes I met the man I was involved with. He had been banished when the children were with me, though I had broken this rule twice, leaving my daughters in a frigid movie-house.

I had known this man before I left my marriage and he was the immediate reason I had left it, though I pretended to him—and to everyone else—that this was not so. When I met him I tried to be carefree and to show an independent spirit. We exchanged news—I made sure I had news—and we laughed, and went for walks in the ravine, but all I really wanted was to entice him to have sex with me, because I thought the high enthusiasm of sex fused people's best selves. I was stupid about these matters, in a way that was very risky, particularly for a woman of my age. There were times when I would be so happy, after our encounters—dazzled and secure—and there were other times when I would lie stone-heavy with misgiving. After he had taken himself off, I would feel tears running out of my eyes before I knew that I was weeping. And this was because of some shadow I had glimpsed in him or some offhandedness, or an oblique warning he'd given me. Outside the windows, as it got dark, the back-yard parties would begin, with music and shouting and provocations that later might develop into fights, and I would be frightened, not of any hostility but of a kind of nonexistence.

In one of these moods I phoned Sunny, and got the invitation to spend the weekend in the country.

"It's beautiful here," I said.

But the country we were driving through meant nothing to me. The hills were a series of green bumps, some with cows. There were low concrete bridges over weed-choked streams. Hay was harvested in a new way, rolled up and left in the fields.

"Wait till you see the house," Sunny said. "It's squalid. There was a mouse in the plumbing. Dead. We kept getting these little hairs in the bathwater. That's all dealt with now, but you never know what will be next."

She did not ask me—was it delicacy or disapproval?—about my new life. Maybe she just did not know how to begin, could not imagine it. I would have told her lies, anyway, or half-lies. *It was hard to make the break but it had to be done. I miss the children terribly but there is always a price to be paid. I am learning to leave a man free and to be free myself. I am learning to take sex lightly, which is hard for me because that's not the way I started out and I'm not young but I am learning.*

A weekend, I thought. It seemed a very long time.

The bricks of the house showed a scar where a verandah had been torn away. Sunny's boys were tromping around in the yard.

"Mark lost the ball," the older one—Gregory—shouted.

Sunny told him to say hello to me.

"Hello. Mark threw the ball over the shed and now we can't find it."

The three-year-old girl, born since I'd last seen Sunny, came running out of the kitchen door and then halted, surprised at the sight of a stranger. But she recovered herself and told me, "There was a bug thing flew in my head."

Sunny picked her up and I took up my overnight bag and we walked into the kitchen, where Mike McCallum was spreading ketchup on a piece of bread.

"It's you," we said, almost on the same breath. We laughed, I rushed towards him and he moved towards me. We shook hands.

"I thought it was your father," I said.

I don't know if I'd got as far as thinking of the well driller. I had thought, Who is that familiar-looking man? A man who carried his body lightly, as if he would think nothing of climbing in and out of wells. Short-cropped hair, going gray, deep-set light-colored eyes. A lean face, good-humored yet austere. A custom-ary, not disagreeable, reserve.

"Couldn't be," he said. "Dad's dead."

Johnston came into the kitchen with the golf bags, and greeted me, and told Mike to hurry up, and Sunny said, "They know each other, honey. They knew each other. Of all things."

"When we were kids," Mike said.

Johnston said, "Really? That's remarkable." And we all said together what we saw he was about to say.

"Small world."

Mike and I were still looking at each other and laughing—we seemed to be making it clear to each other that this discovery which Sunny and Johnston might think remarkable was to us a comically dazzling flare-up of good fortune.

All afternoon while the men were gone I was full of happy energy. I made a peach pie for our supper and read to Claire so that she would settle for her nap, while Sunny took the boys fishing, unsuccessfully, in the scummy creek. Then she and I sat on the floor of the front room with a bottle of wine and became friends again, talking about books instead of life.

The things Mike remembered were different from the things I remembered. He remembered walking around on the narrow top of some old cement foundation and pretending it was as high as the tallest building and that if we stumbled we would fall to our deaths. I said that must have been somewhere else, then I remembered the foundations for a garage that had been poured, and the garage never built, where our lane met the road. Did we walk on that?

We did.

I remembered wanting to holler loudly under the bridge but being afraid of the town kids. He did not remember any bridge.

We both remembered the clay cannonballs, and the war.

We were washing the dishes together, so that we could talk all we wanted without being rude.

He told me how his father had died. He had been killed in a road accident, coming back from a job near Bancroft.

"Are your folks still alive?"

I said that my mother was dead and that my father had married again.

At some point I told him that I had separated from my husband, I was living in Toronto. I said that my children had been with me for a while but were now on a holiday with their father.

He told me that he lived in Kingston, but had not been there very long. He had met Johnston recently, through his work. He was, like Johnston, a civil engineer. His wife was an Irish girl, born in Ireland but working in Canada when he met her. She was a nurse. Right now she was back in Ireland, in County Clare, visiting her family. She had the kids with her.

"How many kids?"

"Three."

When the dishes were finished we went into the front room and offered to play Scrabble with the boys, so that Sunny and Johnston could go for a walk. One game—then it was supposed to be bedtime. But they persuaded us to start another round, and we were still playing when their parents came back.

"What did I tell you?" said Johnston.

"It's the same game," Gregory said. "You said we could finish the game and it's the same game."

"I bet," said Sunny.

She said it was a lovely night, and she and Johnston were getting spoiled, having live-in baby-sitters.

"Last night we actually went to the movie and Mike stayed with the kids. An old movie. *Bridge over the River Kwai.*"

"*On,*" Johnston said. "*On the River Kwai.*"

Mike said, "I'd seen it anyway. Years ago."

"It was pretty good," said Sunny. "Except I didn't agree with the ending. I thought the ending was wrong. You know when Alec Guinness sees the wire in the water, in the morning, and he realizes somebody's going to blow up the bridge? And he goes berserk and then it gets so complicated and everybody has to get killed and everything? Well, I think he just should have seen the wire and known what was going to happen and stayed on the bridge and got blown up with it. I think that's what his character would have done and it would have been more dramatically effective."

"No, it wouldn't," Johnston said, in the tone of somebody who had been through this argument before. "Where's the suspense?"

"I agree with Sunny," I said. "I remember thinking the ending was too complicated."

"Mike?" said Johnston.

"I thought it was pretty good," Mike said. "Pretty good the way it was."

"Guys against the women," Johnston said. "Guys win."

Then he told the boys to pack up the Scrabble game and they obeyed. But Gregory thought of asking to see the stars. "This is the only place we can ever see them," he said. "At home it's all the lights and crap."

"Watch it," his father said. But he said, Okay then, five minutes, and we all went outside and looked at the sky. We looked for the Pilot Star, close beside the second star in the handle of the Big Dipper. If you could see that one, Johnston said, then your eyesight was good enough to get you into the Air Force, at least that was the way it was during the Second World War.

Sunny said, "Well, I can see it, but then I knew beforehand that it's there."

Mike said, the same with him.

"I could see it," said Gregory scornfully. "I could see it whether I knew it was there or not."

"I could see it too," Mark said.

Mike was standing a little ahead of me and to one side. He was actually closer to Sunny than he was to me. Nobody was behind us, and I wanted to brush against him—just lightly and accidentally against his arm or shoulder. Then if he didn't stir away—out of courtesy, taking my touch for a genuine accident?—I wanted to lay a finger against his bare neck. Was that what he would have done, if he had been standing behind me? Was that what he would have been concentrating on, instead of the stars?

I had the feeling, however, that he was a scrupulous man, he would refrain.

And for that reason, certainly, he would not come to my bed that night. It was so risky as to be impossible, in any case. There were three bedrooms upstairs—the guest room and the parents' room both opening off the larger room where the children slept. Anybody approaching either of the smaller bedrooms had to do so through the children's room. Mike, who had slept in the guest room last night, had been moved downstairs, to the foldout sofa in the front room. Sunny had given him fresh sheets rather than unmaking and making up again the bed he had left for me.

"He's pretty clean," she said. "And after all, he's an old friend."

Lying in those same sheets did not make for a peaceful night. In my dreams, though not in reality, they smelled of water-weeds, river mud, and reeds in the hot sun.

I knew that he wouldn't come to me no matter how small the risk was. It would be a sleazy thing to do, in the house of his friends, who would be—if they were not already—the friends of his wife as well. And how could he be sure that it was what I wanted? Or that it was what he really wanted? Even I was not sure of it. Up till now, I had always been able to think of myself as a woman who was faithful to the person she was sleeping with at any given time.

My sleep was shallow, my dreams monotonously lustful, with

irritating and unpleasant subplots. Sometimes Mike was ready to cooperate, but we met with obstacles. Sometimes he got sidetracked, as when he said that he had brought me a present, but he had mislaid it, and it was of great importance to him to find it. I told him not to mind, that I was not interested in the present, for he himself was my present, the person I loved and always had loved, I said that. But he was preoccupied. And sometimes he reproached me.

All night—or at least whenever I woke up, and I woke often—the crickets were singing outside my window. At first I thought it was birds, a chorus of indefatigable night-birds. I had lived in cities long enough to have forgotten how crickets can make a perfect waterfall of noise.

It has to be said, too, that sometimes when I woke I found myself stranded on a dry patch. Unwelcome lucidity. What do you really know of this man? Or he of you? What music does he like, what are his politics? What are his expectations of women?

"Did you two sleep well?" Sunny said.

Mike said, "Out like a light."

I said, "Okay. Fine."

Everybody was invited to brunch that morning at the house of some neighbors who had a swimming pool. Mike said that he thought he would rather just go round the golf course, if that would be okay.

Sunny said, "Sure," and looked at me. I said, "Well, I don't know if I—" and Mike said, "You don't play golf, do you?"

"No."

"Still. You could come and caddy for me."

"I'll come and caddy," Gregory said. He was ready to attach himself to any expedition of ours, sure that we would be more liberal and entertaining than his parents.

Sunny said no. "You're coming with us. Don't you want to go in the pool?"

"All the kids pee in that pool. I hope you know that."

Johnston had warned us before we left that there was a prediction of rain. Mike had said that we'd take our chances. I liked his saying "we" and I liked riding beside him, in the wife's seat. I felt a pleasure in the idea of us as a couple—a pleasure that I knew was light-headed as an adolescent girl's. The notion of being a wife beguiled me, just as if I had never been one. This had never happened with the man who was now my actual lover. Could I really have settled in, with a true love, and somehow just got rid of the parts of me that did not fit, and been happy?

But now that we were alone, there was some constraint.

"Isn't the country here beautiful?" I said. And today I meant it. The hills looked softer, under this cloudy white sky, than they had looked yesterday in the brazen sunlight. The trees, at the end of summer, had a raggedy foliage, many of their leaves beginning to rust around the edges, and some had actually turned brown or red. I recognized different leaves now. I said, "Oak trees."

"This is sandy soil," Mike said. "All through here—they call it Oak Ridges."

I said I supposed that Ireland was beautiful.

"Parts of it are really bare. Bare rock."

"Did your wife grow up there? Does she have that lovely accent?"

"You'd think she did, if you heard her. But when she goes back there, they tell her she's lost it. They tell her she sounds just like an American. American's what they always say—they don't bother with Canadian."

"And your kids—I guess they don't sound Irish at all?"

"Nope."

"What are they anyway—boys or girls?"

"Two boys and a girl."

I had an urge now to tell him about the contradictions, the griefs and necessities of my life. I said, "I miss my kids."

But he said nothing. No sympathetic word, no encouragement. It might be that he thought it unseemly to talk of our partners or our children, under the circumstances.

Soon after that we pulled into the parking lot beside the clubhouse, and he said, rather boisterously, as if to make up for his stiffness, "Looks like the rain scare's kept the Sunday golfers home." There was only one car in the lot.

He got out and went into the office to pay the visitor's fee.

I had never been on a golf course. I had seen the game being played on television, once or twice and never by choice, and I had an idea that some of the clubs were called irons, or some of the irons clubs, and that there was one of them called a niblick, and that the course itself was called the links. When I told him this Mike said, "Maybe you're going to be awfully bored."

"If I am I'll go for a walk."

That seemed to please him. He laid the weight of his warm hand on my shoulder and said, "You would, too."

My ignorance did not matter—of course I did not really have to caddy—and I was not bored. All there was for me to do was to follow him around, and watch him. I didn't even have to watch him. I could have watched the trees at the edges of the course—they were tall trees with feathery tops and slender trunks, whose name I was not sure of—acacia?—and they were ruffled by occasional winds that we could not feel at all, here below. Also there were flocks of birds, blackbirds or starlings, flying about with a communal sense of urgency, but only from one treetop to another. I remembered now that birds did that; in August or even late July they began to have noisy mass meetings, preparing for the trip south.

Mike talked now and then, but it was hardly to me. There was no need for me to reply, and in fact I couldn't have done so. I thought he talked more, though, than a man would have done if he'd been playing here by himself. His disconnected words were reproaches or cautious congratulations or warnings to himself, or they were hardly words at all—just the kind of noises that are meant to convey meaning, and that do convey meaning, in the long intimacy of lives lived in willing proximity.

This was what I was supposed to do, then—to give him an amplified, an extended notion of himself. A more comfortable notion, you might say, a reassuring sense of human padding around his solitude. He wouldn't have expected this in quite the same way, or asked it quite so naturally and easily, if I had been another man. Or if I had been a woman with whom he did not feel some established connection.

I didn't think this out. It was all there in the pleasure I felt come over me as we made our way around the links. Lust that had given me shooting pains in the night was all chastened and trimmed back now into a tidy pilot flame, attentive, wifely. I followed his setting up and choosing and pondering and squinting and swinging, and watched the course of the ball, which always seemed to me triumphant but to him usually problematic, to the site of our next challenge, our immediate future.

Walking there, we hardly talked at all. Will it rain? we said. Did you feel a drop? I thought I felt a drop. Maybe not. This was not dutiful weather talk—it was all in the context of the game. Would we finish the round or not?

As it turned out, we would not. There was a drop of rain, definitely a drop of rain, then another, then a splatter. Mike looked along the length of the course, to where the clouds had changed color, becoming dark blue instead of white, and he said without particular alarm or disappointment, "Here comes our weather." He began methodically to pack up and fasten his bag.

We were then about as far away as we could be from the clubhouse. The birds had increased their commotion, and were wheeling about overhead in an agitated, indecisive way. The tops of the trees were swaying, and there was a sound—it seemed to be above us—like the sound of a wave full of stones crashing on the beach. Mike said, "Okay, then. We better get in here," and he took my hand and hurried us across the mown grass into bushes and the tall weeds that grew between the course and the river.

The bushes right at the edge of the grass had dark leaves and an almost formal look, as if they had been a hedge, set out there. But they were in a clump, growing wild. They also looked impenetrable, but close up there were little openings, the narrow paths that animals or people looking for golf balls had made. The ground sloped slightly downward, and once you were through the irregular wall of bushes you could see a bit of the river—the river that was in fact the reason for the sign at the gate, the name on the clubhouse. Riverside Golf Club. The water was steel gray, and looked to be rolling, not breaking in a chop the way pond water would do, in this rush of weather. Between it and us there was a meadow of weeds, all of it seemed in bloom. Goldenrod, jewelweed with its red and yellow bells, and what I thought were flowering nettles with pinkish-purple clusters, and wild asters. Grapevine, too, grabbing and wrapping whatever it could find, and tangling underfoot. The soil was soft, not quite gummy. Even the most frail-stemmed, delicate-looking plants had grown up almost as high as, or higher than, our heads. When we stopped and looked up through them we could see trees at a little distance tossing around like bouquets. And something coming, from the direction of the midnight clouds. It was the real rain, coming at us behind this splatter we were getting, but it appeared to be so much more than rain. It was as if a large portion of the sky had detached itself and was bearing down, bustling and resolute, taking a not quite recognizable but animate shape. Curtains of rain—not veils but really thick and wildly slapping curtains—were driven ahead of it. We could see them distinctly, when all we were feeling, still, were these light, lazy drops. It was almost as if we were looking through a window, and not quite believing that the window would shatter, until it did, and rain and wind hit us, all together, and my hair was lifted and fanned out above my head. I felt as if my skin might do that next.

I tried to turn around then—I had an urge, that I had not felt before, to run out of the bushes and head for the clubhouse. But I could not move. It was hard enough to stand up—out in the open the wind would have knocked you down at once.

Stooping, butting his head through the weeds and against the wind, Mike got around in front of me, all the time holding on to my arm. Then he faced me, with his body between me and the storm. That made as much difference as a toothpick might have done. He said something, right into my face, but I could not hear him. He was shouting, but not a sound from him could reach me. He had hold of both my arms now, he worked his hands down to my wrists and held them tight. He pulled me down—both of us staggering, the moment we tried to make any change of position—so that we were crouched close to the ground. So close together that we could not look at each other—we could only look down, at the miniature rivers already breaking up the earth around our feet, and the crushed plants and our soaked shoes. And even this had to be seen through the waterfall that was running down our faces.

Mike released my wrists and clamped his hands on my shoulders. His touch was still one of restraint, more than comfort.

We remained like this till the wind passed over. That could not have been more than five minutes, perhaps only two or three. Rain still fell, but now it was ordinary heavy rain. He took his hands away, and we stood up shakily. Our shirts and slacks were stuck fast to our bodies. My hair fell down over my face in long witch's tendrils and his hair was flattened in short dark tails to his forehead. We tried to smile, but had hardly the strength for it. Then we kissed and pressed together briefly. This was more of a ritual, a recognition of survival rather than of our bodies' inclinations. Our lips slid against each other, slick and cool, and the pressure of the embrace made us slightly chilly, as fresh water was squished out of our clothing.

Every minute, the rain grew lighter. We made our way, slightly staggering, through the half-flattened weeds, then between the thick and drenching bushes. Big tree branches had been hurled all over the golf course. I did not think until later that any one of them could have killed us.

We walked in the open, detouring around the fallen limbs. The rain had almost stopped, and the air brightened. I was walking with my head bent—so that the water from my hair fell to the ground and not down my face—and I felt the heat of the sun strike my shoulders before I looked up into its festival light.

I stood still, took a deep breath, and swung my hair out of my face. Now was the time, when we were drenched and safe and confronted with radiance. Now something had to be said.

"There's something I didn't mention to you."

His voice surprised me, like the sun. But in the opposite way. It had a weight to it, a warning—determination edged with apology.

"About our youngest boy," he said. "Our youngest boy was killed last summer."

Oh.

"He was run over," he said. "I was the one ran over him. Backing out of our driveway."

I stopped again. He stopped with me. Both of us stared ahead.

"His name was Brian. He was three.

"The thing was, I thought he was upstairs in bed. The others were still up, but he'd been put to bed. Then he'd got up again.

"I should have looked, though. I should have looked more carefully."

I thought of the moment when he got out of the car. The noise he must have made. The moment when the child's mother came running out of the house. *This isn't him, he isn't here, it didn't happen.*

Upstairs in bed.

He started walking again, entering the parking lot. I walked a little behind him. And I did not say anything—not one kind, common, helpless word. We had passed right by that.

He didn't say, It was my fault and I'll never get over it. I'll never forgive myself. But I do as well as I can.

Or, My wife forgives me but she'll never get over it either.

I knew all that. I knew now that he was a person who had hit rock bottom. A person who knew—as I did not know, did not come near knowing—exactly what rock bottom was like. He and his wife knew that together and it bound them, as something like that would either break you apart or bind you, for life. Not that they would live at rock bottom. But they would share a knowledge of it—that cool, empty, locked, and central space.

It could happen to anybody.

Yes. But it doesn't seem that way. It seems as if it happens to this one, that one, picked out specially here and there, one at a time.

I said, "It isn't fair." I was talking about the dealing out of these idle punishments, these wicked and ruinous swipes. Worse like this, perhaps, than when they happen in the midst of plentiful distress, in wars or the earth's disasters. Worst of all when there is the one whose act, probably an uncharacteristic act, is singly and permanently responsible.

That's what I was talking about. But meaning also, *It is not fair. What has this got to do with us?*

A protest so brutal that it seems almost innocent, coming out of such a raw core of self. Innocent, that is, if you are the one it's coming from, and if it has not been made public.

"Well," he said, quite gently. Fairness being neither here nor there.

"Sunny and Johnston don't know about it," he said. "None of the people know, that we met since we moved. It seemed as if it might work better that way. Even the other kids—they don't hardly ever mention him. Never mention his name."

I was not one of the people they had met since they moved. Not one of the people amongst whom they would make their new, hard, normal life. I was a person who knew—that was all. A person he had, on his own, who knew.

"That's strange," he said, looking around before he opened the trunk of the car to stow away the golf case.

"What happened to the guy who was parked here before? Didn't you see another car parked here when we came in? But I never saw one other person on the course. Now that I think of it. Did you?"

I said no.

"Mystery," he said. And again, "Well."

That was a word that I used to hear fairly often, said in that same tone of voice, when I was a child. A bridge between one thing and another, or a conclusion, or a way of saying something that couldn't be any more fully said, or thought.

"A well is a hole in the ground." That was the joking answer.

The storm had brought an end to the swimming-pool party. Too many people had been there for everybody to crowd into the house, and those with children had mostly chosen to go home.

While we were driving back, Mike and I had both noticed, and spoken about, a prickling, an itch or burning, on our bare forearms, the backs of our hands, and around our ankles. Places that had not been protected by our clothing when we crouched in the weeds. I remembered the nettles.

Sitting in Sunny's farmhouse kitchen, wearing dry clothes, we told about our adventure and revealed our rashes.

Sunny knew what to do for us. Yesterday's trip with Claire, to the emergency room of the local hospital, had not been this family's first visit. On an earlier weekend the boys had gone down into the weedy mud-bottomed field behind the barn and come back covered with welts and blotches. The doctor said they must have got into some nettles. Must have been rolling in them, was what he said. Cold compresses were prescribed, an antihistamine lotion, and pills. There was still part of a bottle of lotion unused, and there were some pills too, because Mark and Gregory had recovered quickly.

We said no to the pills—our case seemed not serious enough.

Sunny said that she had talked to the woman out on the highway, who put gas in her car, and this woman had said there was a plant whose leaves made the best poultice you could have, for nettle rash. You don't need all them pills and junk, the woman said. The name of the plant was something like calf's foot. Coldfoot? The woman had told her she could find it in a certain road cut, by a bridge.

"I could go and ask her to tell me again, exactly. I could go and get some."

She was eager to do that, she liked the idea of a folklore remedy. We had to point out that the lotion was already there, and paid for.

Sunny enjoyed ministering to us. In fact, our plight put the whole family into a good humor, brought them out of the doldrums of the drenched day and cancelled plans. The fact that we had chosen to go off together and that we had this adventure—an adventure that left its evidence on our bodies—seemed to rouse in Sunny and Johnston a teasing excitement. Droll looks from him, a bright solicitousness from her. If we had brought back evidence of real misdoing—welts on the buttocks, red splashes on the thighs and belly—they would not of course have been so charmed and forgiving.

The children thought it was funny to see us sitting there with our feet in basins, our arms and hands clumsy with their wrappings of thick cloths. Claire especially was delighted with the sight of our naked, foolish, adult feet. Mike wriggled his long toes for her, and she broke into fits of alarmed giggles.

Well. It would be the same old thing, if we ever met again. Or if we didn't. Love that was not usable, that knew its place. (Some would say not real, because it would never risk getting its neck wrung, or turning into a bad joke, or sadly wearing out.) Not risking a thing yet staying alive as a sweet trickle, an underground resource. With the weight of this new stillness on it, this seal.

I never asked Sunny for news of him, or got any, during all the years of our dwindling friendship.

Those plants with the big pinkish-purple flowers are not nettles. I have discovered that they are called joe-pye weed. The stinging nettles that we must have got into are more insignificant plants, with a paler purple flower, and stalks wickedly outfitted with fine, fierce, skin-piercing and inflaming spines. Those would be present too, unnoticed, in all the flourishing of the waste meadow.

Post and Beam

Lionel told them how his mother had died.

She had asked for her makeup. Lionel held the mirror.

"This will take about an hour," she said.

Foundation cream, face powder, eyebrow pencil, mascara, lip-liner, lipstick, blusher. She was slow and shaky, but it wasn't a bad job.

"That didn't take you an hour," Lionel said.

She said, no, she hadn't meant that.

She had meant, to die.

He had asked her if she wanted him to call his father. His father, her husband, her minister.

She said, What for.

She was only about five minutes out, in her prediction.

They were sitting behind the house—Lorna and Brendan's house—on a little terrace that looked across at Burrard Inlet and the lights of Point Grey. Brendan got up to move the sprinkler to another patch of grass.

Lorna had met Lionel's mother just a few months ago. A pretty little white-haired woman with a valiant charm, who had come down to Vancouver from a town in the Rocky Mountains, to see the touring Comédie Française. Lionel had asked Lorna to go with them. After the performance, while Lionel was holding open her blue velvet cloak, the mother had said to Lorna, "I am so happy to meet my son's *belle-amie*."

"Let us not overdo it with the French," said Lionel.

Lorna was not even sure what that meant. *Belle-amie*. Beautiful friend? Mistress?

Lionel had raised his eyebrows at her, over his mother's head. As if to say, whatever she's come up with, it's no fault of mine.

Lionel had once been Brendan's student at the university. A raw prodigy, sixteen years old. The brightest mathematical mind Brendan had ever seen. Lorna wondered if Brendan was dramatizing this, in hindsight, because of his unusual generosity towards gifted students. Also because of the way things had turned out. Brendan had turned his back on the whole Irish package—his family and his Church and the sentimental songs—but he had a weakness for a tragic tale. And sure enough, after his blazing start, Lionel had suffered some sort of breakdown, had to be hospitalized, dropped out of sight. Until Brendan had met him in the supermarket and discovered that he was living within a mile of their house, here in North Vancouver. He had given up mathematics entirely and worked in the publishing office of the Anglican Church.

"Come and see us," Brendan had said. Lionel looked a bit seedy to him, and lonely. "Come and meet my wife."

He was glad to have a home now, to ask people to.

"So I didn't know what you'd be like," Lionel said when he reported this to Lorna. "I considered you might be awful."

"Oh," said Lorna. "Why?"

"I don't know. Wives."

He came to see them in the evenings, when the children were in bed. The slight intrusions of domestic life—the cry of the baby reaching them through an open window, the scolding Brendan sometimes had to give Lorna about toys left lying about on the grass, instead of being put back in the sandbox, the call from the kitchen asking if she had remembered to buy limes for the gin and tonic—all seemed to cause a shiver, a tightening of Lionel's tall, narrow body and intent, distrustful face. There had to be a pause then, a shifting back to the level of worthwhile human contact. Once he sang very softly, to the tune of "O Tannenbaum," *"O married life, o married life."* He smiled slightly, or Lorna thought he did, in the dark. This smile seemed to her like the smile of her four-year-old daughter, Elizabeth, when she whispered some mildly outrageous observation to her mother in a public place. A secret little smile, gratified, somewhat alarmed.

Lionel rode up the hill on his high, old-fashioned bicycle—this at a time when hardly anybody but children rode bicycles. He would not have changed out of his workday outfit. Dark trousers, a white shirt that always looked grubby and worn around the cuffs and collar, a nondescript tie. When they had gone to see the Comédie Française he had added to this a tweed jacket that was too wide across the shoulders and too short in the sleeves. Perhaps he did not own any other clothes.

"I labor for a pittance," he said. "And not even in the vineyards of the Lord. In the Diocese of the Archbishop."

And, "Sometimes I think I'm in a Dickens novel. And the funny thing is, I don't even go for Dickens."

He talked with his head on one side, usually, his gaze on something slightly beyond Lorna's head. His voice was light and quick, sometimes squeaky with a kind of nervous exhilaration. He told everything in a slightly astonished way. He told about the office where he worked, in the building behind the Cathedral. The small high Gothic windows and varnished woodwork (to give things a churchy feeling), the hat rack and umbrella stand (which for some reason filled him with deep melancholy), the typist, Janine, and the Editor of Church News, Mrs. Penfound. The occasionally appearing, spectral, and distracted Archbishop. There was an unresolved

battle over teabags, between Janine, who favored them, and Mrs.
Penfound, who did not. Everybody munched on secret eats and
never shared. With Janine it was caramels, and Lionel himself
favored sugared almonds. What Mrs. Penfound's secret pleasure
was he and Janine had not discovered, because Mrs. Penfound did
not put the wrappers in the wastepaper basket. But her jaws were
always surreptitiously busy.

He mentioned the hospital where he had been a patient for a
while and spoke of the ways it resembled the office, in regard to
secret eats. Secrets generally. But the difference was that every
once in a while in the hospital they came and bound you up and
took you off and plugged you in, as he said, to the light socket.

"That was pretty interesting. In fact it was excruciating. But I
can't describe it. That is the weird part. I can remember it but not
describe it."

Because of those events in the hospital, he said, he was rather
short of memories. Short of details. He liked to have Lorna tell
him hers.

She told him about her life before she married Brendan. About
the two houses exactly alike, standing side by side in the town
where she grew up. In front of them was a deep ditch called Dye
Creek because it used to run water colored by the dye from the
knitting factory. Behind them was a wild meadow where girls were
not supposed to go. One house was where she lived with her
father—in the other lived her grandmother and her Aunt Beatrice
and her cousin Polly.

Polly had no father. That was what they said and what Lorna
had once truly believed. Polly had no father, in the way that a
Manx cat had no tail.

In the grandmother's front room was a map of the Holy Land,
worked in many shades of wool, showing Biblical locations. It was
left in her will to the United Church Sunday School. Aunt Beatrice
had had no social life involving a man, since the time of her
blotted-out disgrace, and she was so finicky, so desperate about the

conduct of life that it really was easy to think of Polly's conception as immaculate. The only thing that Lorna had ever learned from Aunt Beatrice was that you must always press a seam from the side, not wide open, so that the mark of the iron would not show, and that no sheer blouse should be worn without its slip to hide your brassiere straps.

"Oh, yes. Yes," said Lionel. He stretched out his legs as if appreciation had reached his very toes. "Now Polly. Out of this benighted household, what is Polly like?"

Polly was fine, Lorna said. Full of energy and sociability, kind-hearted, confident.

"Oh," said Lionel. "Tell me again about the kitchen."

"Which kitchen?"

"The one without the canary."

"Ours." She described how she rubbed the kitchen range with waxed bread-wrappers to make it shine, the blackened shelves behind it that held the frying pans, the sink and the small mirror above it, with the triangular piece of glass gone from one corner, and the little tin trough beneath it—made by her father—in which there was always a comb, an old cup-handle, a tiny pot of dry rouge that must have once been her mother's.

She told him her only memory of her mother. She was down-town, with her mother, on a winter day. There was snow between the sidewalk and the street. She had just learned how to tell time, and she looked up at the Post Office clock and saw that the moment had come for the soap opera she and her mother listened to every day on the radio. She felt a deep concern, not because of missing the story but because she wondered what would happen to the people in the story, with the radio not turned on, and her mother and herself not listening. It was more than concern she felt, it was horror, to think of the way things could be lost, could not happen, through some casual absence or chance.

And even in that memory, her mother was only a hip and a shoulder, in a heavy coat.

Lionel said that he could hardly get more of a sense of his father than that, though his father was still alive. A swish of a surplice? Lionel and his mother used to make bets on how long his father could go without speaking to them. He had asked his mother once what made his father so mad, and she had answered that she really didn't know.

"I think perhaps he doesn't like his job," she said.

Lionel said, "Why doesn't he get another job?"

"Perhaps he can't think of one he'd like."

Lionel had then remembered that when she had taken him to the museum he had been frightened of the mummies, and that she had told him they were not really dead, but could get out of their cases when everybody went home. So he said, "Couldn't he be a mummy?" His mother confused mummy with mommy, and later repeated this story as a joke, and he had been too discouraged, really, to correct her. Too discouraged, at his early age, about the whole mighty problem of communication.

This was one of the few memories that had stayed with him.

Brendan laughed—he laughed at this story more than Lorna or Lionel did. Brendan would sit down with them for a while, saying, "What are you two gabbling about?" and then with some relief, as if he had paid his dues for the time being, he would get up, saying that he had some work to deal with, and go into the house. As if he was happy about their friendship, had in a way foreseen it and brought it about—but their conversation made him restless.

"It's good for him to come up here and be normal for a while instead of sitting in his room," he said to Lorna. "Of course he lusts after you. Poor bugger."

He liked to say that men lusted after Lorna. Particularly when they'd been to a department party, and she had been the youngest wife there. She would have been embarrassed to have anybody hear him say that, lest they think it a wishful and foolish exaggeration. But sometimes, especially if she was a little drunk, it roused her as well as Brendan, to think that she might be so universally appealing. In Lionel's case, though, she was pretty sure that it was not true, and she hoped very much that Brendan would never hint at such a thing in front of him. She remembered the look that he had given her over his mother's head. A disavowal there, a mild warning.

She did not tell Brendan about the poems. Once a week or so a poem arrived quite properly sealed and posted, in the mail. These were not anonymous—Lionel signed them. His signature was just a squiggle, quite difficult to make out—but then so was every word of every poem. Fortunately, there were never many words—sometimes only a dozen or two in all—and they made a curious path across the page, like uncertain bird tracks. At first glance Lorna could never make out anything at all. She found that it was best not to try too hard, just to hold the page in front of her and look at it long and steadily as if she had gone into a trance. Then, usually, words would appear. Not all of them—there were two or three in every poem that she never figured out—but that did not matter much. There was no punctuation but dashes. The words were mostly nouns. Lorna was not a person unfamiliar with poetry, or a person who gave up easily on whatever she did not quickly understand. But she felt about these poems of Lionel's more or less as she did about, say, the Buddhist religion—that they were a resource she might be able to comprehend, to tap into, in the future, but that she couldn't do that just now.

After the first poem she agonized about what she should say. Something appreciative, but not stupid. All she managed was, "Thank you for the poem"—when Brendan was well out of earshot. She kept herself from saying, "I enjoyed it." Lionel gave a jerky nod, and made a sound that sealed off the conversation. Poems continued to arrive, and were not mentioned again. She began to think that she could regard them as offerings, not as messages. But not love-offerings—as Brendan, for instance, would assume. There was nothing in them about Lionel's feelings for her,

nothing personal at all. They reminded her of those faint impres-
sions you can sometimes make out on the sidewalks in spring—
shadows, left by wet leaves plastered there the year before.

There was something else, more urgent, that she did not speak
about to Brendan. Or to Lionel. She did not say that Polly was
coming to visit. Polly, her cousin, was coming from home.

Polly was five years older than Lorna and had worked, ever
since she graduated from high school, in the local bank. She had
saved up almost enough money for this trip once before, but
decided to spend it on a sump pump instead. Now, however, she
was on her way across the country by bus. To her it seemed the
most natural and appropriate thing to do—to visit her cousin and
her cousin's husband and her cousin's family. To Brendan it would
seem almost certainly an intrusion, something nobody had any
business doing unless invited. He was not averse to visitors—look
at Lionel—but he wanted to do the choosing himself. Every day
Lorna thought of how she must tell him. Every day she put it off.

And this was not a thing she could talk about to Lionel. You
could not speak to him about anything seen seriously as a problem.
To speak of problems meant to search for, to hope for, solutions.
And that was not interesting, it did not indicate an interesting attitude towards life. Rather, a shallow and tiresome hopefulness.
Ordinary anxieties, uncomplicated emotions, were not what he
enjoyed hearing about. He preferred things to be utterly bewildering and past bearing, yet ironically, even merrily, borne.

One thing she had told him that might have been chancy. She
told him how she had cried on her wedding day and during the
actual wedding ceremony. But she was able to make a joke of that,
because she could tell how she tried to pull her hand out of
Brendan's grip to get her handkerchief, but he would not let go, so
she had to keep on snuffling. And in fact she had not cried because
she didn't want to be married, or didn't love Brendan. She had
cried because everything at home seemed suddenly so precious to

her—though she had always planned to leave—and the people there seemed closer to her than anyone else could ever be, though she had hidden all her private thoughts from them. She cried because she and Polly had laughed as they cleaned the kitchen shelves and scrubbed the linoleum the day before, and she had pretended she was in a sentimental play and said good-bye, old linoleum, good-bye, crack in the teapot, good-bye, the place where I used to stick my gum under the table, good-bye.

Why don't you just tell him forget it, Polly had said. But of course she didn't mean that, she was proud, and Lorna herself was proud, eighteen years old and never had a real boyfriend, and here she was, marrying a good-looking thirty-year-old man, a professor.

Nevertheless, she cried, and cried again when she got letters from home in the early days of her marriage. Brendan had caught her at it, and said, "You love your family, don't you?"

She thought he sounded sympathetic. She said, "Yes."

He sighed. "I think you love them more than you love me."

She said that was not true, it was only that she felt sorry for her family sometimes. They had a hard time, her grandmother teaching Grade Four year after year though her eyes were so bad that she could hardly see to write on the board, and Aunt Beatrice with too many nervous complaints to ever have a job, and her father—Lorna's father—working in the hardware store that wasn't even his own.

"A hard time?" said Brendan. "They've been in a concentration camp, have they?"

Then he said that people needed gumption in this world. And Lorna lay down on the marriage bed and gave way to one of those angry weeping fits that she was now ashamed to remember. Brendan came and consoled her, after a while, but still believed that she cried as women always did when they could not win the argument any other way.

Some things about Polly's looks Lorna had forgotten. How tall she was and what a long neck and narrow waist she had, and an almost perfectly flat chest. A bumpy little chin and a wry mouth. Pale skin, light-brown hair cut short, fine as feathers. She looked both frail and hardy, like a daisy on a long stalk. She wore a ruffled denim skirt with embroidery on it.

For forty-eight hours Brendan had known she was coming. She had phoned, collect, from Calgary, and he had answered the phone. He had three questions to ask afterwards. His tone was distant, but calm.

How long is she staying?

Why didn't you tell me?

Why did she phone collect?

"I don't know," said Lorna.

Now from the kitchen where she was preparing dinner, Lorna strained to hear what they would say to each other. Brendan had just come home. His greeting she could not hear, but Polly's voice was loud and full of a risky jollity.

"So I really started out on the wrong foot, Brendan, wait till you hear what I said. Lorna and I are walking down the street from the bus stop and I'm saying, Oh, shoot, this is a pretty classy neighborhood you live in, Lorna—and then I say, But look at that place, what's it doing here? I said, It looks like a barn."

She couldn't have started out worse. Brendan was very proud of their house. It was a contemporary house, built in the West Coast style called Post and Beam. Post and Beam houses were not painted; the idea was to fit in with the original forests. So the effect was plain and functional from the outside, with the roof flat and protruding beyond the walls. Inside, the beams were exposed and none of the wood was covered up. The fireplace in this house was set in a stone chimney that went up to the ceiling, and the windows were long and narrow and uncurtained. The architecture is always preeminent, the builder had told them, and Brendan repeated this, as well as the word "contemporary," when introducing anybody to the house for the first time.

He did not bother to say this to Polly, or to get out the magazine in which there was an article about the style, with photographs—though not of this particular house.

Polly had brought from home the habit of starting off her sentences with the name of the person specifically addressed. "Lorna—" she would say, or "Brendan—" Lorna had forgotten about this way of talking—it seemed to her now rather peremptory and rude. Most of Polly's sentences at the dinner table began with "Lorna—" and were about people known only to her and Polly. Lorna knew that Polly did not intend to be rude, that she was making a strident but brave effort to seem at ease. And she had at first tried to include Brendan. Both she and Lorna had done so, they had launched into explanations of whoever it was they were talking about—but it did not work. Brendan spoke only to call Lorna's attention to something needed on the table, or to point out that Daniel had spilled his mashed food on the floor around his high chair.

Polly went on talking while she and Lorna cleared the table, and then as they washed the dishes. Lorna usually bathed the children and put them to bed before she started on the dishes, but tonight she was too rattled—she sensed that Polly was near tears—to attend to things in their proper order. She let Daniel crawl around on the floor while Elizabeth, with her interest in social occasions and new personalities, hung about listening to the conversation. This lasted until Daniel knocked the high chair over—fortunately not on himself, but he howled with fright—and Brendan came from the living room.

"Bedtime seems to have been postponed," he said, as he removed his son from Lorna's arms. "Elizabeth. Go and get ready for your bath."

Polly had moved on from talking about people in town to describing how things were going at home. Not well. The owner of the hardware store—a man whom Lorna's father had always spoken of as more of a friend than an employer—had sold the business without a word of what he was intending until the deed was done. The new man was expanding the store at the same time business was being lost to Canadian Tire, and there was not a day that he did not stir up some kind of a row with Lorna's father. Lorna's father came home from the shop so discouraged that all he wanted to do was lie on the couch. He was not interested in the paper or the news. He drank bicarbonate of soda but wouldn't discuss the pains in his stomach.

Lorna mentioned a letter from her father in which he made light of these troubles.

"Well, he would, wouldn't he?" said Polly. "To you."

The upkeep of both houses, Polly said, was a continual nightmare. They should all move into one house and sell the other, but now that their grandmother had retired she picked on Polly's mother all the time, and Lorna's father could not stand the idea of living with the two of them. Polly often wanted to walk out and never come back, but what would they do without her?

"You should live your own life," said Lorna. It felt strange to her, to be giving advice to Polly.

"Oh, sure, sure," said Polly. "I should've got out while the going was good, that's what I guess I should have done. But when was that? I don't ever remember the going being so particularly good. I was stuck with having to see you through school first, for one thing."

Lorna had spoken in a regretful, helpful voice, but she refused to stop in her work, to give Polly's news its due. She accepted it as if it concerned some people she knew and liked, but was not responsible for. She thought of her father lying on the couch in the evenings, dosing himself for pains he wouldn't admit to, and Aunt Beatrice next door, worried about what people were saying about her, afraid they were laughing behind her back, writing things about her on walls. Crying because she'd gone to church with her slip showing. To think of home caused Lorna pain, but she could not help feeling that Polly was hammering at her, trying to bring her to some capitulation, wrap her up in some intimate misery. And she was bound that she would not give in.

Just look at you. Look at your life. Your stainless-steel sink. Your house where the architecture is preeminent.

"If I ever went away now I think I'd just feel too guilty," Polly said. "I couldn't stand it. I'd feel too guilty leaving them."

Of course some people never feel guilty. Some people never feel at all.

"Quite a tale of woe you got," said Brendan, when they were lying side by side in the dark.

"It's on her mind," Lorna said.

"Just remember. We are not millionaires."

Lorna was startled. "She doesn't want money."

"Doesn't she?"

"That's not what she's telling me for."

"Don't be too sure."

She lay rigid, not answering. Then she thought of something that might put him in a better mood.

"She's only here for two weeks."

His turn not to answer.

"Don't you think she's nice-looking?"

"No."

She was about to say that Polly had made her wedding dress. She had planned to be married in her navy suit, and Polly had said, a few days before the wedding, "This isn't going to do." So she got out her own high-school formal (Polly had always been more popular than Lorna, she had gone to dances) and she put in gussets of white lace and sewed on white lace sleeves. Because, she said, a bride can't do without sleeves.

But what could he have cared about that?

Lionel had gone away for a few days. His father had retired, and Lionel was helping him with the move from the town in the Rocky Mountains to Vancouver Island. On the day after Polly's arrival, Lorna had a letter from him. Not a poem—a real letter, though it was very short.

> I dreamt that I was giving you a ride on my bicycle. We were going quite fast. You did not seem to be afraid, though perhaps you should have been. We must not feel called upon to interpret this.

Brendan had gone off early. He was teaching summer school, he said he would eat breakfast at the cafeteria. Polly came out of her room as soon as he was gone. She wore slacks instead of the flounced skirt, and she smiled all the time, as if at a joke of her own. She kept ducking her head slightly to avoid Lorna's eyes.

"I better get off and see something of Vancouver," she said, "seeing it isn't likely I'll ever get here again."

Lorna marked some things on a map, and gave her directions, and said she was sorry she couldn't go along, but it would be more trouble than it was worth, with the children.

"Oh. Oh, no. I wouldn't expect you to. I didn't come out here to be on your hands all the time."

Elizabeth sensed the strain in the atmosphere. She said, "Why are we trouble?"

Lorna gave Daniel an early nap, and when he woke up she got him into the stroller and told Elizabeth they were going to a playground. The playground she had chosen was not the one in a nearby park—it was down the hill, close to the street Lionel lived on. Lorna knew his address, though she had never seen the house. She knew that it was a house, not an apartment building. He lived in one room, upstairs.

It did not take her long to get there—though no doubt it would take her longer to get back, pushing the stroller uphill. But she had already passed into the older part of North Vancouver, where the houses were smaller, perched on narrow lots. The house where Lionel lived had his name beside one bell, and the name B. Hutchison beside the other. She knew that Mrs. Hutchison was the landlady. She pressed that bell.

"I know Lionel's away and I'm sorry to bother you," she said. "But I lent him a book, it's a library book and now it's overdue, and I just wondered if I could run up to his apartment and see if I could find it."

The landlady said, "Oh." She was an old woman with a bandanna round her head and large dark spots on her face.

"My husband and I are friends of Lionel's. My husband was his professor at college."

The word "professor" was always useful. Lorna was given the key. She parked the stroller in the shade of the house and told Elizabeth to stay and watch Daniel.

"This isn't a playground," Elizabeth said.

"I just have to run upstairs and back. Just for a minute, okay?"

Lionel's room had an alcove at the end of it for a two-burner gas stove and a cupboard. No refrigerator and no sink, except for the one in the toilet. A venetian blind stuck halfway down the window, and a square of linoleum whose pattern was covered by brown paint. There was a faint smell of the gas stove, mixed with a smell of unaired heavy clothing, perspiration, and some pine-scented decongestant, which she accepted—hardly thinking of it and not at all disliking it—as the intimate smell of Lionel himself.

Other than that, the place gave out hardly any clues. She had come here not for any library book, of course, but to be for a moment inside the space where he lived, breathe his air, look out of his window. The view was of other houses, probably like this one chopped up into small apartments on the wooded slope of Grouse Mountain. The bareness, the anonymity of the room were severely challenging. Bed, bureau, table, chair. Just the furniture that had to be provided so that the room could be advertised as furnished. Even the tan chenille bedspread must have been there when he moved in. No pictures—not even a calendar—and most surprisingly, no books.

Things must be hidden somewhere. In the bureau drawers? She couldn't look. Not only because there was no time—she could hear Elizabeth calling her from the yard—but the very absence of whatever might be personal made the sense of Lionel stronger. Not just the sense of his austerity and his secrets, but of a watchfulness—almost as if he had set a trap and was waiting to see what she would do.

What she really wanted to do was not to investigate anymore but to sit down on the floor, in the middle of the square of linoleum. To sit for hours not so much looking at this room as sinking into it. To stay in this room where there was nobody who knew her or wanted a thing from her. To stay here for a long, long time, growing sharper and lighter, light as a needle.

On Saturday morning, Lorna and Brendan and the children were to drive to Penticton. A graduate student had invited them to his wedding. They would stay Saturday night and all day Sunday and Sunday night as well, and leave for home on Monday morning.

"Have you told her?" Brendan said.

"It's all right. She isn't expecting to come."

"But *have you told her?*"

Thursday was spent at Ambleside Beach. Lorna and Polly and the children rode there on buses, changing twice, encumbered with towels, beach toys, diapers, lunch, and Elizabeth's blow-up dolphin. The physical predicaments they found themselves in, and the irritation and dismay that the sight of their party roused in other passengers, brought on a peculiarly feminine reaction—a mood of near hilarity. Getting away from the house where Lorna was installed as wife was helpful too. They reached the beach in triumph and ragtag disarray and set up their encampment, from which they took turns going into the water, minding the children, fetching soft drinks, Popsicles, french fries.

Lorna was lightly tanned, Polly not at all. She stretched a leg out beside Lorna's and said, "Look at that. Raw dough."

With all the work she had to do in the two houses, and with her job in the bank, she said, there was not a quarter hour when she was free to sit in the sun. But she spoke now matter-of-factly, without her undertone of virtue and complaint. Some sour atmosphere that had surrounded her—like old dishrags—was falling away. She had found her way around Vancouver by herself—the first time she had ever done that in a city. She had talked to strangers at bus stops and asked what sights she should see and on somebody's advice had taken the chairlift to the top of Grouse Mountain.

As they lay on the sand Lorna offered an explanation.

"This is a bad time of year for Brendan. Teaching summer school is really nerve-racking, you have to do so much so fast."

Polly said, "Yeah? It's not just me, then?"

"Don't be stupid. Of course it isn't you."

"Well, that's a relief. I thought he kind of hated my guts."

She then spoke of a man at home who wanted to take her out.

"He's too serious. He's looking for a wife. I guess Brendan was too, but I guess you were in love with him."

"Was and am," said Lorna.

"Well, I don't think I am." Polly spoke with her face pressed into her elbow. "I guess it might work though if you liked somebody okay and you went out with them and made up your mind to see the good points."

"So what are the good points?" Lorna was sitting up so that she could watch Elizabeth ride the dolphin.

"Give me a while to think," said Polly, giggling. "No. There's lots. I'm just being mean."

As they were rounding up toys and towels she said, "I really wouldn't mind doing all this over again tomorrow."

"Me neither," said Lorna, "but I have to get ready to go to the Okanagan. We're invited to this wedding." She made it sound like a chore—something she hadn't bothered speaking about till now because it was too disagreeable and boring.

Polly said, "Oh. Well, I might come by myself then."

"Sure. You should."

"Where is the Okanagan?"

The next evening, after putting the children to bed, Lorna went into the room where Polly slept. She went to get a suitcase out of the closet, expecting the room to be empty—Polly, as she thought, still in the bathroom, soaking the day's sunburn in lukewarm water and soda.

But Polly was in bed, with the sheet pulled up around her like a shroud.

"You're out of the bath," said Lorna, as if she found all this quite normal. "How does your burn feel now?"

"I'm okay," said Polly in a muffled voice. Lorna knew at once that she had been and probably still was weeping. She stood at the foot of the bed, not able to leave the room. A disappointment had come over her that was like sickness, a wave of disgust. Polly didn't really mean to keep hiding, she rolled over and looked out, with her face all creased and helpless, red from the sun, and her weeping. Fresh tears came welling up in her eyes. She was a mound of misery, one solid accusation.

"What is it?" Lorna said. She feigned surprise, she feigned compassion.

"You don't want me."

Her eyes were on Lorna all the time, brimming not just with her tears, her bitterness and accusation of betrayal, but with her outrageous demand, to be folded in, rocked, comforted.

Lorna would sooner have hit her. What gives you the right, she wanted to say. What are you leeching onto me for? What gives you the right?

Family. Family gives Polly the right. She has saved her money and planned her escape, with the idea that Lorna should take her in. Is that true—has she dreamed of staying here and never having to go back? Becoming part of Lorna's good fortune, Lorna's transformed world?

"What do you think I can do?" said Lorna quite viciously and to her own surprise. "Do you think I have any power? He never even gives me more than a twenty-dollar bill at a time."

She dragged the suitcase out of the room.

It was all so false and disgusting—setting her own lamentations up in that way, to match Polly's. What did the twenty dollars at a time have to do with anything? She had a charge account, he never refused her when she asked.

She couldn't go to sleep, berating Polly in her mind.

The heat of the Okanagan made summer seem more authentic than the summer on the coast. The hills with their pale grass, the sparse shade of the drylands pine trees, seemed a natural setting for so festive a wedding with its endless supplies of champagne, its dancing and flirtation and overflow of instant friendship and goodwill. Lorna got rapidly drunk and was amazed at how easy it was, with alcohol, to get loose from the bondage of her spirits. Forlorn vapors lifted. She went to bed still drunk, and lecherous, to Brendan's benefit. Even her hangover the next day seemed mild, cleansing rather than punishing. Feeling frail, but not at all displeased with herself, she lay by the shores of the lake and watched Brendan help Elizabeth build a sand castle.

"Did you know that your daddy and I met at a wedding?" she asked.

"Not much like this one, though," said Brendan. He meant that the wedding he had attended, when a friend of his married the McQuaig girl (the McQuaigs being a top family in Lorna's hometown) had been officially dry. The reception had been in the United Church Hall—Lorna was one of the girls recruited to pass sandwiches—and the drinking had been done in a hurry, in the parking lot. Lorna was not used to smelling whisky on men and thought that Brendan must have put on too much of some unfamiliar hairdressing. Nevertheless, she admired his thick shoulders, his bull's neck, his laughing and commanding golden-brown eyes. When she learned that he was a teacher of mathematics she fell in love with what was inside his head also. She was excited by whatever knowledge a man might have that was utterly strange to her. A knowledge of auto mechanics would have worked as well.

His answering attraction to her seemed to be in the nature of a miracle. She learned later that he had been on the lookout for a wife; he was old enough, it was time. He wanted a young girl. Not a colleague, or a student, perhaps not even the sort of girl whose parents could send her to college. Unspoiled. Intelligent, but unspoiled. A wildflower, he said in the heat of those early days, and sometimes even now.

On the drive back, they left this hot golden country behind, somewhere between Keremeos and Princeton. But the sun still shone, and Lorna had only a faint disturbance in her mind, like a hair in her vision that could be flicked away, or could float out of sight on its own.

But it did keep coming back. It grew more ominous and persistent, till at last it made a spring at her and she knew it for what it was.

She was afraid—she was half certain—that while they were away in the Okanagan Polly would have committed suicide in the kitchen of the house in North Vancouver.

In the kitchen. It was a definite picture Lorna had. She saw exactly the way in which Polly would have done it. She would have hanged herself just inside the back door. When they returned, when they came to the house from the garage, they would find the door locked. They would unlock it and try to push it open but be unable to because of the lump of Polly's body against it. They would hurry around to the front door and come into the kitchen that way and be met by the full sight of Polly dead. She would be wearing the flounced denim skirt and the white drawstring blouse—the brave outfit in which she had first appeared to try their hospitality. Her long pale legs dangling down, her head twisted fatally on its delicate neck. In front of her body would be the kitchen chair she had climbed onto, and then stepped from, or jumped from, to see how misery could finish itself.

Alone in the house of people who did not want her, where the very walls and the windows and the cup she drank her coffee from must have seemed to despise her.

Lorna remembered a time when she had been left alone with Polly, left in Polly's charge for a day, in their grandmother's house. Perhaps her father was at the shop. But she had an idea that he too had gone away, that all three adults were out of town. It must have been an unusual occasion, since they never went on shopping trips, let alone trips for pleasure. A funeral—almost certainly a funeral. The day was a Saturday, there was no school. Lorna was too young to be in school anyway. Her hair had not grown long enough to be put into pigtails. It blew in wisps around her head, as Polly's did now.

Polly was going through a stage then in which she loved to make candy or rich treats of any kind, from her grandmother's cookbook. Chocolate date cake, macaroons, divinity fudge. She was in the middle of mixing something up, on that day, when she found out that an ingredient she needed was not in the cupboard. She had to ride uptown on her bicycle, to charge it at the store. The weather was windy and cold, the ground bare—the season must have been late fall or early spring. Before she left, Polly pushed in the damper on the wood stove. But she still thought of stories she had heard about children who perished in house fires when their mothers had run out on similar quick errands. So she directed Lorna to put on her coat, and took her outside, around to the corner between the kitchen and the main part of the house, where the wind was not so strong. The house next door must have been locked, or she could have taken her there. She told her to stay put, and rode off to the store. Stay there, don't move, don't worry, she said. Then she kissed Lorna's ear. Lorna obeyed her to the letter. For ten minutes, maybe fifteen, she remained crouched behind the white lilac bush, learning the shapes of the stones, the dark and light ones, in the house's foundation. Until Polly came tearing back and flung the bike down in the yard and came calling her name. Lorna, Lorna, throwing down the bag of brown sugar or walnuts and kissing her all around her head. For the thought had occurred to her that Lorna might have been spotted in her corner by lurking kidnappers—the bad men who were the reason that girls must not go down into the field behind the houses. She had prayed all her way back for this not to have happened. And it hadn't. She bustled Lorna inside to warm her bare knees and hands.

Oh, the poor little handsies, she said. Oh, were you scared? Lorna loved the fussing and bent her head to have it stroked, as if she was a pony.

———

The pines gave way to the denser evergreen forest, the brown lumps of hills to the rising blue-green mountains. Daniel began to whimper and Lorna got out his juice bottle. Later she asked Brendan to stop so that she could lay the baby down on the front seat and change his diaper. Brendan walked at a distance while she did this, smoking a cigarette. Diaper ceremonies always affronted him a little.

Lorna also took the opportunity of getting out one of Elizabeth's storybooks and when they were settled again she read to the children. It was a Dr. Seuss book. Elizabeth knew all the rhymes and even Daniel had some idea of where to chime in with his made-up words.

Polly was no longer that person who had rubbed Lorna's small hands between her own, the person who knew all the things Lorna did not know and who could be trusted to take care of her in the world. Everything had been turned around, and it seemed that in the years since Lorna got married Polly had stayed still. Lorna had passed her by. And now Lorna had the children in the back seat to take care of and to love, and it was unseemly for a person of Polly's age to come clawing for her share.

It was no use for Lorna to think this. No sooner had she put the argument in place than she felt the body knock against the door as they tried to push it open. The dead weight, the gray body. The body of Polly, who had been given nothing at all. No part in the family she had found, and no hope of the change she must have dreamed was coming in her life.

"Now read *Madeleine*," said Elizabeth.

"I don't think I brought *Madeleine*," said Lorna. "No. I didn't bring it. Never mind, you know it off by heart."

She and Elizabeth started off together.

"In an old house in Paris that was covered with vines,
Lived twelve little girls in two straight lines.

In two straight lines they broke their bread
Brushed their teeth and went to bed—"

This is stupidity, this is melodrama, this is guilt. This will not have happened.

But such things do happen. Some people founder, they are not helped in time. They are not helped at all. Some people are pitched into darkness.

"In the middle of the night,
Miss Clavel turned on the light.
She said, 'Something is not right—'"

"Mommy," said Elizabeth. "Why did you stop?"
Lorna said, "I had to, for a minute. My mouth got dry."

At Hope they had hamburgers and milkshakes. Then down the Fraser Valley, the children asleep in the back seat. Still some time left. Till they got to Chilliwack, till they got to Abbotsford, till they saw the hills of New Westminister ahead and the other hills crowned with houses, the beginnings of the city. Bridges still that they had to go over, turns they had to take, streets they had to drive along, corners they had to pass. All this in the time before. The next time she saw any of it would be in the time after.

When they entered Stanley Park it occurred to her to pray. This was shameless—the opportune praying of a nonbeliever. The gibberish of let-it-not-happen, let-it-not-happen. *Let it not have happened.*

The day was still cloudless. From the Lion's Gate Bridge they looked out at the Strait of Georgia.

"Can you see Vancouver Island today?" said Brendan. "You look, I can't."

Lorna craned her neck to look past him.

"Far away," she said. "Quite faint but it's there."

And with the sight of those blue, progressively dimmer, finally almost dissolving mounds that seemed to float upon the sea, she thought of one thing there was left to do. Make a bargain. Believe that it was still possible, up to the last minute it was possible to make a bargain.

It had to be serious, a most final and wrenching promise or offer. Take this. I promise this. If it can be made not true, if it can not have happened.

Not the children. She snatched that thought away as if she was grabbing them out of a fire. Not Brendan, for an opposite reason. She did not love him enough. She would say she loved him, and mean it to a certain extent, and she wanted to be loved by him, but there was a little hum of hate running along beside her love, nearly all the time. So it would be reprehensible—also useless—to offer him in any bargain.

Herself? Her looks? Her health?

It occurred to her that she might be on the wrong track. In a case like this, it might not be up to you to choose. Not up to you to set the terms. You would know them when you met them. You must promise to honor them, without knowing what they are going to be. Promise.

But nothing to do with the children.

Up Capilano Road, into their own part of the city and their own corner of the world, where their lives took on true weight and their actions took on consequences. There were the uncompromising wooden walls of their house, showing through the trees.

"The front door would be easier," Lorna said. "Then we wouldn't have any steps."

Brendan said, "What's the problem with a couple of steps?"

"I never got to see the bridge," Elizabeth cried, suddenly wide awake and disappointed. "Why did you never wake me up to see the bridge?"

Nobody answered her.

"Daniel's arm is all sunburnt," she said, in a tone of incomplete satisfaction.

Lorna heard voices which she thought were coming from the yard of the house next door. She followed Brendan around the corner of the house. Daniel lay against her shoulder still heavy with sleep. She carried the diaper bag and the storybook bag and Brendan carried the suitcase.

She saw that the people whose voices she had heard were in her own back yard. Polly and Lionel. They had dragged two lawn chairs around so that they could sit in the shade. They had their backs to the view.

Lionel. She had forgotten all about him.

He jumped up and ran to open the back door.

"The expedition has returned with all members accounted for," he said, in a voice which Lorna did not believe she had ever heard before. An unforced heartiness in it, an easy and appropriate confidence. The voice of the friend of the family. As he held the door open he looked straight into her face—something he had almost never done—and gave her a smile from which all subtlety, secrecy, ironic complicity, and mysterious devotion had been removed. All complications, all private messages had been removed.

She made her voice an echo of his.

"So—when did you get back?"

"Saturday," he said. "I'd forgotten you were going away. I came laboring up here to say hello and you weren't here, but Polly was here and of course she told me and then I remembered."

"Polly told you what?" said Polly, coming up behind him. This was not really a question, but the half-teasing remark of a woman who knows that almost anything she says will be well received.

Polly's sunburn had turned to tan, or at least to a new flush, on her forehead and her neck.

"Here," she said to Lorna, relieving her of both of the bags carried over her arm and the empty juice bottle in her hand. "I'll take everything but the baby."

Lionel's floppy hair was now more brownish-black than black—of course she was seeing him for the first time in full sunlight—and his skin too was tanned, enough for his forehead to have lost its pale gleam. He wore the usual dark pants, but his shirt was unfamiliar to her. A yellow short-sleeved shirt of some much-ironed, shiny, cheap material, too big across the shoulders, maybe bought at the church thrift sale.

Lorna carried Daniel up to his room. She laid him in his crib and stood beside him making soft noises and stroking his back.

She thought that Lionel must be punishing her for her mistake in going to his room. The landlady would have told him. Lorna should have expected that, if she had stopped to think. She hadn't stopped to think, probably, because she had the idea that it would not matter. She might even have thought that she would tell him herself.

I was going past on my way to the playground and I just thought I would go in and sit in the middle of your floor. I can't explain it. It seemed like that would give me a moment's peace, to be in your room and sit in the middle of the floor.

She had thought—after the letter?—that there was a bond between them, not to be made explicit but to be relied on. And she had been wrong, she had scared him. Presumed too much. He had turned around and there was Polly. Because of Lorna's offense he had taken up with Polly.

Perhaps not, though. Perhaps he had simply changed. She thought of the extraordinary bareness of his room, the light on its walls. Out of that might come such altered versions of himself, created with no effort in the blink of an eye. That could be in response to something that had gone a little wrong, or to a realization that he could not carry something through. Or to nothing that definite—just the blink of an eye.

When Daniel had fallen into true sleep she went downstairs. In the bathroom she found that Polly had rinsed the diapers properly and put them in the pail, covered with the blue solution that would disinfect them. She picked up the suitcase that was sitting in the middle of the kitchen floor, carried it upstairs and laid it on the big bed, opening it to sort out which clothes had to be washed and which could be put away.

The window of this room looked out on the back yard. She heard voices—Elizabeth's raised, almost shrieking with the excitement of homecoming and perhaps the effort of keeping the attention of an enlarged audience, Brendan's authoritative but pleasant, giving an account of their trip.

She went to the window and looked down. She saw Brendan go over to the storage shed, unlock it, and start to drag out the children's wading pool. The door was swinging shut on him and Polly hurried to hold it open.

Lionel got up and went to uncoil the hose. She would not have thought he knew even where the hose was.

Brendan said something to Polly. Thanking her? You would think they were on the best of terms.

How had that happened?

It could be that Polly was now fit to be taken account of, being Lionel's choice. Lionel's choice, and not Lorna's imposition.

Or Brendan might simply be happier, because they had been away. He might have dropped for a while the burden of keeping his household in order. He might have seen, quite rightly, that this altered Polly was no threat.

A scene so ordinary and amazing, come about as if by magic. Everybody happy.

Brendan had begun to blow up the rim of the plastic pool. Elizabeth had stripped off to her underpants and was dancing around impatiently. Brendan hadn't bothered to tell her to run and put on her bathing suit, that underpants were not suitable. Lionel had turned the water on, and until it was needed for the pool he stood watering the nasturtiums, like any householder. Polly spoke to Brendan and he pinched the hole shut that he had been blowing into, passing the half-inflated heap of plastic over to her.

Lorna recalled that Polly had been the one to blow up the dolphin at the beach. As she said herself, she had good wind. She blew steadily and with no appearance of effort. She stood there in her shorts, her bare legs firmly apart, skin gleaming like birch bark. And Lionel watched her. Exactly what I need, he might be thinking. Such a competent and sensible woman, pliant but solid. Someone not vain or dreamy or dissatisfied. That might well be the sort of person he would marry someday. A wife who could take over. Then he would change and change again, maybe fall in love with some other woman, in his way, but the wife would be too busy to take notice.

That might happen. Polly and Lionel. Or it might not. Polly might go home as planned, and if she did, there wouldn't be any heartbreak. Or that was what Lorna thought. Polly would marry, or not marry, but whichever way it was, the things that happened with men would not be what broke her heart.

In a short time the rim of the wading pool was swollen and smooth. The pool was set on the grass, the hose placed inside it, and Elizabeth was splashing her feet in the water. She looked up at Lorna as if she had known she was there all the time.

"It's cold," she cried in a rapture. "Mommy—it's cold."

Now Brendan looked up at Lorna too.

"What are you doing up there?"

"Unpacking."

"You don't have to do that now. Come on outside."

"I will. In a minute."

Since she had entered the house—in fact since she had first understood that the voices she heard came from her own back yard and
belonged to Polly and Lionel—Lorna had not thought of the
vision she'd had, mile after mile, of Polly lashed to the back door.
She was surprised by it now as you sometimes are surprised, long
after waking, by the recollection of a dream. It had a dream's
potency and shamefulness. A dream's uselessness, as well.

Not quite at the same time, but in a lagging way, came the memory of her bargain. Her weak and primitive neurotic notion of a
bargain.

But what was it she had promised?

Nothing to do with the children.

Something to do with herself?

She had promised that she would do whatever she had to do,
when she recognized what it was.

That was hedging, it was a bargain that was not a bargain, a
promise that had no meaning at all.

But she tried out various possibilities. Almost as if she was
shaping this story to be told to somebody—not Lionel now—but
somebody, as an entertainment.

Give up reading books.

Take in foster children from bad homes and poor countries.
Labor to cure them of wounds and neglect.

Go to church. Agree to believe in God.

Cut her hair short, stop putting on makeup, never again haul her
breasts up into a wired brassiere.

She sat down on the bed, tired out by all this sport, this
irrelevance.

What made more sense was that the bargain she was bound to was
to go on living as she had been doing. The bargain was already in

force. To accept what had happened and be clear about what would happen. Days and years and feelings much the same, except that the children would grow up, and there might be one or two more of them and they too would grow up, and she and Brendan would grow older and then old.

It was not until now, not until this moment, that she had seen so clearly that she was counting on something happening, something that would change her life. She had accepted her marriage as one big change, but not as the last one.

So, nothing now but what she or anybody could sensibly foresee. That was to be her happiness, that was what she had bargained for. Nothing secret, or strange.

Pay attention to this, she thought. She had a dramatic notion of getting down on her knees. This is serious.

Elizabeth called again, "Mommy. Come here." And then the others—Brendan and Polly and Lionel, one after the other, were calling her, teasing her.

Mommy.

Mommy.

Come here.

It was a long time ago that this happened. In North Vancouver, when they lived in the Post and Beam house. When she was twenty-four years old, and new to bargaining.

What Is Remembered

In a hotel room in Vancouver, Meriel as a young woman is putting on her short white summer gloves. She wears a beige linen dress and a flimsy white scarf over her hair. Dark hair, at that time. She smiles because she has remembered something that Queen Sirikit of Thailand said, or was quoted as saying, in a magazine. A quote within a quote—something Queen Sirikit said that Balmain had said.

"Balmain taught me everything. He said, 'Always wear white gloves. It's best.'"

It's best. Why is she smiling at that? It seems so soft a whisper of advice, such absurd and final wisdom. Her gloved hands are formal, but tender-looking as a kitten's paws.

Pierre asks why she's smiling and she says, "Nothing," then tells him.

He says, "Who is Balmain?"

They were getting ready to go to a funeral. They had come over on the ferry last night from their home on Vancouver Island to be sure of being on time for the morning ceremony. It was the first time they'd stayed in a hotel since their wedding night. When they went on a holiday now it was always with their two children, and they looked for inexpensive motels that catered to families.

This was only the second funeral they had been to as a married couple. Pierre's father was dead, and Meriel's mother was dead, but these deaths had happened before Pierre and Meriel met. Last year a teacher at Pierre's school died suddenly, and there was a fine service, with the schoolboy choir and the sixteenth-century words for the Burial of the Dead. The man had been in his mid-sixties, and his death seemed to Meriel and Pierre only a little surprising and hardly sad. It did not make much difference, as they saw it, whether you died at sixty-five or seventy-five or eighty-five.

The funeral today was another matter. It was Jonas who was being buried. Pierre's best friend for years and Pierre's age— twenty-nine. Pierre and Jonas had grown up together in West Vancouver—they could remember it before the Lion's Gate Bridge was built, when it seemed like a small town. Their parents were friends. When they were eleven or twelve years old they had built a rowboat and launched it at Dundarave Pier. At the university they had parted company for a while—Jonas was studying to be an engineer, while Pierre was enrolled in Classics, and the Arts and Engineering students traditionally despised each other. But in the years since then the friendship had to some extent been revived. Jonas, who was not married, came to visit Pierre and Meriel, and sometimes stayed with them for a week at a time.

Both of these young men were surprised by what had happened in their lives, and they would joke about it. Jonas was the one whose choice of profession had seemed so reassuring to his parents, and had roused a muted envy in Pierre's parents, yet it was Pierre who had married and got a teaching job and taken on ordinary responsibilities, while Jonas, after university, had never settled down with a girl or a job. He was always on a sort of probation that did not end up in a firm attachment to any company, and the girls—at least to hear him tell it—were always on a sort of probation with him. His last engineering job was in the northern part of the province, and he stayed on there after he either quit or was fired. "Employment terminated by mutual consent," he wrote to Pierre, adding that he was living at the hotel, where all the high-class people lived, and might get a job on a logging crew. He was also learning to fly a plane, and thinking of becoming a bush pilot. He promised to come down for a visit when present financial complications were worked out.

Meriel had hoped that wouldn't happen. Jonas slept on the living-room couch and in the morning threw the covers on the floor for her to pick up. He kept Pierre awake half the night talking about things that had happened when they were teenagers, or even younger. His name for Pierre was Piss-hair, a nickname from those years, and he referred to other old friends as Stinkpool or Doc or Buster, never by the names Meriel had always heard—Stan or Don or Rick. He recalled with a gruff pedantry the details of incidents that Meriel did not think so remarkable or funny (the bag of dog shit set on fire on the teacher's front steps, the badgering of the old man who offered boys a nickel to pull down their pants), and grew irritated if the conversation turned to the present.

When she had to tell Pierre that Jonas was dead she was apologetic, shaken. Apologetic because she hadn't liked Jonas and shaken because he was the first person they knew well, in their own age group, to have died. But Pierre did not seem to be surprised or particularly stricken.

"Suicide," he said.

She said no, an accident. He was riding a motorcycle, after dark, on gravel, and he went off the road. Somebody found him, or was with him, help was at hand, but he died within an hour. His injuries were mortal.

That was what his mother had said, on the phone. *His injuries were mortal.* She had sounded so quickly resigned, so unsurprised. As Pierre did when he said, "Suicide."

After that Pierre and Meriel had hardly spoken about the death itself, just about the funeral, the hotel room, the need for an all-night sitter. His suit to be cleaned, a white shirt obtained. It was Meriel who made the arrangements, and Pierre kept checking up on her in a husbandly way. She understood that he wished her to be controlled and matter-of-fact, as he was, and not to lay claim to any sorrow which—he would be sure—she could not really feel. She had asked him why he had said, "Suicide," and he had told her, "That's just what came into my head." She felt his evasion to be some sort of warning or even a rebuke. As if he suspected her of deriving from this death—or from their proximity to this death—a feeling that was discreditable and self-centered. A morbid, preening excitement.

Young husbands were stern, in those days. Just a short time before, they had been suitors, almost figures of fun, knock-kneed and desperate in their sexual agonies. Now, bedded down, they turned resolute and disapproving. Off to work every morning, clean-shaven, youthful necks in knotted ties, days spent in unknown labors, home again at suppertime to take a critical glance at the evening meal and to shake out the newspaper, hold it up between themselves and the muddle of the kitchen, the ailments and emotions, the babies. What a lot they had to learn, so quickly. How to kowtow to bosses and how to manage wives. How to be authoritative about mortgages, retaining walls, lawn grass, drains, politics, as well as about the jobs that had to maintain their families for the next quarter of a century. It was the women, then, who could slip back—during the daytime hours, and always allowing for the stunning responsibility that had been landed on them, in the matter of the children—into a kind of second adolescence. A lightening of spirits when the husbands departed. Dreamy rebellion, subversive get-togethers, laughing fits that were a throwback to high school, mushrooming between the walls that the husband was paying for, in the hours when he wasn't there.

After the funeral some people had been invited back to Jonas's parents' house in Dundarave. The rhododendron hedge was in bloom, all red and pink and purple. Jonas's father was complimented on the garden.

"Well, I don't know," he said. "We had to get it in shape in a bit of a hurry."

Jonas's mother said, "This isn't a real lunch, I'm afraid. Just a pickup." Most people were drinking sherry, though some of the men had whisky. Food was set out on the extended dining-room table—salmon mousse and crackers, mushroom tarts, sausage rolls, a light lemon cake and cut-up fruit and pressed-almond cookies, as well as shrimp and ham and cucumber-and-avocado sandwiches. Pierre heaped everything onto his small china plate, and Meriel heard his mother say to him, "You know, you could always come back for a second helping."

His mother didn't live in West Vancouver anymore but had come in from White Rock for the funeral. And she wasn't quite confident about a direct reprimand, now that Pierre was a teacher and a married man.

"Or didn't you think there'd be any left?" she said.

Pierre said carelessly, "Maybe not of what I wanted."

His mother spoke to Meriel. "What a nice dress."

"Yes, but look," said Meriel, smoothing down the wrinkles that had formed while she sat through the service.

"That's the trouble," Pierre's mother said.

"What's the trouble?" said Jonas's mother brightly, sliding some tarts onto the warming-dish.

"That's the trouble with linen," said Pierre's mother. "Meriel was just saying how her dress had wrinkled up"—she did not say, "during the funeral service"—"and I was saying that's the trouble with linen."

Jonas's mother might not have been listening. Looking across the room, she said, "That's the doctor who looked after him. He flew down from Smithers in his own plane. Really, we thought that was so good of him."

Pierre's mother said, "That's quite a venture."

"Yes. Well. I suppose he gets around that way, to attend people in the bush."

The man they were talking about was speaking to Pierre. He was not wearing a suit, though he had a decent jacket on, over a turtlenecked sweater.

"I suppose he would," said Pierre's mother, and Jonas's mother said, "Yes," and Meriel felt as if something—about the way he was dressed?—had been explained and settled, between them.

She looked down at the table napkins, which were folded in quarters. They were not as big as dinner napkins or as small as cocktail napkins. They were set in overlapping rows so that a corner of each napkin (the corner embroidered with a tiny blue or pink or yellow flower) overlapped the folded corner of its neighbor. No two napkins embroidered with the same color of flower were touching each other. Nobody had disturbed them, or if they had—for she did see a few people around the room holding napkins—they had picked up napkins from the end of the row in a careful way and this order had been maintained.

At the funeral service, the minister had compared Jonas's life on earth to the life of a baby in the womb. The baby, he said, knows nothing of any other existence and inhabits its warm, dark, watery cave with not an inkling of the great bright world it will soon be thrust into. And we on earth have an inkling, but are really quite unable to imagine the light that we will enter after we have survived the travail of death. If the baby could somehow be informed of what would happen to it in the near future, would it not be incredulous, as well as afraid? And so are we, most of the time, but we should not be, for we have been given assurance. Even so, our blind brains cannot imagine, cannot conceive of, what we will pass into. The baby is lapped in its ignorance, in the faith of its dumb, helpless being. And we who are not entirely ignorant or entirely knowing must take care to wrap ourselves in our faith, in the word of our Lord.

Meriel looked at the minister, who stood in the hall doorway with a glass of sherry in his hand, listening to a vivacious woman with blond puffed hair. It didn't seem to her that they were talking about the pangs of death and the light ahead. What would he do if she walked over and tackled him on that subject?

Nobody would have the heart to. Or the bad manners.

Instead she looked at Pierre and the bush doctor. Pierre was talking with a boyish liveliness not often seen in him these days. Or not often seen by Meriel. She occupied herself by pretending that she was seeing him for the first time, now. His curly, short-cropped, very dark hair receding at the temples, baring the smooth, gold-tinged ivory skin. His wide, sharp shoulders and long, fine limbs and nicely shaped rather small skull. He smiled enchantingly but never strategically and seemed to distrust smiling altogether since he had become a teacher of boys. Faint lines of permanent fret were set in his forehead.

She thought of a teachers' party—more than a year ago—when she and he had found themselves, at opposite sides of the room, left out of the nearby conversations. She had circled the room and got close to him without his noticing, and then she had begun to talk to him as if she were a discreetly flirtatious stranger. He smiled as he was smiling now—but with a difference, as was natural when talking to an ensnaring woman—and he took up the charade. They exchanged charged looks and vapid speeches until they both broke down laughing. Someone came up to them and told them that married jokes were not allowed.

"What makes you think we're really married?" said Pierre, whose behavior at such parties was usually so circumspect.

She crossed the room to him now with no such foolishness in mind. She had to remind him that they must soon go their separate ways. He was driving to Horseshoe Bay to catch the next ferry, and she would have to get across the North Shore to Lynn Valley by bus. She had arranged to take this chance to visit a woman her dead mother had loved and admired, and in fact had named her daughter for, and whom Meriel had always called Aunt, though they were not related by blood. Aunt Muriel. (It was when she went away to college that Meriel had changed the spelling.) This old woman was living in a nursing home in Lynn Valley, and Meriel had not visited her for over a year. It took too much time to get there, on their infrequent family trips to Vancouver, and the children were upset by the atmosphere of the nursing home and the looks of the people who lived there. So was Pierre, though he did not like to say so. Instead, he asked what relation this person was to Meriel, anyway.

It's not as if she was a real aunt.

So now Meriel was going to see her by herself. She had said that she would feel guilty if she didn't go when she had the chance. Also, though she didn't say so, she was looking forward to the time that this would give her to be away from her family.

"Maybe I could drive you," Pierre said. "God knows how long you'll have to wait for the bus."

"You can't," she said. "You'd miss the ferry." She reminded him of their arrangement with the sitter.

He said, "You're right."

The man he'd been talking to—the doctor—had not had any choice but to listen to this conversation, and he said unexpectedly, "Let me drive you."

"I thought you came here in an airplane," said Meriel, just as Pierre said, "This is my wife, excuse me. Meriel."

The doctor told her a name which she hardly heard.

"It's not so easy landing a plane on Hollyburn Mountain," he said. "So I left it at the airport and rented a car."

Some slight forcing of courtesy, on his part, made Meriel think that she had sounded obnoxious. She was either too bold or too shy, much of the time.

"Would that really be okay?" Pierre said. "Do you have time?"

The doctor looked directly at Meriel. This was not a disagreeable look—it was not bold or sly, it was not appraising. But it was not socially deferential, either.

He said, "Of course."

So it was agreed that this was how it would be. They would start saying their good-byes now and Pierre would leave for the ferry and Asher, as his name was—or Dr. Asher—would drive Meriel to Lynn Valley.

What Meriel planned to do, after that, was to visit with Aunt Muriel—possibly even sitting through supper with her, then catch the bus from Lynn Valley to the downtown bus depot (buses to "town" were relatively frequent) and board the late-evening bus which would take her on to the ferry, and home.

The nursing home was called Princess Manor. It was a one-story building with extended wings, covered in pinkish-brown stucco. The street was busy, and there were no grounds to speak of, no hedges or screen-fences to shut out noise or protect the scraps of lawn. On one side there was a Gospel Hall with a joke of a steeple, on the other a gas station.

"The word 'Manor' doesn't mean anything at all anymore, does it?" said Meriel. "It doesn't even mean there's an upstairs. It just means that you're supposed to think that a place is something it doesn't even pretend to be."

The doctor said nothing—perhaps what she had said didn't make any sense to him. Or just wasn't worth saying even if it was true. All the way from Dundarave she had listened to herself talking and she had been dismayed. It wasn't so much that she was prattling—saying just anything that came into her head—rather that she was trying to express things which seemed to her interesting, or that might have been interesting if she could get them into shape. But these ideas probably sounded pretentious if not insane, rattled off in the way she was doing. She must seem like one of those women who were determined not to have an ordinary conversation but a *real* one. And even though she knew nothing was working, that her talk must seem to him an imposition, she was unable to stop herself.

She didn't know what had started this. Unease, simply because she so seldom talked to a stranger nowadays. The oddity of riding alone in a car with a man who wasn't her husband.

She had even asked, rashly, what he thought of Pierre's notion that the motorcycle accident was suicide.

"You could float that idea around about any number of violent accidents," he had said.

"Don't bother pulling into the drive," she said. "I can get out here." So embarrassed, so eager she was to get away from him and his barely polite indifference, that she put her hand on the door handle as if to open it while they were still moving along the street.

"I was planning to park," he said, turning in anyway. "I wasn't going to leave you stranded."

She said, "I might be quite a while."

"That's all right. I can wait. Or I could come in and look around. If you wouldn't mind that."

She was about to say that nursing homes can be dreary and unnerving. Then she remembered that he was a doctor and would see nothing here that he had not seen before. And something in the way he said "if you wouldn't mind that"—some formality, but also an uncertainty in his voice—surprised her. It seemed that he was making an offering of his time and his presence that had little to do with courtesy, but rather something to do with herself. It was an offer made with a touch of frank humility, but it was not a plea. If she had said that she would really rather not take up any more of his time, he would not have tried any further persuasion, he would have said good-bye with an even courtesy and driven away.

As it was, they got out of the car and walked side by side across the parking lot, towards the front entrance.

Several old or disabled people were sitting out on a square of pavement that had a few furry-looking shrubs and pots of petunias around it, to suggest a garden patio. Aunt Muriel was not among them, but Meriel found herself bestowing glad greetings. Something had happened to her. She had a sudden mysterious sense of power and delight, as if with every step she took, a bright message was travelling from her heels to the top of her skull.

When she asked him later, "Why did you come in there with me?" he said, "Because I didn't want to lose sight of you."

Aunt Muriel was sitting by herself, in a wheelchair, in the dim corridor just outside her own bedroom door. She was swollen and glimmering—but that was because of being swathed in an asbestos apron so she could smoke a cigarette. Meriel believed that when she had said good-bye to her, months and seasons ago, she had been sitting in the same chair in the same spot—though without the asbestos apron, which must accord with some new rule, or reflect some further decline. Very likely she sat here every day beside the fixed ashtray filled with sand, looking at the liverish painted wall—it was painted pink or mauve but it looked liverish, the corridor being so dim—with the bracket shelf on it supporting a spill of fake ivy.

"Meriel? I thought it was you," she said. "I could tell by your steps. I could tell by your breathing. My cataracts have got to be bloody hell. All I can see is blobs."

"It's me, all right, how are you?" Meriel kissed her temple. "Why aren't you out in the sunshine?"

"I'm not fond of sunshine," the old woman said. "I have to think of my complexion."

She might have been joking, but it was perhaps the truth. Her pale face and hands were covered with large spots—dead-white spots that caught what light there was here, turning silvery. She had been a true blonde, pink-faced, lean, with straight well-cut hair that had gone white in her thirties. Now the hair was ragged, mussed from being rubbed into pillows, and the lobes of her ears hung out of it like flat teats. She used to wear little diamonds in her ears—where had they gone? Diamonds in her ears, real gold chains, real pearls, silk shirts of unusual colors—amber, aubergine—and beautiful narrow shoes.

She smelled of hospital powder and the licorice drops she sucked all day between the rationed cigarettes.

"We need some chairs," she said. She leaned forward, waved the cigarette hand in the air, tried to whistle. "Service, please. Chairs."

The doctor said, "I'll find some."

The old Muriel and the young one were left alone.

"What's your husband's name?"

"Pierre."

"And you have the two children, don't you? Jane and David?"

"That's right. But the man who's with me—"

"Ah, no," the old Muriel said. "That's not your husband."

Aunt Muriel belonged to Meriel's grandmother's generation, rather than her mother's. She had been Meriel's mother's art teacher at school. First an inspiration, then an ally, then a friend. She had painted large abstract pictures, one of which—a present to Meriel's mother—had hung in the back hall of the house where Meriel grew up and had been moved to the dining room whenever the artist came to visit. Its colors were murky—dark reds and browns (Meriel's father called it "Manure Pile on Fire")—but Aunt Muriel's spirit seemed always bright and dauntless. She had lived in Vancouver when she was young, before she came to teach in this town in the interior. She had been friends with artists whose names were now in the papers. She longed to go back there and eventually did, to live with and manage the affairs of a rich old couple who were friends and patrons of artists. She seemed to have lots of money while she lived with them, but she was left out in the cold when they died. She lived on her pension, took up water-colors because she could not afford oils, starved herself (Meriel's mother suspected) so that she could take Meriel out to lunch—Meriel being then a university student. On these occasions she talked in a rush of jokes and judgments, mostly pointing out how works and ideas that people raved about were rubbish, but how here and there—in the output of some obscure contemporary or half-forgotten figure from another century—there was something extraordinary. That was her stalwart word of praise—"extraordinary." A hush in her voice, as if there and then and rather to her own surprise she had come upon a quality in the world that was still to be absolutely honored.

The doctor returned with two chairs and introduced himself, quite naturally, as if there'd been no chance to do it till now.

"Eric Asher."

"He's a doctor," said Meriel. She was about to start explaining about the funeral, the accident, the flight down from Smithers, but the conversation was taken away from her.

"But I'm not here officially, don't worry," the doctor said.

"Oh, no," said Aunt Muriel. "You're here with her."

"Yes," he said.

At this moment he reached across the space between their two chairs and picked up Meriel's hand, holding it for a moment in a hard grip, then letting it go. And he said to Aunt Muriel, "How could you tell that? By my breathing?"

"I could tell," she said with some impatience. "I used to be a devil myself."

Her voice—the quaver or titter in it—was not like any voice of hers that Meriel remembered. She felt as if there was some betrayal stirring, in this suddenly strange old woman. A betrayal of the past, perhaps of Meriel's mother and the friendship she had treasured with a superior person. Or of those lunches with Meriel herself, the rarefied conversations. Some degradation was in the offing. Meriel was upset by this, remotely excited.

"Oh, I used to have friends," Aunt Muriel said, and Meriel said, "You had lots of friends." She mentioned a couple of names.

"Dead," Aunt Muriel said.

Meriel said no, she had seen something just recently in the paper, a retrospective show or an award.

"Oh? I thought he was dead. Maybe I'm thinking of somebody else—Did you know the Delaneys?"

She spoke directly to the man, not to Meriel.

"I don't think so," he said. "No."

"Some people who had a place where we all used to go, on Bowen Island. The Delaneys. I thought you might have heard of them. Well. There were various goings-on. That's what I meant when I said I used to be a devil. Adventures. Well. It looked like adventures, but it was all according to script, if you know what I mean. So not so much of an adventure, actually. We all got drunk as skunks, of course. But they always had to have the candles lit in a circle and the music on, of course—more like a ritual. But not altogether. It didn't mean you mightn't meet somebody new and let the script go all to hell. Just meet for the first time and start kissing like mad and run off into the forest. In the dark. You couldn't get very far. Never mind. Struck down."

She had started to cough, tried speaking through the cough, gave up and hacked violently. The doctor got up and struck her expertly a couple of times, on her bent back. The coughing ended with a groan.

"Better," she said. "Oh, you knew what you were doing, but you pretended not to. One time they had a blindfold on me. Not out in the woods, this was inside. It was all right, I consented. It didn't work so well, though—I mean, I did know. There probably wasn't anybody there that I wouldn't have recognized, anyway."

She coughed again, though not so desperately as before. Then she raised her head, breathed deeply and noisily for a few minutes, holding up her hands to stall the conversation, as if she would soon have something more, something important, to say. But all she did, finally, was laugh and say, "Now I've got a permanent blindfold. Cataracts. Doesn't get me taken advantage of now, not in any debauch that I know about."

"How long have they been growing?" the doctor said with a respectful interest, and to Meriel's great relief there began an absorbed conversation, an informed discussion about the ripening of cataracts, their removal, the pros and cons of this operation, and Aunt Muriel's distrust of the eye doctor who was shunted off—as she said—to look after the people in here. Salacious fantasy—that was what Meriel now decided it had been—slid without the smallest difficulty into a medical chat, agreeably pessimistic on Aunt Muriel's side and carefully reassuring on the doctor's. The sort of conversation that must take place regularly within these walls.

In a little while there was a glance exchanged between Meriel and the doctor, asking whether the visit had lasted long enough. A stealthy, considering, almost married glance, its masquerade and its bland intimacy arousing to those who were after all not married.

Soon.

Aunt Muriel took the initiative herself. She said, "I'm sorry, it's rude of me, I have to tell you, I get tired." No hint in her manner, now, of the person who had launched the first part of the conversation. Distracted, play-acting, and with a vague sense of shame, Meriel bent over and kissed her good-bye. She had a feeling that she would never see Aunt Muriel again, and she never did.

Around a corner, with doors open on rooms where people lay asleep or perhaps watching from their beds, the doctor touched her between her shoulder blades and moved his hand down her back to her waist. She realized that he was picking at the cloth of her dress, which had stuck to her damp skin when she sat pressed against the chairback. The dress was also damp under her arms.

And she had to go to the bathroom. She kept looking for the Visitors' Washrooms, which she thought she had spotted when they were on their way in.

There. She was right. A relief, but also a difficulty, because she had to move suddenly out of his range and to say, "Just a moment," in a voice that sounded to herself distant and irritated. He said, "Yes," and briskly headed for the Men's, and the delicacy of the moment was lost.

When she went out into the hot sunlight she saw him pacing by the car, smoking. He hadn't smoked before—not in Jonas's parents' house or on the way here or with Aunt Muriel. The act seemed to isolate him, to show some impatience, perhaps an impatience to be done with one thing and get on to the next. She was not so sure now, whether she was the next thing or the thing to be done with.

"Where to?" he said, when they were driving. Then, as if he thought he had spoken too brusquely, "Where would you like to go?" It was almost as if he was speaking to a child, or to Aunt Muriel—somebody he was bound to entertain for the afternoon. And Meriel said, "I don't know," as if she had no choice but to let herself become that burdensome child. She was holding in a wail of disappointment, a clamor of desire. Desire that had seemed to be shy and sporadic but inevitable, yet was now all of a sudden declared inappropriate, one-sided. His hands on the wheel were all his own, reclaimed as if he had never touched her.

"How about Stanley Park?" He said. "Would you like to go for a walk in Stanley Park?"

She said, "Oh, Stanley Park. I haven't been there for ages," as if the idea had perked her up and she could imagine nothing better. And she made things worse by adding, "It's such a gorgeous day."

"It is. It is indeed."

They spoke like caricatures, it was unbearable.

"They don't give you a radio in these rented cars. Well, sometimes they do. Sometimes not."

She wound her window down as they crossed the Lion's Gate Bridge. She asked him if he minded.

"No. Not at all."

"It always means summer to me. To have the window down and your elbow out and the breeze coming in—I don't think I could ever get used to air-conditioning."

"Certain temperatures, you might."

She willed herself to silence, till the forest of the park received them, and the high, thick trees could perhaps swallow witlessness and shame. Then she spoiled everything by her too appreciative sigh.

"Prospect Point." He read the sign aloud.

There were plenty of people around, even though it was a weekday afternoon in May, with vacations not yet started. In a moment they might remark on that. There were cars parked all along the drive up to the restaurant, and line-ups on the viewing platform for the coin-use binoculars.

"Aha." He had spotted a car pulling out of its place. A reprieve for a moment from any need for speech, while he idled, backed to give it room, then maneuvered into the fairly narrow spot. They got out at the same time, walked around to meet on the sidewalk. He turned this way and that, as if deciding where they were to walk. Walkers coming and going on any path you could see.

Her legs were shaking, she could not put up with this any longer.

"Take me somewhere else," she said.

He looked her in the face. He said, "Yes."

There on the sidewalk in the world's view. Kissing like mad.

Take me, was what she had said. *Take me somewhere else,* not *Let's go somewhere else.* That is important to her. The risk, the transfer of power. Complete risk and transfer. *Let's go*—that would have the risk, but not the abdication, which is the start for her—in all her reliving of this moment—of the erotic slide. And what if he had abdicated in his turn? *Where* else? That would not have done, either. He has to say just what he did say. He has to say, *Yes*.

He took her to the apartment where he was staying, in Kitsilano. It belonged to a friend of his who was away on a fish boat, somewhere off the west coast of Vancouver Island. It was in a small, decent building, three or four stories high. All that she would remember about it would be the glass bricks around the front entrance and the elaborate, heavy hi-fi equipment of that time, which seemed to be the only furniture in the living room.

She would have preferred another scene, and that was the one she substituted, in her memory. A narrow six- or seven-story hotel, once a fashionable place of residence, in the West End of Vancouver. Curtains of yellowed lace, high ceilings, perhaps an iron grill over part of the window, a fake balcony. Nothing actually dirty or disreputable, just an atmosphere of long accommodation of private woes and sins. There she would have to cross the little lobby with head bowed and arms clinging to her sides, her whole body permeated by exquisite shame. And he would speak to the desk clerk in a low voice that did not advertise, but did not conceal or apologize for, their purpose.

Then the ride in the old-fashioned cage of the elevator, run by an old man—or perhaps an old woman, perhaps a cripple, a sly servant of vice.

Why did she conjure up, why did she add that scene? It was for the moment of exposure, the piercing sense of shame and pride that took over her body as she walked through the (pretend) lobby, and for the sound of his voice, its discretion and authority speaking to the clerk the words that she could not quite make out.

That might have been his tone in the drugstore a few blocks away from the apartment, after he had parked the car and said,

"Just a moment in here." The practical arrangements which seemed heavy-hearted and discouraging in married life could in these different circumstances provoke a subtle heat in her, a novel lethargy and submission.

After dark she was carried back again, driven through the park and across the bridge and through West Vancouver, passing only a short distance from the house of Jonas's parents. She arrived at Horseshoe Bay at almost the very last moment, and walked onto the ferry. The last days of May are among the longest of the year, and in spite of the ferry-dock lights and the lights of the cars streaming into the belly of the boat, she could see some glow in the western sky and against it the black mound of an island—not Bowen but one whose name she did not know—tidy as a pudding set in the mouth of the bay.

She had to join the crowd of jostling bodies making their way up the stairs, and when the passenger deck was reached she sat in the first seat she saw. She did not even bother as she usually did to look for a seat next to a window. She had an hour and a half before the boat docked on the other side of the strait, and during this time she had a great deal of work to do.

No sooner had the boat started to move than the people beside her began to talk. They were not casual talkers who had met on the ferry but friends or family who knew each other well and would find plenty to say for the entire crossing. So she got up and went out on deck, climbed to the top deck, where there were always fewer people, and sat on one of the bins that contained life preservers. She ached in expected and unexpected places.

The job she had to do, as she saw it, was to remember everything—and by "remember" she meant experience it in her mind, one more time—then store it away forever. This day's experience set in order, none of it left ragged or lying about, all of it gathered in like treasure and finished with, set aside.

She held on to two predictions, the first one comfortable, and the second easy enough to accept at present, though no doubt it would become harder for her, later on.

Her marriage with Pierre would continue, it would last.

She would never see Asher again.

Both of these turned out to be right.

Her marriage did last—for more than thirty years after that, until Pierre died. During an early and fairly easy stage of his illness, she read aloud to him, getting through a few books that they had both read years ago and meant to go back to. One of these was *Fathers and Sons*. After she had read the scene in which Bazarov declares his violent love for Anna Sergeyevna, and Anna is horrified, they broke off for a discussion. (Not an argument—they had grown too tender for that.)

Meriel wanted the scene to go differently. She believed that Anna would not react in that way.

"It's the writer," she said. "I don't usually ever feel that with Turgenev, but here I feel it's just Turgenev coming and yanking them apart and he's doing it for some purpose of his own."

Pierre smiled faintly. All his expressions had become sketchy. "You think she'd succumb?"

"No. Not succumb. I don't believe her, I think she's as driven as he is. They'd do it."

"That's romantic. You're wrenching things around to make a happy ending."

"I didn't say anything about the ending."

"Listen," said Pierre patiently. He enjoyed this sort of conversation, but it was hard on him, he had to take little rests to collect his strength. "If Anna gave in, it'd be because she loved him. When it was over she'd love him all the more. Isn't that what women are like? I mean if they're in love? And what he'd do—

he'd take off the next morning maybe without even speaking to her. That's his nature. He *hates* loving her. So how would that be any better?"

"They'd have something. Their experience."

"He would pretty well forget it and she'd die of shame and rejection. She's intelligent. She knows that."

"Well," said Meriel, pausing for a bit because she felt cornered. "Well, Turgenev doesn't say that. He says she's totally taken aback. He says she's cold."

"Intelligence makes her cold. Intelligent means cold, for a woman."

"No."

"I mean in the nineteenth century. In the nineteenth century, it does."

That night on the ferry, during the time when she thought she was going to get everything straightened away, Meriel did nothing of the kind. What she had to go through was wave after wave of intense recollection. And this was what she would continue to go through—at gradually lengthening intervals—for years to come. She would keep picking up things she'd missed, and these would still jolt her. She would hear or see something again—a sound they made together, the sort of look that passed between them, of recognition and encouragement. A look that was in its way quite cold, yet deeply respectful and more intimate than any look that would pass between married people, or people who owed each other anything.

She remembered his hazel-gray eyes, the close-up view of his coarse skin, a circle like an old scar beside his nose, the slick breadth of his chest as he reared up from her. But she could not have given a useful description of what he looked like. She believed that she had felt his presence so strongly, from the very beginning, that ordinary observation was not possible. Sudden recollection of even their early, unsure, and tentative moments could still make her fold in on herself, as if to protect the raw surprise of her own body, the racketing of desire. *My-love-my-love,* she would mutter in a harsh, mechanical way, the words a secret poultice.

When she saw his picture in the paper, no immediate pangs struck her. The clipping had been sent by Jonas's mother, who as long as she lived insisted on keeping in touch, and reminding them, whenever she could, of Jonas. "Remember the doctor at Jonas's funeral?" she had written above the small headline. "Bush Doctor Dead in Air Crash." It was an old picture, surely, blurred in its newspaper reproduction. A rather chunky face, smiling—which she would never have expected him to do for the camera. He hadn't died in his own plane but in the crash of a helicopter on an emergency flight. She showed the clipping to Pierre. She said, "Did you ever figure out why he came to the funeral?"

"They might have been buddies of a sort. All those lost souls up north."

"What did you talk to him about?"

"He told me about one time he took Jonas up to teach him to fly. He said, 'Never again.'"

Then he asked, "Didn't he drive you someplace? Where?"

"To Lynn Valley. To see Aunt Muriel."

"So what did you talk about?"

"I found him hard to talk to."

The fact that he was dead did not seem to have much effect on her daydreams—if that was what you could call them. The ones in which she imagined chance meetings or even desperately arranged reunions, had never had a foothold on reality, in any case, and were not revised because he was dead. They had to wear themselves out in a way she did not control and never understood.

When she was on her way home that night it had started to rain, not very hard. She had stayed out on the deck of the ferry. She got up and walked around and could not sit down again on the lid of the life-jacket bin without getting a big wet spot on her dress. So she stayed looking at the froth stirred up in the wake of the boat, and the thought occurred to her that in a certain kind of story—not the kind that anybody wrote anymore—the thing for her to do would be to throw herself into the water. Just as she was, packed full of happiness, rewarded as she would surely never be again, every cell in her body plumped up with a sweet self-esteem. A romantic act that could be seen—from a forbidden angle—as supremely rational.

Was she tempted? She was probably just letting herself imagine being tempted. Probably nowhere near yielding, though yielding had been the order of that day.

It wasn't until after Pierre was dead that she remembered one further detail.

Asher had driven her to Horseshoe Bay, to the ferry. He had got out of the car and come around to her side. She was standing there, waiting to say good-bye to him. She made a move towards him, to kiss him—surely a natural thing to do, after the last few hours—and he had said, "No."

"No," he said. "I never do."

Of course that wasn't true, that he never did. Never kissed out in the open, where anybody could see. He had done it just that afternoon, at Prospect Point.

No.

That was simple. A cautioning. A refusal. Protecting her, you might say, as well as himself. Even if he hadn't bothered about that, earlier in the day.

I never do was something else altogether. Another kind of cautioning. Information that could not make her happy, though it might be intended to keep her from making a serious mistake. To save her from the false hopes and humiliation of a certain kind of mistake.

How did they say good-bye, then? Did they shake hands? She could not remember.

But she heard his voice, the lightness and yet the gravity of his tone, she saw his resolute, merely pleasant face, she felt the slight shift out of her range. She didn't doubt that the recollection was true. She did not see how she could have suppressed it so successfully, for all this time.

She had an idea that if she had not been able to do that, her life might have been different.

How?

She might not have stayed with Pierre. She might not have been able to keep her balance. Trying to match what had been said at the ferry with what had been said and done earlier the same day would have made her more alert and more curious. Pride or contrariness might have played a part—a need to have some man eat those words, a refusal to learn her lesson—but that wouldn't have been all. There was another sort of life she could have had—which was not to say she would have preferred it. It was probably because of her age (something she was always forgetting to take account of) and because of the thin cool air she breathed since Pierre's death, that she could think of that other sort of life simply as a kind of research which had its own pitfalls and achievements.

Maybe you didn't find out so much, anyway. Maybe the same thing over and over—which might be some obvious but unsettling fact about yourself. In her case, the fact that prudence—or at least some economical sort of emotional management—had been her guiding light all along.

The little self-preserving movement he made, the kind and deadly caution, the attitude of inflexibility that had grown a bit stale with him, like an outmoded swagger. She could view him now with an everyday mystification, as if he had been a husband.

She wondered if he'd stay that way, or if she had some new role waiting for him, some use still to put him to in her mind, during the time ahead.

Queenie

"Maybe you better stop calling me that," Queenie said, when she met me at Union Station.

I said, "What? Queenie?"

"Stan doesn't like it," she said. "He says it reminds him of a horse."

It was more of a surprise to me to hear her say "Stan" than it was to have her let me know she wasn't Queenie anymore, she was Lena. But I could hardly have expected that she would still be calling her husband Mr. Vorguilla after a year and a half of marriage. During that time I hadn't seen her, and when I'd caught sight of her a moment ago, in the group of people waiting in the station, I almost hadn't recognized her.

Her hair was dyed black and puffed up around her face in whatever style it was that in those days succeeded the beehive. Its beautiful corn-syrup color—gold on top and dark underneath—as well as its silky length, was forever lost. She wore a yellow print dress that skimmed her body and ended inches above her knees. The Cleopatra lines drawn heavily around her eyes, and the purply shadow, made her eyes seem smaller, not larger, as if they were deliberately hiding. She had pierced ears now, gold hoops swinging from them.

I saw her look at me with some surprise as well. I tried to be bold and easygoing. I said, "Is that a dress or a frill around your bum?" She laughed, and I said, "Was it ever hot on the train. I'm sweating like a pig."

I could hear how my voice sounded, as twangy and hearty as my stepmother Bet's.

Sweating like a pig.

Now on the streetcar going to Queenie's place I couldn't stop sounding stupid. I said, "Are we still downtown?" The high buildings had been quickly left behind, but I didn't think you could call this area residential. The same sort of shops and buildings went on over and over again—a dry cleaner, a florist, a grocery store, a restaurant. Boxes of fruit and vegetables out on the sidewalk, signs for dentists and dressmakers and plumbing suppliers in the second-story windows. Hardly a building higher than that, hardly a tree.

"It's not the real downtown," said Queenie. "Remember I showed you where Simpson's was? Where we got on the streetcar? That's the real."

"So are we nearly there?" I said.

She said, "We got a ways to go yet."

Then she said, "'Way.' Stan doesn't like me saying 'ways' either."

The repetition of things, or maybe the heat, was making me feel anxious and rather sick. We were holding my suitcase on our knees and only a couple of inches ahead of my fingers was a man's fat neck and bald head. A few black, sweaty long hairs clung to his scalp. For some reason I had to think of Mr. Vorguilla's teeth in the medicine cabinet, which Queenie showed me when she worked for the Vorguillas next door. That was long before Mr. Vorguilla could ever be thought of as Stan.

Two joined teeth sitting beside his razor and shaving brush and the wooden bowl holding his hairy and disgusting shaving soap.

"That's his bridge," Queenie had said.

Bridge?

"Bridge of teeth."

"Yuck," I said.

"These are his extras," she said. "He's wearing his others."

"Yuck. Aren't they yellow?"

Queenie put her hand over my mouth. She didn't want Mrs. Vorguilla to hear us. Mrs. Vorguilla was lying downstairs on the dining-room couch. Her eyes were closed most of the time, but she might not be sleeping.

When we got off the streetcar at last we had to walk up a steep hill, trying awkwardly to share the weight of the suitcase. The houses were not quite all the same, though at first they looked like it. Some of the roofs came down over the walls like caps, or else the whole second story was like a roof, and covered in shingles. The shingles were dark green or maroon or brown. The porches came to within a few feet of the sidewalk, and the spaces between the houses seemed narrow enough for people to reach out the side windows and shake hands. Children were playing on the sidewalk, but Queenie took no more notice of them than if they were birds pecking in the cracks. A very fat man, naked from the waist up, sat on his front steps staring at us in such a fixed and gloomy way that I was sure he had something to say. Queenie marched on past him.

She turned in partway up the hill, following a gravel path between some garbage tins. Out of an upstairs window a woman called something that I found unintelligible. Queenie called back, "It's just my sister, she's visiting."

"Our landlady," she said. "They live in the front and upstairs. They're Greeks. She doesn't speak hardly any English."

It turned out that Queenie and Mr. Vorguilla shared a bathroom with the Greeks. You took your roll of toilet paper with you—if you forgot, there wasn't any. I had to go in there at once, because I was menstruating heavily and had to change my pad. For years afterwards, the sight of certain city streets on hot days, certain shades of brown brick and dark-painted shingles, and the noise of streetcars, would bring back to me the memory of cramps low in the belly, waves of flushing, bodily leaks, hot confusion.

There was one bedroom where Queenie slept with Mr. Vorguilla, and another bedroom turned into a small living room, and a narrow kitchen, and a sunporch. The cot on the sunporch was where I was to sleep. Close outside the windows the landlord and another man were fixing a motorcycle. The smell of oil, of metal and machinery mixed with the smell of ripe tomatoes in the sun. There was a radio blaring music out an upstairs window.

"One thing Stan can't stand," said Queenie. "That radio." She pulled the flowered curtains closed, but the noise and sun still came through. "I wish I could've afforded lining," she said.

I had the bloody pad wrapped up in toilet paper, in my hand. She brought me a paper bag and directed me to the outdoor garbage pail. "Every one of them," she said. "Out there right away. You won't forget, will you? And don't leave your box any place he can see it; he hates being reminded."

I still tried to be nonchalant, to act as if I felt at home. "I need to get a nice cool dress like yours," I said.

"Maybe I could make you one," said Queenie, with her head in the fridge. "I want a Coke, do you? I just go to this place they sell remnants. I made this whole dress for around three dollars. What size are you now, anyway?"

I shrugged. I said that I was trying to lose weight.

"Well. We could maybe find something."

"I am going to marry a lady that has a little girl about your age," my father had said. "And this little girl has not got her father around. So you have to promise me one thing and that is that you will never tease her or say anything mean to her about that.

There'll be times when you may get in a fight and disagree with each other the way sisters do, but that is one thing you must never say. And if other kids say it you never take their side."

For the sake of argument, I said that I did not have a mother and nobody said anything mean to me.

My father said, "That's different."

He was wrong about everything. We did not seem anywhere near the same age, because Queenie was nine when my father married Bet and I was six. Though later, after I had skipped a grade and Queenie had failed one, we came closer together in school. And I never knew anyone to try to be mean to Queenie. She was somebody everybody wanted to be friends with. She was chosen first for a baseball team even though she was a careless baseball player, and first for a spelling team though she was a poor speller. Also, she and I did not get into fights. Not once. She showed plenty of kindness towards me and I had plenty of admiration for her. I would have worshipped her for her dark-gold hair and her sleepy-looking dark eyes—for her looks and her laugh alone. Her laugh was sweet and rough like brown sugar. The surprise was that with all her advantages she could be tenderhearted and kind.

As soon as I woke up on the morning of Queenie's disappearance, that morning in early winter, I felt her gone.

It was still dark, between six and seven o'clock. The house was cold. I pulled on the big woolly brown bathrobe that Queenie and I shared. We called it Buffalo Bill and whichever of us got out of bed first in the morning would grab it. A mystery where it came from.

"Maybe a friend of Bet's before she married your dad," Queenie said. "But don't say anything, she'd kill me."

Her bed was empty and she wasn't in the bathroom. I went down the stairs not turning any lights on, not wanting to wake Bet. I looked out the little window in the front door. The hard pavement, the sidewalk, and the flat grass in the front yard all glittering with frost. The snow was late. I turned up the hall thermostat and the furnace rolled over in the dark, gave its reliable growl. We had just got the oil furnace and my father said he still woke up at five every morning, thinking it was time to go down to the cellar and build up the fire.

My father slept in what had been a pantry, off the kitchen. He had an iron bed and a broken-backed chair he kept his stack of old *National Geographic*s on, to read when he couldn't sleep. He turned the ceiling light off and on by a cord tied to the bed frame. This whole arrangement seemed to me quite natural and proper for the man of the house, the father. He should sleep like a sentry with a coarse blanket for cover and an unhousebroken smell about him of engines and tobacco. Reading and wakeful till all hours and alert all through his sleep.

Even so, he hadn't heard Queenie. He said she must be somewhere in the house. "Did you look in the bathroom?"

I said, "She's not there."

"Maybe in with her mother. Case of the heebie-jeebies."

My father called it the heebie-jeebies when Bet woke up—or didn't quite wake up—from a bad dream. She would come blundering out of her room unable to say what had frightened her, and Queenie had to be the one to guide her back to bed. Queenie would curl against her back, making comforting noises like a puppy lapping milk, and Bet would not remember anything in the morning.

I had turned the kitchen light on.

"I didn't want to wake her," I said. "Bet."

I looked at the rusty-bottomed bread tin swiped too often by the dishcloth, and the pots sitting on the stove, washed but not put away, and the motto supplied by Fairholme Dairy: *The Lord Is the Heart of Our House.* All these things stupidly waiting for the day to begin and not knowing that it had been hollowed out by catastrophe.

The door to the side porch had been unlocked.

"Somebody came in," I said. "Somebody came in and took Queenie."

My father came out with his trousers on over his long underwear. Bet was slapping downstairs in her slippers and her chenille robe, flicking on lights as she came.

"Queenie not in with you?" my father said. To me he said, "The door had to've been unlocked from the inside."

Bet said, "What's this about Queenie?"

"She might just have felt like a walk," my father said.

Bet ignored this. She had a mask of some pink stuff dried on her face. She was a Sales Representative for beauty products, and she never sold any cosmetic she had not tried on herself.

"You get over to Vorguillas'," she said to me. "She might've thought of something she was supposed to do over there."

This was a week or so after Mrs. Vorguilla's funeral, but Queenie had kept on working there, helping to box up dishes and linens so that Mr. Vorguilla could move into an apartment. He had the Christmas concerts at school to get ready for and could not do all the packing himself. Bet wanted Queenie to just quit, so that she could get taken on for Christmas help at one of the stores.

I put on my father's rubber boots that were by the door, instead of going upstairs for my shoes. I stumbled across the yard to the Vorguillas' porch and rang the bell. It was a chime, which seemed to proclaim the musicality of the household. I hugged Buffalo Bill tight around me and prayed. Oh, Queenie, Queenie, turn the lights on. I forgot that if Queenie was working in there, the lights would be on already.

No answer. I pounded on the wood. Mr. Vorguilla was going to be in a bad temper when I finally woke him. I pressed my head to the door, listening for stirrings.

"Mr. Vorguilla. Mr. Vorguilla. I'm sorry to wake you, Mr. Vorguilla. Is anybody home?"

A window was heaved up in the house on the other side of the Vorguillas'. Mr. Hovey, an old bachelor, lived there with his sister.

"Use your eyes," Mr. Hovey called down. "Look in the driveway."

Mr. Vorguilla's car was gone.

Mr. Hovey slammed down the window.

When I opened our kitchen door I saw my father and Bet sitting at the table with cups of tea in front of them. For a minute I thought that order had been restored. There had been a phone call, perhaps, with some pacifying news.

"Mr. Vorguilla isn't there," I said. "His car's gone."

"Oh, we know that," Bet said. "We know all about that."

My father said, "Look at here," and pushed a piece of paper across the table.

I am going to marry Mr. Vorguilla, it said. *Yours truly, Queenie.*

"Underneath the sugar bowl," said my father.

Bet dropped her spoon.

"I want him prosecuted," she shouted. "I want her in Reform School. I want the police."

My father said, "She's eighteen years old and she can get married if she wants to. The police aren't going to set up a roadblock."

"Who says they're on the road? They're shacked up in some motel. That fool of a girl and that bug-eyed pickle-ass Vorguilla."

"Talk like that isn't going to bring her back."

"I don't want her back. Not if she comes crawling. She's made her bed and she can lie in it with her bug-eyed bugger. He can screw her in the ear for all I care."

My father said, "That's enough."

Queenie brought me a couple of 222's to take with my Coke.

"It's amazing how your cramps clear up, once you get married. So—your dad went and told you about us?"

When I had let my father know that I wanted to get a summer job before entering Teachers' College in the fall, he had said that maybe I should go to Toronto and look up Queenie. He said that she had written to him in care of his trucking business, asking if he could let them have some money to tide them over the winter.

"I would've never had to write to him," Queenie said, "if Stan hadn't got sick last year with pneumonia."

I said, "It was the first I knew where you were." Tears came into my eyes, I didn't know why. Because I'd felt so happy when I found out, so lonely before I found out, because I wished right now that she would say, "Of course, I always meant to get in touch with *you*," and she didn't say it.

"Bet doesn't know," I said. "She thinks I'm on my own."

"I hope not," Queenie said calmly. "I mean I hope she doesn't know."

I had a lot of things to tell her, about home. I told her that the trucking firm had gone from three vehicles to a dozen, and that Bet had bought a muskrat coat and expanded her business, holding Beauty Clinics now in our house. For these purposes she had fixed up the room where my father used to sleep, and he had moved his cot and the *National Geographic*s to his office—an Air Force billet he had towed to the trucking yard. Sitting at the kitchen table studying for my Senior Matric I had listened to Bet say, "A skin this delicate, you should never go near it with a washcloth," prior to loading up some raw-faced woman with lotions and creams. And sometimes in a no less intense, but less hopeful tone, "I'm telling you I had Evil, I had Evil living right next door to me and I never suspected it, because you don't, do you? I always think the best of people. Right up till they kick me in the teeth."

"That's right," the customer would say. "I'm the same."

Or, "You think you know what sorrow is, but you don't know half."

Then Bet would come back from seeing the woman to the door

and groan and say, "Touch her face in the dark and you'd never know the difference from sandpaper."

Queenie didn't seem interested in hearing about these things. And there was not much time, anyway. Before we had finished our Cokes there were quick hard steps on the gravel and Mr. Vorguilla came into the kitchen.

"So look who's here," cried Queenie. She half got up, as if to touch him, but he veered towards the sink.

Her voice was full of such laughing surprise that I wondered if he had been told anything about my letter or the fact that I was on my way.

"It's Chrissy," she said.

"So I see," said Mr. Vorguilla. "You must like hot weather, Chrissy, if you come to Toronto in the summer."

"She's going to look for a job," said Queenie.

"And do you have some qualifications?" Mr. Vorguilla asked. "Do you have qualifications for finding a job in Toronto?"

Queenie said, "She's got her Senior Matric."

"Well, let's hope that's good enough," said Mr. Vorguilla. He ran a glass of water and drank it all down, standing with his back to us. Exactly as he used to do when Mrs. Vorguilla and Queenie and I were sitting at the kitchen table in that other house, the Vorguillas' house next door. Mr. Vorguilla would come in from a practice somewhere, or he would be taking a break from teaching a piano lesson in the front room. At the sound of his steps Mrs. Vorguilla would have given us a warning smile. And we all looked down at our Scrabble letters, giving him the option of noticing us or not. Sometimes he didn't. The opening of the cupboard, the turning of the tap, the setting of the glass down on the counter were like a series of little explosions. As if he dared anybody to breathe while he was there.

When he taught us music at school he was just the same. He came into the classroom with the step of a man who had not a minute to lose and he rapped the pointer once and it was time to start. Up and down the aisles he strutted with his ears cocked, his bulgy blue eyes alert, his expression tense and quarrelsome. At any moment he might stop by your desk to listen to your singing, to see if you were faking or out of tune. Then he'd bring his head slowly down, his eyes bulging into yours and his hands working to shush the other voices, to bring you to your shame. And the word was that he was just as much a dictator with his various choirs and glee clubs. Yet he was a favorite with his singers, particularly with ladies. They knit him things at Christmas. Socks and mufflers and mitts to keep him warm on his trips between school and school and choir and choir.

When Queenie had the run of the house, after Mrs. Vorguilla got too sick to manage, she fished out of a drawer a knitted object that she flapped in front of my face. It had arrived without the name of its donor.

I couldn't tell what it was.

"It's a peter-heater," Queenie said. "Mrs. Vorguilla said don't show it to him, he would just get mad. Don't you know what a peter-heater is?"

I said, "Ugh."

"It's just a joke."

Both Queenie and Mr. Vorguilla had to go out to work in the evenings. Mr. Vorguilla played the piano in a restaurant. He wore a tuxedo. And Queenie had a job selling tickets in a movie theater. The theater was just a few blocks away, so I walked there with her. And when I saw her sitting in the ticket booth I understood that the makeup and the dyed puffed hair and the hoop earrings were not so strange after all. Queenie looked like some of the girls passing on the street or going in to see the movie with their boyfriends. And she looked very much like some of the girls portrayed in the posters that surrounded her. She looked to be connected to the world of drama, of heated love affairs and dangers, that was being depicted inside on the screen.

She looked—in my father's words—as if she didn't have to take a back seat to anybody.

"Why don't you just wander around for a while?" she had said to me. But I felt conspicuous. I couldn't imagine sitting in a cafe drinking coffee and advertising to the world that I had nothing to do and no place to go. Or going into a store and trying on clothes that I had no hope of buying. I climbed the hill again, I waved hello to the Greek woman calling out her window. I let myself in with Queenie's key.

I sat on the cot on the sunporch. There was nowhere to hang up the clothes I had brought, and I thought it might not be such a good idea to unpack, anyway. Mr. Vorguilla might not like to see any sign that I was staying.

I thought that Mr. Vorguilla's looks had changed, just as Queenie's had. But his had not changed, as hers had, in the direction of what seemed to me a hard foreign glamour and sophistication. His hair, which had been reddish-gray, was now quite gray, and the expression of his face—always ready to flash with outrage at the possibility of disrespect or an inadequate performance or just at the fact of something in his house not being where it was supposed to be—seemed now to be one of more permanent grievance, as if some insult was being offered or bad behavior going unpunished all the time, in front of his eyes.

I got up and walked around the apartment. You can never get a good look at the places people live in while they are there.

The kitchen was the nicest room, though too dark. Queenie had ivy growing up around the window over the sink, and she had wooden spoons sticking up out of a pretty, handleless mug, just the way Mrs. Vorguilla used to have them. The living room had the piano in it, the same piano that had been in the other living room. There was one armchair and a bookshelf made with bricks and planks and a record player and a lot of records sitting on the floor.

No television. No walnut rocking chairs or tapestry curtains. Not even the floor lamp with the Japanese scenes on its parchment shade. Yet all these things had been moved to Toronto, on a snowy day. I had been home at lunchtime and had seen the moving truck. Bet couldn't keep away from the window in the front door. Finally she forgot all the dignity she usually liked to show to strangers and opened the door and yelled at the moving men. "You go back to Toronto and tell him if he ever shows his face around here again he'll wish he hadn't."

The moving men waved cheerfully, as if they were used to scenes like this, and maybe they were. Moving furniture must expose you to a lot of ranting and raging.

But where had everything gone? Sold, I thought. It must have been sold. My father had said that it sounded as if Mr. Vorguilla was having a hard time getting going down in Toronto in his line of work. And Queenie had said something about "getting behind." She would never have written to my father if they hadn't gotten behind.

They must have sold the furniture before she wrote.

On the bookshelf I saw *The Encyclopedia of Music,* and *The World Companion to Opera,* and *The Lives of the Great Composers.* Also the large, thin book with the beautiful cover—the *Rubaiyat of Omar Khayyám*—that Mrs. Vorguilla often had beside her couch.

There was another book with a similarly decorated cover whose exact title I don't remember. Something in the title made me think I might like it. The word "flowered" or "perfumed." I opened it up, and I can remember well enough the first sentence I read.

"The young odalisques in the harim were also instructed in the exquisite use of their fingernails."

I was not sure what an odalisque was, but the word "harim" (why not "harem"?) gave me a clue. And I had to read on, to find out what they were taught to do with their fingernails. I read on and on, maybe for an hour, and then let the book fall to the floor. I had feelings of excitement, and disgust, and disbelief. Was this the sort of thing that really grown-up people took an interest in? Even the design on the cover, the pretty vines all curved and twisted, seemed slightly hostile and corrupt. I picked the book up to put it back in its place and it fell open to show the names on the flyleaf. Stan and Marigold Vorguilla. In a feminine handwriting. Stan and Marigold.

I thought of Mrs. Vorguilla's high white forehead and tight little gray-black curls. Her pearl-button earrings and blouses that tied with a bow at the neck. She was taller by quite a bit than Mr. Vorguilla and people thought that was why they did not go out together. But it was really because she got out of breath. She got out of breath walking upstairs, or hanging the clothes on the line. And finally she got out of breath even sitting at the table playing Scrabble.

At first my father would not let us take any money for fetching her groceries or hanging up her washing—he said it was only neighborly.

Bet said she thought she would try laying around and see if people would come and wait on her for nothing.

Then Mr. Vorguilla came over and negotiated for Queenie to go and work for them. Queenie wanted to go because she had failed her year at high school and didn't want to repeat it. At last Bet said all right, but told her she was not to do any nursing.

"If he's too cheap to hire a nurse that's not your lookout."

Queenie said that Mr. Vorguilla put out the pills every morning and gave Mrs. Vorguilla a sponge bath every evening. He even tried to wash her sheets in the bathtub, as if there was not such a thing as a washing machine in the house.

I thought of the times when we would be playing Scrabble in the kitchen and Mr. Vorguilla after drinking his glass of water would put a hand on Mrs. Vorguilla's shoulder and sigh, as if he had come back from a long, wearying journey.

"Hello, pet," he would say.

Mrs. Vorguilla would duck her head to give his hand a dry kiss.

"Hello, pet," she would say.

Then he would look at us, at Queenie and me, as if our presence did not absolutely offend him.

"Hello, you two."

Later on Queenie and I would giggle in our beds in the dark.

"Good night, pet."

"Good night, pet."

How much I wished that we could go back to that time.

Except for going to the bathroom in the morning and sneaking out to put my pad in the garbage pail, I sat on my made-up cot in the sunporch until Mr. Vorguilla was out of the house. I was afraid he might not have any place to go, but apparently he did. As soon as he was gone Queenie called to me. She had set out a peeled orange and cornflakes and coffee.

"And here's the paper," she said. "I was looking at the Help Wanteds. First, though, I want to do something with your hair. I want to cut some off the back and I want to do it up in rollers. Okay with you?"

I said okay. Even while I was eating, Queenie kept circling me and looking at me, trying to work out her idea. Then she got me up on a stool—I was still drinking my coffee—and she began to comb and snip.

"What kind of a job are we looking for, now?" she asked. "I saw one at a dry cleaner's. At the counter. How would that be?"

I said, "That'd be fine."

"Are you still planning on being a schoolteacher?"

I said I didn't know. I had an idea that she might think that a drab sort of occupation.

"I think you should be. You're smart enough. Teachers get paid more. They get paid more than people like me. You've got more independence."

But it was all right, she said, working at the movie theater. She had got the job a month or so before last Christmas, and she was really happy then because she had her own money at last and could buy the ingredients for a Christmas cake. And she became friends with a man who was selling Christmas trees off the back of a truck. He let her have one for fifty cents, and she hauled it up the hill herself. She hung streamers of red and green crepe paper, which was cheap. She made some ornaments out of silver foil on cardboard and bought others on the day before Christmas when they went on sale in the drugstore. She made cookies and hung them on the tree as she had seen in a magazine. It was a European custom.

She wanted to have a party, but she didn't know who to ask. There were the Greek people, and Stan had a couple of friends. Then she got the idea of asking his students.

I still couldn't get used to her saying "Stan." It wasn't just the reminder of her intimacy with Mr. Vorguilla. It was that, of course. But it was also the feeling it gave, that she had made him up from scratch. A new person. Stan. As if there had never been a Mr. Vorguilla that we had known together—let alone a Mrs. Vorguilla—in the first place.

Stan's students were all adults now—he really preferred adults to schoolchildren—so they didn't have to worry about the sort of games and entertainment you plan for children. They held the party on a Sunday evening, because all the other evenings were taken up with Stan's work at the restaurant and Queenie's at the theater.

The Greeks brought wine they had made and some of the students brought eggnog mix and rum and sherry. And some brought records you could dance to. They had thought that Stan wouldn't have any records of that kind of music, and they were right.

Queenie made sausage rolls and gingerbread and the Greek woman brought her own kind of cookies. Everything was good. The party was a success. Queenie danced with a Chinese boy named Andrew, who had brought a record she loved.

"Turn, turn, turn," she said, and I moved my head as directed. She laughed and said, "No, no, I didn't mean you. That's the record. That's the song. It's by the Byrds."

"Turn, turn, turn," she sang. "To everything, there is a season—"

Andrew was a dentistry student. But he wanted to learn to play the *Moonlight Sonata*. Stan said that was going to take him a long time. Andrew was patient. He told Queenie that he could not afford to go home to Northern Ontario for Christmas.

"I thought he was from China," I said.

"No, not Chinese Chinese. From here."

They did play one children's game. They played musical chairs. Everybody was boisterous by that time. Even Stan. He pulled Queenie down into his lap when she was running past, and he wouldn't let her go. And then when everybody had gone he wouldn't let her clean up. He just wanted her to come to bed.

"You know the way men are," Queenie said. "Do you have a boyfriend yet, or anything?"

I said no. The last man my father had hired as a driver was always coming to the house to deliver some unimportant message, and my father said, "He just wants a chance to talk to Chrissy." I was cool to him, however, and so far he hadn't got up the nerve to ask me out.

"So you don't really know about that stuff yet?" said Queenie.

I said, "Sure I do."

"Hmm hmm," she said.

The guests at the party had eaten up nearly everything but the cake. They did not eat much of that, but Queenie wasn't offended. It was very rich, and by the time they got to it they were filled up with sausage rolls and other things. Also, it had not had time to ripen the way the book said it should, so she was just as glad to have some left over. She was thinking, before Stan pulled her away, that she should get the cake wrapped up in a wine-soaked cloth and put it in a cool place. She was either thinking of doing that or she was actually doing it, and in the morning she saw that the cake was not on the table, so she thought she had done it. She thought, Good, the cake was put away.

A day or so later Stan said, "Let's have a piece of that cake." She said, Oh, let it ripen a bit more, but he insisted. She went to the cupboard and then to the refrigerator, but it was not there. She looked high and low and she could not find it. She thought back to seeing it on the table. And a memory came to her, of getting a clean cloth and soaking it in wine and wrapping it carefully around the leftover cake. And then of wrapping waxed paper around the outside of the cloth. But when had she done that? Had she done it at all or only dreamed about it? Where had she put the cake when she finished wrapping it? She tried to see herself putting it away, but her mind went blank.

She looked all through the cupboard, but she knew the cake was too big to be hidden there. Then she looked in the oven and even in insane places like her dresser drawers and under the bed and on the closet shelf. It was nowhere.

"If you put it somewhere, then it must be somewhere," Stan said.

"I did. I put it somewhere," said Queenie.

"Maybe you were drunk and you threw it out," he said.

She said, "I wasn't drunk. I didn't throw it out."

But she went and looked in the garbage. No.

He sat at the table watching her. If you put it somewhere it must be somewhere. She was getting frantic.

"Are you sure?" said Stan. "Are you sure you didn't just give it away?"

She was sure. She was sure she hadn't given it away. She had wrapped it up to keep. She was sure, she was almost sure she had wrapped it to keep. She was sure she had not given it away.

"Oh, I don't know about that," Stan said. "I think maybe you gave it away. And I think I know who to."

Queenie was brought to a standstill. Who to?

"I think you gave it to Andrew."

To Andrew?

Oh, yes. Poor Andrew, who was telling her he couldn't afford to go home for Christmas. She was sorry for Andrew.

"So you gave him our cake."

No, said Queenie. Why would she do that? She would not do that. She had never thought of giving Andrew the cake.

Stan said, "Lena. Don't lie."

That was the beginning of Queenie's long, miserable struggle. All she could say was no. No, no, I did not give the cake to anybody. I did not give the cake to Andrew. I am not lying. No. No.

"Probably you were drunk," Stan said. "You were drunk and you are not remembering very well."

Queenie said she was not drunk.

"You were the one who was drunk," she said.

He got up and came at her with his hand raised, saying not to tell him that he'd been drunk, never to tell him that.

Queenie cried out, "I won't. I won't. I'm sorry." And he didn't hit her. But she began to cry. She kept crying while she tried to persuade him. Why would she give away the cake she had worked so hard to make? Why would he not believe her? Why would she lie to him?

"Everybody lies," Stan said. And the more she cried and begged him to believe her, the more cool and sarcastic he became.

"Use a little logic. If it's here, get up and find it. If it isn't here, then you gave it away."

Queenie said that wasn't logic. It did not have to be given away just because she could not find it. Then he came close to her again in such a calm, half-smiling way that she thought for a moment he was going to kiss her. Instead he closed his hands around her throat and just for a second cut off her breath. He didn't even leave any marks.

"Now," he said. "Now—are you going to teach me about logic?"

Then he went to get dressed to go and play at the restaurant.

He stopped speaking to her. He wrote her a note saying he would speak to her again when she told the truth. All over Christmas she could not stop crying. She and Stan were supposed to go and visit the Greek people on Christmas Day, but she couldn't go her face was such a mess. Stan had to go and say that she was sick. The Greek people probably knew the truth anyway. They had probably heard the hullabaloo through the walls.

She put on a ton of makeup and went to work, and the manager said, "You want to give people the idea this is a sob story?" She said she had infected sinuses and he let her go home.

When Stan came home that night and pretended she didn't exist she turned over and looked at him. She knew that he would get into bed and lie beside her like a post and that if she moved against him he would continue to lie like a post until she moved away. She saw that he could go on living like this and she could not. She thought that if she had to go on in this way she would die. Just as if he really had choked off her breath, she would die.

So she said, Forgive me.

Forgive me. I did what you said. I'm sorry.

Please. Please. I'm sorry.

He sat down on the bed. He didn't say anything.

She said that she had really forgotten about giving the cake away but that now she remembered that she had done it and she was sorry.

"I wasn't lying," she said. "I forgot."

"You forgot you gave the cake to Andrew?" he said.

"I must have. I forgot."

"To Andrew. You gave it to Andrew."

Yes, Queenie said. Yes, yes, that was what she had done. And she began to howl and hang on to him and beg him to forgive her.

All right, stop the hysterics, he said. He did not say that he forgave her, but he got a warm washcloth and wiped her face and lay down beside her and cuddled her and pretty soon he wanted to do everything else.

"No more music lessons for Mr. Moonlight Sonata."

And then to top if all off, later she found the cake.

She found it wrapped up in a dish towel and then wrapped in waxed paper just as she had remembered. And put into a shopping bag and hung from a hook on the back porch. Of course. The sunporch was the ideal place because it got too cold to use in winter, but it wasn't freezing cold. She must have been thinking that when she hung the cake there. That this was the ideal place. And then she forgot. She had been a little drunk—she must have been. She had forgotten absolutely. And there it was.

She found it, and she threw it all out. She never told Stan.

"I pitched it," she said. "It was just as good as ever and all that expensive fruit and stuff in it, but there was no way I wanted to get that subject brought up again. So I just pitched it out."

Her voice, which had been so woeful in the bad parts of the story, was now sly and full of laughter, as if all the time she had been telling me a joke, and throwing out the cake was the final, ridiculous point of it.

I had to pull my head out of her hands and turn around and look at her.

I said, "But he was wrong."

"Well, of course he was *wrong*. Men are not *normal*, Chrissy. That's one thing you'll learn if you ever get married."

"I never will, then. I never will get married."

"He was just jealous," she said. "He was just so jealous."

"Never."

"Well, you and me are very different, Chrissy. Very different." She sighed. She said, "I am a creature of love."

I thought that you might see these words on a movie poster. "A creature of love." Maybe on a poster of one of the movies that had played at Queenie's theater.

"You are going to look so good when I take these rollers out," she said. "You won't be saying you haven't got a boyfriend for very long. But it'll be too late to go looking today. Early bird tomorrow. If Stan asks you anything, say you went to a couple of places and they took your phone number. Say a store or a restaurant or anything, just so long as he thinks you're looking."

I was hired the next day at the first place I tried, though I hadn't managed to be such an early bird after all. Queenie had decided to do my hair still another way and to make up my eyes, but the result was not what she had hoped for. "You're really more the natural type after all," she said, and I scrubbed it all off and put on my own lipstick, which was ordinary red, not glimmering-pale like hers.

By this time it was too late for Queenie to go out with me to check on her Post Office box. She had to get ready to go to the movie theater. It was a Saturday, so she had to work in the afternoon as well as in the evening. She got out her key and asked me to check the box for her, as a favor. She explained to me where it was.

"I had to get my own box when I wrote to your dad," she said.

The job I got was in a drugstore in the basement of an apartment building. I was hired to work behind the lunch counter. When I first came in I felt fairly hopeless. My hairstyle was drooping in the heat and I had a moustache of sweat on my upper lip. At least my cramps had moderated.

A woman in a white uniform was at the counter, drinking coffee.

"Did you come about the job?" she said.

I said yes. The woman had a hard, square face, pencilled eyebrows, a beehive of purplish hair.

"You speak English, do you?"

"Yes."

"I mean you didn't just learn it? You're not a foreigner?"

I said I wasn't.

"I tried out two girls in the last two days and I had to let them both go. One let on she could speak English, but she couldn't and the other I had to tell her everything ten times over. Wash your hands good at the sink and I'll get you an apron. My husband is the pharmacist and I do the till." (I noticed for the first time a gray-haired man behind a high counter in the corner looking at me and pretending not to.) "It's slow now, but it'll get busy in a while. It's all old people in this block and after their naps they start coming down here wanting coffee."

I tied on an apron and took my place behind the counter. Hired for a job in Toronto. I tried to find out where things were without asking questions and had to ask only two—how to work the coffeemaker and what to do about the money.

"You make out the bill and they bring it to me. What did you think?"

It was all right. People came in one or two at a time mostly wanting coffee or a Coke. I kept the cups washed and wiped, the counter clean, and apparently I made out the bills properly, since there was no complaint. The customers were mostly old people, as the woman had said. Some spoke to me in a kindly way, saying I was new here and even asking where I came from. Others seemed to be in a kind of trance. One woman wanted toast and I managed that. Then I did a ham sandwich. There was a little flurry with four people there at once. A man wanted pie and ice cream, and I found the ice cream hard as cement to scoop out. But I did it. I got more confident. I said to them, "Here you are" when I set down their orders, and "Here's the damage" when I presented the bill.

In a slow moment the woman from the till came over.

"I see you made somebody toast," she said. "Can you read?"

She pointed to a sign stuck on the mirror behind the counter.

NO BREAKFAST ITEMS SERVED AFTER 11 A.M.

I said that I thought it was okay to make toast, if you could make toasted sandwiches.

"Well, you thought wrong. Toasted sandwiches, yes, ten cents extra. Toast, no. Do you understand now?"

I said yes. I wasn't so crushed as I might have been at first. All the time I was working I thought what a relief it would be to go back and tell Mr. Vorguilla that yes, I had a job. Now I could go and look for a room of my own to live in. Maybe tomorrow, Sunday, if the drugstore was closed. If I even had one room, I thought, Queenie would have some place to run away to if Mr. Vorguilla got mad at her again. And if Queenie ever decided to leave Mr. Vorguilla (I persisted in thinking of this as a possibility in spite of how Queenie had finished her story), then with the pay from both our jobs maybe we could get a little apartment. Or at least a room with a hot plate and a toilet and shower to ourselves. It would be like when we lived at home with our parents except that our parents would not be there.

I garnished each sandwich with a bit of torn-off lettuce and a dill pickle. That was what another sign on the mirror promised. But when I got the dill pickle out of a jar I thought it looked like too much, so I cut it in half. I had just served a man a sandwich in this way when the woman from the till came over and got herself a cup of coffee. She took her coffee back to the till and drank it standing up. When the man had finished his sandwich and paid for it and left the store she came over again.

"You gave that man half a dill pickle. Have you been doing that with every sandwich?"

I said yes.

"Don't you know how to slice a pickle? One pickle ought to last ten sandwiches."

I looked at the sign. "It doesn't say a slice. It says a pickle."

"That's enough," the woman said. "Get out of that apron. I don't take any back talk from my employees, that's one thing I won't do. You can get your purse and get out of here. And don't go asking me where's your pay because you haven't been any use to me anyway and this was just supposed to be training."

The gray-haired man was peeking out, with a nervous smile.

So I found myself out on the street again, walking to the street-car stop. But I knew the way some streets went now and I knew how to use a transfer. I had even had experience at a job. I could say that I had worked behind a lunch counter. If anybody wanted a reference it would be tricky—but I could say the lunch counter was in my hometown. While I waited for the streetcar I took out the list of other places where I meant to apply, and the map that Queenie had given me. But it was later than I'd thought, and most places seemed too far away. I dreaded having to tell Mr. Vorguilla. I decided to walk back, in the hopes that when I got there he'd have gone.

I had just turned up the hill when I remembered the Post Office. I found my way back to it and got a letter out of the box and walked home again. Surely he would be gone by now.

But he wasn't. When I walked past the open living-room window that overlooked the path beside the house, I heard music. It wasn't what Queenie would play. It was the sort of complicated music that we had heard sometimes coming through the open windows of the Vorguillas' house—music that demanded your attention and then didn't go anywhere, or at least didn't go anywhere soon enough. Classical.

Queenie was in the kitchen, wearing another of her skimpy dresses, and all her makeup. She had bangles on her arms. She was setting teacups on a tray. I was dizzy for a moment, coming out of the sunlight, and every inch of my skin bloomed with sweat.

"Shh," Queenie said, because I'd closed the door with a crash. "They're in there listening to records. It's him and his friend Leslie."

Just as she said this the music came to an abrupt halt and there was a burst of excited talk.

"One of them plays a record and the other has to guess what it is just from a little bit of it," Queenie said. "They play these little bits and then stop, over and over. It drives you crazy." She started cutting slices off a delicatessen chicken and putting them on buttered slices of bread. "Did you get a job?" she said.

"Yes, but it wasn't permanent."

"Oh, well." She didn't seem very interested. But as the music started again she looked up and smiled and said, "Did you go to the—" And she saw the letter I was carrying in my hand.

She dropped the knife and came to me in a hurry, saying softly, "You walked right in with it in your hand. I should have told you, put it in your purse. My private letter." She grabbed it from my hand and right at that moment the kettle on the stove began to shriek.

"Oh, get the kettle. Chrissy, quick, quick! Get the kettle or he'll be out here, he can't stand the sound."

She had turned her back and was tearing open the envelope.

I took the kettle off the burner, and she said, "Make the tea, please—" in the soft, preoccupied voice of somebody reading an urgent message. "Just pour the water on, it's measured."

She laughed as if she'd read a private joke. I poured the water on the tea leaves and she said, "Thanks. Oh, thanks, Chrissy; thanks." She turned around and looked at me. Her face was rosy and all the bangles on her arms jingled with a delicate agitation. She folded up the letter and pulled up her skirt and tucked it under the elastic waistband of her underpants.

She said, "Sometimes he goes through my purse."

I said, "Is the tea for them?"

"Yes. And I have to get back to work. Oh, what am I doing? I have to cut the sandwiches. Where's the knife?"

I picked up the knife and cut the sandwiches and put them on a plate.

"Don't you want to know who my letter's from?" she said.

I couldn't think.

I said, "Bet?"

Because I had a hope that a private forgiveness from Bet could be the thing that had made Queenie burst into flower.

I had not even looked at the writing on the envelope.

Queenie's face changed—for a moment she looked as if she didn't know who that was. Then she recovered her happiness. She came and put her arms around me and spoke into my ear, in a voice that was shivering and shy and triumphant.

"It's from Andrew. Can you take the tray in to them? I can't. I can't right now. Oh, thank you."

Before Queenie went off to work she came into the living room and kissed both Mr. Vorguilla and his friend. She kissed both of them on their foreheads. She gave me a butterfly wave. "Bye bye."

When I had brought the tray in I saw the annoyance on Mr. Vorguilla's face, that I wasn't Queenie. But he spoke to me in a surprisingly tolerant way and introduced me to Leslie. Leslie was a stout bald man who at first looked to me almost as old as Mr. Vorguilla. But when you got used to him and took his baldness into account he seemed much younger. He was not the sort of friend I would have expected Mr. Vorguilla to have. He was not brusque or know-it-all but comfortable and full of encouragement. For example, when I told about my employment at the lunch counter he said, "Well you know that's something. Getting hired the first place you tried. It shows you know how to make a good impression."

I had not found the experience hard to talk about. The presence of Leslie made everything easier and seemed to soften the behavior of Mr. Vorguilla. As if he had to show me a decent courtesy in the presence of his friend. It could also have been that he sensed a change in me. People do sense the difference when you are not afraid of them anymore. He would not be sure of this difference and he would have no idea how it came about, but it would puzzle him and make him more careful. He agreed with Leslie when Leslie said I was well out of that job, and he even went on to say that the woman sounded like the sort of hard-bitten chiseler you sometimes found in that kind of hole-in-corner establishment in Toronto.

"And she had no business not paying you," he said.

"You'd think the husband might have come forward," said Leslie. "If he was the druggist, he was the boss."

Mr. Vorguilla said, "He might brew up a special dose someday. For his wife."

It wasn't so hard to pour out tea and offer milk and sugar and pass sandwiches, and even talk, when you knew something another person didn't know, about a danger he was in. It was just because he didn't know, that I could feel something other than loathing for Mr. Vorguilla. It wasn't that he had changed in himself—or if he had changed it was probably because I had.

Soon he said that it was time for him to get ready to go to work. He went to change his clothes. Then Leslie asked me if I would like to have supper with him.

"Just around the corner there's a place I go," he said. "Nothing fancy. Nothing like Stan's place."

I was glad enough to hear that it wouldn't be anyplace fancy. I said, "Sure." And after we had dropped off Mr. Vorguilla at the restaurant we drove in Leslie's car to a fish and chips place. Leslie ordered the Super Dinner—though he had just consumed several chicken sandwiches—and I ordered the Regular. He had a beer and I had a Coke.

He talked about himself. He said he wished he had gone to Teachers' College himself instead of choosing music, which did not make for a very settled life.

I was too absorbed in my own situation even to ask him what kind of musician he was. My father had bought me a return ticket, saying, "You never know how things are going to sit with him and her." I had thought of that ticket at the moment I watched Queenie tucking Andrew's letter under the waistband of her underpants. Even though I didn't yet know that it was Andrew's letter.

I hadn't just come to Toronto, or come to Toronto to get a summer job. I had come to be part of Queenie's life. Or if necessary, part of Queenie's and Mr. Vorguilla's life. Even when I had the fantasy about Queenie living with me, the fantasy had something to do with Mr. Vorguilla and how she would be serving him right.

And when I'd thought of the return ticket I was taking something else for granted. That I could go back and live with Bet and my father and be part of their life.

My father and Bet. Mr. and Mrs. Vorguilla. Queenie and Mr. Vorguilla. Even Queenie and Andrew. These were couples and each of them, however disjointed, had now or in memory a private burrow with its own heat and disturbance, from which I was cut off. And I had to be, I wished to be, cut off, for there was nothing I could see in their lives to instruct me or encourage me.

Leslie too was a person cut off. Yet he talked to me about various people he was connected to by ties of blood or friendship. His sister and her husband. His nieces and nephews, the married couples he visited and spent holidays with. All of these people had problems, but all had value. He talked about their jobs, lack of jobs, talents, strokes of luck, errors in judgment, with great interest but a lack of passion. He was cut off, it seemed, from love or rancor.

I would have seen flaws in this, later in my life. I would have felt the impatience, even suspicion a woman can feel towards a man who lacks a motive. Who has only friendship to offer and offers that so easily that even if it is rejected he can move along as cheerfully as ever. Here was no solitary fellow hoping to hook up with a girl. Even I could see that. Just a person who took comfort in the moment and in a sort of reasonable facade of life.

His company was just what I needed, though I hardly realized it. Probably he was being deliberately kind to me. As I had thought of myself as being kind to Mr. Vorguilla, or at least protecting him, so unexpectedly, a little while before.

I was at Teachers' College when Queenie ran away again. I got the news in a letter from my father. He said that he did not know just how or when it happened. Mr. Vorguilla hadn't let him know for a while, and then he had, in case Queenie had come back home. My father had told Mr. Vorguilla he didn't think there was much chance of that. In the letter to me he said that at least it wasn't the kind of thing we could say now that Queenie wouldn't do.

For years, even after I was married, I would get a Christmas card from Mr. Vorguilla. Sleighs laden with bright parcels; a happy family in a decorated doorway, welcoming friends. Perhaps he thought these were the sorts of scenes that would appeal to me in my present way of life. Or perhaps he picked them blindly off the rack. He always included a return address—reminding me of his existence and letting me know where he was, in case of any news.

I had given up expecting that kind of news, myself. I never even found out if it was Andrew that Queenie went away with, or somebody else. Or whether she stayed with Andrew, if he was the one. When my father died there was some money left, and a serious attempt was made to trace her, but without success.

But now something has happened. Now in the years when my children are grown up and my husband has retired, and he and I are travelling a lot, I have a notion that sometimes I see Queenie. It's not through any particular wish or effort that I see her, and it's not as if I believe it is really her, either.

Once it was in a crowded airport, and she was wearing a sarong and a flower-trimmed straw hat. Tanned and excited, rich-looking, surrounded by friends. And once she was among the women at a church door waiting for a glimpse of the wedding party. She wore a spotty suede jacket and she did not look either prosperous or well. Another time she was stopped at a crosswalk, leading a string of nursery-school children on their way to the swimming pool or the park. It was a hot day and her thick middle-aged figure was frankly and comfortably on view, in flowered shorts and a sloganed T-shirt.

The last and the strangest time was in a supermarket in Twin Falls, Idaho. I came around a corner carrying the few things I had collected for a picnic lunch, and there was an old woman leaning on her shopping cart, as if waiting for me. A little wrinkled woman with a crooked mouth and unhealthy-looking brownish skin. Hair in yellow-brown bristles, purple pants hitched up over the small mound of her stomach—she was one of those thin women who have nevertheless, with age, lost the convenience of a waistline. The pants could have come from some thrift shop and so could the gaily colored but matted and shrunken sweater buttoned over a chest no bigger than a ten-year-old's.

The shopping cart was empty. She was not even carrying a purse.

And unlike those other women, this one seemed to know that she was Queenie. She smiled at me with such a merry recognition, and such a yearning to be recognized in return, that you would have thought that this was a great boon—a moment granted to her when she was let out of the shadows for one day in a thousand.

And all I did was stretch my mouth pleasantly and impersonally, as at a loony stranger, and keep on going towards the checkout.

Then in the parking lot I made an excuse to my husband, said I'd forgotten something, and hurried back into the store. I went up and down the aisles, looking. But in just that little time the old woman seemed to have gone. She might have gone out right after I did; she might be making her way now along the streets of Twin Falls. On foot, or in a car driven by some kind relative or neighbor. Or even in a car she drove herself. There was the bare chance, though, that she was still in the store and that we kept going up and down the aisles, just missing each other. I found myself going in one direction and then in another, shivering in the icy climate of the summer store, looking straight into people's faces, and probably frightening them, because I was silently beseeching them to tell me where I could find Queenie.

Until I came to my senses and convinced myself that it wasn't possible, and that whoever was or was not Queenie had left me behind.

The Bear Came Over
the Mountain

Fiona lived in her parents' house, in the town where she and Grant went to university. It was a big, bay-windowed house that seemed to Grant both luxurious and disorderly, with rugs crooked on the floors and cup rings bitten into the table varnish. Her mother was Icelandic—a powerful woman with a froth of white hair and indignant far-left politics. The father was an important cardiologist, revered around the hospital but happily subservient at home, where he would listen to strange tirades with an absentminded smile. All kinds of people, rich or shabby-looking, delivered these tirades, and kept coming and going and arguing and conferring, sometimes in foreign accents. Fiona had her own little car and a pile of cashmere sweaters, but she wasn't in a sorority, and this activity in her house was probably the reason.

Not that she cared. Sororities were a joke to her, and so was politics, though she liked to play "The Four Insurgent Generals" on the phonograph, and sometimes also she played the "Internationale," very loud, if there was a guest she thought she could make nervous. A curly-haired, gloomy-looking foreigner was courting her—she said he was a Visigoth—and so were two or three quite respectable and uneasy young interns. She made fun of them all and of Grant as well. She would drolly repeat some of his small-town phrases. He thought maybe she was joking when she proposed to him, on a cold bright day on the beach at Port Stanley. Sand was stinging their faces and the waves delivered crashing loads of gravel at their feet.

"Do you think it would be fun—" Fiona shouted. "Do you think it would be fun if we got married?"

He took her up on it, he shouted yes. He wanted never to be away from her. She had the spark of life.

Just before they left their house Fiona noticed a mark on the kitchen floor. It came from the cheap black house shoes she had been wearing earlier in the day.

"I thought they'd quit doing that," she said in a tone of ordinary annoyance and perplexity, rubbing at the gray smear that looked as if it had been made by a greasy crayon.

She remarked that she would never have to do this again, since she wasn't taking those shoes with her.

"I guess I'll be dressed up all the time," she said. "Or semi dressed up. It'll be sort of like in a hotel."

She rinsed out the rag she'd been using and hung it on the rack inside the door under the sink. Then she put on her golden-brown fur-collared ski jacket over a white turtle-necked sweater and tailored fawn slacks. She was a tall, narrow-shouldered woman, seventy years old but still upright and trim, with long legs and long feet, delicate wrists and ankles and tiny, almost comical-looking ears. Her hair, which was light as milkweed fluff, had gone from pale blond to white somehow without Grant's noticing exactly when, and she still wore it down to her shoulders, as her mother had done. (That was the thing that had alarmed Grant's own mother, a small-town widow who worked as a doctor's receptionist. The long white hair on Fiona's mother, even more than the state of the house, had told her all she needed to know about attitudes and politics.)

Otherwise Fiona with her fine bones and small sapphire eyes was nothing like her mother. She had a slightly crooked mouth which she emphasized now with red lipstick—usually the last thing she did before she left the house. She looked just like herself on this day—direct and vague as in fact she was, sweet and ironic.

Over a year ago Grant had started noticing so many little yellow notes stuck up all over the house. That was not entirely new. She'd always written things down—the title of a book she'd heard mentioned on the radio or the jobs she wanted to make sure she did that day. Even her morning schedule was written down—he found it mystifying and touching in its precision.

7 a.m. Yoga. 7:30–7:45 teeth face hair. 7:45–8:15 walk. 8:15 Grant and Breakfast.

The new notes were different. Taped onto the kitchen drawers—Cutlery, Dishtowels, Knives. Couldn't she have just opened the drawers and seen what was inside? He remembered a story about the German soldiers on border patrol in Czechoslovakia during the war. Some Czech had told him that each of the patrol dogs wore a sign that said *Hund*. Why? said the Czechs, and the Germans said, Because that is a *hund*.

He was going to tell Fiona that, then thought he'd better not. They always laughed at the same things, but suppose this time she didn't laugh?

Worse things were coming. She went to town and phoned him from a booth to ask him how to drive home. She went for her walk across the field into the woods and came home by the fence line—a very long way round. She said that she'd counted on fences always taking you somewhere.

It was hard to figure out. She said that about fences as if it was a joke, and she had remembered the phone number without any trouble.

"I don't think it's anything to worry about," she said. "I expect I'm just losing my mind."

He asked if she had been taking sleeping pills.

"If I have I don't remember," she said. Then she said she was sorry to sound so flippant.

"I'm sure I haven't been taking anything. Maybe I should be. Maybe vitamins."

Vitamins didn't help. She would stand in doorways trying to figure out where she was going. She forgot to turn on the burner under the vegetables or put water in the coffeemaker. She asked Grant when they'd moved to this house.

"Was it last year or the year before?"

He said that it was twelve years ago.

She said, "That's shocking."

"She's always been a bit like this," Grant said to the doctor. "Once she left her fur coat in storage and just forgot about it. That was when we were always going somewhere warm in the winters. Then she said it was unintentionally on purpose, she said it was like a sin she was leaving behind. The way some people made her feel about fur coats."

He tried without success to explain something more—to explain how Fiona's surprise and apologies about all this seemed somehow like routine courtesy, not quite concealing a private amusement. As if she'd stumbled on some adventure that she had not been expecting. Or was playing a game that she hoped he would catch on to. They had always had their games—nonsense dialects, characters they invented. Some of Fiona's made-up voices, chirping or wheedling (he couldn't tell the doctor this), had mimicked uncannily the voices of women of his that she had never met or known about.

"Yes, well," the doctor said. "It might be selective at first. We don't know, do we? Till we see the pattern of the deterioration, we really can't say."

In a while it hardly mattered what label was put on it. Fiona, who no longer went shopping alone, disappeared from the supermarket while Grant had his back turned. A policeman picked her up as she walked down the middle of the road, blocks away. He asked her name and she answered readily. Then he asked her the name of the prime minister of the country.

"If you don't know that, young man, you really shouldn't be in such a responsible job."

He laughed. But then she made the mistake of asking if he'd seen Boris and Natasha.

These were the Russian wolfhounds she had adopted some years ago as a favor to a friend, then devoted herself to for the rest of their lives. Her taking them over might have coincided with the discovery that she was not likely to have children. Something about her tubes being blocked, or twisted—Grant could not remember now. He had always avoided thinking about all that female apparatus. Or it might have been after her mother died. The dogs' long legs and silky hair, their narrow, gentle, intransigent faces made a fine match for her when she took them out for walks. And Grant himself, in those days, landing his first job at the university (his father-in-law's money welcome in spite of the political taint), might have seemed to some people to have been picked up on another of Fiona's eccentric whims, and groomed and tended and favored. Though he never understood this, fortunately, until much later.

She said to him, at suppertime on the day of the wandering-off at the supermarket, "You know what you're going to have to do with me, don't you? You're going to have to put me in that place. Shallowlake?"

Grant said, "Meadowlake. We're not at that stage yet."

"Shallowlake, Shillylake," she said, as if they were engaged in a playful competition. "Sillylake. Sillylake it is."

He held his head in his hands, his elbows on the table. He said that if they did think of it, it must be as something that need not be permanent. A kind of experimental treatment. A rest cure.

There was a rule that nobody could be admitted during the month of December. The holiday season had so many emotional pitfalls. So they made the twenty-minute drive in January. Before they reached the highway the country road dipped through a swampy hollow now completely frozen over. The swamp-oaks and maples threw their shadows like bars across the bright snow.

Fiona said, "Oh, remember."

Grant said, "I was thinking about that too."

"Only it was in the moonlight," she said.

She was talking about the time that they had gone out skiing at night under the full moon and over the black-striped snow, in this place that you could get into only in the depths of winter. They had heard the branches cracking in the cold.

So if she could remember that so vividly and correctly, could there really be so much the matter with her?

It was all he could do not to turn around and drive home.

There was another rule which the supervisor explained to him. New residents were not to be visited during the first thirty days. Most people needed that time to get settled in. Before the rule had been put in place, there had been pleas and tears and tantrums, even from those who had come in willingly. Around the third or fourth day they would start lamenting and begging to be taken home. And some relatives could be susceptible to that, so you would have people being carted home who would not get on there any better than they had before. Six months later or sometimes only a few weeks later, the whole upsetting hassle would have to be gone through again.

"Whereas we find," the supervisor said, "we find that if they're left on their own they usually end up happy as clams. You have to practically lure them into a bus to take a trip to town. The same with a visit home. It's perfectly okay to take them home then, visit for an hour or two—they're the ones that'll worry about getting back in time for supper. Meadowlake's their home then. Of course, that doesn't apply to the ones on the second floor, we can't let them go. It's too difficult, and they don't know where they are anyway."

"My wife isn't going to be on the second floor," Grant said.

"No," said the supervisor thoughtfully. "I just like to make everything clear at the outset."

They had gone over to Meadowlake a few times several years ago, to visit Mr. Farquar, the old bachelor farmer who had been their neighbor. He had lived by himself in a drafty brick house unaltered since the early years of the century, except for the addition of a refrigerator and a television set. He had paid Grant and Fiona unannounced but well-spaced visits and, as well as local matters, he liked to discuss books he had been reading—about the Crimean War or Polar explorations or the history of firearms. But after he went to Meadowlake he would talk only about the routines of the place, and they got the idea that their visits, though gratifying, were a social burden for him. And Fiona in particular hated the smell of urine and bleach that hung about, hated the perfunctory bouquets of plastic flowers in niches in the dim, low-ceilinged corridors.

Now that building was gone, though it had dated only from the fifties. Just as Mr. Farquar's house was gone, replaced by a gimcrack sort of castle that was the weekend home of some people from Toronto. The new Meadowlake was an airy, vaulted building whose air was faintly pleasantly pine-scented. Profuse and genuine greenery sprouted out of giant crocks.

Nevertheless, it was the old building that Grant would find himself picturing Fiona in during the long month he had to get through without seeing her. It was the longest month of his life, he thought—longer than the month he had spent with his mother visiting relatives in Lanark County, when he was thirteen, and longer than the month that Jacqui Adams spent on holiday with her family, near the beginning of their affair. He phoned Meadowlake every day and hoped that he would get the nurse whose name was Kristy. She seemed a little amused at his constancy, but she would give him a fuller report than any other nurse he got stuck with.

Fiona had caught a cold, but that was not unusual for newcomers.

"Like when your kids start school," Kristy said. "There's a whole bunch of new germs they're exposed to, and for a while they just catch everything."

Then the cold got better. She was off the antibiotics, and she didn't seem as confused as she had been when she came in. (This was the first time Grant had heard about either the antibiotics or the confusion.) Her appetite was pretty good, and she seemed to enjoy sitting in the sunroom. She seemed to enjoy watching television.

One of the things that had been so intolerable about the old Meadowlake had been the way the television was on everywhere, overwhelming your thoughts or conversation wherever you chose to sit down. Some of the inmates (that was what he and Fiona called them then, not residents) would raise their eyes to it, some talked back to it, but most just sat and meekly endured its assault. In the new building, as far as he could recall, the television was in a separate sitting room, or in the bedrooms. You could make a choice to watch it.

So Fiona must have made a choice. To watch what?

During the years that they had lived in this house, he and Fiona had watched quite a bit of television together. They had spied on the lives of every beast or reptile or insect or sea creature that a camera was able to reach, and they had followed the plots of what seemed like dozens of rather similar fine nineteenth-century novels. They had slid into an infatuation with an English comedy about life in a department store and had watched so many reruns that they knew the dialogue by heart. They mourned the disappearance of actors who died in real life or went off to other jobs, then welcomed those same actors back as the characters were born again. They watched the floorwalker's hair going from black to gray and finally back to black, the cheap sets never changing. But these, too, faded; eventually the sets and the blackest hair faded as if dust from the London streets was getting in under the elevator doors, and there was a sadness about this that seemed to affect Grant and Fiona more than any of the tragedies on *Masterpiece Theatre*, so they gave up watching before the final end.

Fiona was making some friends, Kristy said. She was definitely coming out of her shell.

What shell was that? Grant wanted to ask, but checked himself, to remain in Kristy's good graces.

If anybody phoned, he let the message go onto the machine. The people they saw socially, occasionally, were not close neighbors but people who lived around the countryside, who were retired, as they were, and who often went away without notice. The first years that they had lived here Grant and Fiona had stayed through the winter. A country winter was a new experience, and they had plenty to do, fixing up the house. Then they had gotten the idea that they too should travel while they could, and they had gone to Greece, to Australia, to Costa Rica. People would think that they were away on some such trip at present.

He skied for exercise but never went as far as the swamp. He skied around and around in the field behind the house as the sun went down and left the sky pink over a countryside that seemed to be bound by waves of blue-edged ice. He counted off the times he went round the field, and then he came back to the darkening house, turning the television news on while he got his supper. They had usually prepared supper together. One of them made the drinks and the other the fire, and they talked about his work (he was writing a study of legendary Norse wolves and particularly of the great Fenris wolf who swallows up Odin at the end of the world) and about whatever Fiona was reading and what they had been thinking during their close but separate day. This was their time of liveliest intimacy, though there was also, of course, the five or ten minutes of physical sweetness just after they got into bed—something that did not often end up in sex but reassured them that sex was not over yet.

In a dream Grant showed a letter to one of his colleagues whom he had thought of as a friend. The letter was from the roommate of a girl he had not thought of for a while. Its style was sanctimonious and hostile, threatening in a whining way—he put the writer down as a latent lesbian. The girl herself was someone he had parted from decently, and it seemed unlikely that she would want to make a fuss, let alone try to kill herself, which was what the letter was apparently, elaborately, trying to tell him.

The colleague was one of those husbands and fathers who had been among the first to throw away their neckties and leave home to spend every night on a floor mattress with a bewitching young mistress, coming to their offices, their classes, bedraggled and smelling of dope and incense. But now he took a dim view of such shenanigans, and Grant recollected that he had in fact married one of those girls, and that she had taken to giving dinner parties and having babies, just as wives used to do.

"I wouldn't laugh," he said to Grant, who did not think he had been laughing. "And if I were you I'd try to prepare Fiona."

So Grant went off to find Fiona in Meadowlake—the old Meadowlake—and got into a lecture theater instead. Everybody was waiting there for him to teach his class. And sitting in the last, highest row was a flock of cold-eyed young women all in black robes, all in mourning, who never took their bitter stares off him and conspicuously did not write down, or care about, anything he was saying.

Fiona was in the first row, untroubled. She had transformed the lecture room into the sort of corner she was always finding at a party—some high-and-dry spot where she drank wine with mineral water, and smoked ordinary cigarettes and told funny stories about her dogs. Holding out there against the tide, with some people who were like herself, as if the dramas that were being played out in other corners, in bedrooms and on the dark verandah, were nothing but childish comedy. As if chastity was chic, and reticence a blessing.

"Oh, phooey," Fiona said. "Girls that age are always going around talking about how they'll kill themselves."

But it wasn't enough for her to say that—in fact, it rather chilled him. He was afraid that she was wrong, that something terrible had happened, and he saw what she could not—that the black ring was thickening, drawing in, all around his windpipe, all around the top of the room.

He hauled himself out of the dream and set about separating what was real from what was not.

There had been a letter, and the word "RAT" had appeared in black paint on his office door, and Fiona, on being told that a girl had suffered from a bad crush on him, had said pretty much what she said in the dream. The colleague hadn't come into it, the black-robed women had never appeared in his classroom, and nobody had committed suicide. Grant hadn't been disgraced, in fact he had got off easily when you thought of what might have happened just a couple of years later. But word got around. Cold shoulders became conspicuous. They had few Christmas invitations and spent New Year's Eve alone. Grant got drunk, and without its being required of him—also, thank God, without making the error of a confession—he promised Fiona a new life.

The shame he felt then was the shame of being duped, of not having noticed the change that was going on. And not one woman had made him aware of it. There had been the change in the past when so many women so suddenly became available—or it seemed that way to him—and now this new change, when they were saying that what had happened was not what they had had in mind at all. They had collaborated because they were helpless and bewildered, and they had been injured by the whole thing, rather than delighted. Even when they had taken the initiative they had done so only because the cards were stacked against them.

Nowhere was there any acknowledgment that the life of a philanderer (if that was what Grant had to call himself—he who had not had half as many conquests or complications as the man who had reproached him in his dream) involved acts of kindness and generosity and even sacrifice. Not in the beginning, perhaps, but at least as things went on. Many times he had catered to a woman's pride, to her fragility, by offering more affection—or a rougher passion—than anything he really felt. All so that he could now find himself accused of wounding and exploiting and destroying self-esteem. And of deceiving Fiona—as of course he had deceived her—but would it have been better if he had done as others had done with their wives and left her?

He had never thought of such a thing. He had never stopped making love to Fiona in spite of disturbing demands elsewhere. He had not stayed away from her for a single night. No making up elaborate stories in order to spend a weekend in San Francisco or in a tent on Manitoulin Island. He had gone easy on the dope and the drink and he had continued to publish papers, serve on committees, make progress in his career. He had never had any intention of throwing up work and marriage and taking to the country to practice carpentry or keep bees.

But something like that had happened after all. He took an early retirement with a reduced pension. The cardiologist had died, after some bewildered and stoical time alone in the big house, and Fiona had inherited both that property and the farmhouse where her father had grown up, in the country near Georgian Bay. She gave up her job, as a hospital coordinator of volunteer services (in that everyday world, as she said, where people actually had troubles that were not related to drugs or sex or intellectual squabbles). A new life was a new life.

Boris and Natasha had died by this time. One of them got sick and died first—Grant forgot which one—and then the other died, more or less out of sympathy.

He and Fiona worked on the house. They got cross-country skis. They were not very sociable, but they gradually made some friends. There were no more hectic flirtations. No bare female toes creeping up under a man's pants leg at a dinner party. No more loose wives.

Just in time, Grant was able to think, when the sense of injustice wore down. The feminists and perhaps the sad silly girl herself and his cowardly so-called friends had pushed him out just in time. Out of a life that was in fact getting to be more trouble than it was worth. And that might eventually have cost him Fiona.

On the morning of the day when he was to go back to Meadowlake for the first visit, Grant woke early. He was full of a solemn tingling, as in the old days on the morning of his first planned meeting with a new woman. The feeling was not precisely sexual. (Later, when the meetings had become routine, that was all it was.) There was an expectation of discovery, almost a spiritual expansion. Also timidity, humility, alarm.

He left home too early. Visitors were not allowed before two o'clock. He did not want to sit out in the parking lot, waiting, so he made himself turn the car in a wrong direction.

There had been a thaw. Plenty of snow was left, but the dazzling hard landscape of earlier winter had crumbled. These pocked heaps under a gray sky looked like refuse in the fields.

In the town near Meadowlake he found a florist's shop and bought a large bouquet. He had never presented flowers to Fiona before. Or to anyone else. He entered the building feeling like a hopeless lover or a guilty husband in a cartoon.

"Wow. Narcissus this early," Kristy said. "You must've spent a fortune." She went along the hall ahead of him and snapped on the light in a closet, or sort of kitchen, where she searched for a vase. She was a heavy young woman who looked as if she had given up in every department except her hair. That was blond and voluminous. All the puffed-up luxury of a cocktail waitress's style, or a stripper's, on top of such a workaday face and body.

"There, now," she said, and nodded him down the hall. "Name's right on the door."

So it was, on a nameplate decorated with bluebirds. He wondered whether to knock, and did, then opened the door and called her name.

She wasn't there. The closet door was closed, the bed smoothed. Nothing on the bedside table, except a box of Kleenex and a glass of water. Not a single photograph or picture of any kind, not a book or a magazine. Perhaps you had to keep those in a cupboard.

He went back to the nurses' station, or reception desk, or whatever it was. Kristy said "No?" with a surprise that he thought perfunctory.

He hesitated, holding the flowers. She said, "Okay, okay—let's set the bouquet down here." Sighing, as if he was a backward child on his first day at school, she led him along a hall, into the light of the huge sky windows in the large central space, with its cathedral ceiling. Some people were sitting along the walls, in easy chairs, others at tables in the middle of the carpeted floor. None of them looked too bad. Old—some of them incapacitated enough to need wheelchairs—but decent. There used to be some unnerving sights when he and Fiona went to visit Mr. Farquar. Whiskers on old women's chins, somebody with a bulged-out eye like a rotted plum. Dribblers, head wagglers, mad chatterers. Now it looked as if there'd been some weeding out of the worst cases. Or perhaps drugs, surgery had come into use, perhaps there were ways of treating disfigurement, as well as verbal and other kinds of incontinence—ways that hadn't existed even those few years ago.

There was, however, a very disconsolate woman sitting at the piano, picking away with one finger and never achieving a tune. Another woman, staring out from behind a coffee urn and a stack of plastic cups, looked bored to stone. But she had to be an employee—she wore a pale-green pants outfit like Kristy's.

"See?" said Kristy in a softer voice. "You just go up and say hello and try not to startle her. Remember she may not— Well. Just go ahead."

He saw Fiona in profile, sitting close up to one of the card tables, but not playing. She looked a little puffy in the face, the flab on one cheek hiding the corner of her mouth, in a way it hadn't done before. She was watching the play of the man she sat closest to. He held his cards tilted so that she could see them. When Grant got near the table she looked up. They all looked up—all the players at the table looked up, with displeasure. Then they immediately looked down at their cards, as if to ward off any intrusion.

But Fiona smiled her lopsided, abashed, sly, and charming smile and pushed back her chair and came round to him, putting her fingers to her mouth.

"Bridge," she whispered. "Deadly serious. They're quite rabid about it." She drew him towards the coffee table, chatting.

"I can remember being like that for a while at college. My friends and I would cut class and sit in the common room and smoke and play like cutthroats. One's name was Phoebe, I don't remember the others."

"Phoebe Hart," Grant said. He pictured the little hollow-chested, black-eyed girl, who was probably dead by now. Wreathed in smoke, Fiona and Phoebe and those others, rapt as witches.

"You knew her too?" said Fiona, directing her smile now towards the stone-faced woman. "Can I get you anything? A cup of tea? I'm afraid the coffee isn't up to much here."

Grant never drank tea.

He could not throw his arms around her. Something about her voice and smile, familiar as they were, something about the way she seemed to be guarding the players and even the coffee woman from him—as well as him from their displeasure—made that not possible.

"I brought you some flowers," he said. "I thought they'd do to brighten up your room. I went to your room, but you weren't there."

"Well, no," she said. "I'm here."

Grant said, "You've made a new friend." He nodded towards the man she'd been sitting next to. At this moment that man looked up at Fiona and she turned, either because of what Grant had said or because she felt the look at her back.

"It's just Aubrey," she said. "The funny thing is I knew him years and years ago. He worked in the store. The hardware store where my grandpa used to shop. He and I were always kidding around and he could not get up the nerve to ask me out. Till the very last weekend and he took me to a ball game. But when it was over my grandpa showed up to drive me home. I was up visiting for the summer. Visiting my grandparents—they lived on a farm."

"Fiona. I know where your grandparents lived. It's where we live. Lived."

"Really?" she said, not paying full attention because the card-player was sending her his look, which was not one of supplication but command. He was a man of about Grant's age, or a little older. Thick coarse white hair fell over his forehead, and his skin was leathery but pale, yellowish-white like an old wrinkled-up kid glove. His long face was dignified and melancholy, and he had something of the beauty of a powerful, discouraged, elderly horse. But where Fiona was concerned he was not discouraged.

"I better go back," Fiona said, a blush spotting her newly fattened face. "He thinks he can't play without me sitting there. It's silly, I hardly know the game anymore. I'm afraid you'll have to excuse me."

"Will you be through soon?"

"Oh, we should be. It depends. If you go and ask that grim-looking lady nicely she'll get you some tea."

"I'm fine," Grant said.

"So I'll leave you then, you can entertain yourself? It must all seem strange to you, but you'll be surprised how soon you get used to it. You'll get to know who everybody is. Except that some of them are pretty well off in the clouds, you know—you can't expect them all to get to know who *you* are."

She slipped back into her chair and said something into Aubrey's ear. She tapped her fingers across the back of his hand.

Grant went in search of Kristy and met her in the hall. She was pushing a cart on which there were pitchers of apple juice and grape juice.

"Just one sec," she said to him, as she stuck her head through a doorway. "Apple juice in here? Grape juice? Cookies?"

He waited while she filled two plastic glasses and took them into the room. Then she came back and put two arrowroot cookies on paper plates.

"Well?" she said. "Aren't you glad to see her participating and everything?"

Grant said, "Does she even know who I am?"

He could not decide. She could have been playing a joke. It would not be unlike her. She had given herself away by that little pretense at the end, talking to him as if she thought perhaps he was a new resident.

If that was what she was pretending. If it was a pretense.

But would she not have run after him and laughed at him then, once the joke was over? She would not have just gone back to the game, surely, and pretended to forget about him. That would have been too cruel.

Kristy said, "You just caught her at sort of a bad moment. Involved in the game."

"She's not even playing," he said.

"Well, but her friend's playing. Aubrey."

"So who is Aubrey?"

"That's who he is. Aubrey. Her friend. Would you like a juice?"

Grant shook his head.

"Oh, look," said Kristy. "They get these attachments. That takes over for a while. Best buddy sort of thing. It's kind of a phase."

"You mean she really might not know who I am?"

"She might not. Not today. Then tomorrow—you never know, do you? Things change back and forth all the time and there's nothing you can do about it. You'll see the way it is once you've been coming here for a while. You'll learn not to take it all so serious. Learn to take it day by day."

Day by day. But things really didn't change back and forth, and he didn't get used to the way they were. Fiona was the one who seemed to get used to him, but only as some persistent visitor who took a special interest in her. Or perhaps even as a nuisance who must be prevented, according to her old rules of courtesy, from realizing that he was one. She treated him with a distracted, social sort of kindness that was successful in holding him back from the most obvious, the most necessary question. He could not demand of her whether she did or did not remember him as her husband of nearly fifty years. He got the impression that she would be embarrassed by such a question—embarrassed not for herself but for him. She would have laughed in a fluttery way and mortified him with her politeness and bewilderment, and somehow she would have ended up not saying either yes or no. Or she would have said either one in a way that gave not the least satisfaction.

Kristy was the only nurse he could talk to. Some of the others treated the whole thing as a joke. One tough old stick laughed in his face. "That Aubrey and that Fiona? They've really got it bad, haven't they?"

Kristy told him that Aubrey had been the local representative of a company that sold weed killer—"and all that kind of stuff"—to farmers.

"He was a fine person," she said, and Grant did not know whether this meant that Aubrey was honest and openhanded and kind to people, or that he was well spoken and well dressed and drove a good car. Probably both.

And then when he was not very old or even retired—she said—he had suffered some unusual kind of damage.

"His wife is the one takes care of him usually. She takes care of him at home. She just put him in here on temporary care so she could get a break. Her sister wanted her to go to Florida. See, she's had a hard time, you wouldn't ever have expected a man like him— They just went on a holiday somewhere and he got something, like some bug, that gave him a terrible high fever? And it put him in a coma and left him like he is now."

He asked her about these affections between residents. Did they ever go too far? He was able now to take a tone of indulgence that he hoped would save him from any lectures.

"Depends what you mean," she said. She kept writing in her record book while deciding how to answer him. When she finished what she was writing she looked up at him with a frank smile.

"The trouble we have in here, it's funny, it's often with some of the ones that haven't been friendly with each other at all. They maybe won't even know each other, beyond knowing, like, is it a man or a woman? You'd think it'd be the old guys trying to crawl in bed with the old women, but you know half the time it's the other way round. Old women going after the old men. Could be they're not so wore out, I guess."

Then she stopped smiling, as if she was afraid she had said too much, or spoken callously.

"Don't take me wrong," she said. "I don't mean Fiona. Fiona is a lady."

Well, what about Aubrey? Grant felt like saying. But he remembered that Aubrey was in a wheelchair.

"She's a real lady," Kristy said, in a tone so decisive and reassuring that Grant was not reassured. He had in his mind a picture of Fiona, in one of her long eyelet-trimmed blue-ribboned nightgowns, teasingly lifting the covers of an old man's bed.

"Well, I sometimes wonder—" he said.

Kristy said sharply, "You wonder what?"

"I wonder whether she isn't putting on some kind of a charade."

"A what?" said Kristy.

Most afternoons the pair could be found at the card table. Aubrey had large, thick-fingered hands. It was difficult for him to manage his cards. Fiona shuffled and dealt for him and sometimes moved quickly to straighten a card that seemed to be slipping from his grasp. Grant would watch from across the room her darting move and quick, laughing apology. He could see Aubrey's husbandly frown as a wisp of her hair touched his cheek. Aubrey preferred to ignore her as long as she stayed close.

But let her smile her greeting at Grant, let her push back her chair and get up to offer him tea—showing that she had accepted his right to be there and possibly felt a slight responsibility for him—and Aubrey's face took on its look of sombre consternation. He would let the cards slide from his fingers and fall on the floor, to spoil the game.

So that Fiona had to get busy and put things right.

If they weren't at the bridge table they might be walking along the halls, Aubrey hanging on to the railing with one hand and clutching Fiona's arm or shoulder with the other. The nurses thought that it was a marvel, the way she had got him out of his wheelchair. Though for longer trips—to the conservatory at one end of the building or the television room at the other—the wheelchair was called for.

The television seemed to be always turned to the sports channel and Aubrey would watch any sport, but his favorite appeared to be golf. Grant didn't mind watching that with them. He sat down a few chairs away. On the large screen a small group of spectators and commentators followed the players around the peaceful green, and at appropriate moments broke into a formal sort of applause. But there was silence everywhere as the player made his swing and the ball took its lonely, appointed journey across the sky. Aubrey and Fiona and Grant and possibly others sat and held their breaths, and then Aubrey's breath broke out first, expressing satisfaction or disappointment. Fiona's chimed in on the same note a moment later.

In the conservatory there was no such silence. The pair found themselves a seat among the most lush and thick and tropical-looking plants—a bower, if you like—which Grant had just enough self-control to keep from penetrating. Mixed in with the rustle of the leaves and the sound of splashing water was Fiona's soft talk and her laughter.

Then some sort of chortle. Which of them could it be?

Perhaps neither—perhaps it came from one of the impudent flashy-looking birds who inhabited the corner cages.

Aubrey could talk, though his voice probably didn't sound the way it used to. He seemed to say something now—a couple of thick syllables. *Take care. He's here. My love.*

On the blue bottom of the fountain's pool lay some wishing coins. Grant had never seen anybody actually throwing money in. He stared at these nickels and dimes and quarters, wondering if they had been glued to the tiles—another feature of the building's encouraging decoration.

Teenagers at the baseball game, sitting at the top of the bleachers out of the way of the boy's friends. A couple of inches of bare wood between them, darkness falling, quick chill of the evening late in the summer. The skittering of their hands, the shift of haunches, eyes never lifted from the field. He'll take off his jacket, if he's wearing one, to lay it around her narrow shoulders. Underneath it he can pull her closer to him, press his spread fingers into her soft arm.

Not like today when any kid would probably be into her pants on the first date.

Fiona's skinny soft arm. Teenage lust astonishing her and flashing along all the nerves of her tender new body, as the night thickens beyond the lighted dust of the game.

Meadowlake was short on mirrors, so he did not have to catch sight of himself stalking and prowling. But every once in a while it came to him how foolish and pathetic and perhaps unhinged he must look, trailing around after Fiona and Aubrey. And having no luck in confronting her, or him. Less and less sure of what right he had to be on the scene but unable to withdraw. Even at home, while he worked at his desk or cleaned up the house or shovelled snow when necessary, some ticking metronome in his mind was fixed on Meadowlake, on his next visit. Sometimes he seemed to himself like a mulish boy conducting a hopeless courtship, sometimes like one of those wretches who follow celebrated women through the streets, convinced that one day these women will turn around and recognize their love.

He made a great effort, and cut his visits down to Wednesdays and Saturdays. Also he set himself to observing other things about the place, as if he was a sort of visitor at large, a person doing an inspection or a social study.

Saturdays had a holiday bustle and tension. Families arrived in clusters. Mothers were usually in charge, they were like cheerful but insistent sheepdogs herding the men and children. Only the smallest children were without apprehension. They noticed right away the green and white squares on the hall floors and picked one color to walk on, the other to jump over. The bolder ones might try to hitch rides on the back of wheelchairs. Some persisted in these tricks in spite of scolding, and had to be removed to the car. And how happily, then, how readily, some older child or father volunteered to do the removing, and thus opt out of the visit.

It was the women who kept the conversation afloat. Men seemed cowed by the situation, teenagers affronted. Those being visited rode in a wheelchair or stumped along with a cane, or walked stiffly, unaided, at the procession's head, proud of the turnout but somewhat blank-eyed, or desperately babbling, under the stress of it. And now surrounded by a variety of outsiders these insiders did not look like such regular people after all. Female chins might have had their bristles shaved to the roots and bad eyes might be hidden by patches or dark lenses, inappropriate utterances might be controlled by medication, but some glaze remained, a haunted rigidity—as if people were content to become memories of themselves, final photographs.

Grant understood better now how Mr. Farquar must have felt. People here—even the ones who did not participate in any activities but sat around watching the doors or looking out the windows—were living a busy life in their heads (not to mention the life of their bodies, the portentous shifts in their bowels, the stabs and twinges everywhere along the line), and that was a life that in most cases could not very well be described or alluded to in front of visitors. All they could do was wheel or somehow propel themselves about and hope to come up with something that could be displayed or talked about.

There was the conservatory to be shown off, and the big television screen. Fathers thought that was really something. Mothers said the ferns were gorgeous. Soon everybody sat down around the little tables and ate ice cream—refused only by the teenagers, who were dying of disgust. Women wiped away the dribble from shivery old chins and men looked the other way.

There must be some satisfaction in this ritual, and perhaps even the teenagers would be glad, one day, that they had come. Grant was no expert on families.

No children or grandchildren appeared to visit Aubrey, and since they could not play cards—the tables being taken over for the ice cream parties—he and Fiona stayed clear of the Saturday parade. The conservatory was far too popular then for any of their intimate conversations.

Those might be going on, of course, behind Fiona's closed door. Grant could not manage to knock, though he stood there for some time staring at the Disney birds with an intense, a truly malignant dislike.

Or they might be in Aubrey's room. But he did not know where that was. The more he explored this place, the more corridors and seating spaces and ramps he discovered, and in his wanderings he was still apt to get lost. He would take a certain picture or chair as a landmark, and the next week whatever he had chosen seemed to have been placed somewhere else. He didn't like to mention this to Kristy, lest she think he was suffering some mental dislocations of his own. He supposed this constant change and rearranging might be for the sake of the residents—to make their daily exercise more interesting.

He did not mention either that he sometimes saw a woman at a distance that he thought was Fiona, but then thought it couldn't be, because of the clothes the woman was wearing. When had Fiona ever gone in for bright flowered blouses and electric blue slacks? One Saturday he looked out a window and saw Fiona—it must be her—wheeling Aubrey along one of the paved paths now cleared of snow and ice, and she was wearing a silly woolly hat and a jacket with swirls of blue and purple, the sort of thing he had seen on local women at the supermarket.

The fact must be that they didn't bother to sort out the wardrobes of the women who were roughly the same size. And counted on the women not recognizing their own clothes anyway.

They had cut her hair, too. They had cut away her angelic halo. On a Wednesday, when everything was more normal and card games were going on again, and the women in the Crafts Room were making silk flowers or costumed dolls without anybody hanging around to pester or admire them, and when Aubrey and Fiona were again in evidence so that it was possible for Grant to have one of his brief and friendly and maddening conversations with his wife, he said to her, "Why did they chop off your hair?"

Fiona put her hands up to her head, to check.

"Why—I never missed it," she said.

He thought he should find out what went on on the second floor, where they kept the people who, as Kristy said, had really lost it. Those who walked around down here holding conversations with themselves or throwing out odd questions at a passerby

("Did I leave my sweater in the church?") had apparently lost only some of it.

Not enough to qualify.

There were stairs, but the doors at the top were locked and only the staff had the keys. You could not get into the elevator unless somebody buzzed for it to open, from behind the desk.

What did they do, after they lost it?

"Some just sit," said Kristy. "Some sit and cry. Some try to holler the house down. You don't really want to know."

Sometimes they got it back.

"You go in their rooms for a year and they don't know you from Adam. Then one day, it's oh, hi, when are we going home. All of a sudden they're absolutely back to normal again."

But not for long.

"You think, wow, back to normal. And then they're gone again." She snapped her fingers. "Like so."

In the town where he used to work there was a bookstore that he and Fiona had visited once or twice a year. He went back there by himself. He didn't feel like buying anything, but he had made a list and picked out a couple of the books on it, and then bought another book that he noticed by chance. It was about Iceland. A book of nineteenth-century watercolors made by a lady traveller to Iceland.

Fiona had never learned her mother's language and she had never shown much respect for the stories that it preserved—the stories that Grant had taught and written about, and still did write about, in his working life. She referred to their heroes as "old Njal" or "old Snorri." But in the last few years she had developed an interest in the country itself and looked at travel guides. She read about William Morris's trip, and Auden's. She didn't really plan to travel there. She said the weather was too dreadful. Also—

she said—there ought to be one place you thought about and knew about and maybe longed for—but never did get to see.

When Grant first started teaching Anglo-Saxon and Nordic Literature he got the regular sort of students in his classes. But after a few years he noticed a change. Married women started going back to school. Not with the idea of qualifying for a better job or for any job but simply to give themselves something more interesting to think about than their usual housework and hobbies. To enrich their lives. And perhaps it followed naturally that the men who taught them these things would become part of the enrichment, that these men would seem to these women more mysterious and desirable than the men they still cooked for and slept with.

The studies chosen were usually Psychology or Cultural History or English Literature. Archaeology or Linguistics was picked sometimes but dropped when it turned out to be heavy going. Those who signed up for Grant's courses might have a Scandinavian background, like Fiona, or they might have learned something about Norse mythology from Wagner or historical novels. There were also a few who thought he was teaching a Celtic language and for whom everything Celtic had a mystic allure.

He spoke to such aspirants fairly roughly from his side of the desk.

"If you want to learn a pretty language, go and learn Spanish. Then you can use it if you go to Mexico."

Some took his warning and drifted away. Others seemed to be moved in a personal way by his demanding tone. They worked with a will and brought into his office, into his regulated, satisfactory life, the great surprising bloom of their mature female compliance, their tremulous hope of approval.

He chose the woman named Jacqui Adams. She was the opposite of Fiona—short, cushiony, dark-eyed, effusive. A stranger to irony. The affair lasted for a year, until her husband was transferred.

When they were saying good-bye, in her car, she began to shake uncontrollably. It was as if she had hypothermia. She wrote to him a few times, but he found the tone of her letters overwrought and could not decide how to answer. He let the time for answering slip away while he became magically and unexpectedly involved with a girl who was young enough to be her daughter.

For another and more dizzying development had taken place while he was busy with Jacqui. Young girls with long hair and sandalled feet were coming into his office and all but declaring themselves ready for sex. The cautious approaches, the tender intimations of feeling required with Jacqui were out the window. A whirlwind hit him, as it did many others, wish becoming action in a way that made him wonder if there wasn't something missed. But who had time for regrets? He heard of simultaneous liaisons, savage and risky encounters. Scandals burst wide open, with high and painful drama all round but a feeling that somehow it was better so. There were reprisals—there were firings. But those fired went off to teach at smaller, more tolerant colleges or Open Learning Centers, and many wives left behind got over the shock and took up the costumes, the sexual nonchalance of the girls who had tempted their men. Academic parties, which used to be so predictable, became a minefield. An epidemic had broken out, it was spreading like the Spanish flu. Only this time people ran after contagion, and few between sixteen and sixty seemed willing to be left out.

Fiona appeared to be quite willing, however. Her mother was dying, and her experience in the hospital led her from her routine work in the registrar's office into her new job. Grant himself did not go overboard, at least in comparison with some people around him. He never let another woman get as close to him as Jacqui had been. What he felt was mainly a gigantic increase in well-being. A tendency to pudginess that he had had since he was twelve years old disappeared. He ran up steps two at a time. He appreciated as never before a pageant of torn clouds and winter sunset seen from his office window, the charm of antique lamps glowing between his neighbors' living-room curtains, the cries of children in the park at dusk, unwilling to leave the hill where they'd been tobogganing. Come summer, he learned the names of flowers. In his classroom, after coaching by his nearly voiceless mother-in-law (her affliction was cancer of the throat), he risked reciting and then translating the majestic and gory ode, the head-ransom, the Hofuolausn, composed to honor King Eric Blood-axe by the skald whom that king had condemned to death. (And who was then, by the same king—and by the power of poetry—set free.) All applauded—even the peaceniks in the class whom he'd cheerfully taunted earlier, asking if they would like to wait in the hall. Driving home that day or maybe another he found an absurd and blasphemous quotation running around in his head.

And so he increased in wisdom and stature—

And in favor with God and man.

That embarrassed him at the time and gave him a superstitious chill. As it did yet. But so long as nobody knew, it seemed not unnatural.

He took the book with him, the next time he went to Meadowlake. It was a Wednesday. He went looking for Fiona at the card tables and did not see her.

A woman called out to him, "She's not here. She's sick." Her voice sounded self-important and excited—pleased with herself for having recognized him when he knew nothing about her. Perhaps also pleased with all she knew about Fiona, about Fiona's life here, thinking it was maybe more than he knew.

"He's not here either," she said.

Grant went to find Kristy.

"Nothing, really," she said, when he asked what was the matter with Fiona. "She's just having a day in bed today, just a bit of an upset."

Fiona was sitting straight up in the bed. He hadn't noticed, the few times that he had been in this room, that this was a hospital bed and could be cranked up in such a way. She was wearing one of her high-necked maidenly gowns, and her face had a pallor that was not like cherry blossoms but like flour paste.

Aubrey was beside her in his wheelchair, pushed as close to the bed as it could get. Instead of the nondescript open-necked shirts he usually wore, he was wearing a jacket and a tie. His natty-looking tweed hat was resting on the bed. He looked as if he had been out on important business.

To see his lawyer? His banker? To make arrangements with the funeral director?

Whatever he'd been doing, he looked worn out by it. He too was gray in the face.

They both looked up at Grant with a stony, grief-ridden apprehension that turned to relief, if not to welcome, when they saw who he was.

Not who they thought he'd be.

They were hanging on to each other's hands and they did not let go.

The hat on the bed. The jacket and tie.

It wasn't that Aubrey had been out. It wasn't a question of where he'd been or whom he'd been to see. It was where he was going.

Grant set the book down on the bed beside Fiona's free hand.

"It's about Iceland," he said. "I thought maybe you'd like to look at it."

"Why, thank you," said Fiona. She didn't look at the book. He put her hand on it.

"Iceland," he said.

She said, "Ice-land." The first syllable managed to hold a tinkle of interest, but the second fell flat. Anyway, it was necessary for her to turn her attention back to Aubrey, who was pulling his great thick hand out of hers.

"What is it?" she said. "What is it, dear heart?"

Grant had never heard her use this flowery expression before.

"Oh, all right," she said. "Oh, here." And she pulled a handful of tissues from the box beside her bed.

Aubrey's problem was that he had begun to weep. His nose had started to run, and he was anxious not to turn into a sorry spectacle, especially in front of Grant.

"Here. Here," said Fiona. She would have tended to his nose herself and wiped his tears—and perhaps if they had been alone he would have let her do it. But with Grant there Aubrey would not permit it. He got hold of the Kleenex as well as he could and made a few awkward but lucky swipes at his face.

While he was occupied, Fiona turned to Grant.

"Do you by any chance have any influence around here?" she said in a whisper. "I've seen you talking to them—"

Aubrey made a noise of protest or weariness or disgust. Then his upper body pitched forward as if he wanted to throw himself against her. She scrambled half out of bed and caught him and held on to him. It seemed improper for Grant to help her, though of course he would have done so if he'd thought Aubrey was about to tumble to the floor.

"Hush," Fiona was saying. "Oh, honey. Hush. We'll get to see each other. We'll have to. I'll go and see you. You'll come and see me."

Aubrey made the same sound again with his face in her chest, and there was nothing Grant could decently do but get out of the room.

"I just wish his wife would hurry up and get here," Kristy said. "I wish she'd get him out of here and cut the agony short. We've got to start serving supper before long and how are we supposed to get her to swallow anything with him still hanging around?"

Grant said, "Should I stay?"

"What for? She's not sick, you know."

"To keep her company," he said.

Kristy shook her head.

"They have to get over these things on their own. They've got short memories usually. That's not always so bad."

Kristy was not hard-hearted. During the time he had known her Grant had found out some things about her life. She had four children. She did not know where her husband was but thought he might be in Alberta. Her younger boy's asthma was so bad that he would have died one night in January if she had not got him to the emergency ward in time. He was not on any illegal drugs, but she was not so sure about his brother.

To her, Grant and Fiona and Aubrey too must seem lucky. They had got through life without too much going wrong. What they had to suffer now that they were old hardly counted.

Grant left without going back to Fiona's room. He noticed that the wind was actually warm that day and the crows were making an uproar. In the parking lot a woman wearing a tartan pants suit was getting a folded-up wheelchair out of the trunk of her car.

The street he was driving down was called Black Hawks Lane. All the streets around were named for teams in the old National Hockey League. This was in an outlying section of the town near Meadowlake. He and Fiona had shopped in the town regularly but had not become familiar with any part of it except the main street.

The houses looked to have been built all around the same time, perhaps thirty or forty years ago. The streets were wide and curving and there were no sidewalks—recalling the time when it was thought unlikely that anybody would do much walking ever again. Friends of Grant's and Fiona's had moved to places something like this when they began to have their children. They were apologetic about the move at first. They called it "going out to Barbecue Acres."

Young families still lived here. There were basketball hoops over garage doors and tricycles in the driveways. But some of the houses had gone downhill from the sort of family homes they were surely meant to be. The yards were marked by car tracks, the windows were plastered with tinfoil or hung with faded flags.

Rental housing. Young male tenants—single still, or single again.

A few properties seemed to have been kept up as well as possible by the people who had moved into them when they were new— people who hadn't had the money or perhaps hadn't felt the need to move on to someplace better. Shrubs had grown to maturity, pastel vinyl siding had done away with the problem of repainting. Neat fences or hedges gave the sign that the children in the houses had all grown up and gone away, and that their parents no longer saw the point of letting the yard be a common run-through for whatever new children were loose in the neighborhood.

The house that was listed in the phone book as belonging to Aubrey and his wife was one of these. The front walk was paved with flagstones and bordered by hyacinths that stood as stiff as china flowers, alternately pink and blue.

Fiona had not got over her sorrow. She did not eat at mealtimes, though she pretended to, hiding food in her napkin. She was being given a supplementary drink twice a day—someone stayed and watched while she swallowed it down. She got out of bed and dressed herself, but all she wanted to do then was sit in her room. She wouldn't have taken any exercise at all if Kristy or one of the other nurses, and Grant during visiting hours, had not walked her up and down in the corridors or taken her outside.

In the spring sunshine she sat, weeping weakly, on a bench by the wall. She was still polite—she apologized for her tears, and never argued with a suggestion or refused to answer a question. But she wept. Weeping had left her eyes raw-edged and dim. Her cardigan—if it was hers—would be buttoned crookedly. She had not got to the stage of leaving her hair unbrushed or her nails uncleaned, but that might come soon.

Kristy said that her muscles were deteriorating, and that if she didn't improve soon they would put her on a walker.

"But you know once they get a walker they start to depend on it and they never walk much anymore, just get wherever it is they have to go."

"You'll have to work at her harder," she said to Grant. "Try and encourage her."

But Grant had no luck at that. Fiona seemed to have taken a dislike to him, though she tried to cover it up. Perhaps she was reminded, every time she saw him, of her last minutes with Aubrey, when she had asked him for help and he hadn't helped her.

He didn't see much point in mentioning their marriage, now.

She wouldn't go down the hall to where most of the same people were still playing cards. And she wouldn't go into the television room or visit the conservatory.

She said that she didn't like the big screen, it hurt her eyes. And the birds' noise was irritating and she wished they would turn the fountain off once in a while.

So far as Grant knew, she never looked at the book about Iceland, or at any of the other—surprisingly few—books that she had brought from home. There was a reading room where she would sit down to rest, choosing it probably because there was seldom anybody there, and if he took a book off the shelves she would allow him to read to her. He suspected that she did that because it made his company easier for her—she was able to shut her eyes and sink back into her own grief. Because if she let go of her grief even for a minute it would only hit her harder when she bumped into it again. And sometimes he thought she closed her eyes to hide a look of informed despair that it would not be good for him to see.

So he sat and read to her out of one of these old novels about chaste love, and lost-and-regained fortunes, that could have been the discards of some long-ago village or Sunday school library. There had been no attempt, apparently, to keep the contents of the reading room as up-to-date as most things in the rest of the building.

The covers of the books were soft, almost velvety, with designs of leaves and flowers pressed into them, so that they resembled jewelry boxes or chocolate boxes. That women—he supposed it would be women—could carry home like treasure.

The supervisor called him into her office. She said that Fiona was not thriving as they had hoped.

"Her weight is going down even with the supplement. We're doing all we can for her."

Grant said that he realized they were.

"The thing is, I'm sure you know, we don't do any prolonged bed care on the first floor. We do it temporarily if someone isn't feeling well, but if they get too weak to move around and be responsible we have to consider upstairs."

He said he didn't think that Fiona had been in bed that often.

"No. But if she can't keep up her strength, she will be. Right now she's borderline."

He said that he had thought the second floor was for people whose minds were disturbed.

"That too," she said.

He hadn't remembered anything about Aubrey's wife except the tartan suit he had seen her wearing in the parking lot. The tails of the jacket had flared open as she bent into the trunk of the car. He had got the impression of a trim waist and wide buttocks.

She was not wearing the tartan suit today. Brown belted slacks and a pink sweater. He was right about the waist—the tight belt showed she made a point of it. It might have been better if she hadn't, since she bulged out considerably above and below.

She could be ten or twelve years younger than her husband. Her hair was short, curly, artificially reddened. She had blue eyes—a lighter blue than Fiona's, a flat robin's-egg or turquoise blue—slanted by a slight puffiness. And a good many wrinkles made more noticeable by a walnut-stain makeup. Or perhaps that was her Florida tan.

He said that he didn't quite know how to introduce himself.

"I used to see your husband at Meadowlake. I'm a regular visitor there myself."

"Yes," said Aubrey's wife, with an aggressive movement of her chin.

"How is your husband doing?"

The "doing" was added on at the last moment. Normally he would have said, "How is your husband?"

"He's okay," she said.

"My wife and he struck up quite a close friendship."

"I heard about that."

"So. I wanted to talk to you about something if you had a minute."

"My husband did not try to start anything with your wife, if that's what you're getting at," she said. "He did not molest her in any way. He isn't capable of it and he wouldn't anyway. From what I heard it was the other way round."

Grant said, "No. That isn't it at all. I didn't come here with any complaints about anything."

"Oh," she said. "Well, I'm sorry. I thought you did."

That was all she was going to give by way of apology. And she didn't sound sorry. She sounded disappointed and confused.

"You better come in, then," she said. "It's blowing cold in through the door. It's not as warm out today as it looks."

So it was something of a victory for him even to get inside. He hadn't realized it would be as hard as this. He had expected a different sort of wife. A flustered homebody, pleased by an unexpected visit and flattered by a confidential tone.

She took him past the entrance to the living room, saying, "We'll have to sit in the kitchen where I can hear Aubrey." Grant caught sight of two layers of front-window curtains, both blue, one sheer and one silky, a matching blue sofa and a daunting pale carpet, various bright mirrors and ornaments.

Fiona had a word for those sort of swooping curtains—she said it like a joke, though the women she'd picked it up from used it seriously. Any room that Fiona fixed up was bare and bright—she would have been astonished to see so much fancy stuff crowded into such a small space. He could not think what that word was.

From a room off the kitchen—a sort of sunroom, though the blinds were drawn against the afternoon brightness—he could hear the sounds of television.

Aubrey. The answer to Fiona's prayers sat a few feet away, watching what sounded like a ball game. His wife looked in at him. She said, "You okay?" and partly closed the door.

"You might as well have a cup of coffee," she said to Grant.

He said, "Thanks."

"My son got him on the sports channel a year ago Christmas, I don't know what we'd do without it."

On the kitchen counters there were all sorts of contrivances and appliances—coffeemaker, food processor, knife sharpener, and some things Grant didn't know the names or uses of. All looked new and expensive, as if they had just been taken out of their wrappings, or were polished daily.

He thought it might be a good idea to admire things. He admired the coffeemaker she was using and said that he and Fiona had always meant to get one. This was absolutely untrue—Fiona had been devoted to a European contraption that made only two cups at a time.

"They gave us that," she said. "Our son and his wife. They live in Kamloops. B.C. They send us more stuff than we can handle. It wouldn't hurt if they would spend the money to come and see us instead."

Grant said philosophically, "I suppose they're busy with their own lives."

"They weren't too busy to go to Hawaii last winter. You could understand it if we had somebody else in the family, closer at hand. But he's the only one."

The coffee being ready, she poured it into two brown-and-green ceramic mugs that she took from the amputated branches of a ceramic tree trunk that sat on the table.

"People do get lonely," Grant said. He thought he saw his chance now. "If they're deprived of seeing somebody they care about, they do feel sad. Fiona, for instance. My wife."

"I thought you said you went and visited her."

"I do," he said. "That's not it."

Then he took the plunge, going on to make the request he'd come to make. Could she consider taking Aubrey back to Meadowlake maybe just one day a week, for a visit? It was only a drive of a few miles, surely it wouldn't prove too difficult. Or if she'd like to take the time off—Grant hadn't thought of this before and was rather dismayed to hear himself suggest it—then he himself could take Aubrey out there, he wouldn't mind at all. He was sure he could manage it. And she could use a break.

While he talked she moved her closed lips and her hidden tongue as if she was trying to identify some dubious flavor. She brought milk for his coffee, and a plate of ginger cookies.

"Homemade," she said as she set the plate down. There was challenge rather than hospitality in her tone. She said nothing more until she had sat down, poured milk into her coffee and stirred it.

Then she said no.

"No. I can't do that. And the reason is, I'm not going to upset him."

"Would it upset him?" Grant said earnestly.

"Yes, it would. It would. That's no way to do. Bringing him home and taking him back. Bringing him home and taking him back, that's just confusing him."

"But wouldn't he understand that it was just a visit? Wouldn't he get into the pattern of it?"

"He understands everything all right." She said this as if he had offered an insult to Aubrey. "But it's still an interruption. And then I've got to get him all ready and get him into the car, and he's a big man, he's not so easy to manage as you might think. I've got to maneuver him into the car and pack his chair along and all that and what for? If I go to all that trouble I'd prefer to take him someplace that was more fun."

"But even if I agreed to do it?" Grant said, keeping his tone hopeful and reasonable. "It's true, you shouldn't have the trouble."

"You couldn't," she said flatly. "You don't know him. You couldn't handle him. He wouldn't stand for you doing for him. All that bother and what would he get out of it?"

Grant didn't think he should mention Fiona again.

"It'd make more sense to take him to the mall," she said. "Where he could see kids and whatnot. If it didn't make him sore about his own two grandsons he never gets to see. Or now the lake boats are starting to run again, he might get a charge out of going and watching that."

She got up and fetched her cigarettes and lighter from the window above the sink.

"You smoke?" she said.

He said no thanks, though he didn't know if a cigarette was being offered.

"Did you never? Or did you quit?"

"Quit," he said.

"How long ago was that?"

He thought about it.

"Thirty years. No—more."

He had decided to quit around the time he started up with Jacqui. But he couldn't remember whether he quit first, and thought a big reward was coming to him for quitting, or thought that the time had come to quit, now that he had such a powerful diversion.

"I've quit quitting," she said, lighting up. "Just made a resolution to quit quitting, that's all."

Maybe that was the reason for the wrinkles. Somebody—a woman—had told him that women who smoked developed a special set of fine facial wrinkles. But it could have been from the sun, or just the nature of her skin—her neck was noticeably wrinkled as well. Wrinkled neck, youthfully full and up-tilted breasts. Women of her age usually had these contradictions. The bad and good points, the genetic luck or lack of it, all mixed up together. Very few kept their beauty whole, though shadowy, as Fiona had done.

And perhaps that wasn't even true. Perhaps he only thought that because he'd known Fiona when she was young. Perhaps to get that impression you had to have known a woman when she was young.

So when Aubrey looked at his wife did he see a high-school girl full of scorn and sass, with an intriguing tilt to her robin's-egg blue eyes, pursing her fruity lips around a forbidden cigarette?

"So your wife's depressed?" Aubrey's wife said. "What's your wife's name? I forget."

"It's Fiona."

"Fiona. And what's yours? I don't think I ever was told that."

Grant said, "It's Grant."

She stuck her hand out unexpectedly across the table.

"Hello, Grant. I'm Marian."

"So now we know each other's name," she said, "there's no point in not telling you straight out what I think. I don't know if he's still so stuck on seeing your—on seeing Fiona. Or not. I don't ask him and he's not telling me. Maybe just a passing fancy. But I don't feel like taking him back there in case it turns out to be more than that. I can't afford to risk it. I don't want him getting hard to handle. I don't want him upset and carrying on. I've got my hands full with him as it is. I don't have any help. It's just me here. I'm it."

"Did you ever consider—it *is* very hard for you—" Grant said—"did you ever consider his going in there for good?"

He had lowered his voice almost to a whisper, but she did not seem to feel a need to lower hers.

"No," she said. "I'm keeping him right here."

Grant said, "Well. That's very good and noble of you."

He hoped the word "noble" had not sounded sarcastic. He had not meant it to be.

"You think so?" she said. "Noble is not what I'm thinking about."

"Still. It's not easy."

"No, it isn't. But the way I am, I don't have much choice. If I put him in there I don't have the money to pay for him unless I sell the house. The house is what we own outright. Otherwise I don't have anything in the way of resources. I get the pension next year, and I'll have his pension and my pension, but even so I could not afford to keep him there and hang on to the house. And it means a lot to me, my house does."

"It's very nice," said Grant.

"Well, it's all right. I put a lot into it. Fixing it up and keeping it up."

"I'm sure you did. You do."

"I don't want to lose it."

"No."

"I'm not *going* to lose it."

"I see your point."

"The company left us high and dry," she said. "I don't know all the ins and outs of it, but basically he got shoved out. It ended up with them saying he owed them money and when I tried to find out what was what he just went on saying it's none of my business. What I think is he did something pretty stupid. But I'm not supposed to ask, so I shut up. You've been married. You are married. You know how it is. And in the middle of me finding out about this we're supposed to go on this trip with these people and can't get out of it. And on the trip he takes sick from this virus you never heard of and goes into a coma. So that pretty well gets *him* off the hook."

Grant said, "Bad luck."

"I don't mean exactly that he got sick on purpose. It just happened. He's not mad at me anymore and I'm not mad at him. It's just life."

"That's true."

"You can't beat life."

She flicked her tongue in a cat's businesslike way across her top lip, getting the cookie crumbs. "I sound like I'm quite the philosopher, don't I? They told me out there you used to be a university professor."

"Quite a while ago," Grant said.

"I'm not much of an intellectual," she said.

"I don't know how much I am, either."

"But I know when my mind's made up. And it's made up. I'm not going to let go of the house. Which means I'm keeping him here and I don't want him getting it in his head he wants to move anyplace else. It was probably a mistake putting him in there so I could get away, but I wasn't going to get another chance, so I took it. So. Now I know better."

She shook out another cigarette.

"I bet I know what you're thinking," she said. "You're thinking there's a mercenary type of a person."

"I'm not making judgments of that sort. It's your life."

"You bet it is."

He thought they should end on a more neutral note. So he asked her if her husband had worked in a hardware store in the summers, when he was going to school.

"I never heard about it," she said. "I wasn't raised here."

Driving home, he noticed that the swamp hollow that had been filled with snow and the formal shadows of tree trunks was now lighted up with skunk lilies. Their fresh, edible-looking leaves were the size of platters. The flowers sprang straight up like candle flames, and there were so many of them, so pure a yellow, that they set a light shooting up from the earth on this cloudy day. Fiona had told him that they generated a heat of their own as well. Rummaging around in one of her concealed pockets of information, she said that you were supposed to be able to put your hand inside the curled petal and feel the heat. She said that she had tried it, but she couldn't be sure if what she felt was heat or her imagination. The heat attracted bugs.

"Nature doesn't fool around just being decorative."

He had failed with Aubrey's wife. Marian. He had foreseen that he might fail, but he had not in the least foreseen why. He had thought that all he'd have to contend with would be a woman's natural sexual jealousy—or her resentment, the stubborn remains of sexual jealousy.

He had not had any idea of the way she might be looking at things. And yet in some depressing way the conversation had not been unfamiliar to him. That was because it reminded him of conversations he'd had with people in his own family. His uncles, his relatives, probably even his mother, had thought the way Marian thought. They had believed that when other people did not think that way it was because they were kidding themselves—they had got too airy-fairy, or stupid, on account of their easy and protected lives or their education. They had lost touch with reality. Educated people, literary people, some rich people like Grant's socialist in-laws had lost touch with reality. Due to an unmerited good fortune or an innate silliness. In Grant's case, he suspected, they pretty well believed it was both.

That was how Marian would see him, certainly. A silly person, full of boring knowledge and protected by some fluke from the truth about life. A person who didn't have to worry about holding on to his house and could go around thinking his complicated thoughts. Free to dream up the fine, generous schemes that he believed would make another person happy.

What a jerk, she would be thinking now.

Being up against a person like that made him feel hopeless, exasperated, finally almost desolate. Why? Because he couldn't be sure of holding on to himself against that person? Because he was afraid that in the end they'd be right? Fiona wouldn't feel any of that misgiving. Nobody had beat her down, narrowed her in, when she was young. She'd been amused by his upbringing, able to think its harsh notions quaint.

Just the same, they have their points, those people. (He could hear himself now arguing with somebody. Fiona?) There's some advantage to the narrow focus. Marian would probably be good in a crisis. Good at survival, able to scrounge for food and able to take the shoes off a dead body in the street.

Trying to figure out Fiona had always been frustrating. It could be like following a mirage. No—like living in a mirage. Getting close to Marian would present a different problem. It would be like biting into a litchi nut. The flesh with its oddly artificial allure, its chemical taste and perfume, shallow over the extensive seed, the stone.

He might have married her. Think of it. He might have married some girl like that. If he'd stayed back where he belonged. She'd have been appetizing enough, with her choice breasts. Probably a flirt. The fussy way she had of shifting her buttocks on the kitchen chair, her pursed mouth, a slightly contrived air of menace—that was what was left of the more or less innocent vulgarity of a small-town flirt.

She must have had some hopes, when she picked Aubrey. His good looks, his salesman's job, his white-collar expectations. She must have believed that she would end up better off than she was now. And so it often happened with those practical people. In spite of their calculations, their survival instincts, they might not get as far as they had quite reasonably expected. No doubt it seemed unfair.

In the kitchen the first thing he saw was the light blinking on his answering machine. He thought the same thing he always thought now. Fiona.

He pressed the button before he got his coat off.

"Hello, Grant. I hope I got the right person. I just thought of something. There is a dance here in town at the Legion supposed to be for singles on Saturday night, and I am on the supper committee, which means I can bring a free guest. So I wondered whether you would happen to be interested in that? Call me back when you get a chance."

A woman's voice gave a local number. Then there was a beep, and the same voice started talking again.

"I just realized I'd forgot to say who it was. Well you probably recognized the voice. It's Marian. I'm still not so used to these machines. And I wanted to say I realize you're not a single and I don't mean it that way. I'm not either, but it doesn't hurt to get out once in a while. Anyway, now I've said all this I really hope it's you I'm talking to. It did sound like your voice. If you are interested you can call me and if you are not you don't need to bother. I just thought you might like the chance to get out. It's Marian speaking. I guess I already said that. Okay, then. Good-bye."

Her voice on the machine was different from the voice he'd heard a short time ago in her house. Just a little different in the first message, more so in the second. A tremor of nerves there, an affected nonchalance, a hurry to get through and a reluctance to let go.

Something had happened to her. But when had it happened? If it had been immediate, she had concealed it very successfully all the time he was with her. More likely it came on her gradually, maybe after he'd gone away. Not necessarily as a blow of attraction. Just the realization that he was a possibility, a man on his own. More or less on his own. A possibility that she might as well try to follow up.

But she'd had the jitters when she made the first move. She had put herself at risk. How much of herself, he could not yet tell. Generally a woman's vulnerability increased as time went on, as things progressed. All you could tell at the start was that if there was an edge of it now, there'd be more later.

It gave him a satisfaction—why deny it?—to have brought that out in her. To have roused something like a shimmer, a blurring, on the surface of her personality. To have heard in her testy, broad vowels this faint plea.

He set out the eggs and mushrooms to make himself an omelette. Then he thought he might as well pour a drink.

Anything was possible. Was that true—was anything possible? For instance, if he wanted to, would he be able to break her down, get her to the point where she might listen to him about taking Aubrey back to Fiona? And not just for visits, but for the rest of Aubrey's life. Where could that tremor lead them? To an upset, to the end of her self-preservation? To Fiona's happiness?

It would be a challenge. A challenge and a creditable feat. Also a joke that could never be confided to anybody—to think that by his bad behavior he'd be doing good for Fiona.

But he was not really capable of thinking about it. If he did think about it, he'd have to figure out what would become of him and Marian, after he'd delivered Aubrey to Fiona. It would not work—unless he could get more satisfaction that he foresaw, finding the stone of blameless self-interest inside her robust pulp.

You never quite knew how such things would turn out. You almost knew, but you could never be sure.

She would be sitting in her house now, waiting for him to call. Or probably not sitting. Doing things to keep herself busy. She seemed to be a woman who would keep busy. Her house had certainly shown the benefits of nonstop attention. And there was Aubrey—care of him had to continue as usual. She might have given him an early supper—fitting his meals to a Meadowlake timetable in order to get him settled for the night earlier and free herself of his routine for the day. (What would she do about him when she went to the dance? Could he be left alone or would she get a sitter? Would she tell him where she was going, introduce her escort? Would her escort pay the sitter?)

She might have fed Aubrey while Grant was buying the mushrooms and driving home. She might now be preparing him for bed. But all the time she would be conscious of the phone, of the silence of the phone. Maybe she would have calculated how long it would take Grant to drive home. His address in the phone book would have given her a rough idea of where he lived. She would calculate how long, then add to that time for possible shopping for supper (figuring that a man alone would shop every day). Then a certain amount of time for him to get around to listening to his messages. And as the silence persisted she would think of other things. Other errands he might have had to do before he got home. Or perhaps a dinner out, a meeting that meant he would not get home at suppertime at all.

She would stay up late, cleaning her kitchen cupboards, watching television, arguing with herself about whether there was still a chance.

What conceit on his part. She was above all things a sensible woman. She would go to bed at her regular time thinking that he didn't look as if he'd be a decent dancer anyway. Too stiff, too professorial.

He stayed near the phone, looking at magazines, but he didn't pick it up when it rang again.

"Grant. This is Marian. I was down in the basement putting the wash in the dryer and I heard the phone and when I got upstairs whoever it was had hung up. So I just thought I ought to say I was here. If it was you and if you are even home. Because I don't have a machine obviously, so you couldn't leave a message. So I just wanted. To let you know.

"'Bye."

The time was now twenty-five after ten.

'Bye.

He would say that he'd just got home. There was no point in bringing to her mind the picture of his sitting here, weighing the pros and cons.

Drapes. That would be her word for the blue curtains—drapes. And why not? He thought of the ginger cookies so perfectly round that she'd had to announce they were homemade, the ceramic coffee mugs on their ceramic tree. A plastic runner, he was sure, protecting the hall carpet. A high-gloss exactness and practicality that his mother had never achieved but would have admired—was that why he could feel this twinge of bizarre and unreliable affection? Or was it because he'd had two more drinks after the first?

The walnut-stain tan—he believed now that it was a tan—of her face and neck would most likely continue into her cleavage, which would be deep, crepey-skinned, odorous and hot. He had that to think of, as he dialled the number that he had already written down. That and the practical sensuality of her cat's tongue. Her gemstone eyes.

Fiona was in her room but not in bed. She was sitting by the open window, wearing a seasonable but oddly short and bright dress. Through the window came a heady, warm blast of lilacs in bloom and the spring manure spread over the fields.

She had a book open in her lap.

She said, "Look at this beautiful book I found, it's about Iceland. You wouldn't think they'd leave valuable books lying around in the rooms. The people staying here are not necessarily honest. And I think they've got the clothes mixed up. I never wear yellow."

"Fiona . . . ," he said.

"You've been gone a long time. Are we all checked out now?"

"Fiona, I've brought a surprise for you. Do you remember Aubrey?"

She stared at him for a moment, as if waves of wind had come beating into her face. Into her face, into her head, pulling everything to rags.

"Names elude me," she said harshly.

Then the look passed away as she retrieved, with an effort, some bantering grace. She set the book down carefully and stood up and lifted her arms to put them around him. Her skin or her breath gave off a faint new smell, a smell that seemed to him like that of the stems of cut flowers left too long in their water.

"I'm happy to see you," she said, and pulled his earlobes.

"You could have just driven away," she said. "Just driven away without a care in the world and forsook me. Forsooken me. Forsaken."

He kept his face against her white hair, her pink scalp, her sweetly shaped skull. He said, Not a chance.

OTHER TITLES FROM
DOUGLAS GIBSON BOOKS

PUBLISHED BY McCLELLAND & STEWART LTD.

LIVES OF MOTHERS AND DAUGHTERS: Growing Up With Alice Munro
by Sheila Munro
"The book will thrill anybody with a serious interest in Alice Munro."
Edmonton Journal "What Sheila Munro says about her mother's writing
could be just as aptly applied to her own book; you trust her every word."
Montreal Gazette
                          Biography/Memoir, 6 × 9, 60 snapshots, 240 pages, hardcover

A PETER GZOWSKI READER *by* Peter Gzowski
The man who affected the reading habits of millions of Canadians gives us
the work of a lifetime in this selection of his best writing, much of it never
before published in book form.
                          Anthology/Essays, 6 × 9, 228 pages, hardcover

RAVEN'S END: A novel of the Canadian Rockies *by* Ben Gadd
This astonishing book, snapped up by publishers around the world, is like
a *Watership Down* set among a flock of ravens managing to survive in the
Rockies. "A real classic." Andy Russell
                          Fiction, 6 × 9, map, 5 drawings, 336 pages, hardcover

CONFESSIONS OF AN IGLOO DWELLER *by* James Houston
The famous novelist and superb storyteller who brought Inuit art to the
outside world recounts his Arctic adventures between 1948 and 1962. "Sheer
entertainment, as fascinating as it is charming." *Kirkus Reviews*
                          Autobiography, 6 × 9, 320 pages, maps, drawings, trade paperback

THREE CHEERS FOR ME: The Journals of Bartholomew Bandy, Volume
One *by* Donald Jack
The classic comic novel about the First World War where our bumbling
hero graduates from the trenches and somehow becomes an air ace.
"Funny? Very." *New York Times*
                          Fiction/Humour, 5½ × 8½, 330 pages, trade paperback

THAT'S ME IN THE MIDDLE: The Journals of Bartholomew Bandy,
Volume Two *by* Donald Jack
Canadian air ace Bandy fights at the front and behind the lines in the U.K.,
gallantly enduring the horrors of English plumbing. "A comical tour-de-
force." *Montreal Gazette*
                          Fiction/Humour, 5½ × 8½, 348 pages, trade paperback

THE GRIM PIG *by* Charles Gordon
The world of news is laid bare in this "very wicked, subversive book . . . it reveals more than most readers should know about how newspapers – or at least some newspapers – are still created. This is exceedingly clever satire, with a real bite." *Ottawa Citizen*

Fiction, 6x9, 256 pages, hardcover

NEXT-YEAR COUNTRY: Voices of Prairie People *by* Barry Broadfoot
"There's something mesmerizing about these authentic Canadian voices." *Globe and Mail* "A good book, a joy to read." *Books in Canada*

Oral history, 5 ⅜ × 8¾, 400 pages, trade paperback

WELCOME TO FLANDERS FIELDS: The First Canadian Battle of the Great War – Ypres, 1915 *by* Daniel G. Dancocks
"A magnificent chronicle of a terrible battle . . . Daniel Dancocks is spellbinding throughout." *Globe and Mail*

Military/History, 4¼ × 7, 304 pages, photos, maps, paperback

ACROSS THE BRIDGE: Stories *by* Mavis Gallant
These eleven stories, set mostly in Montreal or in Paris, were described as "Vintage Gallant – urbane, witty, absorbing." *Winnipeg Free Press* "We come away from it both thoughtful and enriched." *Globe and Mail*

Fiction, 6 × 9, 208 pages, trade paperback

AT THE COTTAGE: A Fearless Look at Canada's Summer Obsession *by* Charles Gordon *illustrated by* Graham Pilsworth
This perennial best-selling book of gentle humour is "a delightful reminder of why none of us addicted to cottage life will ever give it up." *Hamilton Spectator*   *Humour, 6 × 9, 224 pages, illustrations, trade paperback*

A PASSION FOR NARRATIVE: A Guide for Writing Fiction *by* Jack Hodgins
"One excellent path from original to marketable manuscript. . . . It would take a beginning writer years to work her way through all the goodies Hodgins offers." *Globe and Mail*

Non-fiction/Writing guide, 5¼ × 8½, 216 pages, updated with a new Afterword, trade paperback

OVER FORTY IN BROKEN HILL: Unusual Encounters in the Australian Outback *by* Jack Hodgins
"Australia described with wit, wonder and affection by a bemused visitor with Canadian sensibilities." *Canadian Press* "Damned fine writing." *Books in Canada*   *Travel, 5½ × 8½, 216 pages, trade paperback*

DANCING ON THE SHORE: A Celebration of Life at Annapolis Basin *by* Harold Horwood, *Foreword by* Farley Mowat
"A Canadian *Walden*" *Windsor Star* that "will reward, provoke, challenge and enchant its readers." *Books in Canada*
Nature/Ecology, 5⅛ × 8¼, 224 pages, 16 wood engravings, trade paperback

HUGH MACLENNAN'S BEST: An anthology *selected by* Douglas Gibson
This selection from all of the works of the witty essayist and famous novelist is "wonderful . . . It's refreshing to discover again MacLennan's formative influence on our national character." *Edmonton Journal*
Anthology, 6 × 9, 352 pages, trade paperback

JAKE AND THE KID: *by* W.O. Mitchell
W.O.'s most popular characters spring from the pages of this classic, which won the Stephen Leacock Award for Humour.
Fiction, 5½ × 8½, 211 pages, trade paperback

THE BLACK BONSPIEL OF WILLIE MACCRIMMON *by* W.O. Mitchell *illustrated by* Wesley W. Bates
A devil of a good tale about curling – W.O.Mitchell's most successful comic play now appears as a story, fully illustrated, for the first time, and it is "a true Canadian classic." *Western Report*
Fiction, 4⅝ × 7½, 144 pages with 10 wood engravings, hardcover

FOR ART'S SAKE *by* W.O. Mitchell
"*For Art's Sake* shows the familiar Mitchell brand of subtle humour in this tale of an aging artist who takes matters into his own hands in bringing pictures to the people." *Calgary Sun*   *Fiction, 6 × 9, 240 pages, hardcover*

LADYBUG, LADYBUG . . . by W.O. Mitchell
"Mitchell slowly and subtly threads together the elements of this richly detailed and wonderful tale . . . the outcome is spectacular . . . *Ladybug, Ladybug* is certainly among the great ones!" *Windsor Star*
Fiction, 4¼ × 7, 288 pages, paperback

ROSES ARE DIFFICULT HERE *by* W.O.Mitchell
"Mitchell's newest novel is a classic, capturing the richness of the small town, and delving into moments that really count in the lives of its people . . ." *Windsor Star*
Fiction, 5½ × 8½, 328 pages, trade paperback